EMPIRE STATE

BATEMAN

D0125200

headline

Copyright © 1997 Colin Bateman

The right of Colin Bateman to be identified as the Author of
the Work has been asserted by him in accordance with the
Copyright, Designs and Patents Act 1988.

First published in Great Britain in 1997
by HarperCollins Publishers

First published in this paperback edition in 2013
by HEADLINE PUBLISHING GROUP

1

Cataloguing in Publication Data is available from the British Library

ISBN 978 1 4722 0127 0

Typeset in Meridien by Palimpsest Book Production Limited,
Falkirk, Stirlingshire

Printed and bound in Great Britain by
CPI Group (UK) Ltd, Croydon CR0 4YY

Headline's policy is to use papers that are natural, renewable
and recyclable products and made from wood grown in sustainable
forests. The logging and manufacturing processes are expected
to conform to the environmental regulations of the
country of origin.

HEADLINE PUBLISHING GROUP
An Hachette UK Company
338 Euston Road
London NW1 3BH

www.headline.co.uk
www.hachette.co.uk

For Andrea and Matthew

Prologue

They were just a couple of tourists, or might have been.

Okay, so there was a stretch parked outside on 34th Street, but that wasn't uncommon, and anyone who cared to look would have seen the scrapes down one side where a drunk had smashed a bottle and then tried and failed to carve his initials, or the cracked brake light; they would have seen a driver as well, tired from being behind the wheel all day, his head nodding forward, then jerking back, then nodding forward. A herd of elephants could have snuck up and checked the oil and he wouldn't have known any different.

Inside, two men joined the queue. It was getting towards eleven. Behind them a security guard produced a rope and looped it over two plastic poles to stop anyone else joining; this would be the last trip of the night.

If anyone had studied the men they would have put twenty years between them. One was tall, black, silk suit, shined-up Oxford shoes, hair cut short, nails manicured, wedding band, earnest look about him; confident, imposing. The other was white, five-ten, skinny, hair like straw, pulled back in a ponytail; he wore a Batman sweatshirt, black jeans with the knees turning white, dirty grey sneakers. His face had a sallow complexion, not helped by the wispy excuse for stubble on his chin. In fact they were the same age.

As they waited for tickets the tall man, Mark Benedict, lifted a free leaflet and began to read. Beside him Michael Tate chewed gum and hummed.

'There's enough steel here to build a double track railroad from New York to Saratoga Springs, it says.'

Tate shrugged.

'There are 6,500 windows. Ten million bricks were used.'

'Uhuh.'

They reached the desk. Although he was closest, Tate waited for his companion to produce the eight bucks for the tickets.

'How many visitors a year?' he asked.

Benedict took the tickets and they followed the directions for the elevators. As he walked Benedict scanned the leaflet. 'Doesn't say. I'll find out. A million, easy, I'd say. Four million dollars a year.'

Tate rolled his eyes. 'It's not the money, Mark,' he said.

Benedict nodded. 'Of course.'

They rode the elevator to the 80th floor. It took less than one minute for them to travel the 1,200 feet. Then they entered a second elevator and rode in silence to the 86th floor observatory.

As Tate led them out onto the floor a smile broke on his face. 'I've been dreaming of this since I was a kid.'

'You never mentioned it.'

'There's a lot I never mentioned.' He stuck his head up into the breeze and breathed it in. 'I always loved the idea of it. An American icon. It's not like Marilyn or Elvis or Kennedy, it's never going to get tarnished. King Kong couldn't do it. Neither could Trump. I never did visit before. I knew

I would love it, but I hated the thought of someone telling me it was time to go. Mom or pop.'

'It's my toy and I'll play with it when I like.'

Tate giggled.

Benedict stopped at the suicide grille, and peered out over the lights of Manhattan. 'Gives an impression of height, doesn't it?'

They both laughed.

'Beautiful view,' Benedict said quietly.

Tate nodded beside him. 'Beautiful view of a horrible and sick place.'

'Pity it couldn't just be shifted to Venice Beach.'

'We could build our own out there.'

'Uhuh. I think maybe City Hall might object.'

They completed two circuits of the floor, Tate grinning all the way, Benedict still picking out pieces of information from the leaflet. Then they moved to a smaller elevator to take them to the enclosed 102nd floor observatory.

As they emerged, Tate clapped his hands together. 'I *love* this,' he exclaimed. The second platform offered even vaster panoramic views. 'I could *live* here.'

Benedict, who had seen these enthusiasms before, nodded tactfully. It felt claustrophobic to him after the coolness of the 86th. 'Originally,' he said, 'there was a dirigible mast up top. Blimps were going to tie up and celebrities get on board. They didn't bank on the updraught caused by a 40 mph wind slapping against the building. The longest they ever managed to tie up was for three minutes. Nearly killed the lot of them.'

'Tell me something I don't know,' Tate said bluntly. He spat his gum out onto the floor, then took out another stick and pushed it into his mouth.

Benedict shrugged. '*Is* there anything you don't know?'

3

Tate curled a lip at him. 'I don't know how I feel about President Keneally.'

Benedict raised an eyebrow. 'You voted for him.'

'I don't know how I feel about free health care for the masses.'

'If you were poor and downtrodden, wouldn't you want free health care?'

'But I'm not. And the more I see of the poor and downtrodden, the less I want them to get healthy.'

'You're a cruel and heartless man, Michael.'

The elevator door opened behind them and an elderly security guard lumbered out. He looked at least as old as the building itself.

'Gentlemen, I'm sorry, but the building is closing for the evening,' he said. His voice was rugged, wind-blasted.

Benedict nodded.

'We're not finished yet,' said Tate.

'I'm sorry, sir. We've all got homes to go to.'

Benedict smiled. 'Of course.'

'How long have you worked here, old man?' Tate asked.

The guard flinched at the *old man*. 'Long enough,' he replied tartly, then added, because he *was* proud of it, 'More than fifty years.'

'God,' said Tate, 'that's fucking ages.'

The guard shook his head slightly, then showed them the palm of his hand, indicating the elevator.

Benedict began to move, but Tate stayed where he was. 'It lights up red and green for Christmas, doesn't it?'

The guard nodded. 'Sure.'

'Red and white for St Valentine's, green for St Patrick's.'

'Red, white and green for Columbus Day. Sure. Now, gentlemen . . .'

Tate was at the windows now, pressing his forehead against

4

the glass. 'And in 1947 they installed the most powerful musical instrument in the world, a set of gargantuan carillon bells, to pump out Christmas carols to the streets below.'

Benedict was turning the leaflet this way and that, looking for *that* information.

The guard held his gaze. 'Except nobody could hear them above the traffic,' he said, 'and, anyhow, it would take more than bells to excite anybody in Times Square. You seem to know a lot about us.'

Tate shrugged. 'I want to talk to you about all of this. Isn't it *fascinating*?'

And it was fascinating to the old guy, but it was late and his head throbbed and he was tired and instinctively he didn't like this young pup with the ponytail and bad attitude. 'Some other time, maybe,' he said.

'*Now,*' Tate said.

'No, son, it's time to go home.'

Tate looked to Benedict.

Benedict produced his wallet. 'If it's a question of . . .'

'It's a question of closing this place up for the night. Now please, gentlemen.'

The grin had dropped off Tate's face. It lay on the floor, shivering.

Tate looked for a moment like he was about to bark something, but then abruptly moved towards the elevator. Benedict gave a resigned smile to the guard, then followed. All three of them rode down to the 86th in silence.

The guard said goodnight to them as they moved across to the high-speed elevator to ground level. Benedict replied. Tate strode purposefully ahead.

Benedict led the way to the car. Tate walked backwards, looking up at the building.

'Well,' Benedict asked, 'what do you think?'

'What about, the President or the health care?'

'About the Empire State Building.'

Tate stopped, craned his head as far back as he could. 'Oh,' he said, that grin slipping back onto his face, 'I think we'll buy the fucker.'

I

EMPIRE STATE

1

'Nathan Jones, you've been gone too long.'

'Oh bloody ha-ha.'

The policeman gave him a thin smile, closed the van door after him and then slapped the side of it twice. The gate opened and they drove out into the darkness.

'Do I get the impression that that grates on you after a while, Nathan?' Coolidge asked from the front.

'It grated on me after the first time,' Nathan said, 'as you well know. You bastard.'

Coolidge laughed. He raised a hand, counted off one-two-three in the air and they all launched tunelessly into Nathan Jones, the old Supremes hit, as the van bumped over the security ramps.

Nathan squirmed down in his seat while the rest of the crew roared at him. The smell of the paint was still thick in his nostrils. He'd been at the job for three months now and he still felt giddy by the end of the day. Coolidge said he'd get used to it. 'By about the tenth year,' Coolidge laughed. 'You're used to it, aren't ya, Tommy?'

Tommy Mateer was sixty-five, and smoked a cigarette for each of his years every day. He reckoned he'd give them up when he was a hundred. 'I couldney afford 'em then,' he reasoned.

Nathan pulled out his Walkman and pushed the earphones in. After a few moments Tommy's nose wrinkled up in disgust. Coolidge reached back and patted Nathan on the knee. Annoyed, Nathan pulled out one of the plugs. 'What?' he said.

'I'll bet that's not the Supremes.'

'As if,' Nathan said with a sarcastic curl of his lip. He replaced the plug.

Coolidge touched his leg again. 'Who is it?'

'Sid Vicious.'

'Sounds like shite,' said Coolidge and turned his attention back to the road ahead.

Nathan turned the sound up and closed his eyes.

Two miles out of the police fortress Marty Magee eased the brake down and shook his head. 'You'd think they'd know us by now, wouldn't ye?'

Coolidge peered into the darkness. Ahead, slowly circling, a red light.

'If he starts singing,' Nathan said, slipping the earphones off and peering forward at the checkpoint, 'I'm gonna fuckin' deck him, I'll tell you that for nothing.'

The rest of them giggled. Magee stopped the van and rolled down the window. The police officer approached cautiously. Coolidge noticed the red-eye of a cigarette nestling in the hedgerow to his side. He nodded at it. It wavered slightly then dropped out of sight.

'Good evening, sir,' said the policeman, resting his hand on the frame of the open window. Coolidge noted the sergeant's stripes.

Magee nodded and handed the policeman his driving licence. As he took it he asked: 'Do you mind telling me where you're coming from, sir?'

'Crossmaheart. At the barracks.'

'And your business there?'

Magee rolled his eyes and thumbed back at the van. 'What do you think? We're an elite SAS undercover team masquerading as a gang of painters and decorators.'

The sergeant nodded and handed back the driving licence. 'Crack painters and decorators propping up the British colonial presence in Ireland.'

It didn't quite sink in at first. Then the sergeant leaned in and shone his torch around them. 'Would you mind getting out of the vehicle, boys?'

Coolidge leaned across. 'We've been painting your bloody . . .'

He stopped. One of the sergeant's stripes had flopped down off his arm. He noticed it at the same time. He tutted. He shook his head. 'You just can't get decent fake uniforms these days,' he said, and produced his pistol. He pushed it through the window. 'Get out. All of youse. Now.'

The big door was slid back and one by one they scrambled from the van. The man in the uniform was joined by three others wearing dark overalls and balaclavas. They carried guns. It was too dark to see what type of guns. Nathan's heart pounded. His legs were suddenly weak. Marty gave him a hand out. 'It's all right, son,' he said. 'Don't worry.'

'Oh Jesus,' said Tommy.

'Line yourselves up there, boys,' said the cop.

The seven employees of the Professional Decorating Company quickly formed up. Coolidge, Marty, Tommy, Bob Evans, Michael Graham, Peter Adair, Nathan, in their paint-spattered overalls, their paint-spotted hair, their pale faces white against the winter chill.

'Now tell me this,' said the fake sergeant. 'Does your boss never pay no heed at all to the warnings we give him?'

Coolidge shrugged. 'It's work.'

'It's supporting an army of occupation, that's what it is.'

'Depends where you stand on it, really,' said Coolidge.

Marty elbowed him. 'For fuck's sake, Coolidge, shut up.'

'Does he think we're only raking him?' asked the fake sergeant.

'I don't know what he thinks,' said Coolidge. 'He just tells us where to go.'

'You're very cool, for someone about to get himself shot.'

'Jesus Christ,' said Tommy. 'We're only painters.'

'Well maybe you'll be decorated for your bravery under fire.'

'Oh Jesus Christ,' said Tommy again.

The fake sergeant walked up the line. He stopped at Nathan. 'How old are you, son?' he asked.

'Sixteen,' Nathan whispered, his eyes fixed on the ground.

'Shouldn't you still be at school?'

Nathan nodded.

The fake sergeant smiled. 'Do you wish you'd stayed on now?'

Nathan nodded.

He pushed his pistol into Nathan's forehead. 'You don't really want to die, do you?'

Nathan shook his head. As he did, tears began to run down his face.

'Okay,' said the fake sergeant, 'seeing as how I'm feeling particularly big-hearted, I'm going to let you go.'

Nathan looked sideways at Mickey Graham. Mickey was

shaking. His eyes were shut tight. He bent forward, saw Coolidge staring defiantly forward.

'Go on, scram. Live to cry another day.'

Slowly Nathan shook his head.

The fake sergeant laughed in his face. 'Take the chance, son,' he said.

Nathan shook his head.

The fake sergeant shook his, then stepped back and spoke to his companions in hushed tones.

Suddenly Marty gave a little cry and took off down the road. One of the balaclavas turned after him, raised his gun and let off a burst of automatic fire. Marty was too old and too fat. He collapsed in a heap. He hadn't made more than ten yards.

And then there was light. Maybe half a mile back the way they'd come. Headlights.

'Shite,' said the fake policeman.

It was an instant of hope, and it was quelled in the moment it took for the shooting to begin again.

Nathan screamed as the air erupted.

The gunmen fired with steady efficiency. And just as efficiently the employees of the Professional Decorating Company fell to the ground, destroyed by bullets with barely a grunt between them.

For several moments the only sound was that of chattering teeth. Nathan, standing among the carnage, could not control his jaw.

The fake sergeant laughed at him. 'Jesus,' he said, 'we must have missed you.'

He turned to the balaclava beside him. 'Time we were off, Seanie.' He slipped his pistol back into his jacket, then peered up the road towards the advancing car. He turned back to Nathan. 'Sunshine,' he said, 'go back to school. And tell Mr Professional Decorator he's not outta the woods yet. Okay?'

And then they were gone, slipped into the darkness.

Nathan stood among his friends. His bits of friends. He didn't know what to do. All he could hear was the echo of the gunfire reverberating around his head. He stood and looked at them, and the tears cascaded down his face. There was Tommy, a cigarette still glowing between his lips, more alive than its host. And his friend Coolidge, except it was Coolidge with no head.

Nathan lifted his earphones and stuck them back in. He switched the Pistols back on. He closed his eyes and began to sing along.

He didn't hear the car pull up beside him, nor the sickened cries from within. He only heard the guitars, the sneering vocals, the steady beat. Just the music . . .

2

. . . just the music, but not *that* music, something altogether more pleasant.

Nathan blinked back into the moment. It was long ago and far away. But not *that* long ago, nor *that* far. His head throbbed; a sweat had broken on him; there was too much alcohol in his system, he knew that; and *she* knew that, the way she was looking at him. He pushed himself up off the table and left without a word, just half-raising a placatory hand.

Nathan had never been able to pee in the presence of other men.

It wasn't that he was too small, or too large, or intimidated. He just couldn't do it. If he was started before the other man came in he was fine, he could fire away like the best of them. If he entered the men's room and there was at least one urinal between him and the next customer, he was grand. Shoot away, shake, reholster. If, however, there was only the one free urinal, it could create problems. Usually he would simply enter a cubicle, sit down girly style and no

15

one was any the wiser. But most pubs, he found, only had the one cubicle and as often as not this was occupied by someone in dire need of something beyond a straight pee: that is, the need for which it was intended; or for boking up too much alcohol, taking drugs and occasionally those making love.

This time it had seemed fine. He had been sitting on five pints of Budweiser for the best part of an hour, and a tight bladder is always a help. And when he entered the men's room was empty. Nathan marched unsteadily up to the urinal and unzipped. Or tried to. Over-enthusiastic. His shirt, too big, got tied up in his zipper. He yanked at it once, twice, got it finally on the third attempt, although not before a shirt button had plopped into the half-full urinal. It floated lazily down to nestle amongst the pineapple cubes at the bottom. They weren't really pineapple cubes, he knew, but someone had called them that at school and the name had stuck. And he knew someone who'd proved they weren't. The more accurate description of their taste was more along the lines of wee cubes of soap someone's pished on, but on the whole he preferred to think of them still as pineapple cubes.

By the time he'd freed his willy from its home the door had opened and a man had entered. Nathan gritted his teeth and thought of waterfalls and rivers and all the usual things, then gave the faintest sigh of relief – but not relieved – as the man tried the cubicle door. Locked. Nathan glanced round. Sure enough. There were two feet, a pair of white socks and a crumpled mass of canvas trouser visible under the door. The occupant hadn't made a sound. He might have only just arrived himself, or been there for hours. He might have been holding off on the big evacuation until Nathan's own feet had disappeared past the cubicle door and back out into Michael's Pub, or might have slowly but surely been making his way through a DIY magazine or a short novel about lemmings. Still, whatever, the new arrival let out a barely muffled sigh of frustration and took his place to Nathan's left.

Nathan gritted his teeth again and pushed. This wasn't always a good thing to do while standing up with five pints on board, but he came through it unscathed, though still as dry as before. He blew air down his nose. He tapped his foot. He shook his willy and willed the torrents forward. Useless.

The newcomer hadn't started either. Shorter than Nathan, he blew some air out of his nose as well. Another dryer.

It was all he needed. Nathan knew from sad past experience that there was nothing worse than two dryers. Bad enough one man shaking his willy. But two men standing, shaking their willies was not only deeply, deeply embarrassing, but also quite possibly grounds for arrest. The only worse thing than two men standing shaking their willies in a public urinal is for the door to open and a third man to enter and pee freely and leave silently. But tell everyone.

Nathan looked to his right. The ceramic tiles were disappointingly graffiti free. He had used graffiti before as a distraction, reading it as he would a menu, lulling himself into a sense of security and then pissing away merrily. But no such luck.

The other guy let out another little sigh. This was decision time. One sigh was acceptable frustration, but a second sigh could go either way: continued frustration or self-propelled gratification. Now he had to decide whether to zip up and limp cross-legged back to Lisa and try again later, dart a non-encouraging glance at the other guy to see if he had grown in any way, or just wait it out, wait for the other guy to pee or piss off.

Nathan glanced left. *Jesus*, he thought.

'You're Woody Allen,' he said.

Woody nodded.

In terms of the size of New York it was a fifteen million to one shot. In terms of the size of Michael's Pub, nestling in the darkened intersection of two buildings on 55th Street it was about three hundred to one. Woody'd blown his Rampone horn here nearly every Monday night for twenty years. And every Monday night for the past month Nathan Jones had sat at a table lapping it up. Lisa wasn't that fussed. She didn't laugh at his comedy, didn't appreciate his serious stuff, and didn't see why she should be subjected more than once to a wee bald man blowing a clarinet. The New Orleans Funeral and Ragtime Orchestra wasn't for her.

'I hate when this happens,' Nathan said, nodding down.

'Mmm,' said Woody.

'Still,' said Nathan, 'loved the show.'

'Thanks.'

'Love that old Jimmy Durante one. What's it? "Inka Pinka Doo"?'

'"Inks Dinka Doo."'

'Yeah, great. Love that.'

'Thanks.'

They stared silently at the tiles for some seconds, neither of them getting anywhere.

'I love music,' Nathan said eventually.

'Good.'

'I was in the school orchestra. I can play the 1812 Overture on a tambourine.'

Woody nodded. Grimaced.

'And I once got stuck inside a double bass for three days.'

'Ah, well, yes,' Woody said.

'What do you think of the crowd tonight, then?' Nathan asked.

'Swell.'

'They adore you.'

Woody shrugged.

Nathan tried once more. Not even a dribble. 'I hate it when this happens,' he said again, and added with barely a breath, 'Do you ever think you'll make a film about Ireland?'

Woody shook his head. 'I make movies about Manhattan.'

'Fair enough. But you should think about expanding your range. You could make a Western.'

Woody nodded his head.

'Listen,' Nathan said, 'one of us had better zip up and move out or we're going to be here all night.'

'I guess so,' said Woody, making no attempt to move.

Nathan zipped and stepped back from the urinal. 'I would consider it an honour to have you pee in front of me.'

'Thanks.'

'Am I all right here, or do you want me to go to the door?'

'How about through the door?' Woody said.

'Excellent. Yes, excellent. I can hold on. It's no problem. Listen, if you've time later, stop by and say hello. I, ahm, I'm in the corner. You can't miss me. When I came in I tried to order a Malibu, but the barman misheard, and I've been stuck in the corner with this bloody caribou all night.'

Woody didn't acknowledge him. As Nathan backed out through the door the genius actor-writer-director-comedian's head was disappearing in a cloud of steam.

3

'Where've you been?' Lisa asked when Nathan, relieved now, finally arrived back at their table. She knocked back the rest of her whiskey and coke and signalled at the waiter for another in one fluid motion.

Nathan pulled his chair into the table and gazed into his girlfriend's eyes. Blue. Swimming-pool eyes, he'd called them on their first meeting.

'Having a piss with Woody Allen.'

'Aye.'

'I was. I swear.'

He nodded back towards the men's room. Woody was just emerging, looking about him warily.

'See?'

Lisa shrugged. 'So what, anyhow?'

The thought of their first meeting also flitted through her mind. They both thought about it so often because it was so perfect. And so long ago. She'd fallen in love with him within an hour of meeting him, slept with him within two hours and promised lifelong devotion by morning time. On good days she still felt pretty much the same, but when she was feeling low, which was more often in recent weeks, she'd look at Nathan and blame it all on a holiday romance that had obviously run its course. It was the full moon high in the sky, the incessant jabber of the Chinese, and mostly the miraculous coincidence of it all, that two lost children from Northern Ireland should bump into each other aboard a battered old ferry chugging along the Yangtze River. They had been the only Westerners on board, but ignoring him wouldn't have bothered her because she wasn't floundering about in the midst of bloody China wanting to meet other Westerners. But a shy voice from home, a cheeky smile, and the offer of shares in a purloined bottle of Tsang Tao beer had her practically falling at his feet. She looked at her watch and tutted.

She snagged Nathan's elbow. 'Nathan, please, let's just go home, eh?'

'They're not finished.'

'I know. But I'm tired. I only have the one night off. Please.'

Nathan took a big gulp of his beer. 'Do you think you could just shut up?' He saw her eyes drop. He sighed. 'I'm sorry. Can't you picture yourself in New Orleans?'

'I can picture myself in bed. With you.' It was a lie, but a sweet one.

'Is that an offer?'

'Might be.'

Nathan looked back to the stage. The New Orleans Funeral and Ragtime Orchestra had returned and was just hitting the first few notes of 'A Shanty in Old Shanty Town'.

Lisa stared at Nathan, who grinned inanely at the orchestra in general and Woody in particular. She leaned across the table to him to deliver a shouted whisper. 'Four weeks in a row this is, Nathan.'

'So? He's class.'

'You don't even like this sort of music. I know you.'

He barely looked round. 'You think you know me,' he hissed out of the corner of his mouth. 'But you know fuck all. Now fuck up.'

Lisa rocked back in her seat. She gulped her drink. 'Bastard,' she snapped.

She let out a sigh, squeezed the stem of her glass like it was his neck. It was time for her to go. She could see from the creeping redness in his cheeks that it was time: she could read him like a petrol gauge; he would be the Nathan she loved for most of the night, witty, thoughtful, romantic: then as the drink began to kick in the redness would start at the tip of his chin and slowly move towards his forehead: empty, quarter-full, half, three-quarters, then before he got to a full tank she'd get clear, go home, avoid a scene. It didn't happen often; but often enough. That restaurant on 52nd: glasses smashed, table overturned, all over a slight discrepancy in the bill; the Embassy rock club, the punch-up with the waiter over a misheard drinks order. An almost otherworldly fury. He knew how it affected him, too, but always in retrospect; always with an apology and flowers and a promise.

She pushed a strand of auburn hair from her eyes. *It's not like I love him*, she thought. *It's not like he's particularly good-looking or has a good job or lots of money or is even particularly good company or a real friend. He's* . . . and she tried to categorize him, but she couldn't. He was Nathan.

The secret, she knew, was to keep her own temper.

She stood up. 'Are you coming?'

A pained expression. 'Will you wise up and sit down? They won't be long.'

'Nathan, I really do have a headache. Look, I'll slip on. I'll see you at home if you want to stay and enjoy them.'

'Sit.'

'You're an inconsiderate arrogant bastard, Nathan Jones.'

'Yeah. Sure. And I've been gone too long. Sit down, Lisa.'

Lisa sat. He smiled. Then she lifted his drink and threw it over him. Then she walked out. Even going out the door she was cursing herself for losing her temper instead of him.

She stood outside for five minutes, waiting to see if he'd come sheepishly out after her, but there was no sign; just the vague beat of the music and the violence of the Monday evening traffic. She caught a cab and went home to wait for him.

Two minutes later, a contrite Nathan Jones staggered through the door of Michael's pub looking for her. Kissing and making up was always the best part of the night. But she wasn't there. He could barely believe it. She *always* waited. God, if he went home now they'd only be rowing until the small hours; she'd need time to calm down. It was a feeble excuse and he knew it; nevertheless, he re-entered the pub for another drink. And another.

Later, on the wrong way home, completely refuelled and walking sideways, Nathan crashed his head off a bus-stop. When he woke someone had stolen his wallet. And one of his shoes.

4

'Mr President? The Ambassador and his team are waiting.'

President Michael Keneally turned from the armour-plated window, set down his Diet Pepsi and turned his sleepy gaze upon Graham Slovenski, the White House Chief of Staff. He sighed, ran his hand through his greying hair then waved at Slovenski to lead the way.

Outside the door a Secret Service agent dropped a hand from his earpiece and nodded. 'It's clear, sir,' he said.

'Where is she?' asked the President.

'First floor library.'

'Very good. Keep me informed.' The President padded along in Slovenski's shadow towards the Oval Office. 'Who is it today, Slo?' he asked wearily. 'We did Slovenia and Croatia yesterday, didn't we? Or was that Armenia and Slovakia?'

'Yesterday was Slovakia and Slovenia. The day before was Croatia and Albania. Today's Northern Ireland.'

'Irelandia. Dublin. Right.'

'Wrong. Belfast.'

'Right. So when was Armenia?'

'Tomorrow.'

The President stopped by the door to the Oval Office. Slovenski turned and ran an appraising eye over him, then reached up and fixed a crooked tie.

'There now,' he said.

'Slo,' the President drawled, 'is it very obvious that I don't have much of a clue what's going on in these countries? I mean, to them?'

'Don't worry about it, sir, your ignorance is lost in the translation.'

'Good job I don't know a word of Irish, then.'

'They speak English, sir.'

'As a second language.'

'As a first language.'

'Good God. Then who speaks Irish?'

'I don't know, sir.'

'Good God. Well, let's find out.'

Slovenski opened the door and ushered the President in. With an expansive smile and suddenly eagle-sharp eyes, Keneally crossed the room towards a tremulous-looking Northern Irish delegation.

There was no doubting that the President was a fine-looking man. He was well into middle age but still had a hint of puppy fat; he looked young enough to be sexy, old enough to be taken seriously. He had a beautiful wife who scared the pants off him.

President Keneally had been elected on a tax-cutting ticket, and he was already halfway to doing that. His literacy programme had been universally hailed as a breakthrough in education and was being adopted worldwide as a model system. He had proposed measures to clamp down on racial, sexual and political discrimination that had been universally applauded. He was the most super-do president in United

States history. Naturally he had the lowest first 100-day rating of any president since such ratings were invented and had already been the subject of three assassination attempts. 'Popularity breeds contempt,' was Slo's thinking on it.

The first had involved a microlight piloted by Marcus Fielding, a disgruntled ex-Black Panther who in his declining years had found his brand of militancy sadly out of favour with the times. He had packed two bags with Czech Semtex explosive, strapped them to his chest and aimed for the presidential living quarters. Sadly he had been too old to benefit from the President's literacy programme and had misread his free tourist map of the White House; although he successfully eluded the ultra-sophisticated Secret Service security system he managed to crash into a public reception area, killing himself, one security guard and a three-year-old llama awaiting presentation to the President as a gift from the President of Peru. Many more people would have been killed – although not the President, who was golfing in Maine – had the Semtex exploded. It didn't because Fielding had spent $3,000 on sixteen pounds of modelling clay. The Secret Service sent a new agent. The President of Peru sent a new llama.

The second attempt occurred when the President visited Dallas to mediate in a dispute between the oil barons and environmental campaigners. A mentally deranged woman, released into the community by one president and taught to be angry about it by another, decided to take it out on a third, and stabbed him in the arm with a used syringe when he took time out of his schedule to visit a day-care centre. The injury wasn't serious. There had been the usual uproar about the performance of the Secret Service and the FBI.

The third attempt had been that morning in the President's living quarters when he had tried to explain to the First Lady why her application to become a roving goodwill ambassador for the United Nations had been turned down.

Officially it was because the First Lady, great beauty and discerning intellectual that she was, had only recently moved to the White House and did not yet have sufficient international experience to take on such a demanding task. Unofficially it was because every nation under the sun hated the United States for being too powerful, too rich and too condescending. The President, unable to fall back on his normal team of speechwriters, had not explained it very well at all and the First Lady's much touted goodwill had suddenly evaporated.

The First Lady liked her eggs hard-boiled. Fortunately the assistant to the assistant to the White House chef was a seventeen-year-old reformed drug pusher called Mario Finelli. Mario had been detailed to perform the boiling of the First Lady's egg, and although he was one of the early beneficiaries of the President's literacy programme, he had still not mastered numeracy and had thus underboiled the egg by some two minutes. Had the egg, travelling at an estimated sixty-five miles per hour, been of the requested consistency when it connected with the President's temple, the First Lady might very well have become the First Widow on Murder Charge.

However, it had merely splattered over his face, damaging only his ego, then dripped into his lap. The President had spent the rest of the morning studiously avoiding her, moving circuitously about the White House guided by Secret Service agents relaying her every move. Eventually, he knew, she would track him down.

The Ambassador, a florid-faced man with an earnest smile, briefed the President on the delicate nature of his new state, the need to support its first steps towards democracy and the risk it ran of falling back into sectarian strife. One of his aides produced a map of the country from a battered leather art-folder and propped it up on a table. Using a pen as a pointer the Ambassador indicated different colourings. 'What we're trying to do, Mr President, is attract investment to the areas of our country most ravaged by the twin blights of sectarianism and unemployment. We must get people working together if we're going to have any hope at all.' He pointed to areas of Belfast, the second city, Londonderry, then drew his pen along the length of the border with the Republic of Ireland. 'The areas marked in green signify a majority Catholic population, i.e. generally sympathetic to a united Ireland. The areas marked in orange represent a Protestant majority, i.e. generally sympathetic to maintaining strong links with Great Britain.'

President Keneally nodded thoughtfully. 'And the blue area in the centre, what does that represent?'

'That's Lough Neagh, Mr President.'

'Yes. Of course. Good for fishing, is it?'

'I'd highly recommend it. Why not come visit, see for yourself?'

The President looked round at Slovenski. 'How about it, Slo, a visit to Ireland likely in the next few months?'

Slovenski shook his head. 'Unlikely, sir. We've so much legislation to push through . . . then there's the South American tour after that. Argentina, Venezuela, Brazil, Peru . . . unless you would consider asking the First Lady to represent you?'

The Ambassador's eyes lit up. 'That would be wonderful.' He beamed.

The President pursed his lips. 'It's certainly a thought.'

'Will I suggest it to her, sir?' Slovenski asked.

'Yes. Do that.' The President turned his head slightly

towards his chief of staff and winked, then wheeled sharply back towards the Ambassador and his aides. He clicked off the charm switch. 'Now, what else can we do for you gentlemen? We seem to be running out of time. As you know, America is keen to support emerging democratic nations, but the money bag isn't bottomless. I think we've already channelled quite a lot of cash in your direction, haven't we?'

The Ambassador clamped his hands together. 'Yes, Mr President, the United States has been most helpful, but the task is a long one, a hard one, and an expensive one.' The Ambassador pulled at his lip. 'And we would like to ask a favour.'

'Ask.'

'I understand you're meeting with Michael Tate next week.'

The President nodded gravely. Tate, president of the computer software giant Magiform, was not his favourite person, but nevertheless he had felt obliged to accept an invitation to attend a reception to mark his $50m purchase of the Empire State Building and to help launch his latest assault on under-exploited overseas markets. The *New York Times* had already predicted that Tate would be the first computer nerd in the White House. The *Washington Post* had said that he already was, such was the influence of the world's richest man in the corridors of power. The President wanted to stay the President, so he didn't mind going along and making a speech, but he would absolutely draw the line at being asked to serve drinks.

President Keneally rubbed absentmindedly at the spot on his temple where the 65 mph egg had splattered, then nodded at the Ambassador. 'And you fancy a Magiform plant in your back yard.'

'We thought a word from . . .'

'The Irish helped build America, didn't they, Ambassador?'

'They certainly did.'

'And the Keneallys are all good Irish stock, aren't they, Ambassador?'

'As I understand, Mr President.'

'Well, we'd be remiss not putting a good word in, wouldn't we then?'

'We'd be most grateful.'

The President dropped his grin, and his voice. 'Really?' he said, pushing his face towards the Ambassador. 'How?'

'Ahm, well, sir . . .' spluttered the Ambassador.

'Money perhaps? Shares? Real estate, Mr Ambassador . . .?'

'Well, sir, I . . .'

The President roared with laughter. 'If you could see your face!'

The Ambassador forced a strangled laugh. His aides giggled along nervously. Leaning against the door, Slovenski shook his head, then pushed himself off it. 'Mr President?' He tapped his watch.

President Keneally nodded. 'We'd better wipe that from the tapes, eh, Slo?' Slovenski grinned. The President extended his hand to the Ambassador, then to his aides, thanked them all sincerely for coming to see him and promised he would do everything in his power to help regenerate their stricken country. Much as he had the Albanian, Slovakian, Slovenian and Croatian ambassadors in the preceding days, and would undoubtedly do to the Armenian representative the next day. There was no point in being negative personally; he could leave that up to the shirts.

In the corridor the Secret Service agent hurriedly diverted the President and Slovenski towards the kitchens until the First Lady had completed another circuit and then they returned to his private study.

Slovenski pulled a chair out for himself and sat, lifting his feet up to rest them on the edge of the table. 'Sending her might mend some bridges.'

'There?'

'Here. It would get her some goodwill experience, too.'

The President nodded thoughtfully for a moment. 'Okay,' he said finally, 'you get the wrapping paper, I'll hunt out the Scotch tape.'

5

He walked and he walked and he walked. The dry nausea of hangover arrived with the creeping dawn, but still he tramped on, his shoeless foot now growing sore at the relentless pace. With what little change he could muster he purchased and devoured an Egg McMuffin in a McDonald's, then brought it up on a jewellery store window on Fifth Avenue. *Breakfast on Tiffany's.*

He limped on, rehearsing the whole way. He would say sorry. He would say sorry with flowers – no, no money. He would apologize and promise a reformation of the soul. No, she'd heard that one before. He'd swear off the drink. Nope. Been there, failed at that. He'd threaten suicide. Murder. Self-mutilation. What can you promise when you've promised it all before? She'd take one look at him coming through the door, every inch the raggedy man, and shut him out of her life. And instead of trying to persuade her he'd lose his temper, there'd be a shouting match and before he knew it he'd be putting the final nail in their relationship with some other major transgression when all he was trying to do was declare his love. *Just like Sid and*

Nancy, fight, fight, fight, love, love, love. Except for the drugs. Unless love is the drug.

When he came to Madison Square Park he took a seat on a park bench, lifting his legs up onto it to give them a rest.

He dropped off into a little doze and regretted it immediately. It was the familiar nightmare: in the dark, the terror of that first blast of gunfire suddenly segueing deliciously into Sid Vicious murdering *My Way* and blocking it all out: he could feel no pain; witness no carnage; no longer was he standing crying in the lonely slaughter yard, waiting to be rescued. He was with Sid. And as long as he was with Sid he didn't have to dream about Coolidge and his exploding head. In his dream Sid was a pretty smart fella and they would have some rare conversations. Which was nice, because he knew that in real life Sid was an empty-head.

Nathan shuddered into consciousness. He checked his watch. It was before eight. The park was starting to get busy. His gaze fell on a plump guy in a trench coat hurrying through, face red from the exertion, a paper cup in one hand, a half-eaten doughnut in the other. He was alone, but not alone. Two men were converging on him from either side. Young men. Dusty like Nathan from roughing it. One of them stuck out a foot and sent the plump guy sprawling, coffee in the air, doughnut after it. A Charlie Chaplin mugging. He landed on his stomach with a whoosh of air then rolled over onto his back. One of the guys stuck a foot on his throat, the other bent to rifle his pockets. They didn't appear to be carrying any weapons. Passers-by, on either side, passed by.

Nathan limped over. It was a few moments before they became aware of him. One first, then he tapped his partner. They exchanged glances, then looked back to him.

'Morning,' Nathan said.

Their eyes betrayed only a hazy drug-fuelled curiosity. They weren't concerned. 'What you want, man?' said one. 'He's ours.'

The plump man's face was turning purple. He whined a strangled 'Aaaaaooooh,' and bubbles came out of his nose.

Nathan shrugged and turned away. Then he turned back and pivoting on his sock-foot, kicked up into the face of the closest drugger just as he removed the man's wallet. He sprawled back, dropping his prize. The other made a dive for the wallet. Got a hand to it, too, but a broken hand once Nathan's shoe crunched down on it. Then they were off and running and the plump man rolled over gasping onto his stomach.

Nathan lifted the wallet. Flicked through it. Maybe two hundred dollars. Driver's licence identifying Leonard Maltman. Nathan knelt, placed a hand on poor Leonard's shoulder. 'You okay, mister?' he asked.

Leonard was still wheezing, but his face was already a better colour. He rubbed at his throat and nodded in the same motion. Nathan held up his hand. 'I got your wallet. I don't think they took anything.'

He helped Leonard sit up, then handed him the wallet. Leonard coughed twice, spat something out onto the grass. 'Jesus!' he said. 'Didn't see them! Jesus!' He shook his head furiously, trying to rid himself of the cobwebs, although it probably wasn't the most effective medicine under the circumstances, then took a closer look at Nathan. 'What the hell are you, undercover?'

Nathan smiled, shook his head, started to dust himself down. 'Nah. I was mugged myself last night, so I know how you feel. I'm only now getting home.'

'Well, thank God . . .' Leonard flicked through his wallet, then slapped the brown leather pouch into the palm of his hand. 'And they didn't get a red cent!' He flipped the wallet open again. 'Let me give you something,' he said.

Nathan shook his head. 'No need,' he said.

'You must. You saved my hide, son, it's the least . . . what in hell's name happened to your shoe?'

'I told you. I got mugged. They stole my shoe.'

'They get your wallet?'

Nathan touched his jacket pocket. 'Yeah, well.'

Leonard offered the money again. 'Listen, take this, it's only . . .'

Nathan held up his hand. 'I have plenty of money at home.'

He hauled Leonard to his feet, which was no easy task.

'At the very least let me buy you a cup of coffee,' said Leonard, carefully testing his weight on each foot. He winced a little. 'And a doughnut.'

Nathan shrugged. 'I'm not a bum,' he said. 'I really do have money at home.'

Leonard clamped a beefy hand on his shoulder. 'Son, I don't care if you're Michael Fucking Tate, I'm gonna buy you a doughnut.'

He did too. And a pair of shoes. By the time Nathan was back on the roundabout path to Greenwich Village, Leonard Maltman, head of security at the Empire State Building, had offered him a job.

6

Lisa was already away to work when he got home. There was no note. It was a bad sign. Usually there was something stuck to the fridge. Something funny. The foundations of a bridge over troubled waters. Nathan stripped off his blood-stained clothes and stuck them into the wash. Then he had a shave and a shower and pulled on his canvas jeans, black v-neck jumper and ancient denim jacket and blinked out into the Village. He bought a cup of coffee, a sandwich and a copy of the *New York Times* and walked across to Washington Square. He found a rare seat that wasn't occupied by a derelict. He had an hour to kill. With all the office workers and their erections out to lunch, Lisa would just be hitting her peak period.

His thoughts turned, for the hundredth time that night, to Lisa. She was such an independent soul, and he was such a dependent one. She had latched onto New York like it was home; it scared him. Sometimes, when they had to meet but were on different sides of the city, she wondered why he always arrived late. She'd taken it as laziness, as carelessness, as nonchalance. She didn't know it was because he couldn't work out how to use the subway system and didn't like to ask. When they'd met in China she'd had half a dozen men salivating round her on the ferry because she was such a chatter, a free spirit who infected others with it. She didn't know that although he'd travelled on four continents in recent years he had barely exchanged sober words with more than half a dozen people in all that time. She thought it was laid-backness, coolness, a moody sullenness. Sometimes he desperately, desperately wanted to tell her things, but couldn't, couldn't put it into words, or when he did it came out wrong, or came out as gibberish, or came out as sarcasm. He'd never told her about his dead friends. She didn't know that he loved her.

He arrived at Star World at a little before three, ignoring the video racks and sex toys and proceeding straight up the stairs to the throbbing first floor. Slim Dharkin was, as ever, wedged into his booth. In the vaguely psychedelic four-colour disco light he looked a little like an enormous genie wedged in the top of a murky bottle.

'Five dollars, five tokens, tips extra,' Dharkin said with the dullness of eternal repetition, as Nathan put his money on the counter. 'Money back on the tokens you don't use.'

'I know this already, Slim,' Nathan said, lifting the tokens. He'd been coming here every day since Lisa had taken on the job. She'd even introduced them one night at the end of her shift.

Slim peered forward. 'Oh. Okay. Hi,' he said without conviction. 'Sure.'

'Where's Lisa today?'

Slim scratched his head for a moment, then nodded slightly. 'Cage three,' he said and pointed along the corridor.

Nathan moved off.

'Tips extra,' Dharkin said after him.

When Nathan reached the cage he opened up the door of the most central booth, then slotted in one of the tokens. This had become the pattern after the mistake of his first visit, when he had put all five tokens in at once and spent the whole five minutes watching his girlfriend's breasts being felt by the ginger-haired teenager on the far side of the cage. He had then followed the teenager for fourteen blocks debating whether to punch him to death. He eventually decided it wasn't practical. If he killed everyone who felt Lisa's breasts he would go down as the biggest mass murderer in history.

Lisa's decision to work in Star World had been taken lightly. At least it seemed that way to Nathan. She'd been working in a succession of fast-food joints, earning barely enough for one, let alone two. Then, cleaning tables, she'd met Cindy and got talking. Cindy was a big, brassy black broad who looked about as sexually alluring as a slice of toast, but who didn't have a problem telling anyone where she worked and what she did. Naturally, Lisa was disgusted.

'And they . . .' Lisa said, open-mouthed. 'And then they . . .'

'Right up. Whole fist sometimes . . .'

'And doesn't it . . .'

'Sure it does. But it hurts at home, too, and *he* don't pay me twelve hundred a week.'

'Twelve hundred dollars?'

'Sure. Lotta lonely guys out there. Look at you, girl, you're slim, you gotta chest. You could make double what a fat old bitch like me makes.'

Lisa had laughed it off, right up to the point where some crack-head had tried to throttle her out of nowhere when she was cleaning the men's room, and she decided she wasn't getting paid enough to go through that any more.

She tried to talk it over sensibly with Nathan, said that her breasts had never given her any sexual pleasure. 'So why shouldn't I make a fortune letting lonely men feel them? They might as well be feeling my elbow for all the thrill I get out of it. I swear to God I won't go any further.'

'It's disgusting,' was Nathan's argument. 'The next stop is prostitution.'

'I have no intention of becoming a prostitute. We need money, Nathan, and you're not earning any.'

'There are other ways to earn it, Lisa. This is . . . sick.'

'Sure there are other ways. I could stay in McDonald's for peanuts, at least until they work out I've no green card and I get slung out on the streets again. I don't want to go back to Ireland, Nathan, I like it here. Cindy says she earns eight hundred a week – twelve hundred in a good one.'

Nathan screwed up his face in disgust. 'Cindy is a slut. She earns that much money because she lets men put their fingers right up her cunt, if you'll excuse the expression.'

'Well, I've no intention of doing that.'

'Yes, and Hitler had no intention of reneging on the Nazi–Soviet Non-Aggression Pact.'

'What?'

'My point is, one thing leads to another.'

'Not in this case.'

'Sure. I've been smoking drugs for twenty years and I'm still not addicted.'

'What?'

'It'll become impossible to give up, Lisa. Don't you see? You'll start earning good money, but it won't be enough. Some bastard will offer you thirty dollars to let him stick his fingers up, and you'll think, well, just once, what's the harm.

And then it'll happen again, and again, so you'll get used to it. And then the next bastard will come along and offer you twice as much for something else, then something more, and before you know it you'll be an HIV hooker with a three hundred dollars a day crack habit and a pimp with a big Afro and huge flares who beats the living daylights out of you for not fucking all his friends and taking the starring role in a snuff movie. All for letting some spotty little geek feel your tits in a sordid little place like that. Jesus, Lisa, what would your mummy say?'

'I'll still want to sleep with you.'

'Sleep being the optimum word. You'll be so sick of sex you won't want to know me. And I probably won't want to know you.'

'So it's not your concern for me at all, it's just sexual jealousy.'

'Of course it's sexual jealousy. And concern. How do you expect me to feel? Gratified? Proud? You want me to offer encouragement at your excellent choice of career?'

'There's no need for sarcasm.'

'No, no, there's not. There's need for a large wooden mallet. To knock some fucking sense into you.'

'I don't see you getting a job. I don't see you helping out.'

'Why don't I get one in the next place along? Men can come in and feel my cock for twenty dollars.'

'Well you could.'

'Oh yeah yeah. I'll get a job when I find the right job.'

'Oh Mr Big Responsible. You just pick and choose while we starve to death.'

He tutted. How could he explain to her about his last job, about Coolidge's head? 'We're not going to fucking starve.'

'No thanks to you.'

'You don't understand, Lisa.'

'I do. You think you're above work.'

'I think I'm above shit work.'

It wasn't something they were ever likely to agree on, but in the end they compromised on her giving it a week's trial. She would quit if at the end of that time she hadn't earned $800. Nathan reserved the right to spy on her at any given time to make sure she wasn't contravening the agreement. He also agreed to look for a job. Three weeks on, with Lisa earning $1,300 a week and sticking to their agreement, Nathan had finally landed one.

As the door slid up Nathan peered through. Lisa got up off her seat, said something to the girl beside her, yawned, then loosened the top of her swimsuit, but held it firmly in place with one hand and put her hand out for the tip with the other.

Nathan reached a chicken salad wholemeal sandwich through to her.

She bent down to peer through the little rectangular door. 'Oh,' she said, 'it's you.'

'I brought you some lunch.'

'Thanks. I'm not really hungry.'

'Oh. Okay.' He withdrew the sandwich. 'I'm sorry about last night. Really sorry.'

'Uhuh.'

'I've got myself a job. I start on Monday. Guarding the Empire State Building. Everything's going to be okay. I want you to quit.'

There was a long pause. Then she said, 'Oh Nathan.'

'What?'

'Oh Nathan,' she said again and she looked to him to be on the verge of tears. She reached down and took his face in her hands and kissed him hard on the lips. The tip of her

41

tongue darted into his mouth. Then she pulled back. There *was* a tear. 'I love you so much. But this is driving me mad.'

'I know. Quit.'

'Not *this*, this fighting. We've got to stop it.'

'I know,' he said. 'I know.'

Then a door slid open on the far side of the cage and she turned quickly from him. 'Please go, Nathan, I've work to do. We'll make up properly later, okay?'

'Okay.'

And the tip was paid and the breasts were out and his door slid down.

7

When the President couldn't sleep, which was often, he would turn to his computer. On this night, with his wife giving him two cold and freckled shoulders, he sought solace in his e-mail.

It had become part of his campaign to answer random questions without fuss or publicity, thus ensuring fuss and publicity. A farmer in Iowa, an insurance clerk in Wyoming, a crack dealer in the Bronx, all had received his words of wisdom, then raced to their local newspaper or TV station. Word had soon spread and before long thirty thousand questions a day were coming into campaign headquarters by e-mail, and that figure had remained constant on the move to the White House. Now he had three members of staff detailed to answer some of these questions on his behalf; it was not an advertised service, and thus no one was ever disappointed if they did not get a reply.

Generally he ignored the boring questions and kept his eye out for the unusual. The 1,000-plus enquiries about the budget deficit could be easily handled by his staff. The 3,600 questions about income tax likewise. Even the eternal NRA debate failed to move him. He liked the personals. He could play Dear Abbey, but not just dole out paternal advice, he could get something done. Answer prayers. Play God.

Mr President: My name is Toni Lopez. I own a bookshop in Des Moines. I voted for you. I'm losing a fortune because people keep stealing my books. Whoever heard of anyone robbing a bookshop? I've complained to the police, but they do nothing. Can you help?

Dear Toni: Mea culpa. I hadn't realized my literacy programme was so successful.

I'll call the Chief of Police and make sure he keeps a personal eye on your shop. Michael Keneally (President).

He liked the brackets. Made it seem like an afterthought. My friend the President. By lunchtime every shopper in Des Moines would have heard all about it. One day, Michael Tate had told him, people would vote via the Internet. Democracy would be a computer. Those without access would be without democracy. The true underclass. Tate was a cheery son-of-a-bitch.

He trawled on: poverty-stricken in Nashville; Vietnam vet in Tulsa; Aids victim in Los Angeles; illegal immigrant in Dallas. He dealt with them quickly: a $500 goodwill payment to Nash; recognition of his valour for the vet; deep concern and sympathy for the Aids victim; a quick call to the right authorities for the Mex and he'd be back over the border before dawn. There were no votes in illegal aliens.

The President looked up at a slight tapping on the door of his study, then a dishevelled mop appeared round it.

'Thought I saw a light on,' Slovenski said. 'Everything okay?'

The President smiled up at his favourite. 'You're a god-damn liar, Slo, you know the door's light-proofed. You're just snooping around again.' He indicated for Slovenski to take a chair, but he stayed where he was. 'Everything okay with you?'

Slovenski shook his head. 'Yeah. Sure.'

'Well, why don't you go on home, then?'

'I'm about to. I was working on some speeches.'

'Yeah? What am I saying these days?'

Slovenski shrugged. 'Just the usual glad tidings of great joy.'

The President nodded his head slowly. 'This health care thing's getting you down, isn't it, Slo?'

The health care *thing* was extremely close to the President's heart. The reforms he was proposing would make first-class medical treatment available to *everyone* for the first time. Naturally, such reforms would also decimate the insurance business. The insurance companies, and who could blame them, weren't happy about this and had bought up half of the Senate in order to fight their corner. Michael Tate didn't seem to care one way or another about the reforms, but he could deliver the required seats if he felt like it. And he seemed to be enjoying keeping the President guessing.

Slovenski shrugged. 'I just hate the thought of going cap in hand to Tate. But it's the only way.'

'Pride comes before a fall, and other mindless clichés. Don't judge Tate too harshly. He's new, he enjoys playing the game. Just think of him as Rockefeller with a ponytail.'

'Uhuh. As I recall, Rockefeller was a son-of-a-bitch as well. Remember Iowa?'

The President nodded. Tate had brought prosperity to Iowa. Ten thousand jobs, twenty thousand more in support indus-tries, even built a house in some godforsaken little outpost so that he could get back to nature. But soon the house wasn't big enough and he decided to extend it, except the mayor of that godforsaken little outpost had ruled against the extension. Insisted that Tate attend a council meeting to personally argue his case, then humiliated him in public. Tate just smiled and shrugged, and next day moved his factories and his jobs to Colorado and the whole Iowan economy had collapsed. Tate's blessings were bountiful, but his revenge was catastrophic and every senator, every representative, ran scared of him, or for him. 'You would have done the same, Slo.'

'I wouldn't have moved to Iowa.' He rolled his eyes. 'Maybe. I just don't like the way he tries to squeeze . . .'

'I don't mind being squeezed. Right up to the point where I *do* mind, and then Mr Tate will discover that I can play hard ball as well.'

Slovenski smiled. 'I'll look forward to that.' He opened the door again. 'Goodnight, Mr President.'

'Night, Slo.'

'You should get some sleep, sir.'

The President smirked. 'The dragon is still smoking, Slo. I'll give her another hour yet.'

Slovenski grinned and closed the door carefully behind him.

In fact the dragon *was* smoking. Tara was perched at the top of the stairs as Slo left the Oval Office. The First Lady, after a long process of elimination, had worked out that this was the only place in the historic old White House that she could enjoy a Marlboro without setting off the god-damn smoke alarms.

Slo stopped suddenly on the third step. 'Oh. I'm sorry. I didn't see you there.'

'Yes you did, or you wouldn't have stopped.'

'It was a figure of speech.'

46

Tara arched her eyebrows. 'Still working?'

'No, I'm a hologram.'

Tara smiled; they both did. 'I asked for that.'

Slo nodded. He looked nervously back towards the Oval Office. 'He did his best, about the United . . .'

Tara raised a hand. 'Don't. I don't want to hear.'

'I'm serious, Tara, he did every . . .'

'Slo!' He stopped. 'Do you want a cigarette?'

'No. No thank you.'

They looked at each other.

'Slo,' Tara said, 'did anyone ever tell you your eyebrows are nearly invisible?'

Slo's eyebrows were nearly invisible, but not nearly as invisible as Michael Tate's moustache. That just barely registered as *fluff*. He had tried shaving twice a day, thinking that would make it grow faster and harder. But it just grew back even fluffier. He controlled the world, but he couldn't control his own facial hair.

'Sort of puts things in perspective, doesn't it, Mark?' Tate said, examining his fluff closely in the mirror. They were in the Magiform Corporate Headquarters in Venice Beach.

Mark Benedict grunted and continued to concentrate on the map of the world on the computer monitor before him. A little red dot signified the countries in which Magiform software was the market leader. Every western country had a little red dot. All but a handful of eastern. Performance was a bit patchier on the African continent, but Tate wasn't concerned about that. 'How can you expect a guy in Rwanda to concern himself with software when he has chopping up his neighbour with a machete to worry about?' he laughed and then turned from the mirror. He stood behind his old friend. 'Mark, it's

47

frightening sometimes how much of the world we control, isn't it?'

'We? *You*. And yes, it is frightening.'

'Extra frightening that I could just send out a virus any time I felt like it, and destroy civilization as we know it.'

'You wouldn't do that. I know you wouldn't because you couldn't survive in the real world.'

'Good point. But if ever I felt like committing suicide. That would be the way to go.'

Benedict nodded thoughtfully. After a few moments he said, 'I think you need to see a shrink.'

'Never,' said Tate.

Dear Mr President: You're an evil cock-sucking bastard. You've betrayed your race by giving in to those power-crazy black bastards. Look what they've done to our cities: hookers and drug pushers everywhere. The sooner you draft laws allowing us to shoot the niggers on sight the better. Jews and Koreans too. Answer this one, you faggot-loving fuck. George Burley.

Dear George: Thank you for your kind thoughts at this difficult time for our nation. While I take on board your sentiments, I cannot say that I wholeheartedly agree with them. Can I give you a word of advice, George? As of 1.35 AM today, July 24, I have informed an FBI SWAT team that you are the high priest of a pseudo-Christian Fundamentalist movement and have been stockpiling arms for an attack on your local mosque. That SWAT team is now travelling by military helicopter to your neighbourhood. They have been instructed to use all necessary firepower. Get out of the house, George! With all best wishes, President Michael Keneally.

President Keneally sat back and laughed. He sent the message, then called the switchboard and checked on George Burley's telephone number in Birmingham, Alabama. He punched in the numbers and let the phone ring for a couple of minutes. Eventually a gruff, sleep-thick voice answered.

'Hey, George?'

'Uuuuuh, yeah?'

'George Burley?'

'Yeah. Yeah. What the . . .'

'You don't know me, George.'

'Well . . . what the hell time is it?'

'It's gone one, George. I thought you'd like to know something.'

'At one in the morning I don't want to know fuck, mister, now get off the fucking . . .'

'Shut the fuck up, George. I'm doing you a favour here. Sticking my neck out. Listen carefully . . . we all gotta stick together. You sent some hate mail to the President . . .'

'I didn't . . .'

'Don't fuck with me, George. The President saw it, read it, he's fuming. I hear on the grapevine he's sending someone to see you. I don't know who, George, but sure as hell won't be fucking Bugs Bunny. Check your e-mail George. Now. Be afraid. Be very afraid.'

The President set the phone down and wished dearly that he was in Birmingham, Alabama.

When he looked up again the First Lady, the former Tara Holmes-Boyce, was yawning in the doorway. Half a smile floated across her face.

'Oh,' said the President.

'Oh indeed,' said the First Lady, running a hand with some difficulty through her sleep-tangled but monstrously expensive hairstyle of the week. 'Are you not coming to bed?'

'Is that an invitation?'

'It's a request.'

'I didn't think you were speaking to me.'

'I'm speaking to you. I'm just not your friend.'

The President tutted and looked back to his computer screen. Tara didn't move from the doorway. 'I did what I could about the UN, you know?'

'I don't want to argue about it now, Michael.' She turned slightly, about to leave, then stopped. 'Beyond saying that you're the most powerful man in the world and you wouldn't lift your hand to get your bored wife a worthwhile job.' As he opened his mouth to reply she put her finger to her lips and shushed him. 'Now come to bed,' she said. 'I'm cold.'

With a dramatic swish of her dressing-gown she was gone. The President hurriedly switched off his computer and followed. He caught up with her just as she entered the bedroom. She turned, untied her belt, then stood naked, tantalizing, before him. Their eyes locked. The President blinked first. She gave him another half-smile then climbed into the bed, gathering the quilt about her until she was wrapped as tightly as an Egyptian mummy.

The President sat on the side of the bed. 'I'm sorry,' he said. 'I did my best.'

'Michael, you've stopped the war in the Middle East. You've brokered a peace settlement in Peru. Thanks to your leadership alone half the world is enjoying an economic boom. And you can't get me an unpaid job distributing M&Ms to the needy. Explain that to me.'

'It's just not that simple.'

'Yes it is, Michael. You just don't want me to have it.'

'I want you to have everything, Tara. I have given you everything I can. And I will give you the UN job . . . just sometimes these things cannot be done overnight. For God's sake, you only dreamt this up last week, I can't reorganize the United Nations on a whim . . .'

Tara arched up out of bed. 'It's not a fucking whim!'

'I know, I'm sorry, I . . .'

'I went through that entire campaign at your side, Michael. Have you any idea how many speeches, how many rallies . . .'

'I thought you enjoyed . . .'

'I enjoyed it for you, Michael . . . but there's got to be more to life than smiling at your side! I want to do something in my own right! Jesus Christ, Michael, look who they do have running about the world as a goodwill ambassador. Michael fucking Jackson!'

'I know, I know . . . what can I say . . .'

'Say nothing, do something.'

'Did Slo say to you about Ireland?'

'I ask for the world, you give me Ireland. Not even all of Ireland, just the squiggly bit at the top everyone fights over.'

'It's a start.'

'It's a finish, Michael, if you can't do better than that.'

'You're saying you won't go.'

'Oh I'll go okay. I just might not come back.'

He closed his eyes and spoke with quiet desperation. 'What the hell do you want me to do, Tara?'

She gave him the long, cool, professional stare of the born politician. 'Better,' she said.

Surprisingly, they made love after that. The easy, cosy love of familiarity. Whispered love and promises. To stop himself coming too soon he thought of greasy, fat, stretch-panted George Burley running through the streets of Birmingham dodging every shadow. To make herself come, the First Lady thought of chief of staff Graham Slovenski.

51

8

On 16 September 1963 at the 16th Street Baptist Church in Birmingham, Alabama, George Burley Snr, a leading Klan member, helped plant a bomb which killed four young black girls attending Bible class. The church still contains a small shrine to the murdered girls which, once or twice a year, is ritually desecrated by his son, George Burley Jnr.

His father, now long dead, his lungs wrecked by overwork producing pig-iron in the Sloss Furnaces, spent many evenings regaling his family with stories of that bombing and other merry Klan japes, so it could be argued that George Burley Jnr had some kind of pedigree for what he managed to achieve in those few minutes between the tip-off and fleeing the state.

The explosives were secreted about the house and took several long minutes to gather together, prime and set the trap, his ears cocked the whole time for the beat of the helicopters. George was forty, slim, well but not overly muscled. His hair, naturally curly, was cut short. His face might have been described as good-looking by another man, but a perceptive woman would have detected an inner conceit and outer vanity which detracted from those looks. The classic detracta-attracta face first defined by Freud. He wore black jeans, a sky-blue cotton shirt and Nike trainers. Although he was divorced he still wore his wedding ring.

George strapped his revolver beneath his black sports jacket, then, from the false bottom of a trunk in his garage he extracted and built in 38 seconds his AK-47 assault rifle. From the plant-pots lining the side of the patio he dug up in rapid succession sixteen hand grenades carefully packed in individual Press 'n' Seal sandwich bags. The rifle and grenades he placed in the back of his jeep along with his long-prepared survival bag. From tip-off to departure it took him twelve minutes. He'd practised it twice before: once at fifteen minutes, once at ten. He was quite pleased. He knew that practice and reality were poles apart. Just like in 'Nam.

He'd never been to 'Nam, of course, but he was a big fan of *Platoon*, *Full Metal Jacket*, *Apocalypse Now* and the first half of *Born on the Fourth of July*, so he knew what it was all about. George was himself a former Green Beret. At least, he had attended a two-week training school administered by the Green Berets, so knew all the tricks of their trade. This was George through and through, the jackdaw mentality. From any chosen field of study he could extract exactly what he needed, ditch the rest. His full-time job was as a computer operator at Birmingham Airport, just four miles from his home, and he could do it with his eyes closed, sometimes did, but in his spare time George allowed his mind to roam. For example, he wanted to know more about God, so he completed a correspondence course with the Pioneer Theological Seminary in Rockford, Illinois, and received a bachelor of divinity degree in a remarkable six-week study-period and for only $25. He followed this up within three months with an MA from the Burton College and Seminary in Manitou Springs in Colorado ($46). Given six more months and a couple of hundred dollars George could've been Bishop of New York. He was a theologian and had the certificates to prove it; he knew exactly what it said in the *God-damn fucking Bible* about the niggers and Keneally being the anti-Christ; he could read between the *God-damn fucking lines* better than anyone.

George drove out of Birmingham at a leisurely pace, taking care not to draw attention to himself. At such a late hour the roads were extremely quiet and he was confident that he wasn't followed. He kept off the main thoroughfares, traversing the city's backroads with a studied nonchalance before meeting the highway and heading north-east towards Atlanta. After an hour on the road he pulled off and booked into a motel, paying cash. He took three grenades and the AK-47 into the room with him and lay down with them by his side. He spent some time addressing a long, involved prayer to God, then lay back on his bed and tried to imagine the scene of utter devastation he'd left behind in Birmingham.

He woke at 7 AM, watched the morning news in vain for some mention of the operation to arrest him, then consulted his Top Ten. He had been maintaining his Top Ten People I Want To Kill since he was a boy. He began by scrolling back through the years on his Apple PowerBook; it had taken him the best part of a year to enter the weekly charts on his computer, but it had been worth it, being able to trace his development like that. Sometimes he squirmed with embarrassment at the early entries. The innocence of boyhood! The fashions of adolescence! The horror of Civil Rights! He stopped at one chart from the Sixties: Cassius Clay, Stevie Wonder, Martin Luther King and Malcolm X. He shook his head and smiled. How refreshing that they were all either dead or disabled. Even then he had been a fine judge of mortality. He wondered how his current chart might fare in the coming months, particularly now that he had decided to kill the President.

1 Oprah Winfrey (fat version)
2 Oprah Winfrey (lo-fat version)
3 Michael Keneally (cock-sucker)
4 'Magic' Jordan
5 Spike Lee
6 Tom Hanks for *Philadelphia* (faggot) and Forrest Gump (insult to intelligence)
7 Woody Allen (Jew)
8 Myron Linklater (Computer Supervisor, Birmingham Airport)
9 Jesse Jackson
10 Rap Music

Rap Music, he appreciated, wasn't a person, but if he had to list all the ugly black rappers he hated, he'd have to make it a top 100 and then some.

He had showed the list to someone else only once before. Mrs Burley was a daughter of an illustrious Klan member and must have known what she was marrying, but even she was a bit taken aback by his Top Ten. She was also a bit taken aback by her experience planting bulbs in the pots on the patio (it was quite fortunate that George was off work that day and was available to replace the safety pin in the hand grenade before it exploded) and he'd had to make several costly concessions to her before she agreed not to mention the grenades in the papers filed with the court for their divorce.

Whereas he might have expected a bit of loyalty from Mrs

Burley, he hadn't expected (and certainly wasn't disappointed by) the reaction of his High School teacher when he came across the weekly variation of the Top Ten in the back of his assignment book. George was frog-marched out of the class. His teacher Errol McCrae (black) had some angry words in the office with the headmaster Mark Goodyear (white) before he was shown in.

Mr Goodyear spent some time flicking through the tightly printed charts, chewing at his bottom lip and occasionally raising a solitary eyebrow as he came across an unexpected name.

George, fidgeting sweaty-assed-on-hot-plastic-chair, studied the veins on Mr Goodyear's bowed head. They reminded him of the river system in South America he'd studied during a geography lesson earlier in the week. Kind of.

Eventually the headmaster looked up from the exercise book and studied George's face intently. George stared resolutely back. Then the headmaster stood up and crossed to a filing cabinet and flicked through several folders until he came to the one he wanted. He returned to his desk with it. As he set it down George could see that it was his class's file; Mr Goodyear flicked through the pages until he came to a copy of George's last report, then ran his finger down it, nodded along with it.

When he'd finished, Mr Goodyear closed the report file and replaced it in the cabinet. Then he flicked through the Top Tens once more, flipped the book closed and passed it back across the table to George.

'Well,' he said, 'your handwriting has certainly improved, George.'

George nodded. 'Thank you, sir,' he said.

'But I should warn you, you must pay a great deal more

attention to your spelling. For example, there are two g's in nigger. Likewise there are two s's in Cassius.'

'Sorry, sir.'

Mr Goodyear pulled at his lower lip. 'You don't much like our coloured friends, do you, George?'

'No, sir.'

'You have a reason for that, George?'

'Daddy always taught me that niggers were the dogs of the earth. That they'd been lucky to be slaves. That they didn't deserve to be treated as well as slaves. Monkeys from the trees, sir, is what my daddy said.'

'And you believe everything your daddy tells you?'

'Yes, sir. Of course, sir.'

Mr Goodyear clasped his hands together. 'I can't tell you, boy, but it's so refreshing to meet a young man who adheres to the old values. He's done a good job, has old George. How's he doing these days, anyhow?'

'Not so good, sir. Bad chest.'

'Of course. Well, give him my regards.' Mr Goodyear stood and reached across the table. George hesitantly took his hand. It was his first handshake. 'Run along now, George, and make out like I've given you a hard time.'

George smiled and turned for the door. As he opened it Mr Goodyear called him back. 'I'd maybe stop bringing that particular notebook into class, eh son?'

George nodded.

'And keep an eye on that spelling. You can't expect to beat the niggers if you're not as smart as them. This is 1972, son, and things are changing. They're creeping in everywhere. Be after my job soon. Get yourself qualified, boy, so you'll never have no nigger telling you what to do.'

And George had got qualified, but he still had a nigger telling him what to do. Myron Linklater. That fat fucking nigger computer supervisor at the airport. *What I should have done was drive over to Myron's fucking house and stick a grenade up his black ass and then ask him to tell me how to do my job again.* But he hadn't gone to Myron's because there were bigger fish in the Top Ten. Nobody was going to remember the man who blew Myron *fucking* Linklater's head off. Those other names, well, they were different. They'd remember him okay if he took any single one of *them* out. And if he managed to kill the whole ten, he'd be the most famous man in history. One day, though, he'd get Myron too.

Keeping Myron in the chart was good for George. It helped him keep his feet on the ground.

George showered and shaved, got dressed in his Rev Doc clerical gear, then repacked the arsenal in his sports bag. He checked out of the motel, then drove several hundred yards along the highway before pulling into a McDonald's for breakfast. By ten he was back on the road and by twelve he was checked into another motel on the outskirts of Atlanta. He checked the TV channels, but there was still no mention of the attempt to arrest him. All he could presume was that the FBI had thrown a security blanket over their whole operation, that they were desperately trying to cover themselves so that they had time to come up with a convincing explanation as to why so many of their men had been taken out in what was surely a straightforward operation.

'But this George Burley was just a computer programmer, how could he have laid such a trap? There's sixteen dead FBI agents out there, and there's a chopper down as well.'

'One thing's for sure, he ain't no computer programmer. He's a warrior, a highly trained fighting machine. We're no match for him!'

The thought did cross his mind that possibly the FBI were

wise to his stockpile of explosives and had been cautious about entering the house. Gone were the days of the honourable arms dealer. Though Genty Morrison had been a family friend and White American Resistance quartermaster for many years there was no telling what pressure he was under.

George left the motel and walked several blocks until he came to a pay-phone. Then he called the former Mrs Burley at her office in Birmingham. She worked as a receptionist/telephonist at the legal firm of Saunders & McKee, had done since they'd handled the divorce for the warring Burleys. They'd been impressed by her coolness under fire in the witness box, though he knew that had more to do with Valium and vodka than any inner strength.

He was thrown almost immediately. He'd expected to hear her dulcet tones, that sophisticated southernness, genteel with a hint of haughtiness, but it was different, duller, thicker, maybe even *black*. 'Good morning, Saunders & McKee Attorneys at Law, Rose Parker speaking, how may I help you?'

'I'd like to speak to Grace, please.'

'I'm sorry, Grace isn't here this morning, can I help you?'

'Will she be in later?'

'No, sir, Grace will not be in today.'

'Sick is she?'

'No, sir, Grace is not sick. But she will not be in this day. She has suffered a family bereavement. May I help you? May I ask who's calling? Or may I take a message for her? Or is it one of the partners you'll be looking for?'

'What sort of a family bereavement?'

'Well, sir, I'm afraid I can't . . .'

'This is Reverend Sam Clarke, Grace's cousin from Walnut Grove. Now what's all this about a family bereavement? I ain't heard a danged thing about it. What is it, girl?'

'Oh, I'm sorry, Reverend, I didn't realize . . . there was some sort of explosion at her former husband's home this morning. It completely demolished the house, killed a postman, and Grace is over there while they search for her husband's body. It's a terrible business, sir, Grace is in an awful state. Do you want to leave a message for her, sir? I'm sure we can get it to her . . . sir?'

George hung up the phone and walked quickly back to the motel, his heart thump-thump-thumping like a steam-hammer. He unlocked the door, bolted it behind him, then sat on the bed with the AK-47 on his lap.

Fuckfuckfuckfuckfuckfuckfuck, he thought.

9

On Monday morning Nathan arrived at the Empire State Building, shared a doughnut with Leonard Maltman, then was fitted for his uniform. He quite liked the outfit, but was a little disappointed that there was no gun. Most nearly every other security guard he'd seen in the city carried a gun, and although he'd proved to Leonard that he could handle himself in a fight against two scaredy-cat crackheads, he was hardly a Master of Kung Fu.

Leonard reassured him: 'Hey, Nathan, we don't just give you a uniform and send you out there to fend for yourself, y'know! Training is the name of the game these days!'

'I'll need something . . .'

'We'll teach you everything you need to know. Self-defence! The history of the Empire! How to deal with awkward customers! Checking ID! Resuscitation techniques! And all in one day! We don't send you out there naked, Nathan, we're your family now!'

Nathan smiled. 'Yeah, sure.'

'Kind of, anyway. You'll spend your first few weeks on patrol with one of our more experienced men. Bobby Tangetta maybe, or old Sam McClintock, or . . . anyway, you get the picture.'

To give him the feel of the place Leonard took Nathan up to the 86th floor. It was a fine, sweaty Manhattan morning and the observatory was crowded. Nathan felt good doing the circuit. He caught a few admiring glances from girls. Leonard exuded a quiet confidence, but there was none of the swagger about him you saw with policemen. Maybe it was the absence of a gun. Maybe it was just Leonard.

While Leonard took a call over his radio, Nathan patrolled the observatory himself. He peered through the high-powered binoculars at the city for a few moments, then let a kid have the last few seconds free. Benevolent Nathan! He preferred to look at the city from a distance. He loved the wispy bits of cloud; he could almost reach up and touch; it was like a toy, a big beautiful toy. He could hold up his hand and blot out Central Park. Raise his fist and crush the United Nations. Wave goodbye to Liberty. He liked New York a lot better from the Empire State.

The kid stepped down from the binoculars. He yanked Nathan's arm. 'Hey, mister, what's the Empire State Building made of, anyhow?'

'Blue cheese,' said Nathan. 'Reinforced blue cheese.'

'It is not.'

'It is too. It took ten million cows six months to produce enough milk for the fermentation process to begin. Honest.'

'You're fulla shit, mister.'

Nathan spread his palms. 'Please yourself.'

The kid rattled his hand against the security fence. 'Nobody's gonna get past this. What the hell are you guarding for?'

'Mice,' said Nathan and started to move towards Leonard, who was shaking his head and looking annoyed. 'I was just . . .'

Leonard cut him off. 'I've a meeting, kid, gotta run. Stay here, I'll send someone up show you some more ropes, okay?'

'Okay.'

The new management team at the Empire State took a few days to get itself settled into place. Trump's people weren't the fastest movers and there was a lot of leather and gold furniture to be junked before the team professed itself happy with its new surroundings. Then it was down to business: analysing the tenants, dealing with the employees, reviewing the rents, drawing up a business plan. Michael Tate had instructed them that he wanted the tenants to start reflecting the fact that the Empire State was *sexy*. He was moving Magiform in as a major tenant, sure, but he wanted more than that: he wanted more TV companies, fewer button-makers, more record companies and recording studios, fewer haberdashers. He wanted the Empire to be young, vibrant, to reflect the freeform Magiform ethos – live fast, die young, leave a good-looking hologram. Warhol or Wilson's Factory. Lucas's Light and Magic. Jackson's Neverland without the child sex slurs. So the management team had a bit of a task: 650 tenants, most of them itty-bitty concerns connected to the garment industry.

Walter Ievers, team leader, knew he had his work cut out, but he was enjoying the challenge. At least he had nothing to worry about on the security front. Leonard looked like what he was, like security chiefs the world over, an ex-cop gone to seed. That said, he ran a tight ship. There had been no major robberies or acts of violence for quite a while, not bad considering there were some 15,000 people working out of the building daily. Despite the fact that there were 2.5 million tourists a year there were no major insurance claims for personal injuries outstanding.

Ievers, running a hand through his receding sandy hair, pointed to the seat on the other side of his table as Maltman, smiling nervously, limped in.

'What happened to the leg, Leonard?' Ievers asked, though he guessed from the way the security chief eyed the Dunkin bag on his table he was suffering from the fat ex-cop's disease, doughnut on the knee. 'Gunshot?'

'Yeah. Coupla hoods in the Bronx. Years ago.'

'Coffee, Leonard?'

'Sure. Thanks.'

'Doughnut, Leonard?'

'Absolutely.'

One up to Sherlock. Ievers passed the bag across to the security chief. He waited until he took the first bite of a strawberry-iced pastry, then said: 'I've been reviewing the performance of your department, Leonard.' It wasn't said with menace, but with enough cool authority to suddenly dry the chewing process, to take all the enjoyment out of it. 'I'm pleased with how everything has been going.'

Leonard chewed quickly now, finishing the mouthful, then took a hasty slurp of coffee. He set the paper cup down again and held the remains of the doughnut awkwardly in his hand. Little pink crumbs danced at the corner of his mouth as he spoke. 'I have a great team working with me, Mr Ievers.'

'So it would seem.'

'Although naturally we're all a little concerned . . . well, you know how it is, a new owner moves in and everyone gets a little worried about their jobs. It's only natural.'

'Of course, I understand that, that is in part why I called this meeting. I can assure you that Mr Tate, Magiform, does not intend to make any redundancies in the foreseeable future. Indeed, he intends investing more money in the

Empire State Building, to build up a, shall we say, wealthier tenant base which will, if anything, require even greater security. Thus I don't think it would be incorrect of me to say that improved security means improved salaries, though I'd keep that under your hat for the meantime.'

'Certainly, certainly. Sounds great.'

'Yes, it does. It is.'

'And the down side?'

'What down side?'

'There's always a down side.'

'Not with Magiform, Leonard, not with Magiform. Michael Tate is one of those rare people, more money *and* sense. Treats his people well, generosity personified, and expects absolute loyalty in return. Now, I'll go through the actual employment packages with you at a later date, Leonard – God knows we've a thousand more complicated things to look at before that – but there are a couple of things I want to check with you first.'

Ievers looked at the sheet of paper and smiled. 'Nothing but good news, Leonard, hard work, but good news. Michael Tate will be hosting a big party here next week, both to mark the purchase of the building and to announce another major expansion of his computer empire.'

'Great,' said Leonard. 'An empire for the Empire.'

Ievers let his grey eyes flit up from the sheet for a moment. Leonard looked suitably embarrassed. 'Indeed. Now, there will be a number of very important guests, one of whom will be the President.'

'Keneally?'

'Yes, the President has kindly agreed to come along.'

'Jeez.'

'So, of course, security will be at a premium. The President, of course, will have his own men, but it's important that we contribute as well. At the moment Mr Tate intends to host a reception for the President here in our own offices, and then have him address the guests on the 86th floor observatory. We will of course be advised by yourself on this, but we hope that most of the security, the screening, can be done on a lower level, and then guests can take the elevator to the 86th with the minimum of fuss. We thought maybe just the two of our own staff on duty up top. How does that sound?'

'That sounds just about right, Mr Ievers.'

'Excellent. You'll want to be there as well, I take it?'

'Yes, I will.'

He made a note. 'The Secret Service will want to have a list of all your employees, just to make sure there are no hidden nuts in there.'

'I can vouch for all of them.'

'I'm sure you can, Leonard, but the SS like to think they know better. You can let me have that list today?'

'You betcha.' Leonard, stroking his face with pleasure, became aware of the crumbs for the first time and hurriedly disposed of them. He coughed lightly. 'We have a well-practised routine for visiting dignitaries. In this case we'll draw one name out of the hat. The other goes without saying. Sam McClintock. Been with the Empire just about since it was built. Fifty years, anyway. He's met every American president up there since . . . and the presidents of just about every country under the sun as well. Shook hands with the Queen. Fidel Castro gave him a cigar.'

Ievers was flicking through a pile of memos on his desk. He pulled one out, read it, nodded, looked up. 'Sam McClintock. I thought that name sounded familiar.'

Leonard leaned forward, peering at the hand-written memo. 'What's Sam been up to?'

Ievers shrugged. 'I dunno. But this is from Mr Tate himself, instructing that McClintock's employment be terminated forthwith.'

'Jesus,' said Leonard. 'Why would he want to do that?' Ievers gave a slight shake of the head. 'That's exactly the sort of question you don't ask Michael Tate. Nevertheless, I trust you'll have Mr McClintock removed as quickly as possible.'

'But he's been here half a century, he's an institution, he's . . .'

Ievers stood and extended his hand. 'That will be all, Leonard. You'll let me have that list of names this afternoon, eh?'

'Of course, Mr Ievers.'

At the end of the afternoon shift Leonard called together as many of his staff as he could and laid out what seemed to be their bright future under Michael Tate. *Too good to be true* was the phrase most bandied about. Nathan sat at the back of the canteen, quietly taking it all in. He loved it: he felt part of the team already. Then Leonard told them about the President. It took a few moments to sink in, then they burst into applause. Wolf whistles. Sam McClintock sat near the front, neither clapping or whistling, but there was a little, knowing smile on his face.

Leonard held up his hands to quiet them. 'So how do you guys want to work this? Draw two names from the hat, right?'

Bobby Tangetta shouted from the back, 'Sam always gets to meet the President. That's how it works.'

Leonard looked up. Kept his voice as friendly as possible. 'That's how it *has* worked, Bobby. Maybe Sam doesn't want to meet the President. Maybe he wants to let some young guy who's never met any President have the opportunity.'

'Maybe you want to ask him anyway?' Bobby stood up. 'Yo, Methuselah, whaddya think? You want to meet the President?'

Sam gave a little shrug, tilted his head slightly to the side and looked sheepishly up at Leonard. 'Well, it might be kind of nice,' Sam said. He sucked on a lip for a moment, then said wistfully, 'I wouldn't want to step on anyone's toes, but I suppose I won't have many more opportunities to meet anyone important. And there's not many I haven't met, y'know. I remember the time . . .'

'Yo, Sam, we didn't ask for a fucking history lesson!'

The rest of them burst into laughter. Leonard didn't have to work too hard to stifle his guffaw. He stuck his hand down into the bag, ran his fingers through the torn strips of paper. Sam's name wasn't in there, that much was certain. He drew out a name. 'Hey, Brian Houston, you're meeting the President!'

Brian flushed. He'd only been at the Empire for eight weeks.

'Okay, Brian's in. What's it to be?' Leonard held up the bag. 'Draw another, according to all the rules of democracy in this great nation of ours or let Sam carry on the tradition of . . . well, Sam meeting important people?'

Minto, raising his hand, yelled: 'All those in favour of Sam the Man meeting the Prez, raise their hands!'

All the hands went up. Nathan's too. Even Leonard's, eventually.

10

Nathan stopped off for a few beers on the way home, just a few, just to rest his legs from the long walk and to give him time to study the training manual Leonard had given him. There wasn't much to it. It was a question of familiarizing himself with the building, the elevators, the tenants, how to recognize trouble-makers, help tourists in distress. Common sense, really. He preferred to read the potted history that prefaced it: the destruction of the old Waldorf-Astoria Hotel by General Motors vice-president John Jacob Raskob and his partners to make way for their skyscraper, the engagement of William Lamb to design it. Lamb had shocked them all at their first meeting by producing his prototype: a child's pencil. And then they'd shocked him by telling him he had just eighteen months from the start of drawings to the snipping of the ribbons.

Nathan tried to imagine the thrill of the challenge, the pride of completing it on time, and under budget. He was excited just reading about it – how must old Sam feel to have been part of it all his life? For the last half-hour he sipped a Diet Coke, just to knock the edge off the alcohol. He felt happier than he'd felt for a long time, certainly since arriving in America. The job looked ideal. He'd fallen instantly in love with the Empire. The money wasn't brilliant, but there was a hint that it was about to improve, and at least it would be clean money, it wouldn't smell of sex. It might even be enough for Lisa to give up her shifts in the sex cages.

He left at a little after four; he always enjoyed the sensation of blinking out into the sunlight, as if somebody had suddenly given him a present of day from night. He even whistled a little on the way home. When he reached the apartment he slipped his key into the front door, calling out to Lisa.

She was in their bedroom, packing.

He stood watching her for a moment, confused. Finally he said, 'Where are you going?'

She straightened. 'I'm going nowhere, Nathan. You are. I'm packing your things. I want you out.'

'Okay,' he said and walked into the kitchen. He opened the fridge and took out a bottle of beer, twisted off the lid and then leaned back against the sink. He drained half of it in one, shook his head, then stalked back to the bedroom. 'What?'

'You heard, Nathan.'

'I don't think I heard right.'

'You did. I want you out.'

'You're trying to tell me something.'

'Nathan, it's over. We're finished. Please don't make this more awkward than it is.'

'Just like that. *It's over.*'

'It's the best way.'

'You don't think it might be reasonable to at least give me some sort of explanation?'

'What explanation do you need? You know what it's been like.'

'Like what? Jesus, we have our ups and downs, doesn't everyone?'

'No, Nathan, we have our downs. I can't remember the last up.'

'That's not fair.'

'Name one. Name an up. I'll match you and raise you twenty-six downs. It's no fun any more, Nathan! I'm not sure if it was even fun in the first place.'

'Oh thanks a lot.'

'I'm sorry, but it's true.'

'You told me you loved me.'

'Once.'

'It should only take once.'

'Oh come off it!'

'So you're throwing me out of my fucking home!'

'It's not your fucking home! I pay for it! You do sod all, Nathan!'

'I got a fucking job, didn't I? That's what you asked me to do all along, and now I've got one, you're fucking dropping me.'

Lisa zipped the canvas bag, then pulled it off the bed and set it on the floor. 'There,' she said, 'all your worldly possessions.'

'You could just do it, like that? Here's your bag Nathan, cheerio?'

She shook her head violently. 'Don't you see it's the only way I can do it?' And then her voice broke and the tears began to cascade. 'It's just not working!' she cried.

He crossed to her, tried to put his arm round her, but she pushed him away, pushed him hard and he fell over the bag, sprawling on the floor on his back. He got to his feet quickly, like a boxer trying to beat the count. She sat down on the bed and looked tearily across at him. The tenderness she'd seen in his eyes as he crossed to her, that she'd had to fight off or be stuck for ever, was gone, well gone, and now his eyes had a hooded, hunted look. When he spoke he almost snarled. 'I'd guess there was another man involved, but there must be fucking thousands of them by now.'

'Nathan . . .'

'You're a fucking conniving little whore. You couldn't even be fucking honest. You just see the easy money and you want me out of the way so you can bring your customers back here and let them fuck you.'

'I don't . . .'

'Fuck you!' He turned and kicked the bedroom door with all the force he could muster. It wasn't much stronger than balsa and his foot shot through it. Lisa let out a little yell. As he tried to pull his boot out it got stuck. He yanked at it, but didn't quite get there, it unbalanced him again and he fell back onto the floor. Frustrated, he sprang to his feet again and began to rain kicks at the door, short, sharp, short, sharp, short, sharp until there were a dozen holes. His face was puffed red. Lisa cowered back on the bed. He turned to her. She brought her knees up under her chin. He moved towards her, stopped, then threw out his arm and swept away a shelf full of paperback books. She raised her arms as they cascaded about her head He slapped out at an electric lamp by their bedside, kicked the clock radio onto the floor. He reached across for the framed photo of her mum. She uncurled in a flash, beating him to it. She clasped it to her chest. His hands shot out, caught the corners of it, they heaved-ho for a moment, but his strength won out and he tore it from her grasp. He turned, held it out in front of him, she made a grab for it. As he pulled his arm back to punch it his elbow rammed into her nose. She screamed and fell back, blood already spouting.

Nathan dropped the photograph. 'Oh Jesus,' he said.

She ran the back of her hand under her nose, looked at it. 'I'm bleeding,' she whispered.

'Oh Jesus,' Nathan said again. 'I'm sorry.'

She found a tissue up her sleeve. Tried to staunch the flow. Nathan moved towards her. 'Keep away from me!' she yelled.

Nathan stopped, his face as white as a ghost. 'I didn't mean to.'

The blood was still flowing. Watered down, mixed with tears. 'That temper will be the death of you, Nathan Jones.'

He nodded. 'Can I get you anything?' he said.

'You can get out.'

'I'm sorry, Lisa, I'm really . . .'

'Out!'

She could see the tears in his eyes. She looked away.

'I love you,' Nathan said.

'It's too late for that, Nathan. Please, go. Leave me alone.'

His gaze dropped from her. He studied the palms of his hands. Then he raised them to his lips, as if in prayer. A slight shake of his head, then he bent and lifted his bag, turned and walked out of the bedroom without looking at her again. A moment later the front door slammed.

She sat where she was for several moments, trying to enjoy the sudden silence, but it was an external silence; her heart was steam-hammering. She began to uncurl slowly, dabbing at her face with the blood-soaked tissue. Then suddenly the panic was upon her. What had she done! He was gone! He was really gone! She had chased him away! He would never survive alone in the city! She had killed him!

Before she really knew it she was racing for the door, crying, crying, 'Nathan!'

And he stopped her in the hallway. 'See,' he said, 'you do care.'

73

11

While George Burley chewed his lips in Atlanta, police in Birmingham called in the FBI to help with the investigation into the explosion at his home. The Special Agent in Charge (SAC) and a team of twelve special agents were soon actively involved. They became aware almost immediately of George's connections with White American Resistance, Aryan Nations and other far right organizations. George's name featured in the FBI's on-line database, the Terrorist Information System. He wasn't alone. There were more than 200,000 individuals on it and over 3,000 organizations. George had never been indicted, but he had been questioned about quasi-terrorist activities on numerous occasions.

It was soon established that the explosion had been no accident and that some sort of device had been detonated. As ever with these cases, there was a sad story attached to it. The postman who had been blown to smithereens was on his last day of work after thirty-five years with the Birmingham Post Office and had volunteered to work an unfamiliar route when a colleague fell ill. What the FBI was trying to establish initially was why someone would want to kill George Burley.

After a few hours of searching for bits of George, forensics declared that there was no other body in the house, much to the relief of Mrs Burley who had had to be restrained from joining in the search of the smouldering rubble. George would have been surprised at the depth of her feelings for him. She had once remarked to her sister Claudette that the only thing stopping her from loving him for ever was the fact that *he wants to kill everyone*. Mrs Burley had suspected that all might not be right with their marriage on their wedding day when George had threatened to kill the offici-ating minister if he didn't have a black choirboy removed from the church. Mrs Burley had put it down to nerves. The minister, who was also minister to the Birmingham Home for the Very Disturbed, knew madness when he saw it, and had the choirboy removed.

It would be 24 hours before the FBI concluded that no one had tried to kill George Burley, but that he had set the explosion himself. Another 48 hours before they worked their way through George's computer disks and printouts, which had survived because he kept them in a fireproof container. They already knew that George was a nut, but were thankful that he was a meticulous nut: everything was documented, every organization, every fascist nigger-hating chicken coop between Alabama and Louisiana was detailed, including more than a dozen the FBI had never even heard of. George, in his military strike against the United States Government, had actually destroyed twenty years of Klan-destine groping towards right-wing revolution. Poor George, battling along the highway towards Washington with his new agenda, blissfully unaware of the long series of raids and arrests being planned at FBI headquarters which would destroy the burgeoning underground. George's own e-mail messages to the President, being his last recorded act before destroying his house, gave the FBI some concern, but not so much that he warranted anything above number 87 on their Most Wanted list.

Eighty-seven would not have pleased George, who considered himself an altogether bigger fish. He had decided to press on from Atlanta with his mind more focused than ever on his ultimate objective, although not before he took time out to update his Top Ten. There were no new entries, but the fat and thin versions of Oprah Winfrey each dropped down a place, elevating President Keneally to the top slot. George had hated Keneally before, but now he *really* hated him. *Keneally has declared war, now he will pay the penalty*, George promised as he gunned his car towards Washington.

Gunned in his own head, at least, as George didn't want to break the speed limit and risk bringing down the wrath of the law upon himself. Of course he could shoot his way out of any given situation, but there was no point in drawing attention to himself just yet. Who would remember George Burley, *traffic cop killer*? He was already finding it difficult to handle the embarrassment of George Burley, *postman killer*. It was no way to build a reputation.

A dozen miles out of Richmond, Virginia, George pulled off the interstate, concerned a little at the jeep's temperature gauge. The first small town he came to he got a mechanic to look the vehicle over, but after some lazy poking about he merely refilled it with water and pronounced it otherwise fit, before charging George $30 for his trouble. George hated being ripped off by white trash, but at least he was *white* trash so he paid up with gruff bad manners and roared angrily out of the garage. He thought briefly about including the mechanic in his Top Ten, but decided it would be a bit petty of him, and this acknowledgement of his own rationality calmed him down. This big fish, who was a small fish to the

FBI, had bigger fish to fry. He put his favourite country tape into the deck and settled back to enjoy the backroads for a while, figuring that if the police were on his trail he'd have a better chance sticking to roads less travelled.

Five miles later the jeep ground to a halt in a cloud of steam and George discovered that the road really was less travelled. There wasn't a farm within sight, and he would be damned if he was going to let the jeep, laden as it was with small arms, out of his sight. He hoked about in the engine for a while, but although he may have been an elite fighting machine himself, he couldn't tell a fanbelt from a crankshaft. After half an hour in the sweltering heat, George delved into the emergency rations he had packed to see him through a nuclear catastrophe. He was quite enjoying his warm Coke and Hershey bar when an ageing tractor pulled up beside him.

'Car trouble, Revrun?' a coal-black face asked from behind the wheel.

He wanted to say *No, I'm driving a fucking steam engine*, but he merely nodded and tapped the hood.

'Ah saw the smoke from up on the farm.'

George peered back down the road, but still couldn't see any farm. 'I'm afraid I'm not very good with engines,' George said and threw his arms up in the air with mock embarrassment.

The farmer smiled broadly and switched off his engine. 'If you want, I'll take a look at it, Revrun.'

'Sure,' said George, 'I'd appreciate that.'

'Name's Luther Madison,' the man said, climbing down to stand in front of George. He looked to be in his middle fifties. His hair was grey, receding, his body farm-tough, his jeans blue-grey with the years. He put out his hand.

George extended his reluctantly and grabbed it back as

soon as possible. He turned and nodded at the jeep. 'Fool mechanic five miles back said it was fine.'

Luther grinned. 'That would be Rikkie Metcalf. Is a mechanic like his daddy before him. His daddy knew nothing about cars either. Made quite a good livin' till they built the interstate.'

Luther peered under the hood. Nodded his head. 'Yeah,' he said after a little, 'I reckon I can fix that. You just let me tow you back up to the farm and I can get to work on it. Maybe get you back on the road before nightfall.'

A pained expression crossed George's face. 'What exactly is the problem?' he asked.

'You got yourself a steam problem,' Luther said and turned for his tractor and a tow-rope.

While Luther worked on the jeep, George perched himself on a fence and surveyed Luther Madison's farm. It wasn't much. It nestled neatly into a fold in the land, the shanty-roof green-mossed with age blending perfectly into the backdrop of trees.

'Yes, sir, Revrun, my family's farmed here since the Civil War. 'Course, it weren't always our land. We had to work for that.'

Luther's wife Rosie fetched out a pitcher of homemade lemonade for George to drink. After inspecting it for bugs, George gulped it down. 'I'm fixing supper soon, Revrun,' Rosie said. 'I'd be mighty pleased if you'd stay and share it with us. We don't have much, but what we have we'd be mighty pleased to share with you.'

George's first reaction was not entirely positive. *What the fuck have I walked into here? It's like fucking* Gone with the Wind. His second was a little more considered. At least they were helping him out. And if eating with them reduced their circumstances further, then where was the harm in it? 'I'd be delighted,' George said. 'I'm just sorry I can't be much help to Luther. I'm not much good at fixin' things.'

'I'm sure you fix plenty of things, Revrun,' Rosie said.

It looked a nice supper too. Chicken, of course. Mashed potatoes. Green beans. Sweetcorn. Chilled milk. George tried not to smirk. The staples of negro life. *They wouldn't know what a god-damn steak looked like.*

'Will you, Revrun?'

'Will I what?'

Luther nodded at the food. It took a few moments for George to cotton on. 'Of course,' he said, 'what am I thinking of? God bless this food. God bless this nation. God bless all of us. Amen.'

As George ripped into a chicken leg he nodded across the room at a small table. Three framed photos of young men in uniform. 'Them your boys?' he asked.

Rosie nodded. Her eyes lingered on the pictures. She chewed on, but her mind was suddenly elsewhere.

'You must be proud of them,' George said.

'We were,' said Luther. 'Still are, of course. Just in a different way. They're all dead, Revrun, all three of them.'

'Oh,' said George, taking another bite. 'I'm sorry to hear that. What happened?'

'We've always served our country, Revrun. My pa, he was in the navy during the Second World War, served on the USS *Mason*, only black ship in the whole navy. Got a medal too. I did two tours in Vietnam. Wounded twice. Nearly didn't make it. My boys, they all joined up too. Josh, the eldest, he got it in Beirut. Car bomb demolished their headquarters, killed hundreds. Anthony, he's the middle one, he died in the Gulf, one of those friendly fire incidents they call 'em, shot by his own side anyways. Billy, only seventeen, he got it in Somalia, a gang surrounded him, cut him to shreds with machetes. All three of them, gone, just like that. They were fine boys, Revrun; I brought them up to believe in the flag, in their country, and they served their country until their dying breath. Yes, damn right I'm proud of them.'

George set down his knife and fork. 'You don't feel bitter at all about losing all of your sons, do you, Luther?'

'Why should I? They were soldiers, they knew what they was doing. They believed in America, Revrun.'

'But at the end of the day, they're gone and you don't appear to have anyone to leave the farm to. Wouldn't you say that's a waste?'

'Serving your country is never a waste. Protecting your freedom is never a waste. What's a farm, anyhow? We just toilin' in the sun, waiting for the next world now. Don't make no difference that we ain't got no kids waiting for it. No, they served their country, they served their God. Can't ask more of a man than that.'

'That's a wonderful, Christian attitude.'

'Why thank you, Revrun.'

'No need to thank me, boy,' George said. He continued to eat, looking at his plate, aware of their surprise, enjoying it. After a few moments he looked up. 'Anything the matter?' he asked.

Luther darted a look at Rosie. She shrugged. 'No, suh,' he said.

'You ever been bothered by the Klan, Luther?'

'No, Revrun, can't say that I have.'

'But you've been the victim of racial abuse. When you were younger.'

'Well, Revrun, I guess all of us have, all of us coloured folk that is.'

'That must have been pretty hard to bear.'

Luther shrugged. 'You learn to live with it. It wasn't so bad.'

'People calling you nigger to your face. Not letting you drink from the same fountain. Trying to lynch you.'

'Some of that, maybe.'

'What I don't understand, Luther,' said George, poking his fork out in the farmer's direction, 'is how or why your family would want to serve in the armed forces at all, after being treated like that.'

Rosie set down her knife and fork. 'My boys were good Americans. They died for their country.'

'Absolutely!' said George, jabbing the fork now towards the farmer's wife. 'They died for a country that exploited them. Sent them to fight in battle zones while white boys went to college.'

'Well,' said Luther, 'I don't know about that.' He looked warily across at the minister, then uncertainly at Rosie. She nodded slightly and he pushed his chair back. 'Thank you for supper, honey. Revrun, shall we see if we can get the jeep started?'

George let a little snigger escape. Then he produced a pistol from the inside pocket of his jacket and aimed it at Luther's groin. 'You just put your black ass back on the seat, boy,' he said, his voice rising.

Luther cautiously lowered himself. 'Revrun?' he said.

'*Revrun*,' George mimicked, his upper lip peeling back in a sneer which instantly removed the thin veneer of piety he had somehow managed to sustain through supper. The old attracta-detracta face. Somehow it scared them even more than the gun.

'Oh sweet Jesus,' said Rosie.

George screwed the gun across to her. 'Sweet Jesus ain't gonna help you, you fat black bitch. Nor Chicken George here.'

'We ain't lookin' for no trouble, Revrun,' said Luther.

'*We ain't lookin' for no trouble, massa,*' George fired back. He cackled. 'What gets me,' he snapped, 'what really gets me is how stupid you all are. So really unbelievably fucking stupid. Look at you. You've lost your whole family to the good ol' US of A, we've taken your boys and we've killed them, and you're not mad about it. You're not fucking mad about it! You're proud of them! We took them away and we killed them!'

'They volunteered, Revrun, they wanted to fight.'

'I don't give a fuck! They were in the front line cause that's where we put the niggers! And you're proud of them!'

'Yes, suh, we are.'

'*Yes suh we* are. You stupid fucking nigger bastard.' George trained the pistol at a spot between Luther's eyes. 'I want you to tell me the truth, boy. I want you to tell me what you really feel way deep down in that thick skull of yours. You hate Uncle Sam, don't you? You hate all of us whites, don't you, for killing your boys. You want to kill us, don't you? You want to take our women and you want to fuck them and then cut their throats. That's what you want, isn't it, Luther? You want to get off this piss-poor fucking dust bowl of a farm and fuck our women and slit their throats. Tell me, Luther. Tell me the truth.'

Luther's denim workshirt was soaked through. 'That's not true, Revrun,' he whispered.

'What was that, boy? Speak up.'

Luther's eyes sparked up angry. 'That's not true.'

'Don't you lose it with me, boy!' George snapped.

Abruptly Rosie burst into tears. 'Please, Revrun, don't kill us!' she wailed.

Luther carefully placed a placatory hand on her shaking arm. 'There, now,' he said, 'it'll be okay.'

'But it won't, Luther,' said George, and pulled the trigger.

* * *

George had never killed anyone before. Now he was quite pleased with himself. You could *practise* killing people, and he had, but this was the first time he'd actually *executed* anyone using real bullets. He'd motored along beside *brothers* and fired blanks, he'd hurled more than a few fire bombs into churches and *disfigured*. But this was the first time he had really *killed*. His gun hand held steady, the bullets entered their skulls dead centre, and they dropped without a word.

He buried them in the back yard. He found a shaded area where the soil wasn't baked hard and dug a shallow grave. Then he conducted the funeral service. It was short and to the point; he mentioned their hard work on the land and the sacrifice of their children's lives to the United States; he thanked the Lord for guiding him to this lonely farm and for providing him with his first taste of battle. He didn't dwell too long on the Madisons themselves; they seemed to have lived reasonably good lives, so they'd probably go to heaven, but it would be that low-rent ghetto section of heaven reserved for niggers.

12

Old Sam McClintock had part of a B-52 bomber embedded in his skull. Only a small part, but sometimes it hurt so bad that it felt like the whole damn plane was in there. It had been there for fifty-three years and he had Lieutenant Colonel William Smith, a highly decorated combat pilot, to thank for it.

Sam's father, Matthew, helped build the Empire State Building. He'd been a leading steelworker, one of the brave band of men battling freezing north winds, rain and fog a thousand feet above Fifth Avenue to complete what was then the world's tallest building. In the end the weather got to him and he exchanged his pneumatic riveting-hammer for pneumonia, but when the building was officially opened on 1 May 1931, Matt McClintock was an honoured guest. Later, when it was decided his chest wasn't up to steelwork any more, John Jacob Raskob himself had offered him a security job.

Sam's first really clear memory was of the Empire State, of the sheer delight of being chased around the 86th floor observatory by his dad, of thinking it was just a walled yard, and then suddenly being yanked up by his lapels and shown the view, the view to end all views, and screaming in fear and then screaming in wonderment, and then laughing. And it had felt the same ever since. Even today, when his own chest was bad, and he coughed his way through an explanation to a bunch of jabbering Japanese, his love for the Empire shone through.

'They always seem to move in gangs,' Nathan whispered at his shoulder.

Sam smiled and continued his explanation. He pointed north at Yankee Stadium – the Japs loved their baseball – south to the Statue, east to the United Nations – hey, we're all friends now – and west to Madison Square where he'd seen Cassius in his prime. He didn't tell them that, of course. In fact, he wasn't meant to tell them anything, he was just a security guard and even that not very often. Most of the time he worked the elevators, usually the final jump up to the enclosed 102nd floor observatory where they reckoned the air was better for him. They'd tried to talk him into retiring, or failing that into work downstairs, but he wasn't having it. The Empire State was his. Top of the world. And he didn't mind who asked him about it. He'd been the Empire Man for half a century.

'They never shut up,' Nathan laughed as the Japs moved off.

'Why should they? It's a wonderful building, it's a wonderful view.'

Nathan quite liked Sam's old sage routine, and it was a routine. Bobby Tangetta had told him all about the old guy: about the Wednesday-night poker games, about Sam chasing a Flashdancer through Times Square. He was about as sage as a bar of soap.

Sam smiled and turned left, running his hand along the security fence. Nathan asked if he'd seen any suicides; Sam'd seen a few, okay, but the best one had been Elvita's 'cause it hadn't quite worked out. She was a nice woman, a nice woman with a problem. Sometimes he wondered what had happened to her since. She'd taken a dive from the 86th one freezing December night nearly twenty years before, and been blown back by a strong gust of wind, landing on a narrow ledge on the 85th. Someone was watching out for her. She broke her hip in the process, but she was still the luckiest woman in the world. If that wasn't reason enough to live, he didn't know what in hell was.

Bobby Tangetta, sweating profusely in his blue zip-jacket, met them on the corner. He was running a handkerchief across the back of his neck. 'Jesus, it's hot,' he said.

They pushed the glass door open and approached the Empire State deli. Bobby ordered a hot-dog and a Coke, same for Nathan. Sam got a Coke. Marilu waved Sam away when he offered up his dollars.

'Something wrong with his money that's right with mine?' Bobby asked.

'That's about it, Bobby T.' Marilu grinned. She'd had a thing with Bobby T, and he hadn't treated her well.

They returned to the guard rail to eat. Sam stared out towards the Battery. He closed his eyes for a moment, tilting his head back to let the breeze shoot up his nose. He didn't know why it helped his head so much – giving his brain an airing seemed much too simple an explanation – but it did. The throb began to subside, then drummed back again as Bobby jarred his elbow.

'Hey, whaddya think about Michael Tate? Good guy, Sam? Minto says the new guys downstairs are a heavy fucking outfit, man.'

Sam shook his head. 'One thing you can guarantee when you have a new owner, he gets out the broom and starts sweeping. Don't matter if he's the richest man in the world. Ain't none of us safe here.'

Sam drained his Coke and threw it into a trash can. He checked his watch, then headed towards the lift to the 102nd floor observatory, Nathan still tagging along behind. It had gone noon and the place was really beginning to pack up. They could only take eight at a time up to the 102nd, and that via a rickety old elevator that hadn't been changed since he was a boy. Sam pulled back the gate and ushered the first eight in and warned them to stay clear of the door. Then they were off. It only took half a minute.

He leaned back against the wall and rubbed at the side of his head. Sometimes, when the pain was particularly bad, he swore he could feel the metal tip, pricking him like a bad conscience; other days, when he breathed in, he could almost smell the acrid smoke, the burning flesh.

'You okay?' Nathan asked.

'Sure,' said Sam, but he kept his eyes closed; his thoughts turned inevitably to Lieutenant Colonel William Smith, hero of the Second World War, more than 500 hours of combat duty under his belt, but couldn't fly between Boston and Newark without crashing into the Empire State.

It was his thirteenth birthday. Money was tight, always, but his dad had allowed him to skip his Saturday job and spend the day with him patrolling the Empire. They'd had a great laugh about it in the security office, kitting him out with a too-big uniform and a hat that flopped down over his ears, but hell, why not, what the hell was there to guard in the Empire State anyway?

Visibility, admittedly, was poor that day. Bad for the pilot, good for the tourists in the end, as not that many had ventured up top. Lieutenant Colonel Smith might have known something about low-level fighting, but the canyons of midtown were not the green fields of France.

Sam was thorough if he was anything – still was. Every door his dad checked, he checked right after. Every office he put his head into to say hello, Sam did that too. In fact, those few girls who were working that Saturday were so taken with him and his too-big uniform that he was besieged with offers of chocolate from all sides and he was soon trailing away behind his father. Which was just as well.

At 9.50 AM the twelve-tonne bomber smashed into the 79th floor. Ten men died instantly as the gas tanks exploded. Shrapnel peppered the corridor, one sliver catching Sam on the side of the head and throwing him back into an office doorway. The whole building, sixty thousand tonnes of steel, shook twice. Sam was unconscious for just a few moments; the screaming brought him round. He rolled himself away just in time as a burning river of fuel cascaded past the open door. His head and hands were thick with blood. He tried to find his father, but there was nothing to see but black, burning smoke, and his only sense was of the stench of sizzled flesh. Then someone grabbed him by the arm – a woman, her own hair all sparky – and they ran for it, following a few others to the 33rd Street side of the building. There they stayed and there they prayed, soon surrounded on all sides by flames. It seemed like an eternity, or that eternity was waiting for them, but they waited and they hugged each other and tried to reconcile themselves to an inevitable death. And then the firemen broke through and led them to safety.

Sam shook himself as Nathan pulled the security gate back. 'Just watch the step there, folks,' Nathan said. He pulled his shoulders back and launched into his carefully rehearsed spiel. 'Welcome to the 102nd floor observatory – that's one thousand two hundred and fifty feet up. On a clear day you can see eighty miles in any direction.' It was hardly *Hamlet*, but it was a start.

A young boy raced across the observatory and pressed his

face against the window. 'Gee,' he squealed, 'wouldn't it be great to live up here?'

'If you look carefully,' Sam called from the lift, 'you can see King Kong's footprints on the side of the building.' He winked at the boy's father, then ushered in the eight waiting to descend. Nathan secured the gate, then leaned back against the side again. Another thirty trips, maybe thirty-five and they'd be finished for the day.

Five minutes later they arrived back on the 102nd with another eight passengers. Those from the last trip didn't have to be persuaded to descend. They were already hovering, bored, by the elevator. It never failed to surprise Sam how bored people could get in such a short space of time. Top of the most famous building in the world, and they'd drunk in the view and spat it out again in a couple of minutes. TV was the problem. Short attention span. When he was a boy they'd had to drag him out.

The young boy was first into the elevator. 'Mister,' he snapped, as Nathan closed the gate, 'there ain't no footprints. And there ain't no King Kong.'

'Who told you that?' Nathan asked, wide-eyed.

'My dad.'

Nathan looked up. Moustache. Cropped hair. Pale about the eyes from wearing sunglasses too much. The man gave a little shrug.

Sam tousled the boy's hair benevolently. 'Don't you believe it, son,' he said. 'I was here the night King Kong attacked, scariest thing I ever saw.'

The boy's jaw dropped just a fraction, his eyes flitted to his father, then back to Sam. Then he reached up and slapped Sam's hand away. 'You just keep your hands off me, you pervert,' he said.

13

Chief of Staff Graham Slovenski's wife Miranda was lovely. Everyone agreed. His marriage seemed almost too good to be true. The President had had her checked out on the grounds that her mother's parents came from Russia and old habits die hard, and also because Tara was insanely jealous of her. But the report had been unequivocal in its praise. *She's your basic princess*, it said. What the hell kind of a statement was that to put into a clandestine report anyway? Tara had been furious. *Not even a fucking abortion? Never caught with dope? Come off it! Look at her! She's had her face lifted so often she's got verrucas behind her ears!*

Tara was on the prowl. Her mind was tick-tick-ticking. Her stomach was knotted up with advance guilt. Her plan was this: talk sweetly to Slo, get him into bed, make love, get pregnant, *have a baby*.

She knew it was insane, but in the world rankings of insane things, it probably didn't rate that highly. Her problem with the President wasn't just that he couldn't provide a goodwill posting for her with the United Nations, but that he couldn't provide her with a child. She was desperate to have a baby, her own child, not adopted, not fostered, her own flesh and blood. God damn it, it was every woman's right! But the President wouldn't play ball, so to speak. The sex, well, the sex was fine, just that nothing ever happened. *She'd* been checked out, and everything was working perfectly. But he, well, *he* wouldn't go. *He* wouldn't have the tests, because the tests required sperm, and getting the sperm meant going to a clinic and sitting in a cubicle with a pornographic magazine and masturbating, and the President of the United States wasn't jacking off in a cubicle for *any* reason. It would be political suicide. *The jack-off in the White House*. There were other ways of extracting semen, but he wasn't having any of them. He wasn't having any freakin' scientist playing with his sperm, because he knew that somehow it, the sperm, would find its way to the open market. That one night he'd be trawling through the Internet and he'd come across someone offering the President's sperm for sale. *If God means us to have a little baby, then we'll have a little baby*. But God was busy elsewhere, and Tara fumed alone. He wouldn't discuss it, not at all. The goodwill post, sure, he'd discuss *that*, but not this. Full stop.

Seeing Slo's wife on an almost weekly basis didn't help. *She* had six children; a seventh on the way; she was Mother Nature. Slo had probably just to enter the same room as her and she got pregnant. It came to her that Slo was probably the most fertile man in Washington. Possibly America.

One little interlude, one little screw, nobody else need ever know. And then a baby.

The President was taking Air Force One to Philadelphia, then on to Chicago and Detroit, before finally swinging back towards the end of the week for New York. Everything was going *averagely*. Before he left the White House he shook Graham Slovenski's hand firmly and asked him to guard the fort. 'Make sure the dogs are fed. See that the llama gets his oats. And while you're there give the First Lady a slap in the face and tell her to wake up to the real world.'

'In that order, Mr President?'

'In any damn order you like, Slo.'

Sometimes Slo resented the President treating him more like a housekeeper than the Chief of Staff, but he enjoyed it more than he enjoyed being treated like the house pet. Sometimes the First Lady simply didn't seem to realize that he wasn't a cocker spaniel. Sometimes she would get so relaxed in his company that she would be practically scratching his ear while she chatted. Thankfully it was generally in the privacy of the presidential quarters, so no one was any the wiser, but he thought that was probably more due to good fortune than design. Neither was he sure which annoyed him more: having to concentrate on being a well-behaved lapdog so that he wouldn't spring a hard-on and fuck her leg, or the fact that she seemed completely impervious to the fact that he was a man at all. He often dreamt about what might happen if he took the scenario just one tiny step further, removed his clothes, rolled over on his back and lay panting, waiting for his chest to be scratched. He was convinced that she'd do just exactly that.

He had often tried to rationalize his feelings towards the First Lady, and how they differed from his feelings for his wife, but they defied him. He *loved* his wife. He *loved* his children – some more than others, admittedly, depending on their behaviour and the state of his exhaustion, but he did love them. And he knew that part of it was that he could hardly ever make love to Miranda because she was either recovering from or preparing for childbirth; he had always had a high sex drive but had been prepared to subjugate that in the interests of nurturing the family they both desired; but he'd been subjugating it for six years, and there were only so many times a man could masturbate. And it wasn't that he wanted *any* other woman, or wanted to philander in general; the only person he desired was Tara. Not because she was beautiful and funny and strange and the First Lady – well yes, all of those things – but because something had snapped in his head the first time he had ever met her. No matter what he had done since that day he had thought of her every single minute: in the most high-level discussions, while making love to his wife, while changing a nappy. It was love of the purest kind, he reckoned, and it only happened once in a lifetime. Sorting out America was easy, sorting out his head was more difficult.

Slovenski spent the morning flitting from one meeting to the next around Capitol Hill. By the time he got back to the White House the headache which had begun with the dawn had spread about his skull like lava. He popped a couple of pills and lay down on the couch in his office and fell into a half-dream fantasy in which he saw Air Force One, with the entire cabinet on board, smashing into the earth after being hit by a ground-to-air missile fired by some Southern rednecks. He imagined the national mourning and international outrage. The huge state funeral. The leaders of every country on earth attending. Walter Cronkite delivering the most solemn commentary. *And now Graham Slovenski, who is steering the nation through this most difficult time, comforts the President's widow. She smiles bravely and reaches into her pocket and hands him some chocolate drops. Good boy, Graham! she says.*

He woke suddenly, sweating, and at first he thought he hadn't woken at all, that it was one of those false dawns, apparently awake, but still dreaming. Tara was standing in his office, looking concerned. She said something, but he was too fuzzed-out to take it on board. He jumped up from the couch, twisting his ankle. He let out a little yell then fell back onto the cushions.

'Jesus!' he said, reaching down to massage his foot.

'Oh Slo, I'm sorry, I didn't mean to startle you.' She stepped softly across the room.

'No . . . of course not,' he flustered, 'sorry . . . probably just a little on edge after so many attempts on the President . . . I didn't hear you . . .'

'I'm sorry, Slo, I should have knocked . . . how is it?'

She knelt down in front of him, reached out and gently began to rub his ankle.

He broke into an instant sweat. 'It's . . . fine . . .' he said breathily.

'Do you want me to get some ice?'

'No, no, that's . . . it's fine.'

She smiled up at him. God, he thought. She was, simply, the most beautiful woman he'd ever seen. And he knew she was difficult. And he knew she was a temper-tantrummed little missy. Little britches. But he adored her for it.

She lifted his leg carefully, undid the shoelace, then neatly slipped off the shoe. Then she positioned the base of his foot against her chest and began to stroke the ankle. 'Is that better?' she said.

And he nodded and smiled and tried desperately to detect a nipple.

But if it was there it wasn't erect. Or too well padded. *She's going to pat my head any moment.*

After another few moments she gently let the foot slip down her chest, then, taking it in both hands, eased it onto the ground. 'There,' she said, 'is that better?'

Gingerly he tested his weight on it. It felt fine. 'That's great.' He beamed. 'You should have been a vet. Doctor, I mean.'

She laughed. 'Maybe I should.'

Slo watched appreciatively as she slowly unfolded her body, then stood erect before him. For a moment he stared directly into her groin. *Erect*. Then he pushed himself up off the couch and stepped hesitantly towards his desk. 'That's great,' he said. 'Good as new.'

He settled himself in behind his desk, picked up a sheaf of papers and straightened them. 'So, anyway, what brings you to this lonely outpost? I'll do anything in my power if you don't tell the President you caught me sleeping on the job.'

She smiled. 'Really?'

She held his gaze for a couple of moments into *uncomfortable*. 'Within reason,' he said, mildly panicked.

'I was wondering about Ireland,' she said, lazily running her finger along the top of his desk and examining the very fine residue of dust.

'Northern Ireland.'

'Whatever. You think it's a good idea to go?'

'I don't think it's a bad idea. Are you having second thoughts?'

'Third thoughts. Oh, I don't know. It's a bit backwoodsy, isn't it? What would I do, Slo, give them food or tractors or what?'

'I don't think they're *that* badly off.'

'Well what do they need?'

'Reassurance.'

'I don't know if I'd be up to that.'

'It's what goodwill is all about. You'll be great. A natural.'

'Oh Slo, sometimes you're just so sweet.'

Well if I'm so fucking sweet why don't you just rip your clothes off here and fuck me on the carpet. He reddened slightly. 'Shucks,' he said, playing on it.

'Oh Slo,' she laughed wistfully. Of course the laugh was

really not a laugh, but a groan, and the only wistful thing about it was that she wanted to get Slo wistfully into bed. *But how to do it? And what if he turns me down?* She knew that he was attracted to her, anyone could see that, but he's a gentleman, he loves Miranda; he can lust after and dream, but would he really do it if given the opportunity?

Tara turned abruptly for the door. *God, no, not here, not now.* They needed to be drunk. That would be their excuse. A moment's drunken passion, never to be mentioned again. *Just once.* She would phone her doctor and find out on exactly what day she was most likely to conceive. And then she would make sure they were alone. They would get drunk. And she would have him.

'Okay,' she said, 'I'll go. It'll be nice to see Dublin.'

'Belfast,' Slo said.

'Belfast,' said the President settling back into his seat on Air Force One. 'Maybe she'll get bombed.'

Fred Troy, a veteran FBI special agent attached to the President's security staff following the recent attempts on his life, shook his head. 'They haven't had a bomb there in months. Things have really quietened down.'

'Really?' The President looked perplexed for a few moments. 'Shouldn't I know that?'

Troy nodded vaguely then picked his way hurriedly through the sheaf of faxes clipped to his file-board. He came to the one he was looking for and ran his index finger down it. 'Mr President, I wanted to let you know about an arrest in Richmond this morning. Our resident agency has arrested a guy apparently on his way to have a pop at you . . . had enough weaponry in his vehicle to flatten the White House, and then some.'

The President yawned. 'Excuse me. Troy, any reason to take him any more seriously than any of the other nuts out there?'

'Difficult to say, sir. He was in a bad way when he was found. They're looking into the theory that he may have fallen out with an accomplice.'

'So there may be another one of them out there?'

'They're looking into it.'

Keneally smiled. He tipped his head back against the seat. 'You look into a mirror. You look into a pond. You don't look into a theory.'

'He's being questioned as fully as his injuries allow.'

'Injuries allow!' the President exclaimed wearily. 'Troy, if it was up to me I'd stick needles in his eyes until he talked. Maybe I should make that part of my crime prevention bill, eh? Our inalienable right to stick needles in the eyes of suspects who refuse to talk.'

'Yes, sir.'

'So what has he said? What's he got against me the other cuckoos haven't?'

'We recovered computer software from his vehicle. One particular file showed your name at the top of a death list.'

'Excellent.' The President rubbed at his chin for a moment. 'Who's beneath me on the list? Always good to know what company I'm in.'

Troy squinted at the fax; the list hadn't reproduced very well. 'Ah, now . . . you're top, of course, and . . . Oprah Winfrey's number two . . . and three . . . oh right, fat and thin versions. Psycho or what, Mr President?'

The President closed his eyes. 'Or maybe he has an uncanny perception of where the real power in this country lies.'

'His name's George Burley. Home address in Birmingham, Alabama.'

A presidential eye winked open. 'Birmingham, eh?'

14

Nathan waited in the car, fiddling with the radio dial while Sam walked slowly towards the Cedar Nursing Home. It was an impressive-looking building for unimpressive-looking people, as dark and brooding as death itself. Which was fitting, really.

Nathan was trying to find something even vaguely punk, but wasn't having much luck. He rolled the window down and drummed his fingers on the door and waited, and waited. After two hours he was beginning to regret volunteering to drive the old man out to see his wife.

Sam had been making the journey to the Cedar Home three times a week for nearly five years. Before, he'd been able to motor over in twenty minutes, but since his sight had started to go he'd given up on the driving and it now meant a complicated journey by bus which he found extremely tiring. He'd got to talking about it over lunch and Nathan, with time to kill until Lisa finished her shift, had offered his services. He'd been close to taking his driving test back home when *that* had happened; brushing up on his driving skills would also help convince Lisa that he was becoming more responsible. But God, was it *boring*.

Two or three hours was a hell of a lot of time to spend speaking to someone who never acknowledged his presence, who kept her eyes glued to the television even though the sound was normally turned off, and whose only movement was dipping a craggy hand into the bag of candy he brought and sucking on whatever delight she extracted. Sometimes it got to him: sometimes he slunk off early, the tears dripping down his face, but mostly he was okay, idly chattering away to her about his life at the Empire. She'd always liked to hear about his work. Sometimes, on good days, she let him hold her hand.

This day was a good day. One hand in his, one searching for candy mice. Her eyes followed a re-run of *Moonlighting*, but when he changed the channel there was no perceptible change in her. He flicked on.

'Did I tell you about the new boss, Mary?' Sam said, rubbing the back of her hand. 'Some computer bigshot. More money than sense.' He laughed. 'Maybe that's not fair. Must be bright to be where he is.'

A familiar face came onto the screen. The jug ears. The navy uniform. The Empire State in the background. Sam looked down at his wife, hoping for a glimmer of recognition, but there was nothing.

He shook his head and a tear sprang. 'Oh Mary,' he whispered and touched her hair lightly.

Sinatra.

How old had he been then? Sixteen? Just three or four years after his father had died in the crash. He was supposedly still at school, but he spent most of his time at the Empire State. He was a part-time guard. A benevolent act by the management. The uniform still looked vaguely ridiculous on him, but he was beginning to fill out, grow into it. He was shaving twice a week. He'd had three or four girlfriends already, had bored them to death with his jabber about the Empire. It didn't worry him. They didn't know what they were missing; besides, they'd bored him to death too with *their* constant jabber. All they cared about were the movies. The stars. They all wanted to be actresses. They all wanted to go to Hollywood. *Whatcha wanna be, Sammy, a security guard all your life?*

Yeah, sure, like you're going to Hollywood.

Sam smiled. Hollywood had come to him. Eventually everyone comes to the Empire State. That summer of 1949 Frank Sinatra came. And Gene Kelly. And all the pretty girls and boys of Hollywood. The first Sam knew of it was late one chilly February night when they were closing up the Empire and there was just one visitor lingering on the 86th floor. They got talking. Eventually he came clean: said he was a film director. Sam had never heard of Stanley Donen, but he had heard of Gene Kelly, and he'd most definitely heard of Frank Sinatra, had a cupboard full of his records at home. Mr Donen was scouting locations for his next film, a musical called *On the Town*.

Sam forgot all about it until, six months later and by now a full-time security guard, his boss had announced that the observatories were to be closed for two days to accommodate a film crew. Dean Crawley, head of security, was a fat guy with thick black curly hair and a permanent sneer. 'You keep the fans out, the stars and the crew in. Let them get on with their work. Don't get in the way. You just let them be, boys,' he told them in his sly-raspy voice. 'Make sure they don't throw their stupid asses over the side either. And don't go harassing Sinatra. Their people told our people that he's a touchy son-of-a-bitch, so keep out of his hair, at least what he has of it. No autographs unless *he* volunteers. And he will.'

Sinatra, then, was still pretty big, but the bobby-soxers were beginning to grow out of him and there were newer, younger, better-looking singers coming along. Frankie Laine was number one. Mel Tormé was shooting up the charts. Even old Bing was outselling him.

Sam had to wait his turn to get up-top, one of those busy, hectic, shitty days which seemed to take for ever, but eventually he got there. Saw them all in action. Sinatra and Kelly and that other one whose name he never remembered. Munchkin. Something like that.

'God, Mary, you remember that day? The first time I saw you, getting into the lift. My lift. You were so small and pretty and I thought at first you'd sneaked by them downstairs and were coming up to melt all over Sinatra. You weren't a bit pleased when I demanded your ID card, were you, my love? And I apologized to you, but you weren't having any of it!' Sam started to cackle. He glanced behind him, but no one was paying him the slightest attention. He could have exploded a grenade and they probably wouldn't have blinked.

Mary's job was to tape Sinatra's ears back.

Sinatra didn't much like this. He didn't much like having padding stuffed down the back of his US Navy uniform to make it look like he had an ass, either. So he was in rare form, snapping at everyone about the set.

'He's a concave little bastard,' Dean Crawley had whispered in Sam's ear, and Sam had nodded, but he'd butterflies in his stomach every time Sinatra grouched past him anyway. Frank Sinatra. Right there. Touching distance. Flesh and blood. And human. And vain. And why not? And then he'd seen Mary trailing after him, pleading with him to keep still

– one ear was flapping wild – and the butterflies had gone and been replaced by something altogether more worrying. Like a drumming on his heart. Like the whisper of a warm wind in the depths of winter. Like he didn't know what the hell like, but he couldn't take his eyes off her.

Sinatra had stopped to talk to Gene Kelly, who was directing the dance sections of the movie. Mary came up behind him and reached up to secure the flapping ear. Sinatra lunged forward, like he was being attacked, then spun round on her, his face purple with rage. He pulled his arm back, almost as if to slap her, then stopped himself and jabbed a finger out instead. Mary, wide-eyed, cowered like a rabbit in headlights.

'You keep your hands off me!' Sinatra roared.

Mary's jaw dropped, her eyes tightened, tears sprang and she turned, stifled a little cry and ran back towards the elevators.

Sinatra watched her run. So did the whole crew. A silence settled over the observatory so that all you could hear was the rapid click-click of her retreating heels on the observatory floor. Sinatra shook his head, then shouted half-heartedly after her. 'Come back here right now – damn it!' But she was well gone, and the whole crew switched their attention to him. He reached up to tape the ear back himself, then turned back to Kelly who had watched the incident with barely disguised distaste. As Sinatra opened his mouth to speak Kelly turned abruptly away. He crossed to the assistant director and they began to study some notes Kelly had made on a clipboard. Sinatra looked desperately around him. 'What the hell are you all looking at?' he shouted, and suddenly they weren't all looking.

Sam offered Mary the candy bag. Her long, bony fingers rifled through it, expertly searching for her favourites; her eyes never left the screen. 'If I knew then what I know now, do you think I would have done the same, Mary, do you?'

She pushed another sweet into her mouth. It was only in the following years that he'd started to read about Sinatra's Mafia connections, about what happened to people who crossed him. He squeezed her hand. ''Course I would,' he said.

So spindly little baby-faced Sam McClintock had stepped up to Sinatra, stuck two hands against his white navy uniform and shoved him right back so that he bounced off the security fence. Sam shocked himself. Shocked himself even more by sticking his hand out and grabbing the singer by the throat and pushing his chin up and shouting into his taped ear: 'You don't treat a lady like that, mister,' like he was in a B movie, like he knew anything at all about how to treat a lady.

Then he was pulled away by the crew members and hustled out towards the elevators, but not before he'd seen the look of shock on Sinatra's face, like no one had dared treat him like that before.

The crew released him into Dean Crawley's custody. Dean trailed him along by the back of his shirt, then threw him against the elevator doors and started to slap him. 'What the fuck do you think you're doing?' Crawley screamed. 'Who the fuck do you think you are?' Sam ducked down under the blows and tried desperately to think of something he could say that might rescue the situation. But it was hopeless. He'd blown it. Crawley pulled him up by the collar again. 'You get down those fucking stairs right now, McClintock! You're fucking outta here!'

Creepy Crawley was just about to let go with another slap when someone caught his hand. He turned angrily, swinging Sam round with him.

'Leave him be.'

Crawley released him. Sam looked up. Sinatra.

'Lemme have a word with him.'

A look somewhere between subservience and fear crossed Crawley's face. 'I'll have his skinny Irish ass out on the streets quicker than—'

Sinatra thumbed behind him. 'Get back out there, mister. Leave him with me.'

'Well, I . . .'

'Shift.'

Crawley glared at Sam, then shuffled quickly away. Sam leaned back against the elevator door. He rubbed at the back of his head for a moment. Sinatra moved forward and Sam tensed. The singer bent to retrieve Sam's guard's cap. He brushed his hand across the top of it then handed it back to him.

Sam accepted it warily and they stood looking at each other for a long moment. Then Sinatra gave him a half-smile. 'You're a cocky little shit, ain't ya?'

Sam surprised himself again. The anger was still on him. 'You shouldn't oughta . . .'

Sinatra held his hands up apologetically. 'Whoa there. I know what I shouldn't have done.' He reached up and ripped a piece of tape away from his ear, examined it for a moment, then threw it behind him. 'I'm having a bad day. I'm dancing about in there like a ten-dollar hooker. I'm sorry. I shouldn't have been mean to your girl.'

'She's not my girl.'

'Well, I shouldn't have been mean to her. Where'd she go anyways?'

Sam shrugged.

'You've a lot of balls, kid. I'll go and find her. Apologize, eh?'

'And he did, didn't he, love?' Mary nodded. Nodded at the screen. He reached across and touched her face. She was still beautiful. 'And where would we have been without him?'

Sinatra had found her all right. Found her and brought her back up to the observatory and apologized to her in front of the whole crew and she'd burst into tears again and he'd given her a big hug. And then he'd called Sam out and insisted that he and Mary get squeezed somehow into the next scene. They'd both tried to run away, but they'd been caught and kitted out, then went through about ten takes trying not to look completely wooden each time they passed arm in arm in front of Sinatra and Kelly and Munchkin just before they broke into one of their big dance numbers. Of course their whole damn scene was cut from the movie, but that didn't matter: they'd met each other properly, that was that.

He didn't lose his job either. Sinatra had a word in Crawley's ear, and the incident was never mentioned again. In fact Crawley moved to a different job within weeks. Sam was never sure if the two were connected. He kind of hoped they were.

On the way out the receptionist handed him an envelope. 'I was going to post this,' she said, 'but what's the point? How is she today?'

'Just fine, Rosemary, just fine.'

He didn't open it until he was back in the car. Nathan was asleep in the driver's seat and didn't wake until Sam slammed the passenger door. Nathan let out a yelp and shot back stiff against the seat. 'What is it? What's wrong?' he gasped, looking around him, all panicked.

Sam smiled at the youngster. 'Nothing, son.'

As Nathan started the car and pulled out into the traffic, Sam read the letter. It wasn't any big surprise. The Cedar Nursing Home was putting up its fees again. Sam crumpled it up and threw it out of the window.

15

George didn't know where he was. His ribs were sore, his head throbbed and his hand was painful from a drip needle, but he was a warrior, made of warrior *stuff*. He had trained himself to ignore pain. *Another man would have gone under by now*, he thought, his head on the pillow, his eyes half-closed against the fluorescent lighting.

The FBI agent sitting by his bed was called John Smith. George disliked him immediately. He had a stocky confidence about him, sitting there with his *New York Times* and his darting-vigilant eyes and his chatter with the nurses which just fell on the charming side of aggressive. And of course he was black. It hadn't come as a particular shock when he drifted out of unconsciousness to find a black man assigned to his case. He knew they would. It was part of their training. Designed to throw him. Designed to really annoy him. Then the white guy would come in and take over and George would be so pleased to see him that he'd tell him everything. *Sure*. In fact John Smith was on duty because Bernard Manso, who'd been by George's bed since he was brought in, had had to go home with stomach cramps.

'Where . . .?' George croaked.

Smith smiled and flashed his ID. 'Mackenzie General in Richmond, George. How you feeling?'

George ignored the question. 'What am I . . .?'

'Highway Patrol found you crashed. Don't know who looks after your car, George, but the damn thing just about exploded. You're lucky to be alive.'

George nodded vaguely.

'Or you would be, if they hadn't found all those guns. And called us. And what do you know, but George Burley ain't exactly mister nobody.'

George blinked innocently. He'd done the right thing. The god-damn nigger didn't even know how to fix an engine without making it ten times worse. Why, George had done everyone a favour by blowing his head off. Or had there been more to it? Had he deliberately sabotaged the car so that it would break down on an even lonelier stretch of road, while he followed at a safe distance? Thinking George was a poor defenceless minister he'd have snuck up and cracked his head open with a spanner and hacked him up and buried him and sold the car for ten thousand bucks and drunk himself into the grave. Or was he working in cahoots with that poor white trash mechanic in that last town? That was it, the greaseball had fixed the car so it would break down again, then tipped off the nigger. Then the nigger'd come along, pretended to be friendly, then was just waiting his opportunity to smash George's face with a fence post. *I sensed the danger, I destroyed the enemy.*

'You find my computer?' George asked, turning his head to where Smith was lolling back on his chair. His jacket was open and George could just see an inviting corner of holster.

Smith flashed a smile at the patient, flicked some non-existent fluff off his left knee. 'Don't know about any computer, George. Found some hand grenades and some assault rifles. But I don't remember any computer.'

George closed his eyes.

'How're you feeling now, George? Can I get you anything?' George opened his eyes again. He sighed, then shook his head slowly.

'Coffee? How about a magazine?'

'No.'

'How about a Coke? Some cookies?'

Okay, if he was going to play the decent upstanding FBI man, George would play the redneck. 'How about one of my guns so's I can blow your fucking head off?'

Smith laughed. 'Now George, that's not nice. What you want to go and shoot me for?'

George's eyes narrowed. ''Cause you exist.'

Smith sucked in some air, mock-shocked. 'George, you are a case.'

'And you can knock that condescending shit off, quota-boy.'

'Oh now, George . . .' Smith folded his paper and set it down beside his chair. He put his right arm across his stomach, settled his left elbow on the wrist and rested his chin in his left hand. Thoughtful, professorial.

'Look at the floor, quota-boy.'

Smith looked at the blue tiles. He gave a little shrug.

'Drip, drip, drip. That's your arrogance in a big blue pool round your feet. Dripping off you, quota-boy, dripping off you like sweat, 'cause it ain't meant to be there in the first place.'

With a slight shake of his head Smith sat back. 'Tell me, George,' he said. 'Where can I get some of those mind-bending drugs for myself? I didn't think a white boy like yourself would ever touch them.'

'Drip, drip, drip.'

Smith smiled. 'You're scaring me, George. Really, scaring me.' He dropped his hand from his mouth. 'Just as well you're going to prison. I don't think I'd have another night's sleep if I knew you were on the loose.' He paused, then fixed George with a cool stare. 'I hear you're after President Keneally, George, that right?'

George turned his head slightly towards the FBI man. 'Well, now how would you know that if you hadn't found my computer?'

'I just heard, George. I didn't say there wasn't no computer, I just said I didn't know anything about it.'

'Oh, how you play with words: You'd almost think you went to school, quota-boy.'

For a second, just a second, George saw the anger flash in the agent's eyes. He held it, though. Just. He was silent for a few moments.

'It's surprising really, how close our backgrounds are,' Smith said.

'I think not.'

'Oh now, George, you might be surprised. We're both from poor Southern stock. Both had parents who worked themselves into the ground for us. Both went to good colleges. Both got good jobs. Both got married.'

Despite his suffering, George managed to point an angry finger at Smith. 'You and me, quota-boy, we ain't got nothing in common.'

'Oh I'd say we're exactly the same, George, except at some point our souls diverged. I decided to serve the community, and you went down route psycho.'

'You think you're so smart, don't you?'

'No smarter'n the next man, George, 'less it's you.'

'Sitting there in your cheap suit with your cheap Eff Bee

Eye badge.' George tilted his head, suddenly sniffing up the stifling antiseptic air. 'I can smell the plantation off you, quota-boy, smell the cotton. You think you can cover it up with that cheap aftershave, don't you, boy? What you call it, eau da-do-dah? I once had a teacher like you, thought he could tell me what to do. You know what I did to him, quota-boy?'

'You ate his liver with a bottle of Gatorade and a Hershey bar?'

Smith, it seemed, had watched the same films. He let go with a big laugh and slapped his leg. 'You really get me, George, you really do!'

George closed his eyes. He was abruptly tired of playing the redneck. He turned his head away. 'I want to sleep now,' he said.

'Aw, now, I was just enjoying that. Tell me what you did to your teacher?'

Silence.

'Do that bit about my cheap suit. Tell me about the eau da-do-dah again.'

Silence.

'At least tell me about the quota, George, don't leave me like this.'

George remained silent.

Smith tutted.

'You asleep, George?'

George remained silent.

'You wouldn't be talking about the FBI having to recruit a certain quota of Afro-Americans into the agency every year, would you?'

George remained silent.

'I think you are, George.'

George remained silent.

'Tell you the truth, I don't know if there is a quota. I don't much care. Who am I to complain about a quota if it gets me to a place like this of a fine summer's day, holding a gun over some poor white trash like you. I just love it, George. You hear me?'

Inside, George was smiling. He'd got him.

16

George liked to think of himself as something of a Renaissance Man. He read widely, he studied hard, he taught himself a hundred skills. When the end of civilization came, George would survive – no, not merely survive, he would prosper – damn it, he would lead.

In reality, of course, he was more Piltdown Man than Renaissance Man, a fraud polymath. He could soak up information like a sponge: in that way he was a genius, but a flawed one, because although he had the capacity to understand *everything*, he only wanted that which he could adapt to his own arcane purposes; the rest was superfluous. If it would be useful come the holocaust, George was game for it. Unarmed combat. The slaughter yard. Building. Irrigation. Farming. He even attended knitting classes; three in fact, from a course of ten; you might never wear what he knitted for fear of arrest by the fashion police, but at least it would keep you warm. George quickly grasped the theory of all things and then abandoned whatever class he had so recently joined, preferring to rely on his own superior mental capacity to master the practicalities rather than be held back by his dilettante classmates.

Or looked at another way, George was a psychotic with a short attention span. He wooed his wife with this same reckless enthusiasm. It was Mrs Burley's misfortune to misinterpret this as romantic passion. On the third night of their honeymoon in Barbados she found herself standing crying alone in the middle of a rain-soaked wood surrounded by giant frogs after being slapped around by her new husband, wondering how it had all gone wrong so quickly. George's mistake was to treat her like one of his learning projects; he grew bored because after a few days of her exclusive company he felt he knew her inside and out. Of course he wasn't going to run out on her; that wasn't the kind of thing a Southern gentleman did; he would look after her in fine style, but she was a trophy wife, and meant as much to him as the framed certificates from the theological colleges that hung on his study wall; she had just cost a little more to buy, that was all. Mrs Burley's departure, then, came as a complete shock to him; it wouldn't have been any greater a shock if the giant moose head on the wall he'd machine-gunned on that Canadian trip with WAR had climbed down and galloped out of the door.

George wasn't in the best of moods. His lawyer had called from Birmingham saying he couldn't make it until the day after tomorrow, but instructing him to say nothing in the meantime. *Well thanks*. He suggested appointing a lawyer from Richmond in the meantime, but George wasn't interested.

Smith's shift ended at four. Someone else took his place, but he never really saw who. He didn't come into the room. He sat on a chair outside the door, leaving it just a little open so that he could keep an eye on him. White guy. *Should be shaking my hand*. He drifted off to sleep for a while. When he woke, about eight, Smith was back.

'How're you feeling now, George? You okay?'

George gave a little nod.

'Can I get you anything, George? A Coke? Some coffee? A magazine or something?'

'How about some cotton? I could stuff it in my ears so I wouldn't have to hear you fucking bleating all the time.'

'Oh, nasty, nasty. Offer withdrawn. You break my heart, George, you really do. I thought you might have lightened up by now.'

'At least I can.'

'Oh bitch, bitch, bitch.'

George tutted. He stretched awkwardly, trying to scratch his right shoulder blade with his left hand. With his right hand handcuffed to the bedpost, it was the only way. Satisfied, just, he lay back on the pillow. It was dark outside, bright inside; quiet both sides.

'I gotta pee,' he said suddenly.

'What's that, George?'

'You heard. I gotta take a leak.'

'Go right ahead.' Smith looked about him for a sample jar. Found a cardboard vessel by the locker, extended it to George.

'Okay, I don't wanna pee, I wanna take a crap.'

Smith examined the cardboard vessel, then looked at George. They both shook their heads. 'What do you normally do, George?'

'I don't normally do it like this. I don't know what goes on in your family, but it's rare I'm handcuffed to the bed.'

Smith stood. 'I'll get the nurse.'

'And what the fuck is she going to do?'

'Well, I imagine she'll . . .'

'Would you just uncuff me and help me to the men's room?'

'Not sure if I can do that, George.'

'What am I gonna do, make a run for it?' He gave a sarcastic little laugh. 'Look at me.'

Smith laughed as well. The prisoner did look pretty pathetic, with his regulation-issue striped pyjamas, his bruised face and the drip coming out of his arm.

'Take your gun out. Cover me. Shoot me if I take off down the corridor like Jesse Owen.'

Smith thought about it for maybe five seconds. He shook his head again, then bent towards the bed and uncuffed George.

'Thank you,' said George, lifting the covers back. He swung his legs round and gingerly rested his feet on the floor. Then he stood, shakily, gave a little wince at the pain in his ribs.

'Should you be doing this, George?' Smith asked.

'When you gotta go, you gotta go.'

'Maybe I should get a nurse.'

George shuffled forward a few feet. 'I'm fine.'

'You don't look fine.'

'If you could just . . .' George indicated the drip stand. Smith nodded and stepped behind him. He lifted it, then followed as George shuffled across the floor towards the hall and then on into the men's room.

There were three cubicles. Smith made George wait in the doorway for a few moments while he drew his gun and checked each one out for occupancy first and then hidden weapons. Then he signalled for George to enter.

George chose the centre cubicle and backed into it.

Smith shook the drip stand. 'You want this in with you, George?'

'What do you think?' George snapped and pushed the door across until Smith was blotted out, but left it open enough for the tube to run through to his hand.

He settled himself on the toilet seat.

Smith backed up to the urinals, holstered his gun and unholstered another one. He started to pee. 'Hey, George, I was looking up your Top Ten when I got back to the office. Fascinating stuff. The psychologists think they've struck gold. But tell me this, what has Oprah Winfrey ever done to annoy you? And what's this business about fat and thin versions? Think it would be kind of nice to have a woman who can just blow up or slim down according to the seasons. Like getting a new wife every fall. Now that show of hers can be a real ball-buster sometimes, but putting her in your Top Ten twice that's just . . . anyway . . . what's behind it, George?'

There was no response.

'George?'

No response. Smith re-zipped and stepped towards the cubicle door. 'You okay there, George?' He bent slightly. He could still see George's bare feet. 'Something stuck there, Georgie-boy? I ain't gonna help you with that, I tell ya.'

Still nothing. Smith shook his head slowly then reached for his gun. He held it out before him and cautiously pushed the door open. George's head was slumped down on his chest. 'Christ,' said Smith, holstering the gun. He stepped into the cubicle. He used two of his fingers carefully to lift George's chin up. 'You okay, man?' he asked.

George's eyes opened. 'Sure,' he said and plunged the drip needle into the agent's heart.

In an instant he was dead.

He toppled in over George without even time for a death groan, just a wide-mouthed look of complete shock. George, nearly spitting with the pain in his chest, held Smith up until he could squeeze out beneath him, then let him fall. His head fell into the toilet bowl.

Rubbing his hand where he'd extracted the needle, George hurried across the men's room and gently closed the door. He locked it. Then he set about getting into the dead man's clothes.

17

Sam had been frequenting Pat Murphy's Broadway bar for forty years. Jesus, he'd practically got married there. He didn't even particularly like it any more, it had become too much of a tourist trap. He still called in for a couple most nights of the week, usually enroute to Cedar Wood to see Mary, or like tonight, putting in time until Bobby Tangetta's party got under way. Bobby never needed much of an excuse to throw a party; this time it was in honour of Nathan Jones joining the security team. His wife didn't take much persuasion. They both liked their drink, and that was that.

Sam tapped his fingers along to the occasional Irish jig on the juke box. He didn't much bother with the staff, mostly pink-faced blow-ins from Kerry or Cork, but when he had a couple of drinks in him he didn't mind talking to some traveller or other. He enjoyed chatting about the city and, of course, the Empire and invariably whoever he talked to would turn up the next day on the 86th, though mostly these days he barely recognized them when they did.

Sam peered up from his sports section as a large figure slid in beside him.

'Hi there, Sam, okay?'

Sam squinted against the sunlight coming through the top window. 'Well now, there's a familiar face,' he said, and immediately felt a little uneasy.

As far as he could remember he'd never shared an after-hours drink with Leonard Maltman. A Christmas party maybe, a wedding possibly, but never like this. He didn't mind Leonard. He'd just never thought about socializing with him.

'I was told this was your local, Sam. Nice spot. Thought I'd catch you before the party. Y'know how it is, never get a chance to talk with Bobby running the show. Anyway, how long you been coming here?'

'About a hundred and forty years.'

Leonard laughed nervously and signalled for a drink. 'You okay there?' he said, nodding at Sam's fresh pint.

'I'll take a short, if you're asking.'

'I'm asking.' He nodded at the barman. 'What'll it be, a Bushmills?'

Sam nodded. Finton set up the drinks. They supped quietly for a few moments.

'Great day today, eh?' said Leonard.

'They're all great days when you get to my age.'

Leonard nodded. 'Hope I get to your age.'

'Don't,' said Sam, 'it's miserable. All I got to live for now is my job.'

Leonard gulped and cursed Sam under his breath. *He knows why I'm here*. He'd thought about it all night and all day, but was still looking for the right way into it. Leonard took another sip of his beer. His gaze travelled along the bottles behind the bar, then on to the Irish pennants and yellowed newspaper clippings of hooded men with guns. A little higher there were some framed photos of celebrities who'd visited the bar over the years. One in particular caught his attention. It wasn't the usual fake-smiled pose you saw in bars across the city; this looked like someone having a good time.

'Hey, Sam,' he said, pointing up, 'that's Sinatra, isn't it?'

Sam glanced up, then back down. 'Sure.'

'What a guy. Musta been taken, what, thirty, forty years ago, eh? I bet he knew how to have a good time?'

'Yeah, he sure did.'

Leonard laughed. 'Sounds like you used to know him, Sam.'

Sam shook his head into his pint. 'Take a closer look at the . . . photo, Leonard,' he said.

'Mmm?' Leonard peered forward, brow furrowed. 'It is Sinatra, isn't it?'

'Of course it is. Look beside him.'

'That's . . . sorry, Sam, my eyes ain't so good any more . . . barman?'

Sam rapped his knuckles on the bar. 'Hey, Finton, hand me down the Sinatra pic, would you?'

Finton walked down the bar and unhooked the picture and handed it to Sam. 'Back on that trip again, Sammy boy?' he laughed and wandered off again.

Sam wiped the dust off the glass with the end of his sleeve then showed it to Leonard. 'Now who's that?' he said, pointing to Sinatra's left.

'Ava Gardner!' He looked up and around the bar for a moment, shaking his head. 'Jeez, she was in here too. Look at them. Happy as Larry.'

'Then what'ya think of the bride?'

Leonard took the picture off him and held it close. A teenager in a plain wedding dress. Bright eyes. Great figure. 'She's beautiful. Another actress?'

Sam clicked his tongue. 'That's my wife.' He felt the familiar little warm glow as he said it.

'Jesus,' said Leonard, 'I mean, sorry, but that's your . . .' He turned the frame a little away from him for the extra light. 'That means . . .'

'Yeah, I'm the geek on the right.'

'Good God.' He looked from Sam to the photo, Sam to the photo, checking the likeness. Finally he nodded, satisfied. 'Sam McClintock and Frank Sinatra – partying the night away! Jesus, Sam, how'd you manage that? I mean, Sinatra and Ava Gardner at your wedding. Were they pissed in the bar or something and you persuaded . . .'

Sam shook his head. He took the photo back from Leonard and placed it on the bar. 'Frank'n me. We're pals from the old days. We had our reception upstairs here, Sinatra came and sang at it. Just turned up. Memorable night, Leonard.'

For a few moments Leonard said nothing, just shook his head in disbelief. 'Shit,' he said finally, 'when me and Verna got hitched we had Ralph from the diner and his banjo.'

Sam gave a little shrug, then changed tack abruptly. 'So what brings you down here, Leonard?'

Leonard set his glass down. Gave a little shake of his head. 'Aw fuck, Sam, you know why I'm here.'

'I've kinda guessed.'

'I thought you might. I'm sorry, Sam, I'm not very good at this sort of thing.'

Sam tossed back one of the shorts. 'That's no bad way to be, Leonard. You're a caring individual. Not many of you about these days.' He brought his hand down lightly on Leonard's fleshy arm. 'Relax! This Magiform outfit, they're a young, thrusting, go-ahead kinda company, they don't want an old fool like me looking after the President. What're they thinking, I'll bore him to death with my old stories?'

'It's not . . .'

'Ha! I probably would Leonard, I probably would! No, listen. I don't mind. Just cause I've met every other president since the war, it isn't written in stone that I have to meet this one. Don't get so worked up about it. I'm fine. I'll stay in the background. I'll stay in the canteen if you want. I'll take the day off if it bothers them that much.'

The second short followed the first. Sam signalled for another two, and one for Leonard.

'Sam, it's not a question of taking a day off . . .'

Sam took a swig of his beer, gave him a wry, dentured smile. 'Okay, then I'll just lurk in the office . . .'

'Sam, for God's sake . . . you shoulda retired years ago.'

'I'll never retire, Leonard. I've already had my hours cut back more than I want.'

'You should be taking it easy.'

'Why?'

'It's what people do when they get to your age.'

'And within about a week they're pushing up the daisies. Not me. Not me!' Sam thumped the bar.

Finton floated by. 'Give 'em hell, Sam!' he crowed.

'And fuck you too, Finton,' Sam growled, then glowered back at Leonard, who was more than a little taken aback at the shift in the old man's mood. 'So they don't want me to meet the President. Okay. Mission accomplished. What else are you trying to say, Leonard, that I should retire, or are you just too chickenshit to retire me?'

'Sam . . .'

'Will you just fucking tell me?'

'I don't think you should retire, Sam. If it was up to me you could stay up there all fucking day and all fucking night till you dropped. But it ain't up to me. It ain't up to me, Sam. The order just came down. You have to go. I don't

122

know why. I wish I did, but I don't. They just told me, he's out.'

'And you didn't stand up for me?'

'Of course I stood up for you. But the boss is the boss.'

'You're my boss, Leonard.'

'And I've a boss, and he has a boss, and his boss has his boss and about a hundred times further removed there's Michael Tate and he's the biggest boss of them all. And that's just about where this order came from. I can't stand up to that, Sam. I thought it better to come down here to tell you, personal like.'

'You mean because the men might support me. You mean because they might have lynched your fucking hide if you'd tried it in work.'

Leonard shook his head ruefully. 'Maybe they would. Jesus, Sam, you're Mr Fucking Empire State. They'd be out on strike quicker than you could click your fingers if you asked them. We both know that. But I'm asking you not to do that to me, Sam, nor to them. They're about to be offered new contracts, a good big hike in wages, all sorts of benefits. But if there's any sort of labour problem, especially with the President visiting – Jesus, Sam, I know what companies like Magiform are like. They'll chuck every last one of us out and start from scratch.'

'They wouldn't dare . . .'

'But they would. They really would. Money doesn't matter to them Sam, they grow it on trees down in Silicon Valley or wherever the fuck it is they come from. What matters is loyalty and obedience. You throw a spanner in the works when the President visits and there'll be blood everywhere.'

Sam took a long drink of his beer, draining the glass. He set it down carefully. 'So what're you asking me, Leonard?'

'To go quietly.'

He held Leonard's eyes for a long moment, then slipped off his stool and moved wordlessly towards the door.

Outside, about a hundred yards up, the tears started to flow and his body began to shudder. He steadied himself against a wall. *What am I going to tell Mary?* was his only thought.

A young couple, both blond, Swedes or Danes, asked him if he was okay. He spluttered into his handkerchief, nodded reassuringly. They smiled pleasantly, turned to leave, then switched back. 'Sir, can you tell us how to get to your Empire State Building from here?'

18

'Miss Winfrey will see you in just a few moments, Mr President.'

President Keneally, reclining in the black leather make-up chair, nodded and tutted at the same time. He'd heard that three times in the past twenty minutes. He'd complained after the first ten and had been rebuffed with, *Miss Winfrey has a very busy schedule.* He turned his head slightly, disturbing the girl with the face powder; she matched his tut. 'Fred, get me Slo, will you?'

Fred Troy punched the numbers into his phone, then handed it to the President. The President waited a few moments, then heard the familiar voice. 'Slo? How's life treating you?'

'Fine, Mr President. Just fine.'

'How's Tara?'

A little pause. 'You haven't spoken to her?'

'She's not taking my calls just at the moment.'

'Oh. I'm sorry. Is there anything I . . .?'

'Actually there is, Slo, if you don't mind. She's still going through with this Ireland thing, isn't she?'

'Yes, sir, Northern Ireland.'

'Slo, I'd like you to go with her.'

'Mr President, I can't just drop every—'

'Yes, you can.'

'Mr President, I'm the White House Chief of Staff.'

'Mr Slovenski, I'm the President of the United States of America. Besides, you could do with the break.'

Pause. 'Is this an order, Mr President?'

'Slo? Now come on. I hate it when you get *all hurt*. Please do this for me. You're the only man I trust, Slo, you know that, don't you? So do this for me, will you?'

Slovenski held his breath for seven seconds. Then he nodded. Then he spoke. 'Okay, Mr President, if you insist.'

He felt all *aglow*.

Senator Michael Keneally's opponents in the race for the White House had attacked him for choosing to appear on syndicated chat shows rather than political discussion programmes. 'It turns the election into a beauty pageant!' wailed Senator Bob Broole, who was already trailing. Keneally had hammed it up brilliantly, pulling his best Ali impression out of the bag. 'He just ain't as pretty as me!' he'd crowed at a press conference, and then rolled out a hammering decimation of Broole's foreign policy stance which just blew the old Texan half out of the race.

And the chat-show route had certainly paid off. At the end of the day, who gave a damn how you got there as long as you got there for the right reasons and were prepared to do the job? Even then they'd used Oprah as an example. The figures were indisputable: prime time, lightweight, good-looking. Market a president like a film star and you'll get excellent ballot box office.

Twenty minutes later the President was ushered into

Oprah's dressing-room. He wasn't the least surprised to find that it was three times the size of his own.

She was in her chair, being pampered by four attendants. She nodded at him in the mirror. 'Michael, how are you?'

'I'm fine,' said the President, reaching out his hand, 'and you're looking wonderful.'

She held hers back, wiggling her fingers. 'I'm sorry,' she said, 'just painted.'

'Of course.' He folded his hands behind his back and smiled at her awkwardly. There were no other seats.

'How's Tara, Michael, keeping well?'

The President nodded. 'Yes. Great. Off to Ireland soon.'

'Really? Who's throwing the party?'

'No party. Just a goodwill visit.'

'This is Tara we're talking about?'

When she was finished she slipped her feet off the chair and allowed Keneally to take her arm as she led him to the studio. He asked her twice what approach she intended taking on the show, but her response was so convoluted on each occasion that he was no wiser when she left him to wait for the green light. 'Don't worry, Michael,' she glowed, 'you'll be fine.'

She had a shy-confidence to her that made her very attractive to the President. A vulnerability totally at odds with her position as the most powerful woman in America. He'd watched her cry live on TV: if it had been any of the others, he wouldn't have believed it. Most times she stood in the audience, one of them, on their side; this time she sat opposite him. Her chair was maybe four centimetres higher than his. He was looking up at her, but only just. He didn't mind. She talked him up a storm, he smiled that toothy smile and the crowd whooped and hollered.

'President Keneally . . .'

'Please call me . . . Mr President.'

Whoop-whoop-whoop.

After that Oprah quizzed him lightly about Tara's trip to Ireland; he spoke knowledgeably about inner-city problems; he recalled his early days growing up in rural Maine. Then he fielded questions from the audience, returning them with the expertise of an international tennis coach training a child, tough enough to let them know he meant business, but soft enough to inspire.

Whoop-whoop-whoop all the way.

Troy watched his President with admiration. He'd been on special assignment with Keneally for three weeks now, ever since the last rash of death threats, and his appreciation of the man had grown with each passing day. With some presidents it was all an act, a show for the people; behind closed doors they were something different; with Keneally it was pretty much the same both ways. Honest, funny, henpecked, concerned, confused, quick-tempered, contrite, anxious to do well, keen to impress. Everyman.

The last man to impress Troy so much had been J. Edgar Hoover, though he'd never met him; at least, not when he was alive. Troy alone had been chosen from the Quantico class of '72 to attend Hoover's funeral in Washington, selected as a representative of the future to stand at the head of the casket in the Rotunda. It had been the making of him; from a trainee on the edge of flunking out, his random selection had instilled in him a new determination to succeed. Standing there, surrounded by members of the Supreme Court, the cabinet, senators, representatives and members of the house as Hoover lay before him on Abraham Lincoln's black wooden catafalque. Troy smiled at the memory and glanced at his watch, then back to the audience. They'd all been searched on the way in. Secret Service agents sat among them.

'Mr President,' said Oprah, 'since we announced that you were to be taking telephone questions, just over an hour ago, we've had over 25,000 callers . . .'

Whoop-whoop-whoop.

'You're sure they haven't got a wrong number, Oprah?'

Whoop-whoop-whoop.

'Well you obviously can't answer them all, but we'll do our best, folks. Caller number one is . . . Joe Mantiveri from Middlebury, Vermont . . . Joe . . . hi . . . what's your question for President Keneally?'

Joe spluttered into his phone. 'First . . . uhma . . . may I say what an honour it is to be talking to you, sir? I voted for you all the way . . .'

'Well, thank you, Joe . . .'

'And then, sir, I'm, uhma, high school teacher here in the great state of Vermont and we're all a hundred per cent behind your education reforms, greatest thing that . . .'

Oprah cut in. 'What's your question, Joe?'

'Uhma, well I don't really have a question, Oprah, save for where in hell has President Keneally been all these years, we coulda done with him ten years ago!'

Whoop-whoop-whoop!

Oprah smiled into the camera. 'Just reminding all you folks at home that the President doesn't know what questions we're throwing him tonight . . . next caller is Ruth O'Mara from Indianapolis. What's your question, Ruth . . .?'

High-pitched: 'Mr President, I don't know an awful lot about politics, but I am a great fan of yours and of your wife's . . . I was wondering if I could ask a question about her . . . Mrs Keneally?'

'Yes of course, Ruth . . .'

'Mr President, you see the way she has her hair . . . it's just beautiful . . . but I was wondering, does she use a colour in it, or is it just naturally that kind of . . . tawny brown?'

The President leaned conspiratorially forward and cupped his hand round his mouth. 'To tell you the truth, Ruth, Tara's hair is exactly the colour it was the day she was born. Conversely,' he continued, running a hand through his own thatch in an exaggerated manner, 'mine has been growing grey for quite a few years now, so I use Wells Color Compound from time to time . . .'

Whoop-whoop-whoop.

'Okay, now we have a call from Washington from someone says he's an old friend of yours. Are you there, George Burley?'

The President took a second to twig, then he glanced at Troy, standing alert behind camera number one. It was probably a coincidence, but there'd be no harm in checking it out. Troy nodded and moved immediately towards the control room.

'Yes, Oprah, I'm here.'

'George, where do you know the President from?'

'The President and I have spoken on the phone. I had a problem, I wrote to the President, he called me up and he fixed it.'

'Okay, George, and what was that problem?'

'I had a problem with, well, Oprah, racism.'

'And the President helped you? How was that? What sort of a problem was it?'

'Well, Oprah, it's all around us. Everywhere we go, everything we do, we can never get away from it.'

'This is in Washington?'

'Everywhere.'

'But it affects you, specifically, in Washington?'

'Yes, Oprah.'

'And what form does this racism take?'

'They're just everywhere.'

'Who are?'

'Niggers, Oprah.'

The President hadn't seen her jarred before, and he'd seen her a thousand times. A big *whooooah* rippled through the audience. Oprah glanced at her producer, who made a cutting motion across her throat. Oprah shook her head, then repeated the action to camera. 'Oh . . . I see, George Burley . . . this racism you complain about, it's actually *your* racism.'

'That's right.'

'And how was it that the President helped you out?'

Keneally started to speak, but Oprah held a finger up and he sat back, nodding slightly. He knew what she was doing. Getting into a slanging match with him wouldn't help. It would only legitimize his argument. She would let him talk himself into a hole.

'He helped me decide to get off my ass and do something about all you monkeys.'

'And how did he do that, *George*?'

'He called me up and told me I was a sick mother and he was going to have me wiped off the face of the planet.'

Oprah turned to the President. 'You tell him that, Mr President?'

The President shrugged. 'I might have said something along those lines, Oprah.'

Whoop, whoop, whoop.

Oprah faced the camera. 'Well tell me, George, what exactly are you going to do about us *monkeys*?'

George gave her a little giggle. It was an intentional giggle, meant to make him sound mad, and thus proving to George that he wasn't mad. 'Heh-heh-heh. Luckily, you ain't my number one right now, Oprah. That privilege I saved for the President. He's the one I'm coming for.'

'Coming for?'

'I'm gonna blow his head clean off, Oprah, clean off.'

Oprah nodded for a few moments, then turned to the audience. 'That's one sick son-of-a-bitch, ladies and gentlemen.'

They roared their approval and Oprah waved them into a commercial break. The President focused his attention on the nearest camera, staring into it as if he was staring out George Burley, daring him to blink; after a few moments it blinked back at him, from green to red, and the President smiled. A little victory.

As the President hurried into the control room Fred Troy was going ballistic. 'Well how in hell did he get through? Is there no vetting system? Jesus, I thought you guys had this kind of thing worked out years ago.'

The director, sweating profusely, shook his head. 'You can only vet so far. We checked his ID with the hotel he called from. He told us exactly what he planned to say. We can't be blamed if he veered off at the last moment. It's called freedom of speech.'

'It's called incitement . . .'

'He said he knew the President.'

'Did you never think of asking the President?'

'We thought it would be a nice surprise.'

'It was.'

Oprah waved soothing hands from the doorway. 'Relax, folks, great TV!'

The President loosened his tie. There was a thin veneer of sweat on his brow. 'Jesus,' he said, shaking his head. 'Did I handle that okay? Maybe I should have said something?'

'Not at all,' said Troy. 'You handled it perfectly – not that you should have had to in the first place.'

'Troy – I thought George Burley was locked up in, where was it? Richmond, or somewhere?'

'Richmond, yeah. Last I heard.'

Oprah came hurrying across. 'Michael, I'm sorry that happened . . .'

'So am I,' said the President coolly. Oprah's mouth fell slightly. 'I'm sorry,' he added quickly, 'I know it's not your fault, goddamn it. What're the chances of a nut like that getting through anyway? How many calls did you say we had?'

'By the time we finished, about 50,000. Three got on air.'

'God-damn lucky bastard.'

Troy, beginning to calm down, nodded his head. 'It happens, Mr President. Look at Lee Harvey Oswald – he shot three people with one bullet.'

'Oh just cheer me up, Troy, just cheer me up.'

19

Lisa was dreading the party.

She'd told Nathan she didn't want to go, but he'd come over all hurt and he was irresistible when he was like that. She'd tried the usual tack.

'But I won't know anyone!'

'Precisely, and if you'd bothered coming down to work you would know them by now and it wouldn't be such a hurdle. You're the one likes meeting people, for God's sake.'

He had her there, of course. She shrugged.

'Lisa, c'mon, they'll all be bringing their partners. We don't have to stay long.'

Partners. She gave him the look: *sure*, Nathan.

'So you'll be on your best behaviour?'

He smiled. 'Of course. Aren't I always?'

'I don't want us to fight. Not any more.'

'So come to the party. I'll be an angel.'

'A teetotal angel?'

'Lisa, c'mon, we have to have a drink. But only a few. I promise. It'll be a good laugh, they're a nice bunch.'

She looked at him doubtfully, but she agreed. She *should*

make the effort, despite the plan that was slowly coming to fruition in her mind.

In her lunch break, Lisa went shopping for something to wear. Cindy tagged along as well, but she was more of a hindrance than a help. Her idea of fashion had little to do with the word *understated.*

'You okay, girl?' Cindy asked as Lisa barked her annoyance at the thirteenth dress she'd tried on in one store.

'Sorry, yes, sure.'

'You better tell me.'

Lisa rolled her eyes. 'What am I going to say? When they ask me what I work at?'

Cindy smiled sympathetically. 'I tell the truth, then I offer a private audience in one of the bedrooms.'

'You . . .?'

''Course not! What you take me for, girl? I say I wait tables.'

'And what if they say where?'

'Make it up. You think they're going to check? There are ten million waitresses in this city.'

'But what if they say, hey, maybe I'll call in and say hello, or . . .'

'Then tell 'em you're part of a flying waitress service. Tell them you're on twenty-four-hour standby to fly anywhere in the world for emergency waitressing duties.'

Lisa laughed. She unzipped the latest effort and threw it on the floor of the changing room. 'I'm not going to get anything. This is pointless.'

'That ain't the attitude, Lisa. What you gotta do is this: what am I trying to say with this dress?' She picked up the crumpled dress from the floor and held it against her. 'Am I trying to say, *hey look at me, little Miss Sexy*? Am I trying to say, *demure, retiring, but there's a sex bomb waiting to get out*? Am I trying to say, *I'm with my partner, so hands off*? Or *I'm with a partner, but I'm open to offers*?'

'I'm trying to say I don't want to be here and can I please go home.'

'Okay. Nun's habit for you, I think.'

They laughed some more and ignored Cindy's advice. Eight shops later Lisa bought something. Plain, knee-length, but they both agreed, extremely sexy.

On the way back to Star World, Cindy asked, 'What *are* you trying to say, Lisa?'

Lisa shrugged. 'I don't know. I really don't know.'

It was a nice place. Twice the size of theirs. A converted loft. Bright.

'God,' Lisa said, 'how'd you . . .'

'Afford it on a security guard's wage?'

Embarrassed, Lisa looked to her toes. 'Sorry, I didn't mean . . .'

Bobby Tangetta squeezed her arm. 'Shit, Lisa, we couldn't afford it on three security guard wages. Shona was left some money by a mad uncle in Boston. That's the only reason we're here.'

'It's lovely,' Lisa said. 'Wish I had a mad uncle.'

Nathan was right. They weren't a bad bunch. There was a bit of macho posturing, but Lisa had learnt to ignore that; she'd seen men, *hundreds* of men by now, at their most vulnerable; she knew what they were really like. Bobby was friendly, Minto was raucous, Leonard reserved, worried-looking, Nathan was helping himself to copious amounts of wine.

She tried to say to him, tried to hint without causing a scene, that maybe he should take it a little easier on the drink, but he just gave her that *I'm in control* look and she held herself back from growling at him because that meant that the opposite was true. She reminded herself: it's his night, his friends, he wants to get drunk, okay. Stay calm, stay pleasant, see it through.

When Lisa was in the bathroom fixing her make-up – it didn't need fixing, but it would take up another twenty minutes, and that was twenty minutes nearer home – Shona came in. She apologized for barging in on her, but then they got talking. She was a pleasant enough girl, very much in love; Lisa could tell that by the way her big brown eyes just seemed to *glow* as they followed Bobby around the apartment.

'So howja meet Nathan?' Shona said, squeezing up beside Lisa at the basin and studying her reflection in the mirror. 'Hope ya don't mind me saying, but he's rilly cute. You met in Ireland, right?'

Lisa smiled. 'Not at all. I know he is. No. We met in China. It's a long story.'

'China? Hey, that's cool. What were you doing out there?'

Waitressing. She nearly said it. Nathan was already primed to answer the inevitable question that way. 'Oh, just travelling.'

'China. Gee. You guys getting hitched?'

Lisa shook her head. 'No.' Then she laughed. 'He hasn't asked me.'

'Oh don't wait for that one. Go out and buy a ring yourself. Then *tell* him. It's the only way.'

'That what you did?'

'No. But I would've if Bobby hadn't been so quick.'

Brian Houston had arrived and managed to get the TV tuned into a sports channel and now the men stood about roaring on one boxer or another. Shona, Lisa, Minto's girlfriend Marlene and three or four others whose names Lisa had forgotten stood around making very small talk while trying to balance paper plates full of the chilli Shona had made. Lisa smiled along, but didn't say much. *Here I am at a party, free drink, free food, congenial company, with the man that I love, when the alternative is standing in a cage on Times Square having my breasts massaged by a maniac, and I'm still pissed off.*

With a roar of disapproval the men turned as one from the television and descended on the food.

Nathan joined Lisa. His face was red right up to his eyebrows. He held his plate, sagging under a mountain of food, up to her. 'Good grub?'

Lisa smiled. 'Lovely.'

Nathan turned. 'Where the fuck's Sam, anyhow?' he asked.

Lisa shook her head. His language always deteriorated in keeping with the amount of alcohol he consumed. It made her fucking mad.

Leonard Maltman set his plate down on the table. 'I saw him earlier,' he said. 'Wasn't feeling well. Didn't think he'd make it.'

This was a lie. Leonard thought he would probably drop dead if Sam walked through the door now and caused a scene.

'Old guy's slowing down, that's for sure,' said Bobby T.

'Must be due to retire soon, eh Leonard?' said Minto.

Leonard raised his eyebrows and lifted his plate. 'Not up to me,' he said.

'So Lisa,' said Bobby T, 'how come you ain't been down to see us at the Empire? That boy of yours sure loves strutting his stuff.'

'I know, I should,' Lisa said. 'I been busy.'

'Doing what?' It wasn't Bobby T. It was Nathan.

'Nathan . . .'

'Hey, Lis, tell the boys what you been busy doing.'

'Nathan, please don't.' She could feel herself starting to sink into the carpet.

'Don't be shy, love. It's nothing to be ashamed of, is it?'

She looked at him. 'Nathan. Shut the fuck up.'

The whole party fell into an embarrassed silence.

'Lisa works in a sex club on Times Square. If any of you wants to give her ten dollars, you can feel her tits.'

Lisa slapped her chilli into his face and ran for the door. Nathan stood dripping, laughing. Shona came after her.

'Lisa, please . . .' and grabbed at her arm.

Lisa shrugged her off. 'Leave me. It's okay. I'm going.'

'But he didn't mean . . .'

'Leave me!'

Shona cowered back. 'Can I get your coat?'

Lisa hovered in the open doorway. 'Yes,' she barked.

Shona ran to get it.

'C'mon, Lisa,' Nathan shouted from the lounge, 'it's better out in the open, isn't it?'

'You bastard!' Lisa howled and flew out the door without her coat.

She ran and she ran, she fell, broke a heel, gouged a hole in her knee. The tears came then, but only when she was sure that he was not following her. A fine rain was falling. *Handbag. Purse. Dammit.* Everything was back there. She was in heels – heel – a nice dress, she was already wet. She wasn't about to hitch, it was too far to walk and she wasn't likely to get a cab on the strength of a promise.

She stood in a shop doorway. *Compose. Composing. Composed.*

He would not do this to her again.

Thirty minutes after leaving, Lisa began to retrace her steps to Bobby Tangetta's apartment. She would look them all in the eye and tell them exactly what she did for a living and why. It was her body and it was up to her what she did with it; that if she wanted to make an absolute fortune from it that was her decision and nobody else's; she wasn't harming anyone, she wasn't going to catch a life-threatening disease and pass it on at a nice party; she also understood completely why Nathan was so completely pissed off about it. *So there.*

It took her a while to figure out which apartment it was, but by standing in the road and looking in what she guessed was its general direction she was able to see that of the three or four in the block with lights on, only one had a dozen figures silhouetted against curtains.

As she was mounting the steps to the first floor she met Nathan. He had an ugly stain on his shirt like he had been shot in a bad Western. And he had a closed and swollen left eye like he'd been punched by someone who cared about her.

Nathan smiled apologetically.

Lisa glared at him.

'You forgot your coat,' Nathan said. It was over his arm. So was her bag.

'Who hit you?' Lisa asked.

'They had a vote and nominated Minto.' He shrugged. Sobriety was forcing itself on him, and with it the familiar contrition. 'It's okay,' he said, and meant it. 'I deserved it.'

She nodded. 'I'm not ashamed of what I do,' she said.

'So why run away?'

'I'm ashamed of what you try to do to me because of what I do. That's what I'm pissed off about.'

'It just came out. And *I am* ashamed of what you do.'

Lisa shrugged. 'Well,' she said.

They looked at each other.

'So what do you want to do now?' Nathan asked.

'Are you talking with my life, or about the party?'

'Either. Neither. Both.'

'Take me home, Nathan.'

'Okay.'

20

They just kinda bumped into each other in the middle of the night, strangers in a bed, apologized, apologized again, kissed and made up, kissed and touched and hugged and made love. They lay in each other's arms. When he moved his arm from beneath her head he found that it was damp and realized that she'd been crying.

'What's wrong?' Nathan asked softly.

'Nothing. I'm just being silly.'

'Tell me. You know you can tell me anything in the whole world.'

She shook her head in the gloom. 'I love making love to you, Nathan. I love being held.'

'And the same to you with bells on.'

She giggled. *Great* giggle. Always was.

In the morning, after they had made love again, they showered together then walked hand in hand to a coffee shop three blocks away. They didn't say much, just smiled at each other. She gave him a lingering kiss goodbye and he went off to work. The warm feeling lasted most of the way back to the apartment. Then she started to cry again. She walked from room to room and she couldn't stop the tears. She called Cindy. She cried down the phone.

'Girl, you gotta get a hold a yourself,' Cindy said.

'Well that's a big help,' Lisa gurgled, and they both laughed and she sniffed up as many of her tears as she could. 'I'm sorry. I've no one else to . . .'

'Did he hit you again?'

'He's never hit me. Not on purpose.'

'He hits you by accident, Lisa?'

'I know it sounds strange, but . . .'

'Sounds like bullshit. But hold on. I ain't running you down. My man hits me once a week, and I'm still with him.'

'Cindy, he doesn't hit me. He just . . . he has this temper. It's like a red haze . . . and he goes from being Mr Sweetness to . . .'

'What's his problem, Lisa? What makes him . . .'

She told her about the party. 'He gets like this when he's drunk. Very drunk. But it's not the drink. And despite what he says, it's not what I do for a living either. Do you know what I mean?'

'No.'

'I know it sounds . . .'

'What're you going to do about it, girl?'

'I don't know . . .'

'You either get out, girl, or you quit whining about it, you hear me?'

Sometimes Lisa doubted if Cindy was the right person to seek moral support from.

Nathan's enthusiasm for the Empire had not dulled any by the end of his second week, which he thought was pretty amazing. *Pretty fucking amazing.* He wanted Lisa to come and see him. Manning the lifts. Patrolling the corridors. Up on the observatory floors. Advising. Describing. Helping. But Lisa's shifts didn't allow it. She kept promising. But she was working longer, harder. He told her it wouldn't be for long. His first pay cheque was only a few weeks away, then they'd be okay. They'd be on an equal footing. She could scale down her work. Maybe find another job. A better job. A job that didn't entail having her breasts felt by complete strangers. Nathan had kept a check on her, sneaking into the booths, and was satisfied at least that that was all that she was doing. *Just the breasts. Sure. That's okay. That's okay. Roll up, roll up, roll fucking up.*

The rest of the crew seemed a nice enough bunch. Brian Houston, the closest to him in years, had immediately tried to strike up a rapport with him, but he was a quiet sort as well and they were having some difficulty making headway. He was a tall fella, glasses, hair thinning already, didn't seem to want to talk about anything but boxing. *Boxing.* That and his new-found worries about meeting the President.

Nathan didn't think there was a problem. 'What would he want to speak to you for anyway?' he laughed. 'Never worry about it. Just nod and smile. He's not going to ask you to dissect American foreign policy towards China, is he?'

'You don't know that.'

'I do know that. Well let Sam do all the talking. Nod and smile and let Sam yitter away.'

Sam and *yitter* didn't seem to be too well acquainted. When Nathan spied him in the canteen at lunch break he plonked himself down beside him and smiled hello. Sam scowled at him for the briefest of moments and then continued staring morosely into his food. Nathan was scarcely one of the great conversational initiators, unless he had a skinful on board, so he just nodded to himself, embarrassed, and picked at his food until Brian joined them and started talking about boxing.

This seemed to annoy Sam as much as it did Nathan. He pushed his plate away and stood up. He seemed on the brink of saying something to Brian, then gave a little shake of his head and shuffled off.

'I wonder what's up with Father Time?' Brian asked, and without waiting for an answer launched into his boxing again. But after a few minutes he stopped and looked curiously at Nathan. 'You okay?' he asked.

Nathan nodded vaguely. 'I just had a thought.'

'Is that a new experience for you?'

'I'm going to ask her to marry me.'

'Who? Anyone I can see from here?'

Nathan stood up. 'I'm going to do it now. Right now. I'm going home.'

'Nathan, this is work, do it later. It'll keep.'

Nathan shook his head. 'No it won't. I'm going now.'

He turned and hurried out of the canteen.

'What'll I tell . . .?' Brian began, but it was too late, Nathan was gone.

He had this giant smile on his face. He clapped his hands together as he hurried along the sidewalk. It had begun to rain, but he didn't mind: he was focused. He looked at his watch. She'd be leaving for her shift in half an hour. He thought about flowers. A ring. *Jesus, yes, a ring.* He checked his wallet: $70. Money she'd given him. She wasn't big on jewellery – but a ring, nevertheless. He found a jeweller's. All the rings looked the same. He asked for one for $69.99, looked at a tray and picked one that wasn't too garish. He didn't wait for the change. It wasn't the ring, it was what it represented. He loved her.

And Lisa loved him, but not enough. She left the envelope on the table. It was a shitty way to do it, but it was the *only* way.

Outside she hailed a cab.

Nathan, soaked, came through the door at a pace. 'Lisa?' he called.

There was no response. What an anticlimax if she was out shopping. He laughed. He thought about how best to do it: take the shopping off her, go down on one knee, propose. Or persuade her to forgo her shift, then take her out for a meal; take the ring out, the whole restaurant would be clapping. A violinist would come and serenade them. They wouldn't even have to pay the bill.

Something . . . *empty.*

He walked into their bedroom. He saw his reflection in the mirror, moved towards the bathroom . . . and went back to the reflection . . . something odd about it. And then he realized that it was the fact that he couldn't see any reflection at all. Normally her dresser was so full of make-ups and perfumes and sprays that he couldn't see a thing. But they were gone. All of them.

He stood for a second, catching his breath, trying to think. He ran a hand through his damp hair. *Oh no.*

He crossed the room and flung open the wardrobe doors. All of her clothes were gone. All of *his* clothes were gone.

Oh God no please.

He ran from room to room, looking desperately for some sign that either of them still lived in their apartment: the washing machine full of clothes, her underwear drying on the radiator; his toothbrush . . . nothing. He rubbed at his head. *What the fuck . . .?*

146

Downstairs a door slammed. He ran into the hallway and peered over the banister. 'Lisa!' he shouted.

But no. Miles Flerscent, their neighbour, going to his apartment. His multi-cheeked face peered up at him. 'Nathan? Can I have a word with you?'

Nathan, panicked, stepped back from the rail. He went back into the apartment. And then he saw it, sitting flat on the table. He lifted the envelope. His name on the front: NATHAN JONES. It sent a little shudder through him. So cold. So impersonal. Like she knew hundreds of Nathans.

Just a few lines.

Dear Nathan: This is a terrible thing to do, but I have to. I can't tell you to your face because it will break my heart. I have to go away. I've saved some money. I don't know where I'm going. But I have to go. Please forgive me. Lisa.

Well fuck.

Nathan crumpled the letter into his pocket. Tears sprang: he angrily wiped them away with his sleeve.

He ran from the apartment, leaving the door open behind him. He thumped down the stairs to Miles's place and banged on the door. It was already open. Miles stood by a bookcase looking apprehensive.

'I'm sorry, Nathan,' he said simply and pointed to a plain green canvas bag sitting at his feet.

'Oh,' said Nathan.

Nathan crossed the room and picked up the bag. It had followed him from Ireland across the world. He had never been one for adorning a travelling bag with souvenirs.

'When did she go?'

'Nathan . . .'

'When did she fuckin' go!'

'This afternoon.'

'When!'

'About half an hour ago.'

'Jesus Christ! Where – where did she go?'

'I don't know.'

Nathan dropped the bag and affixed two hands to Miles's jumper. 'You know. Tell me. Tell me where she fucking went.'

'Nathan, please . . .'

'Tell me!'

'I don't know!'

'I was going to marry her!' he cried. 'In the name of God, tell me where she went!'

'I'm sorry – all I know is she left your things down here, said she was going away. She didn't say where. Just that she was getting a bus and wouldn't be back.'

Nathan was gasping for breath. 'A bus. A bus. It's the Port Authority, isn't it? The Port Authority?'

Miles nodded. Nathan grabbed his bag and hurried to the door.

'Nathan . . . can you leave your key?'

Nathan stopped, turned, he pulled the key from his pocket and threw it at Miles. 'Take your fucking key, you fat bastard.'

Lisa bought her ticket. When she had first thought of it, weeks ago, the plan had been to go west, fly to LA, start again out there. But as time had passed she had whittled away at that plan, her bravery and her heart gradually failing her: first she pinned it back to the Midwest, then further down the east coast, then another part of New York . . . she knew if she didn't get out soon she'd be reduced to living in the same block, then the same apartment and eventually she'd be back in bed with Nathan.

Lisa looked listlessly through the magazines on the news

stand. Nothing took her interest. Nathan was quite happily working at the Empire State; *God, if only he knew.* She bought some candy, then checked her watch. Less time than she thought: five minutes. Five minutes to find the departure gate. She looked at her ticket. Gate 57.

He ran as if his life depended on it. And it did.

Through the rain, pouring now out of the black skies. Through the traffic. Through the shoppers. The rain masked his tears. The bag bouncing off his sodden back all the way. It wasn't much more than a mile, but it was the longest mile. It stretched from murderous Ireland to China to America to a sex club to the top of the Empire State Building and he ran every fucking inch of it.

Deep down, she knew what she was doing. *Walking too slowly.* That if somehow she missed the bus it would be a signal that she wasn't meant to leave at all.

Nathan burst through the doors of the Port Authority bus terminal, scattering a gang of trainee hoods in from New Jersey for a day's shoplifting. They scowled at him, but he was gone, dashing across the concourse, looking desperately around him. He came from a town where the bus station was a bus-stop. There was one bus. Here there were hundreds. Every day, in all directions. He could hardly breathe. He ran some more. A bank of ticket desks, destinations above them. North, south, east, west . . . *Jesus Christ!*

It wasn't the tickets that mattered . . . the buses. He jumped onto an escalator, pushed through its passengers. The gates . . . one after the other, as far as the eye could see . . .

She was surprised to find herself standing by Gate 57. She expected to walk for several minutes yet . . . to get lost, to wander aimlessly, and then go home. But there it was, and there was the driver pushing luggage into the hold. She stopped, stared; looked back for whatever reason.

'Ma'am?' the driver said, 'you going on this one?'

Lisa stared at him.

'We're leaving now, ma'am.'

She nodded. He stepped forward and lifted her bags. 'Just you get on board. I'll get your ticket in a moment.'

She nodded again.

So many fucking numbers!

'Lisa!'

He shouted. He shouted again. Hundreds of passengers looked round.

'Lisa!'

A bus to his right revved its engine. He jumped on board. 'Lisa!' he yelled down the aisle. No. No!

He was off again, yelling again.

'Lisa!'

Thirty minutes later he sat exhausted on the bottom step of an escalator. She was gone. And every time he went to move he stopped and gave her ten more minutes, just in case she would pop up and surprise him and tell him it was all a misunderstanding.

It was a long time before he realized that she was really gone.

21

Looking at the map in her *USA Rough Guide* Cape Cod had only seemed about an inch away. But it was an eight-hour trip, including a stop-off for a half-cooked hot-dog in a bus station outside Providence, Rhode Island. The first couple of hours she cried, just a vague kind of crying, a mountain stream of emotion as opposed to a swollen Mississippi. The second couple she slept. The rest of the time she sat bus-sweaty and bored, reduced to reading a *National Enquirer* someone had left behind. She didn't speak to anyone, nobody spoke to her. Quiet as a mouse, or a Nathan . . .

Once she got her feet on the ground, a base, a *home, dammit*, she would write to him properly, explain what she was feeling. Of course, she would first have to work out exactly what she was feeling. She hated him, she loved him, simple as that. She couldn't stand being with him, but now, bus-fatigued, she wanted to curl up against him. Finally she drifted off into a big sleep, the *National Enquirer* torn to shreds in her lap.

The bus arrived in Provincetown on the Cape Cod knuckle in darkness. Lisa disembarked last, stood stretching for a few moments, sucking in the sea breeze, surprised at the pleasantness of the summer after the humidity of New York. The harbour area was busy with tourists coming off the last whaling boats of the day on MacMillan Wharf, the air alive with the chatter of children and gulls, the smell of burgers and pizza. She heaved her bag over her shoulder and began to walk away from the harbour, turning left onto Commercial Street with an exhilarated step. She suddenly felt cut out again for independence; she'd been like that before, travelling the world, but she'd allowed it to be suppressed by Nathan: *no, that wasn't fair*. She hadn't wanted to leave him.

Lisa picked her way through the gift shops for half an hour until thirst got the better of her. She found a pub called the Governor Bradford. Lisa pulled up a stool and ordered a beer. A curly haired woman, no make-up, smiled pleasantly as she poured. 'Just arrived?' she asked.

Lisa nodded. 'Aye. Off the bus.'

'First time?'

'Mmm? Here?'

'Yeah, whatever.'

'Sure.'

'Good place for it. The first time.'

Lisa nodded vaguely and paid for her drink. The barmaid wandered off and Lisa downed half the glass. There was baseball on the TV and she passed twenty minutes staring at the screen, barely focused. She couldn't remember the last time she had sat by herself in a pub and not felt either alone or intimidated. Alone because *he* wasn't with her, intimidated in case some guy recognized her cleavage. Now she felt relaxed; she smiled at nothing, but the barmaid saw it and came back towards her. Lisa tipped her glass. 'I'm looking for somewhere to stay,' she said.

The girl nodded, finished pouring her drink, then stepped back to the racks of spirit bottles and withdrew two cards from a metal spike.

'This one,' the barmaid said, 'is for Intown Reservations, mostly for gay and lesbian accommodation, this one, the Provincetown Reservation Service, is for all the other poor uneducated souls.'

Lisa went to hand the Intown back and then thought: *Fuck it, right now I don't need any man hassle.* She held onto it, and the barmaid gave her a little smile and reached her hand across the bar. 'Hi,' she said, 'I'm Mona.'

Lisa shook back. The clasp was a little too lingering for her, but she felt embarrassed about reclaiming her hand. 'Lisa,' she said.

'You on vacation, Lisa, or looking for a job?'

Lisa shrugged. 'A bit of both, I suppose. Is there much work going?'

'This time of year, sure. Waitressing mostly, 'less you want to work on one of the boats.'

Lisa shook her head. 'Waitressing sounds okay.'

'Tips are good, and you don't get much hassle, less you're looking for it. What you do before, anyhow?'

Lisa looked at Mona for a few moments, deciding. Then she gave another little shrug. 'For the past three months I've been letting men feel my tits for tips in a sex club off 42nd Street in New York.'

A guy, three stools down, turned and looked at her, then at her tits.

Mona nodded her head slowly. 'And you decided that wasn't the career for you.'

Lisa nodded.

'And you've come up here to get away from it all, and although you know this is one of the gay capitals of America, you haven't a gay notion in your head. Is that just about it?'

Lisa nodded. Gave a little laugh. 'How'd you get inside my head, Mona?'

'I ain't been inside nothing. It's written all over you. Besides, I hear it every night, it's that sort of a bar, and that sort of a town.'

'You mean like a Rick's Café for the sexually confused?' Mona nodded. 'And what happens to these people?'

'Mostly they've converted before the week's out.'

'Really?'

'Really. The subconscious is a wonderful thing, Lisa. You think people come here by accident when they've got fifty-two states to choose from? Ask yourself that.'

Lisa tugged at a lip. 'But it's a holiday resort. There's good beaches.'

Mona raised an eyebrow. 'Hey. Lisa, the beaches ain't that good. You *know why you're here.*'

Lisa opened her purse to pay for the drink. Mona raised a hand.

'On the house.'

'No, really, I . . .'

'On the house. Alternatively, once you're settled in, come down to the Atlantic House later. It's where all the *gals* meet.'

Mona tutted, then slipped down the bar as a fourteen-part family appeared through the swing doors. Lisa sipped steadily at her beer; then flicked the two accommodation cards off each other for a few moments. She went and made a call. When she got back to her seat she drained her glass and lifted her bag. She set the two cards back on the bar. Mona came back down to her.

'Get a room okay?'

'Sure.'

'Good.' Mona gave her a little smile. 'Which card did you use?' Lisa threw the bag up onto her shoulder. 'Can't remember,' she said. 'I guess I'm a little confused.'

22

Lisa took a room for three nights at the Elephant Strides By Inn, a couple of turns off the main drag. It was a bright, roomy boarding house with a nice veranda. She went up to her room and lay down in the dark. She thought about the beach and making a lazy day of it tomorrow. She was just drifting off when a knock on the door brought her suddenly awake and for a moment she was frightened – not of the dark or the flap of the net curtain in the salty breeze, but at the thought that it might be Nathan. *Frightened? What was he, a monster?* She shook herself awake, managed a garbled *Hold on* while she searched for the lamp switch, then cautiously approached the door.

For a moment she was taken aback. She shouldn't have been, for in her three months in Star World she'd seen everything. The man in the doorway, and it was very definitely a man, wore a gorgeous shoulder-length blond wig, a silver-shimmering blouse, knee-length skirt, black leather boots and a cracker of a smile.

'Sorry to bother you, love, but you wouldn't happen to have any nail varnish on you, would you?'

She realized quickly what it was that shocked her. The

incongruity of it. The lack of neon. The roar of a thousand cabs. He held up an empty bottle of Mary Quant Wild Cherry.

Lisa shook her head. 'Sorry, I don't . . .'

'I mean, it doesn't have to be this colour. Anything'll do, within reason.'

'I'm sorry, I don't wear it.'

Before she could move he reached out and lifted her hand. He examined her nails, or lack of them. 'Oh dear,' he said, 'have we got a problem.'

'They've always been short,' Lisa said, surprising herself at the note of apology in her voice.

He threw his head back. 'Falsies! Urgently required!'

Lisa laughed in spite of herself. 'You're from Liverpool.'

'I'm from Blackburn, but it makes bugger all difference to them here.' He stuck out his own beautifully manicured hand this time. 'Alex Maskey,' he said, 'by day, Alexis Mascara by night.'

'Lisa . . . Alexis Masc . . .'

'You mean you haven't caught my show yet? Tssk, tsssk. I'm at the Crown and Anchor every Tuesday and Thursday. Best show in town!'

'Well, I've just arrived . . .'

'Tonight's the night!'

'I'm a little tired . . .'

'Bugger tiredness, luv! You're only young once!' He stepped forward, although taking care not to cross the threshold. He examined her face. 'Where you from anyway, Dublin is it?'

'The north.'

'Oh aye? We're practically neighbours, then. Seriously, you should come down and see the show. You ain't heard nothing till you've heard my "Hello Dolly"! Come on down!' He suddenly threw his head back and bellowed: 'But I need varnish!'

He turned and stomped back to his room across the hall.

'See ya later!' he called, crashing the door closed behind him with the heel of his boot.

Lisa laughed aloud as she closed the door.

She had a bath. Spent an hour in it. She hadn't had a bath in a year. The old apartment only had a shower; before that she'd been travelling fast and cheap and baths were a luxury seldom encountered.

Refreshed, naked, with the breeze still fluffing up the curtains, she tried to rescue something that didn't need ironing from her bag. She settled on a pink skirt and a white buttoned jersey. She was just finishing her make-up when the door opposite slammed, followed a few seconds later by the rapid *bite-bite-bite* of stiletto boots on the wooden stairs.

Fifteen minutes later Lisa stepped out onto the road and began to walk the few hundred yards back to Commercial Street. She walked slowly, luxuriating in the cool sea breeze about her ankles. She felt good: *lighter.* She deserved this, a good night out, a night to get drunk, to make friends if she wanted, to hang out, to not worry about some bastard slipping her a crumpled five-dollar bill and expecting to suck her nipples.

She walked with her left hand swinging by her side, but it didn't feel right. Not numb, or anything, like she'd had a stroke, but different, strange . . . she tried to work it out, what the difference was, but couldn't quite get it. She held it stiffly to one side. Then folded it up behind her back. Then slipped it into the slit-pocket in the side of her skirt, but none of these positions felt right, so she swung it again by her side, happy again that that was the way it should be, but confused because it still wasn't quite right.

It was only as she pushed through the doors of the Governor Bradford that she realized what it was. She wasn't holding Nathan's hand.

23

Nathan spent most of the night in the bar. Three times he scrunched up the letter and threw it into an ashtray. Three times he changed his mind and brushed the ash off it and straightened it out again and read it through once more.

Fuck.

He shivered. He cursed to himself, then he cursed himself. He caught sight of himself in the bar mirror and shook his head. *Look at me. Look at me. Look at me. Sitting here in my wee blue uniform. Mister important. Mister fucking important and she's gone, just like that.* As the hours wore on the bar began to crowd up, get rowdy. He needed space to think. While he could still walk, he decided to. He changed into his jeans and a black sweatshirt in the men's room. Then he went back out onto the street and began pounding the sidewalk, trying to think, trying to think out the whys and wherefores, but not getting anywhere because it was all too fresh and it made perfect sense and perfect nonsense at the same time; it didn't matter what he thought or what he did, because whatever decision had been made had been made by her and there was nothing he could do about it. It was the finality of it that got him. Really got him. That she had ended the lease, just like that, then thrown herself out of the relationship and him out of his home. And the joke of it was that she'd probably left because he had refused to treat their relationship seriously, and she didn't even know that he was about to propose to her. He took the ring out of his pocket and slipped it over his little finger.

By midnight his feet were sore walking and his mind was sore thinking. He had walked blindly, in circles, the bag of his belongings a deadweight over his shoulders. His body's every fibre throbbed. He had nowhere to go and no one to talk to. He didn't have a friend in the whole of America. He had only felt this alone, so miserably gut-wrenchingly afraid, once before. Nathan closed his eyes, but it didn't stop the tears tripping down his face.

At home his mother would have told him to pray to God for help. But on that lonely road he had not once thought of God. Now he opened his eyes and looked to the skies; God was not there, but *something* was. Just for a moment: silhouetted against the stars, a winged shape, *huge*, silent, ghostly. *God, I'm going mental.*

He jammed his eyes shut again. Counted dizzily to thirty, and when he opened them again the shape was gone. He shook his head, turned to his left, and was confronted by the dark hulk of the Chelsea Hotel.

It was an omen. Once before in a moment of crisis he had closed his eyes and Sid had rescued him, blocking out the pain. Now he had done it again. God's winged messenger had led him to where his musical saviour had lived; this was where Sid had had his moment of crisis, where his girlfriend Nancy had been stabbed. *It was meant to be.*

This was a place where troubled artistes came to sort themselves out. He had passed it many times on his foot-padding trips out to Greenwich Village, had always promised himself that one day he would walk in and enquire after Sid.

Nathan walked into the lobby and set his bag down. He was immediately disappointed. There was a certain dour quality about the place. It smelt *nice*. He'd expected it to smell like a mortuary. Like alcohol and vomit. He'd expected seediness and got designer rock. He'd imagined the floor littered with syringes and the reception crowded with doom-eyed rock victims. The bald guy on the desk looked up. 'Yes?' he said, his tone Italian.

'I'd like a room.'

The man nodded. The plastic clip in the desk read: Silvan Rozzi, deputy manager. 'Okay,' he said and bent to a computer.

'Room 100 if you have it.'

Silvan looked up. 'The Sid Vicious suite?' he said. Nathan nodded. Silvan glanced to his left. Nathan followed his gaze. 'You'll have to join the queue.'

In a red plastic-chaired lounge there sat half a dozen young men in various stages of punk: three wore white dinner jackets and leather bondage trousers, their hair spiked up. The other three wore combinations of leather and tartan and bicycle chains.

'They all want . . .?'

'They always want. They'll be waiting a long time. Room 100's been taken this last six months. They live in hope. Now do you want to join those losers or can I offer you something else?'

Nathan shook his head. 'What else have you got?'

Silvan looked to his computer again. 'Well, now, let me see . . . the Leonard Cohen room is free. A bit gloomy, but rather a pleasant ambience. The room's not bad either.'

Nathan shook his head again. 'No, I . . .'

'You're Irish, aren't you? How about the Dylan Thomas room?'

'He was . . . I'm not really into celebrity squares . . .'

'You're not?' Silvan looked doubtful. 'How refreshing. Well then, we can offer . . .'

'What about 99?'

'99?'

'99.'

Silvan checked his screen. He shook his head. Then: '96?'

'That'll do rightly.'

Nathan gave his details. Paid in cash for one night. He went upstairs to his room. He lay on the bed. He needed a good night's sleep, to rest and not think about her any more until tomorrow. She was gone and there was nothing he could do about it. But he couldn't escape her and sleep was a million sheep away.

He went back out into the night. Found a deli, bought as many beers as he could carry. And then he went back to the Chelsea and drank as many of them as he could before falling asleep.

In his dream Lisa stood by the foot of his bed, taunting him about his sexual inadequacies. Then she was chasing him up the stairs. The Empire stairs. His legs were leaden; she seemed scarcely to notice; with each flight she gained on him, finally grabbing his shirt collar as he emerged at the 86th floor observatory. She spun him round and kissed him and suddenly all was right with the world. And then she plunged the hunting knife into his stomach and threw him over the side. Hands reached out to him as he fell floor after floor, but he was too embarrassed to reach out for them, and certainly too shy to scream.

He woke, still drunk, head throbbing, mouth dry, sick. He rolled out of bed, scattering the empty bottles of Budweiser at his feet. His sweatshirt was stuck to his body, his hair plastered back on his head. He sat at the edge of the bed and hugged himself. He was *so cold*. It was the room; through the fog he realized that the hotel manager had been playing with him; he'd wanted to give him Sid's room, but he couldn't with all those punks hovering nearby. All he had to do was slip along the corridor to . . .

Nathan pulled on his Oxfords and staggered to the door. He checked he had his key with him, then pulled the door shut behind him. He moved the few metres along the corridor to room 100. He steadied himself against the doorframe, straightened up, then knocked sharply, three times.

The chain was pulled back, the door yanked sharply open.

Her hair was blond-spiky. Her lipstick scarlet. Her legs black-stockinged.

'Nancy?' he said.

She smiled. 'Come on in,' she purred, 'I've been expecting you.'

24

Mary was sitting in her chair watching the TV. For all Sam knew she'd been sitting there since the day before. He leaned over and kissed her brow: she smelt of soap and there was a vague hint of the perfume he'd bought her at Christmas. The nurses here were good, at any rate. Or not at *any* rate: an increasing rate. Max Fleisher, director of the Cedar Home, called Sam in as he arrived and told him the prices were going up.

'Oh yeah?' said Sam. He took a seat in Max's cluttered office.

'Oh yeah, yeah. I gave you a letter last week. I figured you never opened it.'

'I figured if you were bringing the prices down you would have told me yourself.'

'Sam, you know how it is.'

'Max, I haven't a clue how it is.'

Max, bald-headed, a self-roller in one corner of his mouth, shrugged and handed Sam a second copy of the letter. 'It's not that much.'

'If it wasn't that much you'd tell me yourself, Max. How much?'

'Not that much.'

'What're we talking here, hundreds?'

'Yeah. Kinda.'

'How many hundreds?'

'Fifteen.'

Sam nodded slowly. 'And Mary gets fifteen hundred dollars better treatment for that.'

'Sam, c'mon, you know she gets the best there is. There isn't anything more we can do.'

'So what's the fifteen . . .'

'Sam, you know what it is. Administration. Inflation.'

'Profit.'

'Sam, we're not a charity.'

'You should be.'

'Well that's as may be.' Max started to roll another cigarette. 'If it were up to me, maybe we would be. But I just do what I'm told. Sam, sometimes you've just gotta accept what's handed down from high office.'

Sam laughed. 'Yeah. Sure.' He stood up. He reached across to shake Max's hand.

Max's brow furrowed at the unfamiliar gesture. He fumbled the cigarette. He raised himself slightly and shook. 'You're getting damned civil in your old age, Sam,' he said.

Sam squeezed Max's fingers. Hard.

'Sam?'

Sam squeezed a little harder, till he could feel the bones straining together. Max let out a little yelp and wriggled his hand free. 'Life in the old dog yet,' said Sam as he turned for the door.

Max, shaking life back into his fingers, slumped into his chair. 'What the fuck was that for?' he called after the old man.

'That was for free,' Sam snapped back, ''cause I am a fucking charity.'

* * *

Mary was watching *Oprah*. The President was being interviewed. Sam pulled up a chair, took her hand, and sat
watching the programme. He liked President Keneally. He
seemed a warm kind of a man. His smile was eager to please,
but not sickeningly so. Sam'd been on top of the Empire for
fifty years and had met every big cheese there was; he knew
a glassy smile when he saw one. He looked about him, at
the sad old wrecks lying in their beds; at the shakers and
nodders and droolers and starers; and at Mary, beautiful
Mary.

He rested his head on her arm. He closed his eyes.
Remembered. The honeymoon in Florida. Walking hand in
hand on the beach. No – not walking, not at first anyway,
running, the sand too hot for them, screaming with laughter.
Walking, later, sure, in the cool evening, the waves lapping,
the moon up high, kissing, making love. They'd talked
even then, in the quiet of the night, of how they would
spend the rest of their lives together, happy lives, and how
they would end up in a happy retirement in somewhere like
Florida. Key West maybe. She'd dreamt of a little cottage, a
veranda, twin rocking chairs, the sun going down, supper,
children, grandchildren. Sam had pretty much the same
dream, except he could never quite work out how to get the
Empire into it.

As he looked at her he began to weep.

'You picture me retired, Mary?' he whispered. 'You want
me to bring you home and look after you myself? I could
wash you and clean you and talk to you and you could sit
and watch your TV for just as long as you want and I could
sit beside you all day and . . . y'know, maybe in your own
time, maybe if we worked at it, you could say something to
me, just a word, just a nod, just anything . . .'

He shook his head and rubbed his sleeve across his face.

He couldn't do any of that for her. Knew it would be madness. 'Fifty years. Fifty. Out on my ass. Just like that. Fifty fucking years.' He rubbed one of her wrinkly knuckles. 'You see the President there, Mary? I was going to meet him next week. Shake his hand.'

Mary stared vacantly at the screen. Sam winced. The pain in his head was getting worse. He'd taken some aspirin but they'd taken half an hour to kick in, and then kicked out again within twenty minutes. Maybe shrapnel wasn't one of the things the makers tested it on.

Sam knew it didn't matter what he did. The end result would be the same. When you've had the same routine for fifty years, then you suddenly change it, it does for you. He'd seen it a dozen times, in friends, in colleagues. Mort Grenswhitz had taken early retirement from the Empire; gone to Florida for the golf; dead within three days, didn't even make the first tee, keeled over tying his shoes in the clubhouse. Amy Smithson, worked the concession stand for thirty years. They'd thrown a surprise retirement bash for her on the 87th floor; bursts of tears, but within ten minutes she was serving the food; it was in her blood, and so was something else that ate her up and they'd buried her within three months. And what about Mo Fienstein? Not been gone three days before he was begging to come back. Ended up with a cleaner's job in the Port Authority. Eight weeks and some crack dealer sliced his throat for no particular reason.

He blew a sigh out of his nose and squeezed her hand. 'I know what you're thinking,' he said, his voice a mix of cry and laugh, 'you're thinking why didn't that old fool bring me any candies today, aren't you?'

He delved into his pocket and produced a bag. He set them on the arm of her chair and opened them up. She ignored them for a couple of minutes; then her hand slowly snaked into the sack and he could see her fingers working out the shapes and sizes. It looked like a giant spider.

That night he dreamt about a giant spider. The size of an Oldsmobile. A big hairy spider the size of an Oldsmobile cascading along its web towards him and was just about to get him . . . he didn't know what spiders had in the way of teeth or whether they just gummed you to death . . . when a B-52 bomber exploded into the creature and he screamed, trying to get away from the flames, but his head was burning and he was stuck fast and then suddenly there was a hand reaching out to him and it was his dad's and he grabbed it and he was pulled free. He was standing on the sidewalk and everyone was charging around in a blind panic, everyone but his dad who pulled a big tartan towel from his coat and threw it over Sam's head to douse the flames. The pain was suddenly gone and Sam pulled the towel away, but it wasn't his dad at all, but the President; the President extended his hand and said, 'Thanks, Sam, I couldn't have done it without you.'

He woke soaked. It was still dark. Gone three. He got up and took another few aspirin. He fixed himself a proper drink, created a scrag-bag sandwich from the slim pickings in the fridge, then sat down in front of the TV. He flicked. He ate. There was nothing to watch. He drank on. He listened to some Sinatra, some Louis Armstrong, even some scratchy Jolson.

He woke in his chair at seven. The drink had eased the pain in his head for a while, but now it was pounding with a vengeance. He took three or more aspirin. A long drink of milk. He stared out of the window for a long while, then lifted the family photograph from the top of the TV. He kissed Mary. Then he called Florida.

It was answered on the fourth ring.

'Hi. Hello.'

He said nothing. He wanted to, but he opened his mouth and choked up.

'Hello, hello, anyone there?'

He sniffed up. That fine chirpy voice.

An annoyed tut, and then: 'Dad?'

He sniffed again.

'Is that you, Dad?'

He nodded. A lot of use. He managed a gruff, 'Hi, Stacey.'

'Oh, Dad, it is . . . is everything okay?'

'Yeah. Yeah. Sure.'

'Dad . . .?'

'Everything's fine. How are . . .'

'Is Mum okay?'

'Yes. Of course.'

'Are you sure?'

'Yes, I'm sure. I just . . .' She could hear the quiver in his voice. 'Stace, I just miss her so much.'

'Oh Dad . . .'

'I know it's stupid . . .'

'It's not stupid, Dad.'

He sniffed back up again. 'How're the kids?'

'They're great. You could find out for yourself, y'know, you could come down.'

'I know. Soon, maybe.'

'Dad, it was soon maybe last year. We do have hospitals down here. We do have old folks' homes. You could bring Mum.'

'I know. I will. Once things get sorted out. I've just been busy, y'know, work.'

'You still stuck up that damn tower? You've been promising to quit for the last ten years, Dad. When're you ever going to learn to take things easy? Relax. Retire. Enjoy yourself. You know we'd love to have you.'

'Stace, I . . .'

'I don't want to hear another excuse.'

'I'm going to meet the President, Stace.'

'The . . . Keneally?'

'Keneally. Sure. Next week.'

'Aw, Dad, gosh. That's really neat.'

'He's coming to the Empire. They want me to meet him.'

'Aw, Dad, wait'll I tell the boys, they'll be thrilled. I suppose there's no point in asking . . .?'

He laughed. 'None at all.'

'Just one measly little . . .'

'Stace, I don't ask for autographs. You know that.'

'But it's the Presid—'

'No, Stace.'

'Oooooooh . . . sometimes you're so annoy . . . hey, listen, Dad, after all these years, maybe he'll ask for yours. What would you say to that?'

He gave a little chuckle. 'Well,' he said, 'I'd have to think about that.'

She'd decided it for him. One way or another, he would meet the President.

II

ESCALATION

1

Nathan regained consciousness just as Nancy began to walk up his chest in her stilettos.

For a few leather-punctuated moments he was too stunned to make a noise, then let out a yelp as she drew blood. She grinned and stepped off him onto the bed. Then she was on him again, grinding into him; she hovered a big shiny heel over his crotch. She bobbed her head from one side to the other. 'Want me to?' she cooed, vampire-unsexy.

'Please, no,' said Nathan.

She jagged his penis. He yelped. She laughed and jumped off the bed. Nathan strained against the handcuffs.

'This isn't funny!'

She roared. 'It's not meant to be!'

'Please, I . . .'

'Who do you love?' she snapped.

'What?'

'Who do you love!'

His mouth was thick with rapidly induced hangover. His head was swimming. 'I love . . .'

She nipped him, hard, twisting her nails into his leg. 'Who do you love?' she demanded.

'Lisa.'

She moved up the bed, slapped him hard across the face. 'Who do you love?'

'Li—'

She slapped him again. She took hold of his cheeks and twisted them. 'Who do you love?'

'I love you.'

Nathan's trousers sat unhappily about his ankles. His t-shirt was ripped and lay open to either side of his nipples. His nipples were clamped by bulldog clips.

She hurried across the room to a dresser. From a drawer she withdrew a whip. She returned to him, running the leather strap through her hands. She smiled. 'Not even an erection. What do you want from me, baby?'

As she spoke she slowly stripped off her black panties. She was completely shaven. For a moment she watched his penis for some reaction. There was none. She lifted the panties to her nose and breathed in, then she raised her other arm and whipped him hard across the legs. As he opened his mouth to scream she rammed them into his mouth.

He screamed anyway, but it was a dull mix of fluff and gag.

She prowled about the bed, running the whip along his sweat-sheened body. 'You love this, don't you? You trail up here begging for it, beg beg begging for it, then you get it and all you can do is lie there and scream. But where's the fucking hard-on?' She lifted his limp penis and rolled it between her forefinger and thumb. 'Exactly how bad do you want me to get?' He shook his head. She squeezed. His eyes crossed. She squeezed a little more. He thrust himself up out of the bed, but the handcuffs, and the feet cuffs, held him firm. Then she twisted the bulldog clips and he screamed until tears shot out of his eyes and a little trickle of blood dripped out of his nose.

She stood at the end of the bed, shaking her head a little. 'Well I'll admit one thing,' she said, 'you're a challenge. Usually they come before I even get the handcuffs on.'

Nathan tried to explain. It came out as: 'Nnnntheatheth-ingyousem tothnkIm.'

She rubbed a hand across her brow, then crossed to a mini-fridge and removed a can of Coke. She took a long drink, then poured a little over his wounds. It wasn't exactly vinegar at Calvary, but it wasn't far off.

'I'm tired, too,' she said, her voice suddenly rising from androgynous low to girly high. She gave him a little smile, wagged a finger. 'Don't worry, I'll soon be back to what you love best. Just let me get my breath.' Perching on the end of the bed, Nancy began to run her finger along the tips of his toes. Another time he would have reared up, ticklish, but now all he felt was numb. 'I'm going to write a book about this, one day,' she said. 'I'd write it as a paper right now, but I don't think I'd get the grades!' She cackled and tweeked his little left toe. Just a little hard. 'Y'know, I'm studying psychology . . . I won't say where, you'd probably look me up and insist I beat you between classes.' She tutted. 'All you . . . guys . . . all you guys and your Sid *thang*, y'know, you just fascinate me. I mean, it's not music, is it? Y'know, half the guys come up here make me play "My Way" while I do this – jeez, that's as cruel to me as I am to them. He just wails! He can't sing a note!'

Nathan tried spitting out the soiled panties. He got them half out. She set down her Coke and jammed them back in.

'Now what am I gonna do to coax that little man of yours into life?' She lifted one leg onto the bed, displaying her vagina. She rubbed a finger along it. 'Is it a little of this?'

She looked expectantly at his moribund penis. Nathan shook his head. She dropped the leg again, then bent over him and slipped her mouth around his manhood. He closed his eyes. He could feel her tongue rubbing the tip. She kept it up for a couple of minutes, working hard, slobbering all over him. She slipped her legs up onto the bed as she sucked, twisting round so that he was staring at her bottom and vagina. There was a pimple on either cheek. The vagina was swollen. It looked as if a bald man with a rugby ball stuck in his mouth was sitting on his chest.

After a little more earnest suction she gave up. She turned her face towards him, drooling. 'What is it you want, honey?'

He shook his head.

'It's the knife, isn't it?'

He shook his head.

She rolled off the bed and padded across to the dresser again, and from the same drawer removed a long-handled knife. She held it up before her; it glinted in the light. He swallowed hard, despite trying hard not to swallow anything at all.

'I don't use this very often,' she said, 'though most of them want me to. Just a little dangerous, I think. I have about eight of them in there. They get carried away, they're drunk, or they've just shot up, and they're fucking away and suddenly out of nowhere comes this fucking big knife, they want the whole gig! They want to stab me too! They've found their Nancy and they want to go the same way! No way, baby! First thing I do, I get them handcuffed, then I search them, then I confiscate. They gimme a hard time, sure, but then a little sucky, a little fucky, then they're as meek as lambs and they sneak on out, most times they forget about their god-damn knives.' She twisted the blade in the light again, studied her own reflection in it for a moment. 'But you, mister, you're a challenge.'

She stepped towards the bed. 'I draw the line at cutting myself, but I'll cut you anywhere you god-damn please. You want your dick cut? You want circumcised? That what you want?'

He shook his head.

She looked at his penis again. 'There just ain't no life in you at all, is there?'

She straddled him again, this time facing him. She placed the tip of the knife just under his left nipple. 'So you just want me to play away, see what turns you on?'

Nathan shook his head.

Nancy started to carve.

Nathan fainted again, and then he was in another nightmare, far away and long ago. He was home.

He woke to the sound of hammering. It took him a moment to focus. Nancy was moving towards the door. He looked down at his chest. It was a mass of blood and slice. He groaned.

Nancy glanced back, 'Shush now, honey. You don't want me thrown out now, d'ya?'

Nathan's head fell back on the pillow.

She pulled the door open a couple of centimetres. 'What?' she snapped.

Somebody said something. 'What?' she snapped again.

Somebody said something else. 'What?' she snapped again.

She glanced at Nathan, then back. 'Hold on a moment,' she said and closed the door. She crossed the room, stood over him. 'What's your name?'

Nathan spluttered into the panties. She tutted, pulled them free, tossing them to one side. He dry-coughed.

'I said, what's your name, buster!'

'Nathan,' he croaked.

'What the hell-fuck's your game, mister?'

'I . . .'

Nancy crossed to the dresser. Nathan tensed up, expecting another weapon to emerge from her armoury. She turned, clutching a notebook, and returned to his side. She flicked through half a dozen pages, stopped, then stabbed a finger at the page. 'I've a Sid at eleven. I've a Sid at eleven-thirty. I've a Johnny at midnight. I've a Johnny Thunders at one. A Mr Smith at two. Another Mr Smith at three, only Mr Three o'clock Mr Smith is standing out there apologizing for being so late because he couldn't get away from his fucking wife. So who the fuck are you?'

'Nathan . . .' he croaked. 'I just wanted to see Sid's room.'

'*Honey*, I've given you the best I have for the last half-hour.' She looked at his bloody chest. 'You paid me.'

'You handcuffed me! You took it!'

'I thought that was what you wanted!'

'You didn't ask!'

'I never ask! That's what they all want! Slapped around and fucked!'

'I just wanted to see . . .'

'What sort of a pervert are you?'

'Please . . . let me go.'

Nancy shook her head. 'How can I let you go? Jesus, I've carved you to ribbons.'

Mr Three o'clock Smith banged on the door again. Nancy shook her head pitifully at Nathan. 'You're going to sue, aren't you?'

Nathan shook his head. 'Just let me go.'

'You'd take me for millions.'

'Please, I . . .'

'All these years, wasted. Even if I win it'll be eaten up in legal costs.' She lifted the knife. 'You came for a Sid session. We should finish it as a Sid session. Except maybe in reverse. You got all frenzied. Came at me with a knife. I managed to push you away. You fell on it. You bled to death. I'm sorry.'

Nathan strained against the cuffs again. 'Nancy, please, just let me go. I won't sue. I swear to God I won't sue. Just release me.'

'I've just cut you up and you're going to walk out of here without saying a word!' She sat on the edge of the bed. 'Why the fuck didn't you come? I'd be okay if you'd come. There would have been evidence. That you'd enjoyed it. But you didn't. Why didn't you come? Am I not attractive?'

Three o'clock Smith banged on the door again.

'Nancy, please, I need a doctor.'

'You need a fucking psychiatrist! You should be locked up! You're sick!'

'Nancy, please, I think I'm bleeding to death.'

'Don't let me stop you.'

Nathan reared up suddenly against the cuffs. 'CALL THE COPS!' he roared, 'CALL THE COPS!'

Nancy's jaw dropped. Three o'clock Smith pushed the door open, peered in, mouthed *Jesus*, turned and hurried off down the corridor.

'He won't get the cops,' Nancy said.

She pulled her arm back, plunged at him with the knife. Nathan shifted to one side. She stabbed the bed. Thick black tears sprang down her face. She stabbed him again, just missed. 'Damn you! Stay still!'

'CALL THE COPS!'

Nancy stood. 'Fuck you!' She hurried to her dresser. She pulled out a leather bag from beneath it, opened the drawers and rapidly began to empty out the contents. Leather gear, knives, whips, dildos, vibrators. 'Fuck you. This has been my gig for six months! Now I gotta start all over! You sick fuck, you've ruined me!'

'I'm sorry,' Nathan said.

'Sorry fuck,' said Nancy. She hurried to the door, peered out into the corridor. Then she was gone.

Nathan slumped back on the bed, wincing at the rips in his chest.

George had greatly enjoyed the *Oprah* show, although he'd much rather have been in the audience with a bazooka under his jacket.

He knew they'd be onto him in minutes, so he made a quick exit from the Montrose Hotel and spent a pleasant early evening shopping in Georgetown. He needed a new wardrobe and enough small arms to start a military coup. This was all accomplished with relative ease; John Smith's credit card was a Godsend for the clothes and a quick flash of his FBI gold badge was exactly what was required to cajole those feigning a little reluctance on the weapons front into providing exactly what was necessary. His final calls were to a pet store, Reptiles R Us, where he purchased for $100 a Nigerian slipper snake and McDonald's, where he bought a large Diet Coke.

Re-armed and re-styled, George spent the early evening getting used to his new weaponry in a rather seedy room in the Ambassador Motel in Washington. He had already strangled the snake. He used a Swiss Army knife to extract the venom. Then, about midnight, when he was packed up and ready to head for New York, he sauntered over to the reception desk and told the guy the phone in his room wasn't working. He used the house phone to call his wife in Birmingham. He kept a close eye on his watch. He suspected the call would be traced, but he only wanted to say a quick goodbye and besides, he was such a master of disguise, such a nimble-footed warrior and class-A strategist that the chances of members of the security forces catching him were so small as to be virtually negligible.

Mrs Burley was more than a little tipsy when she answered. She'd been at a low ebb for several days, but her sister Claudette had tried to liven her up a little by taking her out to a singles night at a local bar. This had not been entirely successful. Claudette, who was a regular, was used to the cut and thrust of jam-packed singles repartee, but Mrs Burley was well rusty. Fuelled by copious amounts of undiluted gin she'd fallen into an argument with a one-legged rodeo rider (retired) which had ended with her punching him across the bar.

Now, slumped at home in a chair in front of the TV, Claudette asleep opposite her, it took her half a minute to find the phone in the drunk-fog. She replied in that peculiar gin-soaked Southern way, as if she was a donkey undergoing elocution lessons. 'Yeah-us, awho is-a call-ging?'

Thrown at first, George said: 'Is Mrs Burley there?'

'Thee-us ais Missus Burrrleigh, awho is-a . . .'

'Jesus! It's me. George!'

Mrs Burley peered through the fog. 'Gee-orge?'

'Yes, for chrissakes, it's me. I'm just calling . . . I'm just calling to say . . . well Jesus, I love you, Grace, and I always will.'

'Awwww, Gee-orge, thay-at's sooh sweet!'

'And I want you to know I'm doing all of this for you.'

'Awwww, Gee-orge, ayalll of what for me-ah?'

'Grace, have you been drinking?'

'Me-ah?'

'Jesus Christ, Grace, I leave you alone for five minutes and you go to pieces. How in hell's name are we going to defeat the niggers if you fall apart like this every time there's a bit of a crisis?'

'Gee-orge . . . what neegars?'

George took a deep breath. He counted to seven. He said, quietly: 'Grace, I want you to remember this, that I did it for you and that I did it for America. Goodnight, Grace. Goodbye. I will not call again.'

George travelled as far as Philadelphia by Greyhound. It was an uncomfortable journey. His body was sore, anyway, but the pain was hardly helped by the three pistols, four grenades and one hundred rounds of spare ammunition located about his body. He had learnt his lesson: the foolhardiness of allowing himself to be distanced, no matter by how little, from his weaponry. He needed to have instant access to his guns. He could put up with a little short-term discomfort.

The call to the White House Press Room had thrown him a bit at first. Missing out on the *Oprah* opportunity was bad enough, but the news that the President's itinerary for the coming week didn't bring him within a hundred miles of the capital meant an urgent re-think of his plans. George wanted to get the job done and return to a normal life as quickly as possible; trailing the President across the States didn't help that ambition any at all, although it did encourage in him the notion that perhaps he had him on the run.

Of course George did not harbour any intentions of returning to Birmingham or of taking his place in the control tower at the airport. That would have been a sure sign of madness. If pushed he might have admitted to a little fantasy of living in a town just outside Birmingham, sneaking into the city late at night to visit Mrs Burley; but he was intelligent enough to realize that that might not be possible for a few months, at least until the furore over the assassination had died down. A year tops. No, in reality George realized the old life was over, and it was no bad thing. It wasn't many men had the opportunity to start afresh, to leave behind the baggage that comes with four decades of living. George had his false social security number. False passport. False employment references. He could go anywhere. Do anything. He wouldn't even have to maintain his Top Ten any more. He'd have the time to make it a Top One Hundred. He didn't think he'd have much trouble filling it.

Glancing through the President's itinerary, he decided that New York would be the best place to strike. The Big Rotten Apple. If anywhere represented the degradation of modern American living it was New York. The melting pot. It was the ideal place for George Burley to turn up the heat. There was a busy New York schedule, but the ideal venue for the execution leapt out at him as soon as he had jotted it down. The top of the Empire State Building. Killing a symbol of everything that was sick about America, in a place that was a symbol of everything that was great about America. It made perfect sense, albeit to a nut.

Plus – it would be a challenge, killing a president in such a confined space. All of those chickenshit efforts on previous presidents had been easy touches. George made a mental note of a new Top Five.

1 Oswald – shot Kennedy across half of Dallas, and still got caught. Jerk.
2 Hinkley – shot Reagan (just) on a crowded sidewalk, got caught. Dick.

3 John Wilkes Booth – shot Abe Lincoln in crowded theatre. Easy. Got caught. The olden days – didn't know any better.

4 Harvey – white rabbit, attacked Jimmy Carter while he was white-water rafting. Escaped. (George wasn't too sure about this one, but he remembered something along those lines.)

5 – any of those dog-eared efforts so far on that cunt Keneally.

He would be different, *so* different. The challenge was, first off, to get into the Empire at all. Security would be tight as a coon's ass. Second was to get the President's ear, explain to him where he'd gone wrong. Third was to cut the fucker off.

George dozed fitfully as the half-empty bus trundled towards Philly. Two hours into the trip a black guy in the seat opposite leaned across the aisle towards him. George stiffened instinctively.

'Can I offer you a sandwich, sir?'

George shook the fug-bugs from his head. 'What?'

'Can I offer you a sandwich?'

'Uhm, no. No. I've no money.'

'I don't mean to sell you one, sir. I've more than enough.' He offered the foil-wrap to George.

George shook his head. 'No. Thanks. Really.' He could see a triangle of white bread, a hint of indeterminate filling. But he knew what the trick was. He knew what silver foil was used for. It was used to smoke heroin. *Accept a sandwich one day, the next you're begging on the streets for your next rock of crack.* George smiled politely and closed his eyes again. One day, he knew, the newspapers would make him out to be a mad racist. *If they could see me now, chatting away like I'm one of the brothers, they'd understand the truth of it. That what I do isn't about individuals, it's about America. One day, not tomorrow, not next year, maybe not for a decade, they'll call me a hero. Saint George. There'll be a national holiday. It won't be fucking Martin Luther King Day. It'll be George Burley Day. Maybe a whole weekend.*

Twenty minutes outside Philly George extracted the McDonald's straw from his jacket pocket. From his wallet he carefully removed a sealed plastic bag. From within it he gingerly picked a sharp brown rose thorn. This he placed just inside one end of the straw. He sat for a few moments with the straw in his mouth until he was sure that nobody was watching. Then he took aim.

The thorn hit the black guy with the sandwiches in the back of the neck. George watched his reflection in the window as he swung round, slapping at his neck. He examined his hand.

'Damn it,' he said, 'I been stung by a bee.'

George nodded across sympathetically. 'Didn't see it,' he said.

'Damn,' said the man, turning away again, still rubbing at his neck.

George sauntered casually down the aisle as the bus pulled into the station in Philly. He was pleased to see the sandwich man's head resting against the window, his eyes staring lifelessly.

3

Silvan Rozzi shook his head, crossed his arms, stepped forward, stepped back, tutted. The manager stepped forward again, craning his neck to examine the headboard for friction marks. 'It's okay,' he said, 'the police and paramedics are on their way.'

'I don't want the . . .'

'But I do.' Rozzi tutted again. 'You know,' he continued, 'even rock'n'roll hotels have certain standards.'

Nathan half-groaned, half-cried. His head throbbed. His chest was tight. 'I just want out of here.' He shook his head wearily, looked down at the congealing mess on his chest. 'I didn't ask for any of this,' he said weakly.

Rozzi wasn't for moving. 'It's important these things are done properly,' he said solemnly.

Nathan pulled at the handcuffs again. A flake of blood dropped onto the pillow. 'I'm sorry,' he said, 'I didn't mean to bleed on the sheets. I'm not here on purpose. All I want you to do is release me. I'll go back to my room. I'll buy you a new sheet, if that's the problem.'

'It's not a question of sheets. There's the question of a

key for your handcuffs. There's a question of who's going to attempt to release you without contracting HIV. There's the question of medical treatment for you. The police will want to know everything. I can't answer these things, or at least not without my attorney present. I'm sorry, but I can't help you.'

'Could you at least get me a drink of water?'

Rozzi shook his head ruefully. 'I'm sorry,' he said, 'it's best not to get involved.' He turned abruptly for the door. 'I'll just go and see if they've arrived.'

Nathan's head lolled back onto the pillow. He dry-swallowed. He blacked out. Just for a few moments, or just for a few days, he couldn't tell. When he blinked back into the real world there was a figure standing by the window.

Nathan croaked out a hello. The figure turned slightly, as if unsure he'd heard, or unwilling to drag himself away from the view. He was tall, thin under a black leather jacket, red t-shirt; face, hair spiked black.

'Oh God,' Nathan groaned.

'Wot?'

'You didn't waste much time. I don't think the Sid Vicious Suite is yet ready for re-occupation.'

'You wot?'

Nathan let out a deep-deep sigh. 'Oh God protect me,' he said.

'Wot?'

'Nothing. Nothing. For fuck's sake, nothing.'

The figure moved from the window and stood by the end of the bed. His eyes narrowed, half-focused on Nathan's chest; he began to roll back and forward on the balls of his feet. 'Oi,' he said after some little time, 'what's your fucking game?'

Nathan closed his eyes. 'It's not a game,' he said simply.

He opened his eyes again and strained once more against the handcuffs. 'Damn it! It's not a fucking game!'

Spike seemed a bit taken aback by this. He gave a little shrug. 'Not my fault, mate,' he said, defensively, and peered forward at the handcuffs. 'Got no fucking key, mate?'

Nathan shook his head, gritted his teeth. 'Yes, of course I've got a fucking key, I slashed myself to ribbons, called the police then handcuffed myself to the bed. Of course I've got one fucking big key!'

Spike rocked back a little too far on his heels, stumbled, righted himself. 'Y'know,' he said, 'you're very sarcastic. Just like John. John was very sarcastic.' He leant forward again, a little too far. He pushed himself off the base of the bed. 'Y'know what they say, don't you?'

Nathan shook his head.

'They say that sarcasm is the lowest form of wit.'

'Do they,' Nathan said flatly.

'Do. I said that to John, too. You know what he said?'

Nathan shook his head.

'He said: Sid, fuck away off and kill yourself. Which I didn't think was much of an argument.' He straightened suddenly, eyes alert, ears straining. 'Wot?'

'I didn't . . .'

'Nancy?' he called. 'Where the bleedin' hell are you?'

His brow furrowed. He turned, peered towards the bathroom. 'Nance?' he called softly.

Nathan rolled his eyes. 'She's gone! Ran for it! Now, please, just . . .'

Spike didn't seem to hear. He moved cautiously, slightly furtively, towards the bathroom. 'Nancy, sweetie, you okay, love?'

'Hey, fuck it,' Nathan called, 'please get these bastards off me . . .'

The guy pushed the bathroom door open. 'Nance . . .?'

And then he yelled. He dived forward. Nathan, shocked, strained to see, but the fella was out of his eyeline now. For a moment there was no noise at all, even the dull throb of traffic seemed edited out, but then gradually there came to him a sound he had only heard once before, and then only in his own mind on a cold night in Crossmaheart, a kind of animal whimpering.

'Hey,' Nathan called, 'you okay . . .?'

The voice was weary. 'Oh Nancy . . . oh Nancy . . . oh, no . . . Nancy . . .

'Hey – look de fuck at dis!'

Nathan's head jerked towards the door. Cops. 'Aaaaah!' Nathan exclaimed and threw his head back on the pillow. 'This is not my day!' he shouted at the ceiling.

There were two bluemen in the doorway. One, small, Hispanic, pushed his cap back on his head. 'Hey,' he said, 'and I thought I knew how to have fun!'

His partner nodded warily and inched into the room, one hand resting on his holstered gun.

Nathan rattled his cuffs, jangled his feet. 'Can you please get me out of these? And you might care to check the bathroom out. I think there's been some sort of an accident.'

Hispanic nodded at his partner. 'You look afta 'im. I'll check the john.'

The other cop winked and moved to the foot of the bed. He blew some air out of his cheeks. 'You kids today,' he said.

Hispanic drew his gun and advanced cautiously towards the bathroom; he held the pistol before him and toed the door slowly open. He stepped forward. Then he straightened, turned, holstered his gun. 'What de fuck you playin' at asshole? There ain't no one in der.'

* * *

Fifteen minutes after the paramedics had pronounced him fit but bloody, the Fire Department arrived to cut Nathan out of the handcuffs. At the height of the activity there were four police officers, three hotel staff, three paramedics and eight firemen crammed into room 100. Three citybeat reporters idled in the corridors, taking turns to shout questions through the door. It was an exceptionally quiet night in the city.

'Man, you pay for this shit?' said one of the paramedics, white-gloved, dabbing his chest with an antiseptic wipe.

'I didn't pay for nuthin',' Nathan croaked. He accepted a drink of water and a sedative, half-choked on it.

'You gotta freebie, yeah? Luck of the Irish.' He cackled.

One of the cops appeared in the doorway, flicking through Nathan's wallet. Then he approached the bed, stepping over and between the legs of the prone firemen.

'Won't be long now,' said one.

The cop held the wallet up for Nathan to see. 'Nathan Jones. Irish. Passport photo doesn't do you justice. Your tourist visa's up, son, and I don't see no green card.'

Nathan closed his eyes. 'What can I say?'

'Not much. You wanna press charges against anyone before we deport you? Who was it, girlfriend, boyfriend . . .?'

Silvan Rozzi, still hovering, gave a little cough and whispered in the cop's ear.

'Or hooker. Or all three, you never know these days. Still, you won't forget her in a hurry, will you?'

Nathan shook his head.

Uncuffed, Nathan quickly pulled up his trousers, but not before one of the photographers outside had popped his camera round the door and sneaked a shot. One of the cops shouted something, but the damage was done. Nathan flexed his legs, stretched himself, winced as the cuts pulled against the light dressing the paramedics had applied. *Oh God*, Nathan thought.

The firemen withdrew, wishing him all the best. The paramedics left, cheery. Rozzi glowered at him, swept up the bloody and by now lubricant-stained and blowtorch-burnt bedding, and hurried from the room. A moment later he returned and dumped Nathan's remaining belongings in the doorway. Three of the police left, leaving him alone in the room with the two original cops.

'Okay, my frien',' Hispanic said, 'let's go down to the squadcar.'

Nathan looked helplessly at the policemen. His bottom lip began to quiver.

'I'm sorry,' the other cop said, 'we've no choice. You've only yourself to blame. No green card, you shouldn't mess around with the hookers.'

'I didn't . . .'

'You a horny lil' devil my frien',' said Hispanic.

Barefoot, topless, they led him to the elevators. Hispanic carried his gear. His partner said: 'In case you're wondering, we'd normally have the cuffs on you right now, but it hardly seemed appropriate.'

Nathan managed a weak smile. 'Thanks,' he said.

'Don't mention it. But try running and I'll shoot you dead.'

'Do I look like I could run anywhere?'

The cop looked him up and down. 'See your point,' he said.

Through the lobby. The Sid convention stared doom-eyed. Nathan examined them closely. Rozzi was back behind the desk. He didn't look up.

Daylight was just coming to the city, but it didn't do much for 23rd Street; the Chelsea hovered dark behind them, a black hole intent on sucking up another American dream.

Nathan stubbed his toe on the door. He let out a *fuck* and

started to hop while the cops cracked up. Something crackled over their radio. Nathan bent to hold his toe. He counted to five; the pain started to subside; as he came out of his slouch he smacked the nearest cop in the balls.

He groaned and doubled up. Hispanic, startled, reached for his nightstick, but Nathan straightened, rammed a fist into his throat and took off up the road as fast as his legs would carry him.

Hispanic gagged, sucked in big gulps of air, shook himself, drew his gun. Raised. Aimed. Hand quivered, anger slipped. 'Fuck it!' he shouted and dropped it again. 'The son-of-a-bitch.'

His partner rolled over on his back on the Chelsea steps, hands between his legs, face contorted.

'You okay, man?' Hispanic asked, kneeling.

'I'm just wonderful,' his partner squeezed out, tears appearing in stereo.

4

Nathan spent the early hours of Tuesday morning kicking the heads off flowers in Strawberry Fields.

He didn't know how he'd ended up there. He'd just run and run and run. He'd tried to find it once while sober and got hopelessly lost; but now here he was, kicking, kicking, kicking. After a while he stopped and slumped to the grass. He cradled the last of the three cans he'd managed to purchase with the few coins that remained in his trouser pockets. They'd hardly given him a second glance in the deli: naked from the waist up, bandaged, barefoot, just your average New York customer.

He hated places like Strawberry Fields. Lennon had been as much of an anarchist as Sid. More, really. He'd been bright and witty about it, Sid had just been a thug with anti-social tendencies, and a pretty hopeless one at that. There were no memorials to Sid – in twenty years no one would remember him at all. Nathan admired Lennon, but how could you remember someone with a *garden*?

And how would he remember Lisa? Making beautiful love, and then she ran away. If he could just talk to her, show her the ring . . . the ring! Jesus, the cops had that too.

'Love, love me do,' Nathan sang quietly to the dead flowers at his feet.

'How sweet,' the flowers replied. Or not. Not the flowers. Nathan looked up. Dawn was pushing through the trees, and so was a small woman in a sheepskin coat. As she drew closer Nathan could see that she was of Oriental extraction, that she had the life-sapped skin of middle age and that her eyes were red, as if from crying.

'Sorry,' Nathan said, 'I'm getting maudlin in my old age.'

The woman gave a little shrug and a tight but friendly smile. 'It's a garden for emotion. Many people come into my garden and shed a tear.'

Nathan looked at her carefully. She glanced behind her. Nathan followed it to the bushes where he could make out the outline of three, maybe four people. Big people.

She saw that he saw. 'I'm sorry,' she said. 'They go with me everywhere, since . . . well, y'know.'

'Yoko,' Nathan said.

She looked shyly to one side. 'I'd like to come here more often, but there's so many people during the day.'

Nathan offered her the can.

She shook her head. 'I don't. Thank you.'

'I know what it's like to lose a friend. To have them shot.' She nodded.

'It stays with you for ever,' said Nathan.

'He's always with me. Always.'

Nathan nodded for several moments. 'Your English is very good,' he said after a few moments.

'So is yours.'

He smiled. 'I'm sorry. That must sound patronizing.'

She shrugged. 'I'm used to it. I've lived here thirty years. People still talk to me as if I'm an imbecile.'

Nathan drained the can, was about to fire it behind him when he thought better of it. He looked at his black feet. 'You couldn't lend me a couple of shoes?'

Yoko tutted, then took a step back towards cover. 'You have to go and spoil it.'

Nathan's brow furrowed. 'I didn't mean . . .'

'Asking for money.'

'I was only . . .'

'You're all the same.'

'I was only joking. I don't expect you carry any shoes on you.'

'I despise dishonesty. You don't want a shoe. You want money for more alcohol. Or crack.'

'What the fuck are you talking about? I was just asking for a little help to get me home.' He hated *assumptions*. She had no idea of the hell he'd been through in the last few hours. He shot a finger out at her. 'You can stuff your money up your hole for all I care.' Nathan struggled to his feet, then threw the can over his head into the bushes. He kicked at the flower-heads on the grass before him. 'And fuck your garden. And fuck John Lennon. And thanks for splitting the Beatles up, you Japanese bitch. And your records are fucking crap. And I hope someone shoots you, too.'

Nathan took a deep breath. He looked at the bushes behind her. The big figures had drawn closer to the edge. He spat on the grass.

Yoko, a little closer still to the bushes, shook her head sadly. 'You've so much anger in you.'

Nathan kicked another flower-head. 'Of course I have,' he spat, and then more quietly, 'I was just trying to be pleasant and you think I'm a drug addict.'

'Look at you. What should I think?'

For a moment, a very brief moment, Nathan had a vision of Coolidge and the rest of his colleagues lying dead on that lonely Ulster road. God, why was he trying to pick a fight with Yoko Ono of all people? He took a deep breath, tried to clear the anger from his head. He bent and picked up one of the dead flowers and tossed it into the bushes. 'You've paid your own price for splitting up the Beatles,' he said quietly.

'I didn't split up the Beatles!' Yoko stamped her foot on the ground, then her hands dipped, searching, into the pockets of her sheepskin jacket and produced a packet of cigarettes. She lifted one with her lips, then replaced the packet. Her hands searched again and she came up with a lighter which lit on the fourth flick. As she bent into the flickering light Nathan saw that her face wasn't just darkly Oriental, but darkly dirty. Her fingers, curled about the lighter, were filthy; the nails, long but chipped, were black.

He shook his head. He'd been where she was; but she had a billion dollars to cushion the blow; the least she could have done was wash her face. Nathan had blown practically all of his £100,000 compensation in a little over three years. And his face had always been clean, except for the blood on it now, and he'd always been presentable, save for the current blood-stains and the missing shoes.

They looked at each other in silence for a few moments. Yoko drew lustily on the cigarette, blowing the fumes out through her nose.

'I suppose I'd better be going,' Nathan said. He nodded goodbye to her, then added: 'At least Woody Allen was nice to me.'

Yoko gave a sarcastic laugh. 'You don't know Woody.'

'Do I not?'

197

'Well, why don't I just call him and ask?'

Yoko rummaged in her pockets again, then produced a portable phone. She turned away so that he couldn't see which buttons she pressed. Then she bent her head down into her sheepskin jacket and began talking quietly.

Nathan shook his head sadly. He looked at his watch. Sobriety was coming to him. Hunger, too. Of course Woody wouldn't remember him. He hadn't told him his name, so how could he?

Nathan glanced back at the rock widow's hunched figure. He could see now that the sheepskin coat was badly ripped along the spine. And that her hair was matted. And that she was wearing odd shoes. He rolled his eyes. Cursed himself. He quickly crossed the few yards of grass to her and, putting his hands on her shoulders, spun her round. She tried to pull away but he held her tight, then in one lightning move he snatched the phone away from her. She screamed and grabbed for it, but he spun away and held it quickly to his ear.

'Woody?' he said.

No reply . . . no static . . . no nothing. He weighed it in his hand while Yoko swiped at it again. Held it to his nose. Then he took a bite out of it.

Chocolate.

Chocolate with a vague taste of sweat and gravel. He spat it out.

Yoko began to cackle. Her teeth were black, those that she had.

'Oh for God's sake,' Nathan said and threw the chocolate phone to the ground. She was on it in an instant.

Nathan turned and started to walk out of Strawberry Fields, angry at himself now that he'd been taken in so badly. First a disappearing Sid, now a bagwoman Yoko lookalike. He had to get a grip. Had to claw back reality. *Survive. Live long and prosper.* He didn't hear the footsteps until the last moment. She moved deceptively quietly for a nut. The chocolate phone cracked across the back of his skull and he tumbled forward. For a moment, just a moment, he was out of it, but then he was back and rolling over onto his back; his vision began to clear; he was just getting up when there was another cackle and then a rush of dark forms about him and he was pinned to the ground. Yoko's security men, yeah, sure. Their communal stench had him gagging. Five of them, heavy breathers, chest infections, their hands shooting into every part of his body capable of hiding anything . . . Nathan screamed and lost it. He kicked out, strong, a grunt of pain, a leg loose, he kicked again, winced at the pain of his toes on tooth enamel. With the leverage of his one leg he was able to twist and shoot out another kick, this time to his left, and then both feet were free and he arched his body back and kicked out again and then his arms were free and four of his attackers were sprawled back on the ground; one, still standing, was already retreating back into the bushes; Yoko not-Yoko stood mesmerized, the chocolate phone held tightly to her chest.

It was like being mugged in a terminal ward. As he sprang to his feet ready to fight on, his assailants lay back on the dewy grass, gasping, crawling, holding themselves. Nathan began to back out of Strawberry Fields, still wary of the chocolate phone.

5

Brian Houston was fixing an omelette and explaining to his sister the importance of the Tyson v Douglas fight in the Tokyo Dome on 11 February 1990. Their apartment was on the third floor of a Brooklyn brownstone.

'Y'see, up until then Tyson was invincible.'

'Invisible?'

'Stop it. He knocked everything over. He was the best heavyweight in history. Youngest, toughest, fastest – well, maybe not as fast as Ali – but fastest since. He was exactly what the division needed, someone who could unify it – a star. I mean, sure Larry Holmes, he was okay, but he had all the charisma of a pine bench.'

'Hey, don't knock pine.' She pushed him gently away from the pan. 'Go and watch the fight again. I'll watch the omelette.'

'Are you sure?'

She flickered her eyes.

'Thanks,' he said. 'Love you.'

'Love you too.'

He turned back to the lounge and the video. She addressed

the eggs. 'If I hear one more word about boxing,' she said, 'I'm going to cave his head in with a brick.'

'Whatssat?' Brian called.

'I said, Tyson looks like he's been hit with a brick.'

'You betcha,' said Brian.

At first, with the excited commentary at full volume, he didn't hear the doorbell. It was only when he flipped out the tape and was ready to replace it with *Champions Forever* that he heard the chimes. As he moved across the lounge Lucy appeared in the kitchen doorway.

Brian shrugged and peered through the spyhole. He stepped back, surprised, then peered again. Then he unlocked the door.

'Nathan?' he said.

'Hi. How're ya doing?'

'Fine,' said Brian. 'Uhm. How are you?'

Nathan smiled. 'Been better.'

'Uhm. Do you want to come in?'

Nathan nodded weakly. 'I wouldn't mind.'

Brian ushered Nathan into the apartment, then helped him into a chair.

Lucy appeared in the kitchen doorway. She looked Nathan up and down. She noted the matted hair, the scab-encrusted chest, the black feet. She gave Brian a look which said: *What is the wild man of Borneo doing in our lounge?*

'God, Nathan, I wondered why you weren't in work today. You look like you've gone six rounds with Tyson.'

Nathan shook his head. 'That would've been easier.'

Lucy reappeared in the doorway. 'This omelette is burning,' she said.

'Put it on three plates then, sister.'

Her eyes narrowed, but she turned.

'Nathan, what the hell's happened to you? Last I saw you dashed out to get married. I take it she didn't say yes.'

Nathan shook his head ruefully. Lucy was back in the doorway. 'I want to hear, too,' she said.

Nathan nodded. He closed his eyes, took a deep breath. 'She left me. Ran out.'

'I'm sorry,' said Brian. 'And?'

'Then a woman I don't know handcuffed me to the bed and carved me up.'

'In your apartment? Jesus.'

'No. In the Chelsea Hotel.'

'In the . . .' began Lucy.

'I got drunk. I decided to look up . . . anyway, it doesn't fucking matter. The woman sliced me up, then she left and the ghost of Sid Vicious came in for a chat. Then half of New York turned up to try and cut me free, then the cops arrested me for having no green card. I escaped. I spent the night talking to someone I thought was Yoko Ono in Strawberry Fields and the rest of the day hiding in a deluxe wardrobe in a furniture shop on Washington Square.'

'*In* a deluxe wardrobe?' said Lucy.

'Sure.'

'And how was that?'

'Claustrophobic.'

'Jeez,' said Brian. He looked at Lucy. They both nodded.

'Acid,' they said together.

'Honestly, no. I don't.' He sighed; it sounded as if it came all the way up from his feet. 'I'm sorry,' said Nathan, 'I'm just so tired. I hardly know you, but I know you better than I know anyone else in New York. I've no clothes. I've no money. I haven't eaten all day. I want to die. I was going to try Sam's, but I heard he wasn't well. The way my luck's running if I went round there he'd probably die on me. And then I'd get done for murder.'

He looked like he was about to cry. Lucy stuck a finger out at him.

'So fuck off and leave us alone then,' she said.

Nathan looked at her for a moment. Then all three of them cackled.

He stood in the shower for as long as the water was hot. He shaved; the blade was ragged; he thought maybe it was the girl's. He soaped then scraped, wincing, at the soft scabs on his chest. He scrubbed the grime from his feet. He washed his hair three times. He left his hair wet, slipped into a scarlet woollen dressing-gown. The bathroom was too steamed up for him to examine himself properly in the mirror; he rubbed enough off the glass with the back of his hand to check that his face was unmarked. Standing there, warm, clean, smelling of shampoo and soap and toothpaste, he could almost believe that it hadn't happened. Then the fresh-forming scab jagged on the wool and he had to carefully detach a strand and dab at the blood and pus, and it was real.

6

Later, Lucy hovered in her bedroom doorway until she was sure that Nathan, sprawled in front of the TV, was asleep. Then she hurried along to Brian's room. 'You awake, bro'?' she whispered.

Brian mumbled something in the dark. Lucy lifted the quilt and slipped beneath it. She snuggled up behind her brother, moving her right hand under his arms and resting it on his chest.

He moved back slightly until they were well spooned. 'You've no clothes on again,' he said.

'Sorry,' she said.

'People will talk.'

'People will.' She ran her hand over his chest. 'Tell me about Nathan Jones, are you buddies or what?'

Brian gave a little shrug. 'Hardly know him. Seems okay.'

'You gave him our address.'

'I gave everyone our address. For the fight next week.'

'Oh God. I'd forgotten. I must arrange to be out of the planet.'

'Don't you dare. You're cooking, my friend. Or you're out on your pretty ass.'

She nipped his ass with her free hand. He squirmed away. 'Back to the subject,' she said. 'Nathan Jones. What're you going to do?'

He shrugged again. 'Help him, I suppose. I mean, he doesn't want much. A couple of t-shirts, a few dollars, a lend of my spare uniform until he can get another. He's down on his luck big style, the least I can do is help the guy through to pay day.'

'He has no green card, is he not going to get dumped out anyway?'

'Doubt it. If he was black or a Mex, maybe, but he's Irish, he has a job for life if he can keep his shirt on for long enough.'

'You've a heart of gold, little bro'.'

Lucy slipped a hand into his shorts.

'Look, Luce, I've warned you before.'

She tutted. 'It doesn't do any harm.'

'Luce.'

'Too late, bro'. I detect a stirring.'

'Luce!'

'Sorry, bro', much too late.'

'Fuck it,' said Brian.

Nathan could hardly sleep with the pain of it all: head pain; heart pain; the jagged pull of the scabs only reminded him of his loss. When he did drift off he saw the massacre of Crossmaheart, but it was not hooded terrorists mowing down his colleagues, it was Lisa. *Please, Lisa, don't do this, I'm sorry, I'll make it up to you* . . . but she just smiled that winning smile and pulled the trigger.

At a little before five Lucy slipped stealthily from Brian's room, and walked into Nathan. He was groggy, disorientated, almost fell back, then steadied himself and stumbled forward, putting a hand out to stop himself and clutching her left breast in the process.

She let out a little yelp, then hurried past.

He mumbled, 'Bathroom,' after her, then stood and tried to shake the cobwebs from his head. Had he really . . .? There was a slight shift in the darkness as she opened and closed her bedroom door. What was she . . .?

7

'Name?'
  'What?'
  'Name.'
  'You know my name. You just called me in.'
  'Name.'
  'Brian.'
  'Full name.'
  'Brian Houston.'
  'Occupation.'
  'I'm the WBA Welterweight Champion.'
  'Occupation.'
  'Security guard. Empire State. New York.'
  'How long have you worked here, Brian?'
  'Six years. Six years in October.'
  'And where did you work before that?'
  'I worked in a comic book shop in Denver.'
  'Why did you leave it?'
  'My sister was moving east.'
  'So?'
  'So I moved to New York with her.'

'What about your parents?'

'What about them?'

'Are they still alive?'

'I hope not, we buried them.'

'Do you think this is a bit of a joke, Brian?'

'A bit.'

'Do you know how many attempts there have been on the President's life since he came to office?'

'No.'

'Thirteen.'

'Lucky for some.'

'So you'll appreciate that we have to investigate the background of any and every person who's going to be in close contact with the President.'

'Sure.'

'So stop trying to be so fucking smart. What happened to your parents?'

'Cancer. Within six months of each other.'

'What does your sister do?'

'Teaches.'

'Teaches what?'

'Creative writing at NYU.'

'Have you ever been convicted of a felony?'

'Convicted?'

'Have you ever been convicted of a felony?'

'No.'

'Has your sister?'

'Not that I know of.'

'Are you now, or have you ever been, a member of the Communist party?'

'No. Neither has my—'

'Have you ever fired a gun, Brian?'

'No.'

'Primed a bomb?'

'No.'

'If I kidnapped your sister and ordered you to shoot the President, would you do it?'

'No.'

'What would you do?'

'Shoot you.'

'But you've never fired a gun before.'

'I can learn.'

'Who would teach you?'

'I'd teach myself.'

'Are you now, or have you ever been, a member of the Aryan Nations or an equivalent far-right organization or militia?'

'No.'

'Do you sympathize with any of these organizations?'

'I do.'

'You do?'

'Sure.'

'In what way?'

'I sympathize with anyone who's that deluded.'

'Favourite comic?'

'Laurel and Hardy.'

'Comic.'

'Jerry Lewis.'

'Comic.'

'Oh. Right. *Amazing Adventures 18: War of the Worlds.*'

'Who wrote it?'

'H.G. Wells wrote the book. But the comic had little to do with that.'

'Who wrote the comic?'

'I can't remember.'

'Your favourite comic and you can't remember?'

'It was a long time ago.'

'Even so.'

'I gave up comics when I came east.'

'Why?'

'Working with them, you kinda lose interest. I took up boxing.'

'You fight?'

'No, I follow boxing.'

'How come?'

'What can I say? Why do we do anything? I enjoy it.'

'Would you say you had a latent violent streak in you?'

'I wouldn't say that.'

'So how do you explain your fascination with boxing?'

'I don't have to explain it.'

'Would you say that you've an obsessive personality?'

'No.'

'What's your favourite fight?'

'Leonard v Hagler.'

'Why?'

'I don't know. So unexpected. Lived up to the hype. A genius comes out of retirement, performs brilliantly.'

'What date was the Joe Louis – Max Schmeling fight at Yankee Stadium?'

'June 22, 1938.'

'Sure?'

'Sure. But you don't know whether I'm right or not, do you?'

'But I will before the President arrives.'

'And if I'm wrong?'

'Who knows? With that and not knowing who wrote *Amazing Adventures 18*, it might add up to something in your psychological profile.'

'Is that what this is? I thought it was an intelligence test. I thought I had to pass.'

'Very funny.'

'I hope you take into account the fact that I might just be a crap fan.'

'I take a lot of things into account.'

'I'm sure you do. Is that it?'

'For now.'

'You mean there's more?'

'I'll get back to you on that.'

Back in the canteen Brian got himself a cup of coffee. The rest of the crew was just starting to drift in for the first shift. Old Sam, as if he had a point to prove, was first in, already onto his second paper cup, eyes roving over the *Times* sports section.

Brian slipped onto the bench beside him. Sam blinked up, down. It was hardly *Hail fellow, well met*, but shit, it was Old Sam; you considered yourself lucky to get a blink; it was Sam's equivalent of a bear hug.

'How's it goin'?' Brian asked.

Sam pulled his paper in protectively. 'It's going okay. And before you ask I haven't got to the boxing yet, and I ain't about to rush.'

Brian shrugged. 'Been for your inquisition yet?'

'What?'

'The Secret Service guy's just given me a grilling. Y'know, about meeting Keneally. I say grilling, it was more like a light poaching.'

Sam folded his paper. He looked about the room. Most of the guys were sitting quietly, bleary-eyed. 'I'm not being grilled.'

'Well they wouldn't need to. You're beyond reproach. Besides, you probably haven't the strength to lift a gun.'

'I'm not meeting the President. They're kicking me out the day before he comes.'

'Kicking . . .?'

'Licence revoked. You want me to write it in blood on the wall?'

'Do the rest of the guys know this?'

Leonard Maltman, who'd been straining to hear the conversation, his back to them at the front of the canteen, glanced round just in time to see Sam do his poor little orphan look.

'Why should they care about an old guy like me?' said Sam. *Here we go*, thought Leonard.

Bobby Tangetta stuck a finger into Leonard's chest. 'No fucking way!'

Leonard took a step back. 'Bobby, c'mon, calm down. Things are not that bad.'

Bobby turned back to the canteen. '*Things are not that bad! Bullshit! Bullshit! Bullshit!*'

Sam kept his head down. He'd made his decision, he'd imparted his information, now he'd let things take their course. Whatever happened, it was gratifying to see the men support him.

'The way I see it,' said Minto, rising slowly to his feet at the back of the canteen, 'is that if we acquiesce on this, then all our jobs are on the line. Management can just point at anyone and say 'bye. We have to stick with Sam.'

Leonard shook his head. 'Guys – you don't understand. It's not a case of pointing the finger. We have a new management structure, they have a new way of doing things. Sam's been a great servant to the Empire, they know that, and they'll look after him in his retirement, but he's well past retirement age. He should have been gone years ago – he knows that. You know that, don't you, Sam?'

'What do I know?' said Sam, shrugging.

Now he's turned Jewish. 'He knows that. It's not a matter of whether he can still do the job. It's his age, it's insurance . . .' He threw his hands up. 'It's life! It happens all the time, guys!'

'Not to you, you fat fuck,' Bobby shouted.

Leonard chose to ignore him.

'But the day before he's due to meet the President!' Bobby was doing his finger pointing again. If he'd tried it in private, Leonard would have flattened him. Sat on him until he burst. 'He's met every President in history. Every celebrity you care to name . . . from Elvis to . . . *hell knows* . . . and you just chuck him out like . . . like . . .'

'The way I see it,' Minto interjected, 'we have three courses of action open to us.'

'We don't need to talk about *action*,' said Leonard.

'One, we can let Sam go, not make a fuss. Thanks for your fifty years, Sam. We'd be betraying the Empire's longest-serving employee and a loyal friend, we'd look like a bunch of pussies and management could jack us around for the rest of eternity. On the plus side, it would doubtless ingratiate us with the new *boy* and our jobs would be perfectly secure until the next time he took a dislike to any one of us.'

'Don't load your argument,' Leonard spat, beginning to lose it a little.

'Two, we can take a vote condemning the decision, take no action, but ask Brian Houston to relay our displeasure to the President when he meets him.'

Brian went pale. 'Well, I'm not sure . . .'

'Three, we can take immediate strike action.'

Leonard raised his hands, palms out. 'Jeez, guys, c'mon. We don't need to strike over this. This is meant to be a big week for us. Let's not get off on the wrong foot with these guys. We gotta work here.'

'You wanna kiss their tight asses, Leonard,' Bobby Tangetta shouted, 'you go ahead and kiss them.'

'Sam – you don't wanna strike, do you? Think what it would do for the image of the Empire. What would the President think, Sam?'

'I'll ask him when I see him, Leonard,' said Sam.

8

The waves lapped up onto the beach like a thousand little kitten tongues. The full moon and the cloudless, windless night made it perfect for walking. They kicked the sand, arm in arm.

Alexis Mascara had invited her backstage to what he described as her personal toilet, then, anxious to party on, she'd forgone getting changed and led Lisa a merry dance around the bars of Provincetown.

Big fake perm, stilettos in hand, he wasn't one for beating about the sandcastle. 'Who're you running from, love?' he asked. He'd big imploring eyes Lisa found irresistible.

Lisa, mostly drunk, shook her head. 'I'm not running from anyone.'

Alexis tutted. 'Come off it. Look at you. You've eyes like stalks. Only one thing does that. Look at mine, I've more bags than Marks and Spencer.'

'Your eyes are lovely.'

'Aw, shucks.'

'Do you have a broken heart as well?'

'Doesn't everyone?'

'I don't know.' Lisa, on the verge of tears, gazed up into those eyes. It was time to deflect the story onto her companion. 'Did you love him?' she asked.

'Him?'

'Your boyfriend?'

'What boyfriend?'

'You said you'd a broken . . .'

'And I 'ave.' He stopped, disengaged his arm. 'Listen, dear, I may wear suspenders and a bra, shave my legs, pull on a blond wig and wear more make-up than Ivana Trump, but I'm 100 per cent man, and I'm more than happy to prove it.'

Lisa bit her lip. 'Oh. I'm sorry. I just thought . . .'

'Yeah, well, y'know what thought did.' He grinned, struck a photo-shoot pose. 'I can see how you might get the wrong impression.' He reached across and prodded her arm gently. 'Basically I see myself as a slumming entertainer. Of course I belong on Broadway, blasting out one of the shows, but for now I'm just earning a living hamming it up for a bunch of boot-faced lesbians.'

Lisa laughed. They had been a bit tough. 'Do they know you're not gay?'

He winked. 'Well a couple of them do.'

'You . . .?'

'I'm ashamed to admit I sometimes play the gay card right up to the point where I get their knickers off.' He pulled camply at his lip. 'Shocked?'

'Not at all.'

They walked on along the beach for ten minutes, then flopped down into the sand. Alexis produced a four-pack of Budweiser from what appeared to Lisa to be a bottomless handbag and they supped quietly, relaxing to the weak pulse of the bay.

Alexis said quietly, 'It's lovely here, isn't it?'

'Beautiful.'

He began to trace an outline in the sand with his finger. 'Bet you wish he was here with you now.'

Lisa shook her head slowly. 'No. Not really.' She gave a little laugh. 'Silly, isn't it? You don't leave someone because things are going well. You leave because you've grown to hate them. Then you want them to experience this . . . beauty with you.'

'There's a thin line between love and hate, my girl.'

Lisa looked at the sand. Alexis had drawn a heart. There, in the moonlight, in full stage regalia, he looked like the most beautiful woman she had ever seen. Abruptly Lisa shivered. Maybe that girl Mona, in the bar, had been correct; maybe she had come here to Provincetown to get in touch with her true sexuality. That would be the joke of it; she would decide she was a lesbian and fall in love with a beautiful woman who was a man.

'So what was he like,' Alexis asked, 'this man of yours, before he became the man you love to hate?'

'I don't know what to say. He was . . . strange.'

'Well we all like a bit of strange. What're we talking here, a hump or a short leg or a long leg or a beard growing out of his arse?'

Lisa began to giggle. 'No! . . .'

'Was he a mental case then? Doo-lally?'

'Mmm. Not so sure on that front. He was just . . . Nathan.' She lay back, folding her arms behind her head, and stared up at the stars. 'He was very quiet. And sometimes very loud. He showed absolutely no consideration for me at all . . . apart from the times he showed all the consideration in the world. Sometimes he was the light at the end of the tunnel – distant, but hopeful; sometimes he was the tunnel, a thing to be fought through before you got to the light. He was funny and sad at the same time; he was very protective, very jealous – but not I think because of love for me, but because he had lost something in the past and was frightened the same would happen again. Yet he was so scared I would go out there and meet someone and not come back. He's so shy with people, so helpless in the wide world; I don't know if he could even survive by himself. Maybe that's why I feel so guilty. But I had to get away. I had to. I just miss him. It's only been a day and I miss him like a mother misses her child.'

Alexis nodded at her for a few moments. 'Jesus,' he said finally, 'was that from *Hamlet* or something?'

'I'm sorry . . .'

'Don't be! That was lovely! I haven't a clue what it all meant, but I feel like crying.'

'That's how Nathan got me. I always felt like crying. At first, because I loved him; then because I felt trapped; now because I feel guilty for leaving him. God, I hope he's all right.'

'He'll be fine, luv. We're all quite capable of surviving under our own steam. He may act dumb, but that's all it is. I expect your Nathan will be firmly on his feet soon enough. It's like someone who's been bedridden for so long, they can't walk because they haven't used their muscles. But chuck them out of the bed, they soon learn how to walk. Slow going. A bit painful. But good for them in the end. Your Nathan will do just fine.'

'You really think so?'

'I know so.'

'I hope you're right.' Lisa finished her can and began to bury it in the sand. 'At least part of me hopes you're right. The other half hopes he can't cope.'

'So that you can race back and mother him.'

'Yeah . . . well.'

Alexis passed her another can.

'So,' said Lisa, opening it up and flinching back from the spray, 'enough of my problems. What of yours. Who broke your heart?'

'Mind your own business.'

She chased him down the beach.

The alcohol struck about 4 AM. She woke, head spinning, room revolving, and was sick down the side of the bed. Then again. And again. She'd never been sick in her life on drink before and it scared her; the mess on the bed and floor scared her even more. In her drunken way she tried to mop it up with her hand. It fell through her fingers like, well, vomit. Then she over-reached and slipped out of the bed, landing on the floor with a thud and a squelch.

Alex, across the hall, sitting with his feet up on the dresser, sipping vodka and listening to Buddy Holly, had heard her being sick, but resolved to leave her be. The wig remained resolutely in place. But when he heard the thud he jumped up and hurried across the hall. He tapped lightly on Lisa's door, then, when there was no reply, a little louder. He pressed his ear against it and called softly to her. After a little he could just make out the faintest of sounds, little-girl sobs. He tried the handle. Unlocked. He slipped in, closed the door and turned the light on.

The poor girl was in a mess, half naked on the floor in a puddle of boke, looking up at him like a puppy that knows it's done wrong but can't do anything about it. He couldn't resist a little smile. 'You poor dear!' he said and bent to her.

'I'm sorry,' Lisa said.

'Don't you worry, girl, I'll soon have you sorted.'

He lifted her under one arm and carried her into the shower like a roll of carpet, although he hadn't carried many rolls of carpet into the shower before. On his way he lifted the wooden dresser stool with his free hand. He set it down in the cubicle, then manoeuvred her onto it.

'I'm sorry,' Lisa said.

He turned the water on, not too hot, not too cold. He stripped off the little of her nightshirt that still clung sweatily to her. Then he stuck his fingers down her throat and made her sick again and again; she fought him at first, but then gave in to it.

'It'll be okay,' Alex whispered repeatedly.

'I'm sorry,' said Lisa.

He kissed the top of her head, then left her in the steam for five minutes. She sat with her head in her hands and let the hot water drum down on her back. When he returned he wrapped her in a large pink bathtowel and patted her down. He walked her slowly back to her bed; she was conscious enough to notice that the sheets had been changed; the sick on the floor was gone as well. The carpet where it had been felt warm and soapy. 'I'm sorry,' she said.

'Never you mind, luv,' he said and helped her onto the bed.

He popped out of the room again but returned in a few moments with two big pint glasses filled with iced water.

'Here,' he said, 'get these down ya. They do say that coffee's a great thing to take when this happens, but personally I think it's a load of shite.'

Lisa shook her head, tried to push the glass away, but Alex persisted – and he was right; it did feel good.

When most of the first pint was gone, Lisa let out a great burp. She laughed. 'I'm sorry,' she said.

Alex put a finger to her lips. 'If you say that once more, girl, I swear, I'll deck ya.'

Lisa smiled meekly. He sat back on the bed beside her and she nestled down into his arms. He had, at least, removed the oversized inflatable breasts. He began to pat her hair. In a few minutes she was asleep.

Somewhere along the line they began to kiss. When Lisa glanced at the mirror she saw the two girl-heads together and it frightened her for a moment, but not so much that she desisted. Further along the line his hands began to massage her body. Right at the end of the line, he entered her.

Alex knew she was probably thinking of Nathan.

Lisa knew Alex knew.

Neither of them cared.

He began to speed up. Press deeper. He snuffled at her ear.

'Oh!' she said, then hugged him again. She whispered: 'I thought you said your heart was broken.'

'Aye, my heart is,' he said, 'but my cock's in fine form.'

9

The delight of George's Top Ten, and the reason why he'd maintained his interest in it all the way through high school, college and his work at the airport, was that it was constantly in a state of flux. If it had become stagnant it would have become boring and he would have trashed it; but it had assumed a beautiful life of its own, constantly changing with each broad demeaning slap of the nation's blackening hand. Every week brought a new transgression; an opinionated actor, politician or sportsman, every news broadcast could be relied upon to offend his delicate sensibilities and suddenly alter the composition of the chart. Myron Linklater, his supervisor at the airport, had entered the chart at number eight the previous week, but was only likely to hang in there for a little longer. Myron's mistake was to chastise George for a wrong call on the air traffic control monitor; George had been furious. He'd made the error, okay, but he sure wasn't going to take any grief for it from the likes of Myron Linklater. Myron was lucky. A saner nut would have stalked Myron and sorted it out with a carving knife; but George remained calm. He had bigger plans.

Half an hour after checking into the Montrose International Hotel, George had his modem plugged into the wall, he'd downloaded the right software, filled in his fake credit card details and was quite happily surfing the Web for the information he needed; what he couldn't find there he managed to locate with some rudimentary hacking; by the early evening most everything he required was in place. He had a detailed itinerary for the President's New York visit with timings right down to the very second; he had a list of invited guests; names and addresses of all the security staff, including two who would meet the President; and a run-down on which members of the press would be present. The press list was small – just one name. Magiform guarded its public image jealously and intimate access to these kinds of events was usually only granted to trusted media friends. On this occasion, with the limited size of the observation platform, the largely private nature of the President's visit and the number of recent assassination attempts on him, Magiform was able to justify the exclusion of the majority of the New York and national and international media. It would of course have its own video team on hand to record the event and release an edited version of the events shortly afterwards. Clark Fuller, a Reuters correspondent who'd written a flattering profile of Michael Tate in a recent issue of *Newsweek*, was 'chosen' from the pool.

George napped for a while, then showered and pulled on a pair of black jeans, a polo-neck sweater and a damson zip-up bomber jacket. It was time to check out New York for himself. He was pleased with his attitude: it would have been easy for him to accept the popular conception of New York in general and Manhattan in particular as the cesspit of the world, a stinking black hole of vice, corruption and disease; but he had to make his own mind up. It was too easy for people to be blinded by what they read in books; so after examining the New Testament for several minutes of inspiration, George left the hotel with a determined step and his interpretation of an open mind.

Thirty minutes later George was emotionally and physically drained. Everything he'd heard was right. The place was a hellhole. He hadn't felt such nausea since the last time he'd smashed up the 16th Street nigger shrine in Birmingham. It wasn't the fact that they were everywhere, it was the fact that they were everywhere and confident with it. It was as if they sensed his horror of it all. They seemed to crush in around him; their sweat clung to him, he gagged on their ghetto stench, they stared at him with their white eyes and dribbled past him with their hungry mouths; his eyes grew tired watching out for assault; his neck strained from the spastic jerks as he tried to walk with eyes alert to the front and back. In his mind he was tripped, pinched, poked; it was all he could do not to remove the Uzi submachine gun from inside his jacket and destroy them all; only the thought of wiping the inane grin off Keneally's face stayed him.

Leaning against a Barnes and Noble bookstore window, getting his breath back, he debated whether to return immediately to the hotel and conserve his anger or to press ahead. It came to him that to retreat now would be to deny his faith; to press on would in its own small way put him on a par with the great humanitarians of history, like Columbus and Cortez, carrying God's word to the sorry heathens.

He took a deep breath and pressed on towards Times Square, glowing in the dark ahead of him like a traffic sign to hell. Of its own accord George's top lip curled up in disgust as he walked along the cracked sidewalk; his hands, plunged firmly into pockets, stroked the outline of the Uzi. Neon sex winked at him from every second doorway. Black-bearded one-shoed *cunts* whispered their shopping list of drugs at every block. Fat cops with glistening nightsticks and bulging stomachs drank coffee from paper cups and laughed amongst themselves, ignoring the filth.

At the corner of 42nd Street George just caught the familiar strains of megaphone rhetoric. He was a past master of it himself. Glory be, he thought, some brave but deluded sucker thinks these worthless souls are worth saving.

He scurried through the midnight traffic towards the source. He could see a group of maybe twenty or thirty negroes standing in a half-moon shape.

'Take God into your soul! Take God into your house! For he is a white God, and he loves all you white children!'

George pushed through the group, suddenly determined to applaud this mighty preacher, confronting the dark hordes in their stronghold. As he reached the front he shouted, 'Praise the Lord!'

His jaw dropped.

General Hastings Bandana, leader of the Moravian Army of Christ and black as the African night, stood erect in full dress uniform; he looked impressive, or would have to a circus ringmaster. He had more medals than Audie Murphy, more stripes than a zebra. He held a wooden staff before him, ramming it down on the sidewalk to emphasize each fresh bellow into the megaphone he held in his other hand. He blinked at George for a moment, confused, then returned to the bad fight.

'Chil'un, he ain't no white God like the white devils tell us! Where was the Holy Garden of Eden? Why it was in Africa. What colour was the good Lord? Why he was a African too. Don't ever accept the word of no white man, brothers, for he don't know no better. He been crackin' the whip for so long, why he's gone and

forgotten all the true facts. He ever see a photo of the Good Lord? So howisit he can say that he's white? Take God into your soul – before the white devil takes it first! He gonna murder your mamma, he gonna murder your pappa! He gonna sell you crack! He gonna stick you in a ghetto!'

George tried to back into the crowd, but they'd closed ranks behind him. He could feel their hot breath on the back of his neck. Not lost souls at all, but dedicated followers. Someone behind him gave him a dedicated slap across the back of the head. George ducked forward.

General Bandana plunged the staff towards him. 'The white devil amongst us!' he yelled.

'The devil himself!' roared the crowd.

A stone hit George on the side of the face, and he knew immediately that they were out for blood. There were no stones in this part of Manhattan. It was a dirty, stinking, hole, but stones did not lie about like they did in the country. The stone that hit him was carried by someone who expected to use it, who had brought it into the centre of the city prepared to break someone's head in the name of the Lord.

George turned, faced them, checked for blood. A smear on the back of his hand. For a few moments they stared at him in angry silence, waiting for one of their number to make another move. The General, wanting to be out of the way when the stones started flying, stepped back onto the road. A cab screeched, avoided him by inches, sounded its horn. Flustered, the General dropped his megaphone. A collective howl went up from the crowd and they moved forward.

He had done nothing wrong, but they were preparing to kill him.

George removed the Uzi from his jacket. He pointed it a little over their heads and began to fire.

Panic stations.

Long before the gunfire had ended the crowd had dispersed in shrieking panic; automobiles crashed, neon crashed, screams of terror mixed with screams of pain as George, hardly thinking about it, dropped the Uzi to waist level towards the end of his volley of warning shots and the scowl on his face changed to a smile as he saw those least able to run at great speed fall to the ground, blood spurting from neat little holes in their legs.

But it was no time for *real* carnage. There was more important work. He slipped the gun back inside his jacket and started to run. Within a block he had reversed his jacket, white lining now to the fore, and ditched his polo-neck, he had turned corners, traversed alleys, lost himself in the easily pleased tourist crowds. He could hear sirens, but there was no chance of him being apprehended. He was a chameleon. He was Mr Camouflage. He had fought the Civil War all over again and this time the Confederacy had triumphed. *And not a soul injured*, thought George, *save for those already lost for all eternity*.

Triumph!

He did then what he hadn't done for a long time; he went to a bar.

George's wife hadn't liked him drinking because it made him bad-tempered.

10

George stayed in Pat Murphy's Broadway bar for a little under three hours. He drank beer. Spirits made his head revolve. He sipped with strength, like he was sucking blood through vampire teeth. After a while he realized that he had bitten his fingernails to the quick; as that dawned on him, he realized that his right leg was sore from constant jerking against the table. Adrenalin city. He had come through his second combat with flying colours; not only had he scattered the enemy, but he had beaten his retreat both unscathed and undetected. He was, truly, a mighty warrior. He fingered the Uzi again. He sucked on his beer and grinned. A woman, on her way to the ladies, smiled back. George nodded, a little embarrassed. He got to thinking about his wife. About the way she looked sometimes in the morning, emerging from the shower, her breasts heavy, her hips heavy, her hand heavy as she slapped him away for trying to paw her. What he would give now to have his hands on those breasts. To sneak into the shower with her, take her with all the animal passion he could muster. George wondered, not for the first time in his life, what it would be like to have sex with a black woman.

Not to romance. Not to date. Just to take. Force. Would she be different? Unrestrained? Would she fight him, or lie there and take it?

It was time for George to go. He knew he was too far gone: to even contemplate a black woman. He waited several minutes, toying with his empty glass, while his erection subsided.

Outside the streets were beginning to empty; the city that never sleeps was getting drowsy, but the harsh neon of Times Square still lit the night; an electric siren. Once again he was drawn to it, but it no longer seemed so scary. He had conquered his fear by scattering its unholy denizens following a pitched battle, now he could stride through it with the bravado of a conquistador.

Someone offered him some grass. George lashed out. The man tumbled into a gutter. *Yeah!*

George roared with laughter, but then got his feet mixed up; he stumbled, righted himself against a neon sign. He looked up. *Star World. Nude Girls! Live Models!* flashed at him. *Why not?* He ran his tongue over his upper teeth. *Why not indeed?* George mounted the stairs carefully; he knew he was drunk, and why not? It was in the glorious tradition: mighty warriors, triumphant in battle, always went out whoring afterwards. *Fucking the vanquished.* Not that he would *fuck*, too dangerous these days, but he would come fucking close. George giggled. At the top of the stairs a big fat guy, squeezed behind a table, gave him five tokens in exchange for his five dollars.

'Any black gals?' George asked.

Slim Dharkin thumbed up the narrow corridor. 'Most'em,' he said.

George nodded and moved between the rows of cubicles.

'Tips extra,' Dharkin called after him.

George slipped into a booth and closed the door. It stank of ammonia and billions of wasted sperm.

He fumbled the tokens. He bent to retrieve them, counted them back, one, two, three, four – damn it, five was stuck to the floor already. He peeled it off. *The world is surely filled with sick puppies*, he thought.

He slipped the tokens into the slot. The booth darkened, a little door about eye level slipped up and he peered into the cage. There were five or six girls reclining on chairs to his left. Another two stood at windows opposite him, servicing their clients. A white girl, plump, big-chested, raised herself wearily and moved towards his window. George shook his head, pointed to the seats. The white girl tutted, reversed. A black girl rose, equally wearily, and tottered across on her heels to the window. The erection sprang again in George's pants.

She wore a yellow bikini. Her stomach spilled out over the rim of her briefs. Her hair was long, straight, a wig. Her breasts were *pretty damn huge*. George stooped down to look up into her face. 'Hi,' he said. Her lipstick was blood red.

'Well hi there,' said the girl, 'I'm Cindy.' She smiled jaggedly and reached out her hand. He reached out his hand to shake it, but withdrew it when he saw her frown. 'Ten dollars,' she said.

'Oh,' said George. 'Sorry.'

'That's okay.'

'What do I get for that?' he flustered.

'Whatever you want, honey.'

She clicked her fingers. George whipped out his wallet. He slipped out a note – $20. He handed it over. He was surprised and a little exhilarated – he wasn't sure whether it was the girl or his erection dictating the pace. She took the note and crumpled it into a little purse which she pulled round from behind her, then swung it back out of sight.

'What you want then, honey?'

George took a deep breath. 'I always wanted to suck me a nigger tit. See if they taste any different.'

She undipped her bikini top. 'That's okay,' she cooed, guessing that George was no longer listening. 'I always wanted to be sucked by a white tit.'

He was, of course. *Sassy*, he thought. George reached gingerly through the window and cupped her left breast in his hand. He weighed it. He weighed the other one. He weighed them both at the same time. This surprised her a little; most everything she encountered was done single-handed.

He squeezed her nipples. They were long and brown, like long and brown nipples. She grimaced a little at this, although she was well used to it.

George lifted the left breast and slipped it into his mouth.

'Easy with those teeth, hon,' she said, and patted his head.

George felt a little dizzy. His tongue traced the outline of the nipple; his mouth closed upon it, sucked it into the back of his throat. So big, yet so soft. *Damn it*.

He let the tit flop out of his mouth. He stepped back. He spat on the floor of the booth. His face had turned suddenly from drunk floppy to hard nasty. 'You're an ugly big mama, aren't ya?'

The girl shrugged. 'You the one suckin' my titty, hon.'

'I ain't your *hon*, whore.'

'Please yourself.'

King of the sneers. George ran a hand across his brow. He was dripping. 'Look at you,' he spat, 'you're fat, you're ugly, and your tits are stretched from here to Alabama through

231

having dozens of bastard children suck off them. Tell me I'm right.'

'The customer is always right.'

'Oh you have a fine smooth way with the talk, you nigger-bitch.'

'I don't mind talking, hon, puts my night in just as quick as someone sucking on me.'

'You have a husband?'

'You have a wife?'

'Hey, I'm paying for this.'

'Complain to the manager, hon.' She put a hand on her hip. Then she lifted a leg and pulled the crotch of her bikini briefs out to show him the dark line within. His eyes dropped to it. 'Let's just put you straight.' George looked up again. 'I don't mind if you stick your arm half-way up my pussy, don't care if yo' shoot yo' stuff right all over me, but don't think for one moment I'm gonna answer personal questions to some cheap bastard john like you.'

'Fair enough,' said George.

''Less you wanna give me another thirty dollars and I'll tell you what my guy does with his big cock.'

'Why do you think I'd want to know about someone's cock?'

The girl shrugged. 'I dunno. Just the look of you, hon.'

'Meaning what?'

'Nothing.' She glanced up at the wall above him. There would be a clock there.

'No, I want to know what you mean. Are you trying to imply that I might be a faggot?'

'Trying?' the girl laughed. 'Implying? Hon, I don't care which way you turn, you paid me, you can do whatever the hell you like. All I'm sayin' is it's a matter of some personal pride that I don't think there's been a man in the last three years hasn't shot his stuff during his time with me. I kinda notice you ain't so much as unzipped. You know there's booths with just men in them further on down. Maybe you wanna . . .'

'I ain't no god-damn fucking faggot, you evil-mouthed whore.'

'Talk dirty to me, baby. Tell me what you really want to do. Your time's running down.'

George gripped the edge of the booth. 'I wanna fuck you till you bleed.'

'Can't do it in there, hon, what else you wanna do?'

'I want to ram it in your mouth till you gag.'

'Can't do that either, hon. Any action down there yet, hon?'

There was action okay. George had it out. There was a dull thudding sound against the side of the booth. 'You need to get the Lord inta your life, girl,' George panted.

'I feel him move inside me already, hon.'

'You need the Lord in your life, girl!'

'I feel him!'

'You need sweet Jesus Christ to save your soul!'

'I need him!'

'You need the laying on of the hands!'

'I want them, hon, I want them now!'

'Good God Jesus!'

'That's it, baby!'

'Gimme a titty!'

'I'm coming baby!'

She thrust her breast back through the window. George suckled greedily. *Beat. Beat. Beat.*

As he began to ejaculate George bit down. Hard.

The girl screamed.

Hard.

Harder.

He tasted blood.

She was beating at him. Screaming. He tugged. He tore.

He finished ejaculating. The other girls rushed to his window, trying to punch him.

With one mighty rip he tore the nipple from her breast. She fainted.

He rezipped. He chewed. He opened the cubicle door. Slim Dharkin was hurrying along the corridor, checking each booth to see where the screams were coming from. Other customers, scared, curious, were emerging from their booths at the same time. Slim beat at them as they appeared, anxious to nail the offender. They ducked, fled.

George walked at Slim. Slim stopped. George let his jacket hang open to reveal the Uzi. 'You gotta problem?' George asked. He swallowed the nipple.

With the lights so dim Slim couldn't see that it was an Uzi, but he quickly registered that it was some sort of a weapon, and whatever sort of a weapon it was, it was of a greater calibre than his fat fists. 'No problem,' he said. He saw a trickle of blood running from the side of George's mouth. Above the disco music he could hear one of the girls screaming. *'Get the paramedics! Get an ambulance! Christ!'*

George marched past him and hurried down the steps. In a few moments he was back out onto the Square. He walked quickly back to his hotel. He was a little more sober now, a little more wary. As always after a sexual experience he felt a mixture of emptiness and guilt. Half of him thought he had compromised the racial beliefs that ran to the very core of his being; the other half argued this wasn't so, that he had had a meaningless sexual encounter with a black whore with the sole purpose of finding out what it was like; he could now argue his beliefs based on actual experience. He knew that others, more hard-line than himself, would taunt him about it if they ever found out, that far from being a good WAR-monger he harboured a secret passion for dark women. George nodded to himself as he walked. They could say what they wanted, but he knew where his passions lay, and the fact that he had eaten part of her surely proved that if anything his taste in women remained very much on the correct side of the Mason-Dixon line.

11

President Keneally hit the floor. His heart was about to explode. His fingers grabbed at the carpet, the nails dug in, trying to hold on. It was no use. He was slipping away.

Tara walked barefoot towards Graham Slovenski's room. It was only a hundred yards, a flight of steps, but every step felt like a mile; the fear of being seen, the fear of what she was about to do. She hugged the shadows; she hugged herself. Twice she stopped, twice she nearly turned back, but then that gnawing feeling in her groin pushed her on. It wasn't lust, she reassured herself, it was duty. She must do this. For herself. For her husband. For America.

'I had a dream.'

'No, Mr President,' said Slo. '*I have* a dream.'

'What are you talking about?'

'Martin Luther King. *I have a dream.*'

'Slo. I'm telling you I had a dream.' The President, reclining in striped boxer shorts on the king-sized bed in the Boston Four Seasons, twisted the phone flex around his hand, then reached across to the bedside cabinet with some difficulty and lifted a can of Diet Pepsi. He slurped, spilt a little, burped. 'I'm sorry,' he said, 'where was I?'

'You had a dream, Mr President.'

'Yes. Of course. Slo?'

'Yes, Mr President?'

'You don't mind me calling you at this time of the morning, do you?'

'No, sir. What else would I be doing?'

'Is that sarcasm?'

'No, sir. What else *would* I be doing?'

'You have a wife, family.'

'So do you, sir.'

'Fair point. And what joys they are. What a pity neither of us are with them. How is Miranda?'

'She's fine. Thank you.'

'It doesn't annoy you that I sound off like this?'

'No, sir, if it helps you, it's fine by me.'

'Half the world goes to see a therapist. What would it do to Wall Street if it got out that the President was in therapy?'

'It would not help the state of the nation.'

'It's a strange word.'

'World?'

'Word.'

'Uhuh? Which one? State or nation?'

'Therapist.'

'Sir?'

'*The rapist*. Is that where it comes from, do you think?'

'I don't know, I hadn't thought about it.'

'I'll bet it is. The rapist. He fucks your mind. Do you think I need therapy, Slo?'

'No, sir. You need a friend.'

'That's nice. Do you know any?'

'Very funny, Mr President.'

'I had this dream. I was being carried through the sky by a gigantic bird. Huge, skeletal . . . maybe it was a lizard. It had wings, anyway. And talons, and they were digging into me, I was bleeding and we were getting higher and higher. We were above New York . . . I could see the Statue of Liberty waving up . . . and then the lizard thing looked round and it didn't have a lizard head at all . . . it was Tara, and she smiled this really cruel smile and said, "Thanks for the coconuts," then dropped me and I just fell down and down and down . . . and then I woke up on the floor.'

'And you're okay?'

'I'm fine. But I have these coconuts and I've no idea where they came from.'

'Sir?'

'Of course I don't! But a strange dream. What would a therapist make from that?'

'About five hundred dollars, Mr President.'

'Good point!'

'You should get some sleep. You've another busy day ahead of you.'

'They're all busy, Slo. But sure, I know, if you can't stand the heat. I miss Tara, y'know.'

'I know that.'

'When do you leave for Dublin?'

'You mean Belfast.'

'Belfast. Yes.'

'That's tomorrow, sir. About eleven.'

'Look after her, Slo. Tell her I love her.'

'You should tell her yourself.'

'I tried. She's not taking calls. Or *my* calls at any rate.'

'I'll tell her. Don't worry. Everything will be okay.'

'Okay, Slo, thanks, 'bye.'

'Goodbye, Mr President.'

Slo replaced the receiver. He looked up at Tara, rocking gently on the end of his bed. Her hair was pulled back off her face. Her nightdress was pink and would have been transparent in a good light. She had a bottle of wine in her hand.

'I'm sorry,' Tara said, 'that must have been embarrassing for you.'

'I've had better moments,' said Slo. She was drunk. His pyjamas were stuck to him.

'Join me in a drink, Slo.'

For the third time he said: 'No. Tara. It's too late. Too early.'

She tutted. Maybe she'd been wrong. Maybe he didn't find her attractive.

'You should lock your door,' she said.

'This is the White House.'

'You should lock your door, nevertheless.'

'I know. Still, as prowlers go . . . uhm.'

'Slo. Were you edging towards a compliment there?'

Slovenski shifted his legs with some difficulty. Tara's position on the quilt effectively stopped him from moving more than a few inches.

'Did anyone see you come in here?'

'Do you care?'

'We should both care.'

'Is the First Lady not allowed to consult the Chief of Staff?'

'Not at 6.35 AM in a see-through pink negligee.'

'Slo?'

'Uhuh?'

'How do you know it's see-through?'

'Because I'm not blind.'

'A better man might have avoided looking at all. But now that you have, what do you think?'

'I think you shouldn't be in here.'

'Of what you saw.'

'Tara, that's not fair.'

'Nevertheless.'

'Tara. Please. You should go.'

She gave him a long, lingering look. *Now, now, now, now. Do it! Climb in beside him! Make love! Fuck him! Twins on the way!* Tara slowly raised herself from the bed. As she stood the light from his bedside table caught her nightdress and he was able to see her properly for the first time. For a few moments he was mesmerized; he was the rabbit caught in headlights. She saw that he saw. He knew that it was her intention.

Tara moved up the bed towards him. 'I'm sorry,' she said softly. 'I just needed to talk. You're right. It's not a good time. We'll talk in Ireland, okay?'

'Okay,' he whispered.

She leaned over the bed. Her lips brushed his cheek. He smelt perfume, wine. A breast, a nipple, pressing against flimsy material, touched his arm.

Then she was gone, gliding across the room.

She couldn't do it. Not here, not in the White House. Not in their *home*. In Ireland. Yes, in Ireland. When there was an ocean between her and the President. She would get him then.

Tara lingered for a few moments by the door, checking that the coast was clear, then slipped out. She raced along the hall, up the stairs, not caring for one moment about shadows and security. *So close, so god-damn close!*

Slovenski collapsed back on the pillow. He puffed out his cheeks. Blew out the air. His heart was racing. He was soaked through. He threw back the covers. He shook his head violently from side to side.

It had been a dream. A fantasy. He punched the pillow.

Slovenski rolled out of bed. He took a deep breath. He unbuttoned his pyjama jacket as he padded across to the bathroom. He switched the light on and ran a hand through his matted hair as he peed. He flushed, washed his hands. When he looked at his groggy visage in the mirror he could see quite clearly the lipstick kiss on his left cheek.

12

The rapist?

The breadth of a continent away, the same thought passed through the mind of Michael Tate as he strolled into the office of John Smedlin, his therapist. The billionaire wore his Batman sweatshirt. The knees of his jeans were frayed. Smedlin indicated a leather chair. *If it's rape,* Tate thought, *how come I enjoy it so much?*

Smedlin smiled benignly, then sneezed. 'Sorry,' he said, 'I've been trying to shake this cold for a month.'

Tate nodded. 'That's my next project. A cure for the common cold.'

'Can I buy shares in that?'

'No.'

Smedlin nodded, then consulted a file resting in his lap.

'So,' he said, 'how have we been?'

'*We?*'

He half-raised a weary eyebrow. 'So,' he said, 'it's going to be one of those days. What's wrong, Michael?'

Tate shrugged. 'I feel . . . *uncomfortable.*'

'Uncomfortable with the chair, or with being here?'

242

'The chair, mostly.'

'It cost me a thousand bucks. What's wrong with it?'

'It's hard. It doesn't *groove.*'

'Is that it?'

'And I don't like the thought of all the loons who might have dribbled over it.'

'You're calling my patients loons.'

'Are they not?'

'Some. Maybe. What does that make you?'

'I don't think I'm a loon. Do you?'

'That depends how you define loon. How would you define it? Besides the drooling?'

'Someone who babbles incessantly. Unwashed. Someone who adds two and two and gets a horse.'

'But not someone who thinks he can take over the world?'

'But *I can* take over the world.'

'Is amassing money the same as taking over the world? Don't world leaders have to be voted in?'

'Possibly.'

'Possibly? What are you suggesting, Michael, seizing power?'

'Not seizing.'

'Even Hitler was voted in.'

'Are you comparing me to Hitler?'

'Would you be annoyed by that comparison?'

'I don't know. I mean, obviously yes, to the wars and camps and all that; but you've got to admire the man on an organizational level. And without so much as a floppy.'

'So,' Smedlin said, making a note, *'admires Hitler.'*

'I'd prefer if you didn't write that down.'

'I'm sure you would.'

'Listen, who pays the bills around here?'

'You do, Michael.' He lifted his pen again. *'But won't admit it.* Satisfied?'

'No.'

'How long have you been coming to see me, Michael?'

'In Earth years?'

'Yes. Earth years.'

'Sixteen.'

'Sixteen years. Yes. And in all that time you've sat on that chair, how come this is the first time you've mentioned *my* loons.'

'I wanted to get to know you first.'

'What is it about them you don't like?'

'Unpredictability.'

'Name a loon.'

'What, in history?'

'No, you've met.'

Tate sat back for the first time. His eyes seemed to get a faraway look for a moment, but he quickly blinked back to reality.

'I'd rather not.'

'Michael.'

'I know what you're playing at. You want me to talk about *that* again.'

'As the single most formative experience of your teenage years, I think it does you good to talk about it.'

'I think you get a kick out of it.'

'Michael, you obviously think it does you good too. Or you wouldn't keep coming back.'

'I might just like your company.'

'Most companies you like, you buy. I'm not for sale.'

Tate nodded.

'You were in the park,' Smedlin began, 'and . . .'

'A coupla guys got me into the bushes and abused me. But I don't blame them, I blame my pop for leaving me in the park while he went for a beer. And from that day

I became an introverted loner, lived only through my computers, became a fucking computer genius, set up a company in my yard, became a millionaire, then billionaire and now I'm the most powerful man in the world, almost. So I should really thank my pop for abandoning me in the park and those loons for jacking me off, otherwise I'd be stacking shelves in the neighbourhood Seven-Eleven.' Tate fake-yawned. 'There you go.'

'Succinctly put. But you never mentioned jacking off, before.'

'Yes I did.'

'No you didn't. You really didn't. But don't worry, it's fine.'

'Fine?'

'It puts the other thing in perspective.'

'What other thing?'

'Buying the Empire State Building.'

'Excuse me, but what tangent did that come in on?'

'You don't see the connection? Michael, come on. You've just admitted for the first time that you were jacked off in the bushes – which means that you had an erection. And now you're compensating for it by buying the Empire State Building, which is the biggest erection money can buy. You see that, don't you?'

Tate pulled at his bottom lip. 'Let me get this straight. The reason I bought the Empire State Building is not that it became available at an extremely good price or will be an asset to my business or is one of the wonders of the world, but because I was manipulated by loons to the point that I got an erection?'

'Exactly!'

They sat and looked at each other for several long moments. Then Tate said: 'And I pay you for this crock of shit?'

13

The President took certain things with him everywhere. The Secret Service to protect him. Fred Troy for extra special protection. Direct access to vast arrays of nuclear arms to protect democracy and the American way of life. His wife, quite often. And almost always an inflatable globe.

The biggest problem, he found, was getting an inflatable globe that was bang up to date. Nations fragmented so often that it was next to impossible to obtain one which was not hopelessly behind the times. He had resolved on several occasions to take up his problem with the Inflatable Globe Manufacturers of America Association, if only it existed. Last thing at night when he was on tour, and occasionally when he was in the White House, and then only when he could get enough breath for Tara laughing at him and he giggling away too, he would inflate the globe and study it. He was, without argument, the most powerful man in the world. And it was his job to fill that world with as much hot air as he possibly could.

The President, still in his boxers, twirled the globe in his hands. He threw it up into the air, then kept it aloft with little punches.

'Belo-Russia,' he sang. 'The Independent People's Republic of Moravia. The Basque Republic.'

He was beginning to have misgivings about not bringing Slo with him on this trip. He missed the company, he missed the advice. The rest of them were yes-men and bullshitters. Policy advisers, communications directors, speechwriters, pollsters, media advisers. Bullshit! Slo had sounded a little odd on the phone: strained, maybe; sulking, possibly. Maybe he'd pushed things a bit far, forcing him to go with Tara to Dublin. Or Belfast. He would give him some time off. Tell him to go on a holiday. A real holiday. Maybe he could stay in Ireland that little bit longer. He could arrange for Slo's wife and family to join them. As he punched the globe again it gave a sudden hiss and shot across the room.

The President called Fred Troy. 'Troy. How are you?'

'Ever vigilant.'

'That's reassuring.'

'Thank you, Mr President.'

'Do you sleep standing up, Troy?'

'No sir. I don't need much rest. Like America, I have a great constitution.'

'You're a source of constant reassurance, Troy. I should promote you.'

'Thank you, sir.'

'It struck me I haven't been told anything about this assassin. Last I heard he'd escaped and was heading my way, then he pops up on *Oprah*. Has he been picked up yet?'

'No, sir, he's pretty much dropped from sight, Mr President. But he'll resurface. They always do.'

'That's what worries me, Troy. I wouldn't like him to resurface under my very eyes. Remember Yitzhak Rabin.'

'Absolutely no chance of that, sir.'

'Tell me he's just a redneck and I don't have to worry.'

'Sir, I could tell you that, but I don't like to lie. If he's smart enough to tap into Oprah's telephone system from a remote location, by-passing 50,000 other calls in the process, then he's smart enough to worry about.'

'Well that's not very reassuring. But honest. Tell me about New York.'

'I foresee no problems in the United Nations. I'll be working closely with James Morton from our New York office. The Empire State Building, as you know from my report, sir, poses a very real security risk.'

'Mmmm,' said the President.

'As you will recall,' said Troy, catching on, 'I'm not happy. Something happens up there, there's no way out. No escape route.'

'But Troy, it's up to you to ensure that nothing happens.'

'Yes, sir, I know, sir. Nevertheless, the reduction of risk is what this game is all about.'

'You think it's a game, Troy?'

'No, sir! Euphemism, sir!'

'Okay. Relax. I'm sure you'll cover all eventualities.'

'I'll do my very best, sir. In fact I'm going up to New York this morning myself to check it out.'

'You mean you're leaving me to fend for myself.'

'You are in safe hands, Mr President.'

'That's what they told Yitzhak.' He put the receiver down. Then he lifted it again and called Tara. He felt alone. He needed a hug.

There was no response.

14

Sam had planned on a long lie-in. All that business at work, the strike vote, the stand-off, the capitulation by the new owners, well, it would take it out of any man, let alone an old fella like him. He'd the day off and he intended lying in bed watching the TV until lunchtime, and then maybe he'd do more of the same in the afternoon. Then up to the Cedar Home for a visit.

It was one of those humid Manhattan nightmare days and his head was bad. He sipped a Coke, swallowed a handful of aspirin. The weather was part of it, the wedge of B-52 bomber didn't help, but the business at work was most of it. He should have been triumphant; the guys had backed him, he was going to meet the President; management hadn't even said another word about his retirement. Leonard had returned with a big smile on his face. *Okay, lads, it's okay. I spoke to Mr levers. He's agreed that Sam can meet the President, and all other matters will be reviewed after the visit.* Simple as that. But it wasn't as simple as that, and Sam knew it; he had felt uncomfortable with the confrontation and guilty about risking everyone's jobs; now he felt a sense of foreboding. He was old enough and wise enough to realize that that wouldn't be the end of it, that managements, even supposedly enlightened managements like Magiform, didn't just cave in like that. Everything that should have smelt of. roses smelt of shit.

The phone rang at a little after nine. Sam had an extension beside the bed, but it still took him a couple of minutes to creak over to it.

A warm voice. 'Oh hello, Mr McClintock. My name's Clark Fuller and I work for Reuters – you know Reuters okay?'

'Sure,' said Sam.

'Okay. I'm covering the presidential visit to the Empire State Building on Friday, and I understand you're one of the employees who'll be looking after him.'

Sam laughed into the mouthpiece. 'Yeah. Sure.'

'I'm writing a feature article on the visit for national syndication, and I just wanted to get a few background details on you. Y'know, how long you've worked there, any experiences there, y'know the kind of thing.'

'Sure. Where'd you get my number?'

'Ahm – Walter levers, is it? At the Empire. Said you were the man to talk to for background. A wealth of experience, he said. Mr Empire, he said. You don't mind me calling, do you?'

'No. I'm just feeling a little . . .'

'Walter levers was telling me your wife has been in hospital for some time.'

'Was he?'

'And that you'd applied to the company for a loan to cover increased medical bills?'

'Did he now? That was nice of him.'

'Sorry. He stressed the confidentiality of it, but he was thinking of you . . . he was suggesting that if I wanted to interview you I – or Reuters – might want to make a contribution to those medical bills.'

'How much would we be talking about?'

'I'd have to check it out. A couple of thousand maybe, for North American rights, anyway. More if it goes international. What I'd like to do is get your story now, over the phone, and then we can tie up any loose ends on Friday when I'm there covering the President's visit. Is that okay?'

Of course it was okay. Sam didn't need to be paid to recall the old days at the Empire but it certainly helped; chatting to Fuller was no problem either; he seemed genuinely interested in what he had to say, and that was a nice change.

An hour later, in the Montrose International Hotel, George Burley replaced the receiver. Things were shaping up very well indeed.

15

Lisa, bags packed, was on the move. Or trying to be. She sat in the sun at Provincetown harbour waiting for the Boston ferry. A few hours up the coast and she'd be back in a big city. A job. A new apartment. A new life. Her head throbbed with hangover, with dehydration, with guilt. She wanted to phone Nathan and apologize to him: not for running away, not for sleeping with someone, but for running away and sleeping with someone and enjoying it. She'd probably leave out the bit about him wearing a slinky cocktail dress and a blond wig.

It was something she'd had to do. Only by sleeping with someone could she break the ties to Nathan. The spell was now broken. She could go out into the world and begin to enjoy it again. She could look for a man who would allow her to be herself. Who wouldn't box her in. She could *choose* a man who didn't drink, who didn't fly into a rage, who wouldn't humiliate her in public. She could choose a woman, if she wanted. That's how free she was. Nothing and no one would ever interfere with her life and how she wanted to live it again.

She'd an hour to kill. She'd bought a tuna sandwich, but she couldn't eat it. She tore strips off and tossed it to the gulls. Crowds were already beginning to form up for the whale watch cruises. The yitter and yelp of excited kids and the frustrated bark of camera-heavy parents wasn't helping her head. She sipped on a bottle of Evian water and half-closed her eyes against the sun. She counted off in her mind all the reasons she hated Nathan. She quit at twenty-three. Then she totted up all the reasons she loved him. Just the one. *He's Nathan.* And she had the bruises – although accidental, she conceded – to prove it.

She shifted slightly as a man sat down beside her. She half-nodded at him, but he ignored her. He unfolded a *Boston Globe* and began to study the front page. Lisa looked at her watch. Still three-quarters of an hour before boarding even started. She gazed out beyond the harbour to the sea: it didn't look particularly rough, but the way she was feeling it didn't need to be. The merest lap of insignificant wave on steel hull and she'd be throwing her guts up. She threw the remains of the tuna sandwich away in a single lump. The gulls descended on it with glee.

The man beside her lowered his paper. 'That was a bit of a waste, luv,' he said.

Lisa tutted. 'I can throw it away if I bloody . . . oh.' She lowered her blazing eyes. 'Alexis. Alex,' she said weakly.

He looked at her. His gaze was cool, emotionless.

'It . . . is you, isn't it?' she ventured.

She studied his face: to be sure it was him, and then for some reaction. Dark-stubbled angled chin, blue-blue eyes, hair short, straight, high cheekbones. He really was astonishingly handsome.

He gave a slight nod. 'I know. Didn't recognize me without my clothes on.'

'God,' said Lisa.

Alex shrugged. 'Where I come from it's polite to say cheerio.'

Lisa bit at a lip. Her hand dropped onto his knee. 'I'm so sorry,' she said. 'I just panicked. It's not you . . . God, there's just so much going on in my head.'

'And quite a lot in your bed.'

'Oh God . . . what a horrible thing to do. I'm sorry. You must feel . . . I don't know what you must feel. What do you feel?'

'Hung over, mate, hung over.' He took her hand. 'Listen, cock, I've been round the block a few times. I know not to get upset when a girl runs out on me. We had a ball. You had two. Who's complaining?'

Lisa took a deep breath. She smiled up into his face. 'You are *so* nice.'

'What can I say? You're not so bad yourself.'

They grinned at each other.

'You're off to Boston?'

Lisa nodded. 'That's the idea.'

'When's it go, luv?'

She shrugged. 'Forty, forty-five.'

'Good.' He stood, then pulled her up after him. 'I know where we can get the perfect hangover cure. C'mon.'

She resisted for just a few steps. Then she bent and picked up her bag and allowed him to drag her along.

They sat at a table in the Governor Bradford. 'From here you can see if the ferry's about to leave,' Alex said, 'if you've x-ray vision.'

Lisa picked up her glass and looked at it doubtfully. 'This is what they call a hair of the dog.'

Alex shook his head. 'Me, I can't stand dogs. I prefer to

think of it as a furball of the cat.' He showed Lisa his teeth and let out a little feline hiss. He raised his glass. 'Here's to ya, kid, and may all your troubles be little ones.'

Lisa clamped a hand over her mouth. 'Oh God, don't say that.'

Alex laughed and emptied his glass in one. Lisa followed suit. She nearly threw it back up. 'Jesus Christ,' she gasped, 'what was in that?'

'Don't ask, kiddo!' Alex boomed.

Myth or no, half an hour later she did feel better. They got some proper drinks. She . . . Jesus, *he* started telling her about his life on the road as a struggling young performer up and down the motorways of Britain, a depressing, hungry existence if ever there was one. And then the break for America and the depressing, hungry existence pounding the highways here. He painted an idyllic picture of summers in Provincetown and tough winters in New York trying to make it on Broadway. But he kept her laughing right through and before she knew it two hours had passed, she was half pissed again, the ferry had long gone and she really didn't want to leave his company.

He carried her bag back to the Elephant Strides and she took her old room again. He watched her unpack. Then he undressed her and took her to bed. They made raucous love. Just before she reached orgasm she opened her eyes, turned her head to the left and watched him make love to her in the mirror. But when she came, grinding her nails into his back, her legs clamped so tight about him, it was not his name that she shouted.

Alex lay back on the bed, breathing hard. She closed her eyes.

'I'm sorry,' she said.

'You spend your life apologizing to me.'

'I know. What a bitch.'

'He must be sensational in bed.'

Lisa shook her head. 'No, he's not. *You're* sensational.'

'So all I have to do is change my name to Nathan and we'll be flying.'

'Oh God. I don't know what came over me.'

And they both roared at that.

'If I go to sleep now,' Alex said after they'd been quiet for a little while, 'will you be here when I wake up?'

Lisa nodded. 'I'm not going anywhere. Not for a while.'

16

They felt sorry for Nathan, but it was more than that. You can feel sorry for a psycho or an alcoholic or a bore, but you wouldn't necessarily want them to stay in your house. They had debated it briefly.

'We could just dump him out on his ass,' said Lucy.

'Tell him to go and annoy someone else.'

'Tell him to take his miserable face and stick it down the toilet.'

'But we won't.'

'Of course not.'

'Because he's a colleague, maybe a friend, and he's down and he needs help.'

'He needs friends. He's been dumped on from a great height. We'll look after him until he's on his feet. We'll even buy him new feet.'

'Because that's the sort of guys we are.'

'Caring.'

Lucy pushed a strand of hair from her face. 'He saw me coming out of your room last night.'

'Oh.'

'Naked as the day I was born.'

'Oh.'

'He didn't mention it at breakfast.'

'What could he say? Great tits?'

'He seemed a little embarrassed.'

'He always seems a little embarrassed. What does he know, anyway – you could have been borrowing something.'

Lucy nodded, unconvinced. 'So we'll keep him,' she said. 'For a while.'

Nathan got hold of a new uniform, Brian lent him some of his own clothes, Lucy bought him some fresh underwear, then visited a thrift store and came back with gear every bit as good as what he'd lost. They scrounged together a couple of hundred dollars cash, just so as he wasn't asking them for a hand-out every half-hour.

When Nathan was dozing on the couch, Lucy nodded at him from the kitchen. 'He is nice, isn't he?' she said, handing her brother another dish to dry.

'He's okay.'

'He's so helpless. It's like having a puppy about the place.'

Brian laughed. 'Funny, isn't it? We're not allowed animals in the apartments, yet we could have Charlie Manson staying here and we wouldn't hear a peep until he produced his pet cat.'

Later Lucy made a salad and Brian and Nathan popped out to the deli for some extras. They returned with four bottles of wine. The salad was wolfed down, they lingered over the wine. It was all very congenial.

'You know,' Nathan said, 'I'm quite jealous of you.' He was looking at Brian, but for a second Lucy was worried that he was going to talk about her. She'd caught his admiring glances several times already. Caught them, juggled them, tossed them back with aplomb. 'Getting to meet the President.'

'*Meet* is hardly the word. I'll be in the background watching out for snipers.'

'Sure it's something to tell your kids, isn't it?'

'And I'd love it too,' said Lucy, 'to be that close to him. Just to be able to reach out and touch him.'

'What would you want to do that for?' Brian asked.

Lucy shrugged. 'I think he's lovely.'

'You'd get arrested for it,' said Brian. 'I saw some of those guys downstairs today. Like orang-utans in suits. They'd have you down on the ground with your arms broken the moment you made a move.'

Lucy gave a little laugh. 'Well, timing would be everything.'

'If he says hello to me,' Brian said, 'I'll say hello back. I'll let Sam do all the talking.'

'Who is this Sam?' Lucy asked.

'I think he helped build the Empire,' said Brian. 'He's worked there all his life. You ought to see him walking down the street, he's got one of those shaky walks people who've spent too long in elevators get.'

'That's old age,' said Nathan.

'Old age and elevator legs both.' Brian began to pour another round of drinks. 'Sam's okay. He's just one of those cantankerous old guys who's been there so long he thinks he owns the place. Everyone's too scared to say something to him in case he drops down dead. And that's just exactly the thing that'll happen. He'll say "Good morning, Mr President," and topple over. Then the Secret Service will check him for unexploded bombs before throwing him over the side.'

'Ach, he's okay,' said Nathan. 'I'd be cantankerous if I was staring death in the face.'

'You *were* staring death in the face,' said Lucy. 'Tell us all about *her.*'

Nathan blushed. 'I'd rather not.'

'Bullshit!' laughed Lucy. 'Give us the dirt!'

Nathan took a big gulp of his wine. 'There are some things in this life I'd prefer to forget. That's one of them.'

'Weren't you turned on at all?'

'Lucy!' said Brian.

'Lucy nothing – did you get an erection?'

Nathan held her gaze. 'It was the least sexual thing that has happened to me in a long time.'

Later, Brian was so legless they had to help him to bed. He flopped onto the top sheet face down like he'd been shot.

Lucy and Nathan stood in the doorway looking at him for a few moments.

Lucy said, 'He doesn't usually drink.'

Nathan smiled. 'He did well for an amateur. What about you?'

'Pacing,' said Lucy, 'is the name of the game.'

Nathan turned from the door and returned to the lounge. He sat on the three-seater that had been his bed for the past few days. Lucy followed him, lifted the TV control from the floor, staggered slightly, then flicked the channel from ESPN to MTV. Then she sat on the floor in front of him, facing the screen; as she leaned back Nathan opened his legs and she rested between them, her back against the seat.

'You don't enjoy the boxing as much as Brian, do you?' Nathan said.

'Does anyone?'

'He doesn't strike me as having much of a social life,' Nathan said.

'He does okay.'

'No girlfriend?'

'Not at the moment. A bit like you.'

'New York's a lonely place without a girlfriend.'

'Is that a chat-up line?'

'No,' said Nathan, glad that she couldn't see him blush, 'an observation.'

She turned, she saw the blush. 'Well why isn't it a chat-up line?'

'Well . . .'

She leaned her elbows on his knees, dropped her arms and rested her chin on them. For the first time he smelt her perfume; very faintly, but very obviously Gio. Lisa wore Gio. Maybe half the world wore Gio, but there and then it was Lisa. She was prettier than Lisa, just; she looked a little more cunning, just. Really, they were remarkably similar. He could almost close his eyes and pretend.

'Don't tell me you've been turned off women, have you?'

'No.'

'Not being dumped by your girlfriend in the most callous fashion?'

'No.'

'Not being tied to a bed and whipped?'

'No.'

'Well why isn't it a chat-up line, then?'

Nathan shrugged. The thought had entered his head, but just in the dreamily unambitious way of a man lacking in self-confidence. Then he yawned.

'Well thanks,' said Lucy.

'Sorry. Nothing personal.'

She smiled, then fake-yawned herself. 'I know. It's getting late. You've work in the morning. So have I.'

She pushed herself back from Nathan's knees, began to get up, then stopped. She dropped her head, then looked coyly up from beneath her fringe. 'You never did tell me what you thought the other night. When you saw me naked. Touched my breast.'

'Well,' said Nathan. 'What can I say?'

'Whatever you want.'

'You were very nice.'

'Nice?'

He bit his lip. 'I'm sorry. That's not the right word.'

She smiled. 'You're just as bad as Brian. You don't say what you really think.'

Nathan shrugged. 'I am what I am.'

'I know. Maybe it's me. I'm very honest. I always have been. I say what I feel, I feel what I say.'

'Well . . . that's admirable.'

'Is it? It doesn't leave a lot of space for the subtleties of life. For example, I could tell you right now that I find you exceedingly attractive. It would be honest, but it would probably scare you half to death. On the other hand with you being so quiet it might take six months for you to realize what I feel, and then you might turn me down anyway. I'm caught between a rock and a hard place.'

'I'm not as bad as all that.'

'Aren't you?'

'Is that how I seem?'

Lucy nodded.

'I've never thought about it,' Nathan said.

'Perhaps you should.'

'You can't change what you are.'

'Yes you can, look at Cher.'

'That's physical; I'm talking mental.'

'Mental too, she reinvented herself. Didn't you see *What's Love Got to Do with It?*'

'That was Tina Turner.'

'Same difference.'

'The point is,' Nathan said, 'I don't think you know me well enough to be advising me on changing my whole outlook on life.'

She stood. 'I think I do.'

'You're a quick judge of character.'

'One of my many talents.'

And there was a sparkle in her eyes which reminded him of Lisa. *Too close for comfort.* 'What're the others?'

She put a finger to her lips, thought for a moment. 'Well, I can cook a mean steak. I can recite the national anthem backwards. I give wonderful blow-jobs.'

They fixed gazes.

'You must fix me a steak some time.'

'I might even sing to you, one time.'

They smiled. Nathan nodded his head slightly. 'How do you know?'

'How do I know what?'

'That you give wonderful blow-jobs.'

She gave a little shrug. 'I haven't had a complaint yet.'

'I'm not suggesting that you don't, but it's not the sort of thing a man would say after getting a blow-job . . . y'know, thanks, but that was crap. He'd say it was wonderful whether it was wonderful or not.'

'You can tell.'

'How? Ejaculation?'

Lucy shrugged. 'You can just *tell.*'

'I doubt it.'

'You do wonders for a girl's self-esteem; first I'm *nice*, now my blow-jobs suck. What do you call that, deflatio?'

Nathan smiled. 'You *are* an English teacher.'

'I suppose the same applies to the steaks. They might be crap, but no one's prepared to say so.'

'It's possible.'

'But then I've tasted the steaks. I know they're nice.'

Nathan shrugged. 'Pity you can't give yourself a blow-job, then.'

'Did I say you were shy, a while ago? I take it back.'

They grinned at each other for several long moments. The air was heavy with . . . something he didn't know . . . lust or the sweat of jousting. She moved to her bedroom doorway.

'Well,' she said, 'all that's left for me to do is sing you the national anthem backwards.'

'Or not, as the case would be.'

She lingered in the doorway. 'The fish that refused to bite,' she said quietly.

'The . . .?' Nathan began.

'Goodnight, Nathan,' said Lucy. She entered her room and closed the door.

'Goodnight,' Nathan said.

An hour later, out of the drunken-fug of sleep, with the dancing MTV shadows still bouncing around the room, he smelt the Gio up close. He was naked under the spare quilt, but not alone. There was a head down there. He peeled the sheet slowly back. She looked up at him, started to . . .

'Don't speak with your mouth full,' he said, and added, 'That feels wonderful.'

He was surprised, touched, turned on, a little bit frightened and a big bit guilty.

17

On a quieter day the police might have picked him up for questioning, or just zapped him with their nightsticks while passing, but this afternoon was busy-busy and they just laughed back at him, the big guy in the panama hat having hysterics against a shopfront.

George regained a semblance of control after a few minutes, but it didn't last for long. Every few steps he burst out again. *It was fate! It was the Lord moving in a mysterious way! The Lord was testing him!* He bought a hot-dog, stuffed it into his mouth as if it could literally plug the laughter. It couldn't, of course, he merely choked on it, then laughed some more, and it nearly killed him. And he laughed about that too.

Not, of course, that it was that funny. Or funny at all.

George arrived, by appointment, at the Reuters building at 3.15 PM exactly. Besides the panama hat he wore a white suit. He had once seen a man dressed exactly like this in the *Alabama Gentleman's Quarterly* and had promised that one day, given the right circumstances, he would kit himself out similarly. It spoke to him of style, of quality, of the charm and elegance of the Old South, of the plantation owner. In truth the man in the *Alabama Gentleman's Quarterly* was not a Southern gent at all, but Tom Wolfe, that foppish pioneer of new journalism, who had as much to do with the Old South as a new Northern thing. Had he only met Tom Wolfe and known of his past literary achievements, George would have immediately granted him a place in his Top Ten, then gutted him with a fish knife.

He sat in a sparsely appointed waiting-room for twenty minutes. He read *Time* and tutted at the state of the world. He hated being kept waiting, but he retained his composure by concentrating on the task ahead. Looking at him, no one could tell that his legs tingled with excitement, that his heart thumped with adrenalin. Every day, every hour, he was getting closer to his goal, and the world would never be the same again.

Eventually a tall, sparely built black guy approached him and extended a hand. George remained seated and offered a limp handshake.

'Would you like to come through?' the guy said.

George nodded. He stood and followed the guy along a corridor, through a couple of right turns, and into a small office. A seat was pulled out for him. George sat. The guy took a seat behind a desk. An Apple PowerBook sat on top of the desk. A yellow legal notebook. Two red felt-tipped pens. They looked at each other for a few moments. The men, not the red felt-tipped pens.

After a little, George said, 'Will Mr Fuller be long? I have a busy schedule while I'm visiting the city.'

The guy smiled. 'I am Mr Fuller.'

'But . . .' George began, then caught himself, 'of course. I'm sorry. It's funny how you get a different impression of someone on the phone.'

Fuller smiled. 'What did you expect, older, younger? Thicker, thinner?'

Whiter, thought George. 'You look so young!'

'Is that a problem?' Fuller asked with a hint of impatience.

George laughed aloud. 'Not at all!' he roared. 'It's quite refreshing! I feel quite at home – tell the truth I wasn't looking forward to this – I was expecting a brash, arrogant, spit-and-sawdust New Yorker. But you seem quite the gentleman.'

'Not always,' said Fuller, 'but nice of you to say. Now, this magazine you run . . .'

'*Computer Generations.*'

'Yeah. You say you want a longer piece than what's likely to go out over the wires. I'm covering the presidential visit for a number of publications and other media, but the chances of me getting time to do a specialized piece for . . .'

'We're a monthly magazine, Mr Fuller, you'd have a week or so to play with. We do pay top dollar.'

'How top is top dollar?'

'Five thousand top dollars. We pay well, Mr Fuller.'

'Very well.' Fuller nodded his head slowly, weighing up. George could tell he was trying to hide his surprise at the extent of the reward. 'No investigative work, no background?'

'We have all the background. We would like answers to some questions from Michael Tate, but he may not choose to play ball. I'll give you a list of those questions prior to the event. Get answers if you can. If not, don't worry.'

Fuller tapped his fingers on the desk for a few moments. He scrolled down something on his PowerBook. Then he nodded to himself, looked up at George and smiled. 'Okay. I'd say we have a deal.' He reached his hand across the table.

'Excellent,' said George. He jiggled the proffered fingers a little. 'Now, one more thing. About the money.'

'Thirty days from publication.'

'Actually, it is company policy to pay for this type of specialized article in advance. May I be discreet with you, Mr Fuller?'

'Of course.'

'Thank you. As I'm sure your people can testify to, we do things a little differently down south.'

'*My* people?'

'Reuters.'

'Sorry. Yes, of course.'

'We don't always like to put transactions of this nature through our books. Do you understand?'

'Yes. Of course. This transaction has nothing to do with Reuters, so you're free to pay as you wish.'

'Might I suggest that on the morning of the presidential visit, I deliver the money to you in person, in cash?'

'I don't see why not. Although I'm not sure I'll be coming into the office before I go to the Empire . . .'

'I'd really rather give you the money outside of your office anyway, away from prying eyes. Perhaps I could drop it off at your home address?'

Fuller thought about it for a few moments, figuring out privacy from profit. George watched his eyes revolve like the dials on a slot machine; saw the dollar signs come up. 'Of course.'

18

George loved a challenge, but this was a CHALLENGE!

A challenge and a learning experience. He knew better than to put all his eggs in one basket. He should have taken on board the possibility that Fuller might not be of Anglo-Saxon origins.

The solution was, at the same time, incredible and impossible to a lesser mortal. But George had completed seven out of fourteen night classes in theatrical make-up held at the University of Alabama. He was convinced that he could physically replicate any man, and not a few women, given the right materials. *Why by the time I'm finished, I'll see my reflection in the mirror and want to shoot myself.* And as far as acting was concerned, he had also taken a starring role in the Birmingham Thespian production of *Pygmalion*, although he had only appeared in seven out of the eighteen performances (he told them he had perfected the role and it was pointless continuing). In short, he was a walking, talking chameleon, Lord Olivier in snakeskin.

Indeed, the fact that Fuller was black had one tremendous advantage. Once his mission was complete he would

269

be able to change colour again and slip back into anonymity. And the cause of black liberation in America would be put back a hundred years! Epic! More than he could ever have dreamt of!

George took a cab to Meril Steiner's Review, a theatrical shop backing onto a dilapidated cinema near Columbus Circle. He told Meril that he was auditioning for the lead role in an off-off-Broadway *Othello*. The owner, manager and only employee, bald, pale, toothy, old, looked like Nosferatu, was more than helpful, wouldn't let him go.

'We used to do a lot of black-face here,' he said, sorting through his lotions and powders, 'but things ain't what they used to be.'

'No, it's not terribly PC, is it?' George said.

'So the secret is, not to look like a white man in black-face, but like a black man in black-face.' He studied George's face from behind the counter. His eyes flitted about from ear to ear and all points in between. 'You do your own make-up?'

George nodded.

'I did Broadway make-up for thirty years before I opened this place. Why I remember . . . well I remember too much, and sometimes not enough. You want I show you how to put this on so that you can go dancing tonight in Harlem, if you want?'

George smiled. 'Would you mind?'

'It would be a pleasure!' Meril Steiner grinned, then ushered George in behind the counter and into a back room. 'And a pleasure for you to watch an artist at work!'

George took a seat, the old guy pulled a smock round him. 'This won't take so long, your face, it's got similar contours to a black man's.'

George grimaced, then explained in detail the look he was

after. He had examined Fuller intently, *and he didn't even know it.*

Meril nodded as the details tumbled out. 'Okay,' he said, 'I can see that the nose will be your problem, sure enough. If you were Bobby de Niro it would be simple; we'd break the nose, flatten it, then fatten it up. But you ain't de Niro, or you sure as hell wouldn't be coming in here looking for help. Just how close an inspection are you going to have to pass? This stage, close to the audience is it?'

'Very close.'

Meril grinned. 'Okay. Well let's see what we can do for you.'

He worked studiously and exclusively. Customers were ignored. They rang the bell, slapped the counter; Meril growled out that he was busy and to come back. George sat with his eyes closed, relaxed, while Meril talked him through the application. George, of course, knew most of it already, so for the most part relaxed himself, enjoyed the free make-over and tried to imagine himself *black.*

When he glanced at his watch, George was surprised to find that two hours had passed. Meril stood back, straightened with some difficulty, and released an appreciative sigh. 'Now that's what I call genius!'

The wig was on. The nose was thick. The skin was milky brown. Meril fetched a mirror and on the count of three George opened his eyes and nearly jumped out of his chair. *I am Mandingo!* And more to the point: *I am Clark Fuller!*

'Excellent. Excellent!' he shouted. 'I am Hamlet!'

Meril laughed. 'No. You are Othello. You want Hamlet, I make you Hamlet.'

George gagged. 'Of course! But wonderful! Excellent! This will do very nicely indeed.'

Meril rubbed his hands together. 'Now you just sit there a while, allow it to dry properly and we'll be able to paper over any cracks that come up. But yes, you do look good.'

George smiled appreciatively. 'How much do I owe you?'

'You owe me everything!' Meril patted George's shoulder. 'But a great performance will suffice! You sit there and dry, my friend, and don't worry about the money. It's been a pleasure. Now I have to pop upstairs and change this . . .' Meril pulled a colostomy bag out from beneath his apron. 'Then I'll come back and finish you off.'

Meril scurried through a doorway. George lifted the mirror and examined himself again. *Excellent!* He didn't need finished off.

George removed the smock, stood and stretched. He nosed about the office for a few minutes. He found a leather shoulder bag. He poured the contents out onto the floor. Then he filled it with the make-ups Meril had used on him and zipped it closed.

He left the office and returned to the shop. He walked across to the till and opened it. There wasn't much there, a cash float of about seventy dollars and some coins, but it was money. He put the notes in his wallet and began to scoop up piles of change for his pockets.

He turned as a figure appeared in the doorway. 'Get away from the till, you black bastard!' Meril screamed, lifting a broom.

George smiled.

Meril shouted again and began to run-shuffle towards him.

When he was close enough George punched him in the mouth. Meril wilted.

When he had settled on the ground George kicked him in the face. Then once in the ribs. Then he lifted the leather bag and left the shop.

19

'I had this incredible dream last night,' Nathan said over breakfast, hoping it would embarrass Lucy. Good-natured, bantering embarrassment, not bad-tempered humiliation. Brian had yet to appear.

She served him scrambled eggs and toast with a thin strip of ham. 'Really?' she said, returning the pan to the kitchen, then taking her seat at the pine bench opposite him. 'What was it about?'

Now Nathan was embarrassed. He thought for a panicked moment that maybe he really had dreamt it, but then he thought about the tenderness down below and knew it was real. 'Well what do you think?' he asked, with the nearest approximation to a cheeky grin he could manage.

She shrugged.

She wasn't cold, exactly. Indifferent, maybe. Hung over, probably. Alcohol affected different people in different ways. In some it kickstarted their libido; in others it dampened it down. With her it had just temporarily removed her inhibitions. Now she was trying to pretend it hadn't happened. There had been no romance about their encounter; no kissing, no whispering of sweet everythings; she appeared mysteriously, there had been the act of oral sex, she departed silently. And now she ate with gusto. Nathan had a pallid sheen about him; she had a vibrant, pink, fresh glow. Quite beautiful, really.

'It was a nice thing to wake up to,' Nathan said, looking at his eggs, poking them with his fork. 'Last night. You.'

She nodded, chewed.

'Well . . .' said Nathan. 'I thought it was . . . well, thanks.' He shovelled in a mouthful while he thought of something to say. He chewed nervously, swallowed loudly. 'You've been very good to me,' he blurted.

Lucy smiled. 'Yeah, I know. Gave you money. Somewhere to sleep. Clothes to wear. Sucked your cock. As the song says, no charge.'

'I didn't mean . . . I mean . . . I don't know what I mean. I mean I'm not used to something like that happening to me. Spontaneously. I'm . . . I'm very pleased that it did. You are very beautiful, Lucy. So you are. Ahm, and now I'll shut up.'

Lucy put her fork down. 'That's very nice of you to say.'

'I do mean it. You are lovely. Maybe we could . . .'

Lucy raised her hand. 'Woah, there. Don't be getting carried away.'

'The movies, or dinner . . .'

'Nathan?'

'A show?'

'I like having oral sex.'

'Okay.'

'The sperm is good for my skin.'

'I'm sorry?'

'Sperm. It's good for my complexion. I like to get as much of it as I can.'

'Oh.'

'Much as I enjoyed last night, it had as much to do with beauty treatment as lust.'

'Oh,' said Nathan.

Lucy laughed. 'Look at you! You look like I've just burst your favourite balloon.'

'You just used me for . . .' Nathan began, confused.

'Nathan, we used each other. Let's not get things out of proportion here. *You're* the one had an orgasm.'

'You didn't give me a chance.'

'I didn't *want* an orgasm.'

'I know,' he snapped, 'you wanted sperm.' He bit his lip, willed himself to calmness. He spoke in more measured tones. 'Would I be correct in thinking that if you could just go into a Superdrug and buy half a litre of it, you wouldn't have anything to do with sex at all?'

'Perhaps.'

Nathan pushed his plate away. He had changed his mind. This Lucy wasn't beautiful at all. She *was* cold. Calculating. He had made a mistake. He had begun to have naive fantasies about her filling the massive void left by Lisa, but she wasn't half the woman Lisa was. A vain ice maiden obsessed with her own beauty. His temperature started to rise again. He had been abused. Sucked dry to satiate this strange woman's crazed need for longevity.

He jabbed a fork at her across the table. 'What is the point in having a great complexion if you don't enjoy sex?'

'Who said I didn't enjoy sex?'

'You *implied* you didn't enjoy sex.'

'No, I *implied* that I didn't want to have sex with you.'

'You just wanted to milk me for sperm.'

'You were here, you were available, you were willing. I don't see what the problem is.'

'I feel . . .'

She snapped this time, waving a warning finger at him. 'Don't dare say that you feel raped. Tied to a bed and thrashed, now that is rape. You're giving me a hard time just because I didn't fall in love with you.'

'Don't talk absolute—'

'You strike me as someone who's just too damn anxious to fall in love. No woman who treats you the least bit well is going to be safe.'

Nathan shook his head. 'Have I woken up yet, or is this all a dream?'

'You're awake. You're alone. We're your only friends in New York. Lighten up.'

Lucy stood, cleared the plates and returned to the kitchen. Brian appeared in the doorway of his room, yawning. 'God,' he said, 'I feel like shit.'

'You look like shit too, hon,' Lucy said without looking. 'You better get showered, you'll be late to work.'

'Breakfast?'

'Too late, hon.'

Brian nodded across to Nathan. 'You look a bit hot under the collar, Nath – suffering?'

'Nah. Not really.' He looked pointedly across to the kitchen. 'We were just discussing life, and how it sucks.'

Brian held his head, grimaced. 'You can say that again,' he said.

On the way to work Brian said: 'You really miss that girl of yours, don't you?'

Nathan nodded. It was sweltering already. His uniform was too small. His head was throbbing. His throat was dry.

'The way I see it,' Brian continued, 'you can do one of two things.'

Nathan looked sullenly ahead. 'Please, no advice. I don't need advice.'

Brian threw an arm round him, gave him a playful hug. 'Hear me out! What harm can it do?'

Nathan shrugged him off. 'I just don't want to think about it right now.'

'But that's exactly what you're doing!'

'I know! But I'm *trying* not to!'

'Hear me out!'

Nathan rolled his eyes. 'I'm going to hear this whether I like it or not, aren't I? Okay, okay! Shoot, Don Juan de Marco.'

Brian smiled triumphantly and clapped his hands together. He walked hunched forward, bouncing from toe to toe, like a boxer on the way to the ring. 'All right – one of two things. You can forget about her completely, decide that that part of your life is over. I know, not easy, but you gotta try.'

'Thus far,' said Nathan, 'I'm not hearing anything original.'

'Wait. If you can't cut her out, you have to go the other way. Get her back in. Do everything in your power to win her back. Prove to her that your love is the strongest love in the world.'

'Is that it?'

'That's it! Win her back!'

'Jesus, I'm glad I didn't pay good money for that! For a start, Brian, I don't know where the fuck in the whole of America she is. I can't win her back if I can't find her. She's not exactly in the telephone directory.'

'I know that. I know she could be anywhere. But this is what I mean about proving to her that she's your true love. You've gotta do something spectacular to win her back.'

'Aye, Brian, sure.'

'I'm serious. I've been thinking about it, and I know how to do it.'

Nathan laughed. 'I don't believe I'm hearing this.'

'Listen, what have you got to lose?'

He shrugged. 'Everything. I'm illegal here, remember?'

'Illegal, shmegal. Love conquers everything.' He clicked his fingers. 'You ever see *Sleepless in Seattle*?'

'Tom Hanks?'

'Yeah. Tom Hanks. His son gets on the radio and appeals for a wife for his widowed father.'

Nathan gave him an incredulous, 'Uhuh.'

'You do the same, except obviously you're appealing to your lost love.'

'Brian . . .'

'Except no one bothers with the fuckin' radio any more. You do it on TV. You do it on *Oprah*.'

'Oprah?'

'Oprah. You call them up. You tell them your story. They'll fall for it. Do a whole programme on you. You'll get her back, I tell ya!'

'You're barking, Brian, barking fucking mad.'

'I'm telling you. Every woman in America watches her. I'll bet your girl did.'

Nathan shrugged. 'Okay, once in a while, maybe . . . but Jesus Christ, Brian, they're not going to make a show about everyone who falls out with their girlfriend.'

'Why the hell not? Look at the crap they do make shows about. Anyway, why the hell not give it a shot?'

'Brian, I thought I was naive, but you take the biscuit.'

'Nathan, you've got nothing to lose, because you've got nothing. Not even a biscuit. You come up with a better idea.'

'Brian, there's an expression we use back home to describe people like you.'

'Yup?'

'You're a fucking mental.'

20

And as these things do, the idea grew on him during the day. Lisa *was* out there somewhere, in wide America. He didn't know the exact number, but there was somewhere in the region of three hundred million people in the States. He was never going to bump into her by chance. Or if he did he would be too decrepit to get out of his wheelchair to kiss her.

Their parting was worse than death, because with death there was a grave to visit, ashes to scatter, the grim reality that they would never meet again. The way he had left it with Lisa was more like a movie showing from which he'd been thrown out halfway through for being too noisy. Somewhere that movie was still running, and he needed to know how it ended.

He had watched *Oprah* himself. More than Lisa, in fact, as she was out most days getting her breasts sucked and he had no job at all. He had sat there with his beers and his pizza watching it day in, day out. Oprah was a caring woman. Maybe if she heard his story, it would touch her deeply and she would fly him to Chicago to make an emotional nationwide appeal.

*   *   *

All I know, Lisa, is that I love you. I've made some mistakes, but I'll change, I promise.

And what were those mistakes, Nathan?

I punched her in the nose. I lived off her money. She became a prostitute to keep us in food.

But you love her deeply? You've changed your ways?

I've changed everything, ma'am, and I'd give anything to have her back.

She'd surprise him then, and Lisa would appear from nowhere and they would kiss and make up and Oprah would close the show with a tear in her eye.

Over lunch Nathan sat quietly with Sam. Both were lost in their thoughts until Brian arrived, grinning, and slipped Nathan a scrap of paper. 'The number you were looking for,' he said.

'Number?' Nathan replied, confused.

'Oprah.'

'Oprah?'

'Oprah.'

'Oprah.'

Sam nodded along with them. 'Did I ever tell you boys about meeting Maria Callas?'

'No,' said Brian, rising from the table again. He squeezed Nathan's shoulder. 'Call them,' he said.

He took the crumpled paper out of his pocket half a dozen times during the afternoon. He strode purposefully around the main observation tower; he helped, he guided, he warned; but his mind was on Lisa. More than once he nearly threw the number over the side, but then he held back; on the fifth time he did throw it, but a gust of wind caught it and blew it back. It landed further down the observatory and he had to ask a very large woman to remove herself so that he could retrieve it from between her legs without being arrested. It was a sign.

Nathan, lost in his thoughts, didn't notice the two FBI guys. No reason why he should have, really, they weren't noticeably protecting the American way of life. They were just a couple of tourists.

Fred Troy yawned, then placed his hands on the security grille. 'Most people look at the view,' he said wearily, 'I look out there and I see attack helicopters swooping in to blow the President to a thousand pieces. What do you see?'

James Morton, in charge of the FBI's New York office, smiled at his old friend. 'I see our helicopters blowing their helicopters out of the sky before they can do a thing. *Relax*, Fred, it's all under control.' His brow furrowed suddenly and he pressed his face tight against the fence. 'No . . . wait, God . . . I see . . . I see a big fat steak, fries, a cold beer . . . Jesus Christ, Fred, they're coming straight towards us . . .'

Fred pushed himself off the fence. 'Okay. Point taken. But I still don't like this place.'

'Fred, I know you. You take a dislike to a place, nothing will dissuade you. When was the last time you were in Dallas?'

'Dallas? I don't think I've ever been to Dallas.'

'But you've had opportunities to work there?'

'Sure, haven't we all?'

'My point exactly. You have this second nature. There's something in you that steers you away from places that might be dangerous to the President. Yet you're always coming to New York to annoy me.'

Fred smiled. 'It's not New York, James, it's *here*.'

They headed back to the elevators. There were twenty-five

years between them, you could see that in their hair, their skin, if not in their clothes: but there was a bond which was above and beyond the mere passage of time. Just as J. Edgar, albeit from beyond the grave, had plucked Fred from an anonymous pack to imbue him with the true spirit of the FBI, so Fred had plucked Morton from the ranks at Quantico and trained him up into the leading agent of his generation. Fred was quite sure that one day Morton would be head of the FBI.

'You thinking about retiring, old man?' Morton asked as they strode back out onto Fifth Avenue.

'No,' said Troy.

He wasn't one for using four hundred words where one would do.

Nathan didn't want to do it anywhere any of his colleagues might overhear him, so when he took another break late in the afternoon he took the elevator back down to the lobby and left the Empire. The streets were, as ever, teeming. He battled through, his stomach churning with nervousness. He made his way to Pat Murphy's Broadway Bar. He was pleased to see that it was mostly empty. He positioned himself by the pay-phone. He had a pile of quarters. He waited for the barman to move off to serve some customers near the door, then dialled.

Lisa, this is where it begins.

A couple of days, tops, and he'd be on national television. Their love would become famous. They would be celebrities in their own right. Some mad fucker in Hollywood would give them a million dollars to film their life story. *Green Card* meets *Love Story* meets *Sleepless in Seattle*.

After being kept on hold for five minutes Nathan was finally put through to *Oprah*'s production office. His nerves were shot, but his voice held steady. He explained his situation to the sweet-voiced girl on the end of the line: not everything of course – not the violence, not the drinking, not his boorishness, not her occupation. The good things.

'She was the most important thing in the world to me. I want her back.' His voice was heavy with the poignancy of the moment; tears sprang. 'I need her back,' he cried.

'I don't think so,' said the girl.

The emotion suddenly drained from his voice. 'What?'

'I said, I don't think so.'

'But why not?'

'I'm afraid, sir, that we did lost love last year. And if I'm not mistaken, two years before that.'

'But—'

'Miss Winfrey very much regrets—'

'But this is fucking important.'

'I appreciate that, sir.'

'I need her back!'

'Sir, I—'

'Let me speak to Oprah herself.'

'I'm sorry, sir, but—'

'Put her on!'

There was a slight intake of breath. 'Thank you for calling *Oprah*. Please call again.'

Click.

Nathan cradled the receiver in his lap for a few moments. Then he lifted it and began to smash it against the coinbox.

21

Sam was in a fairly jaunty mood when he arrived at the Cedar Nursing Home. The money would be *very* handy. Shit, he would have told the whole story for nothing, or a couple of drinks.

Things weren't that bad.

He'd been a fighter all his life. There weren't many kids his age would have come through an air crash in better shape. There weren't many young bucks would have picked a fight with Sinatra and come out in possession of all his faculties. There wasn't a man alive had met more famous people than he had. And he'd had fifty years with the best wife in the world: a beautiful, charming, intelligent, lively woman, who could have had her pick of men, and she'd picked him, a lowly security guard. She could have had money, a life in the fast lane, *things*, but she got him and was content with it. He had a beautiful daughter in Florida, grandkids. He had as much health as a man his age could expect to have, and if his head was a constant reminder of mortality, so be it. He could still walk and talk and hear and think. He still had respect: he could give it and receive it. There was still a life to be lived; two lives.

How are you, Sam?
Just fine, Mr President.
I hear you've been here for fifty years.
Yes sir, Mr President.
Sam, could I have your autograph?
Of course, Mr President.

He hurried up the steps into the lobby. He had a lot to tell Mary.

Mary wasn't in her usual position before the television. Nor was she in her bed; another woman lay in it, sleeping. He checked her chart anyway, in case he was seeing things; then he looked up and down the ward. He went to the bathroom, checking to see if any of the nurses were sorting her out in there. No.

He stood uncertainly in the middle of the floor, his hands unconsciously fingering the candy sack in his pocket, fearing the worst but knowing just as well that there was probably a simple explanation. All he had to do was ask, but he felt paralysed, every bit as helpless as the poor devils lying helpless all around him.

After a few minutes he became aware that a nurse had arrived at the far end of the ward. She was changing the sheets on an empty bed. He watched her, mesmerized.

Mary has died, and they have forgotten to tell me.

There was a tug on his arm. He turned slowly.

'Sam?' Max Fleisher stood beside him, looking a little concerned. 'You okay?'

Sam nodded.

'I saw you slip by downstairs. I wanted to catch you before you came up.'

Sam nodded again, then surveyed the ward. 'Where is she?'

Max took him by the elbow. 'Come on down to the office, Sam, we need to talk.'

Sam took his elbow back. 'What's the matter?'

'Nothing's the matter, I just need to have a word with you. C'mon, will you? Everything's fine.'

'So where's my wife?'

'Sam, we moved her. But she's fine.'

'She's taken a turn? You were supposed to phone me. You didn't phone.'

'She's fine.'

'Why didn't someone phone?'

Max tried the elbow again. 'Sam, c'mon, we moved her to a different floor, that's all. Now will you come down to the office with me?'

'Which floor?'

'The ground floor.'

'The terminal floor.'

'Will you come on? It's not the terminal floor, Sam, you know that.'

'I don't know anything. I know you've moved my wife.' Sam nodded across at the bed opposite him. 'They've taken my wife,' he said to the occupant, who stared vacantly back at him, 'and they never phoned.'

'There was nothing to phone about!'

'Wouldn't even spend a dime to let me know she was gone.'

'She's not gone!'

'She's gone to the ground floor.' He nodded at the woman in the bed. 'And they won't even let me see her.'

'I'm trying to get you down to see her!'

Sam set off for the ground floor, leaving a surprised Max several paces behind.

Max's tut was heard at the far end of the ward. 'Sam!'

he called as he set off in pursuit, trying to run and look dignified at the same time, which wasn't easy. At the end of the ward he tagged Sam's shoulder. 'Why don't you take the elevator?'

'Why don't *you* take the elevator?' Sam shot back and began to take the steps two at a time.

Max took the steps one at a time, but faster, so that he was just ahead of Sam when he reached the bottom. He turned on his heel, put his hand out and placed it firmly on the old man's chest. 'Sam, we need to talk, and we need to talk now. Now listen to me, your wife is fine, there has been no change in her condition. C'mon, Sam, you've known me long enough to know that I wouldn't lie to you.'

Sam held his gaze for a good half-minute. Max gave him a little encouraging smile. It was probably the wrong thing to do.

'Take me to my wife now,' Sam said, 'or I'll kill you.'

'Now there's no need for that, Sam.'

Sam slapped the hand away from his chest and pushed the nursing home manager back. He hurried along the corridor to the ward.

Max stood watching him for a few moments, then with a weary shake of his head returned to his office. He sat behind his desk and called a file up on his computer, any file. He stared at it for a few minutes, trying to absorb the information, but it wasn't working; he closed down the computer and sat back on his swivel chair, hands folded behind his head. He waited.

After fifteen minutes Sam appeared in the doorway. His face was like thunder. 'Why?' he said simply.

Max unfolded his arms and indicated that Sam should take a chair. Sam ignored him. 'Sam, c'mon, she's fine.'

'Sure. *Sure*. She's lying in bed. Staring into space.'

'She always stares into space.'

'She watches TV.'

'She watches. She doesn't see. We know this.'

'*We* know nothing. I know what I know. She watches TV. She listens to what goes on around her. But not down there. There's no light. There's one window. Everybody else is on life support machines. That's death row you have her on.'

'It's not death row.'

'Well it's half a breath from it.'

They stared at each other for several long moments; the only sound was the clock on the wall and the squeak-squeak of a visitor's canvas shoes on the linoleum floors. For the first time Sam's voice sounded like it was about to break. 'For God's sake, man, she didn't even want her candy.'

Max leaned back in his seat, rubbed the palm of his hand into his crumpled brow. 'Sam, I have a boss too, y'know. It's not like this is my home.' He broke off suddenly, thumped the top of the desk with his fist. 'For Chrissakes, Sam, will you sit down!'

Sam stood resolutely by the door. 'What's your obsession with sitting down? You think it makes bad news any better? They teach you that at bedside manner school, Max, or did you flunk that one completely? I thought maybe the least you could do was a phone call.'

Max rose from his chair. He moved round to the front of his desk and perched himself on the corner. 'Sam, we're not a public service here, we're a private nursing home. People pay to stay here.'

'I know this. I pay for the best treatment for my wife. And you shovel her into the terminal ward.'

'Sam, c'mon, she hasn't been shovelled anywhere. The truth of the matter is it's as much to do with you as it is with me. You gotta pay your bills, Sam.'

'I pay my bills.'

'You pay some, Sam, not all.'

'I posted you a cheque last week.'

'You posted me a cheque for the wrong amount. I told you the fees were going up, Sam, I gave you a note of it personally. So why pay the old sum?'

'I forgot, okay?'

'You didn't forget, Sam, I know you. You're meticulous about Mary, you always have been.'

'So I get the figure wrong. I'm a few days late with it. What the hell difference does it make?'

'It makes a difference. These are changed times, my friend. My boss, he keeps a tight rein on the accounts. Where Mary was, that's premium space; you don't keep up your payments, you get shifted down. That's his decision. I'm sorry, Sam, but that's the way it is. A couple of old dames, last week he threw them out on the street. That's the kind of guy he is.'

Sam shook his head. 'Who is he, this guy, Joe Stalin?'

Max shook his head too. 'He's an accountant, Sam. He doesn't have a name. He has a budget.'

Sam pushed himself off the doorframe. 'Okay,' he said, 'you move her back home, I'll get you the extra money.'

'You get me the money, I'll move her back home.'

'It's like that, is it?'

'Fraid so.'

'I'll have the money on Friday.'

'I'll move her on Friday.'

'You know she'll die in there. With all those dead people.'

'She'll be fine, Sam. She's checked all the time, you know that. There's been no difference at all since we moved her.'

'I think I know more than any damn doctor, Max.'

'Okay.'

Sam turned to leave. Then he stopped and wagged a finger

back at Max. 'This is going to sound just great on Friday,' he said.

'What is?' Max asked wearily. 'What's Friday?'

'Shifting my wife to the terminal ward. Friday I'm meeting the President.'

Max smiled. 'Sure, Sam, I'm sure you see him all the time.'

'Laugh if you want. But I'm telling you the truth. He's coming to the Empire all right. All presidents come to the Empire eventually.'

'I'm not surprised, you're a regular presidential magnet.'

'The problem with you kids,' Sam snapped, 'is that you have no respect.' The wagging finger stiffened.

Sam turned back down the corridor to see his wife. He chewed at his lower lip. The problem was, Max was right. She was staring at a wall, but it might just as well have been *Oprah*.

22

Brian was worried about Nathan. Ever since he'd come back off his break he'd been staring morosely out over Manhattan, his arms folded on the observatory wall, his head resting on his arms. Tourists edged past him warily.

'C'mon, Nathan, things aren't that bad,' Brian said, putting an arm round his shoulders, giving him a little squeeze. 'Look at you. We're up here, supposed to be discouraging people from jumping; anyone gets a look at that face, even the happiest little camper will go flying over the side. C'mon, will ya? It's not that bad.'

Nathan shook his head. 'Listen,' he said, his voice mud-slow, 'go and *patrol* or something. I'm fine.'

'So *Oprah* didn't go for it. There are plenty more chat shows.'

'It was a stupid fucking idea in the first place.'

'Maybe it was, but it was worth a try, wasn't it?'

'Was it? You get me all fired up about it, then I get slapped down, and I'm worse off than ever.'

'You're going to let one little rebuff get you down?'

'Yes.'

'Where's the get up and go in you, man?'

'It got up and went.'

'So you're giving up the search for Lisa just like that?'

Nathan shook his head. 'No, I'm giving up listening to stupid cunts like you, just like that.'

Brian gave him one more squeeze. 'Okay, so one idea didn't pan out. Here's another one.'

'Please, don't.'

'Listen. We finish work, we get into our street duds, then we go out and get drunk as skunks.'

'And?'

'And that's it. Maybe another idea will pop into our heads. Maybe it won't. Let's go and have a good time anyway.'

Nathan managed a hint of a smile. 'Are you a relentless optimist, or what?'

'Or what. Remember, the President's coming tomorrow and I have the doubtful pleasure of escorting him. I intend to do it unencumbered by the power of cogent thought. I'm going to get gloriously drunk and then stumble through tomorrow with the worst hangover in the world.'

'Is that wise?'

'Of course not. C'mon, it'll be fun. I'll even allow you to talk about that girl of yours for a couple of hours, as long as you don't try to slit your wrists.'

Nathan straightened, stretched, lifted his cap and ran a hand through his hair. 'You're very good to me, y'know,' he said. 'I do appreciate it.'

Brian shrugged. 'What are friends for?'

'Betraying,' said Nathan.

Brian punched his arm and moved back on to patrol. Nathan leaned back on the parapet and stared out over the city. His stomach was resolutely knotted. He sensed that somewhere, way beyond that endless vista, his girl was making love to another man, and it was killing him.

They got drunk. Uproariously drunk. Nathan knew already that Brian wasn't much of a drinker, but what he lacked in talent he made up for in determination: like a hapless but spirited boxer, he didn't know when to quit, didn't know when to stay down. Nathan was with him all the way, like a trainer, ready to throw the towel in on his behalf if he took too much punishment.

They confined themselves mostly to the Irish bars. Nathan lost himself in his thoughts while Brian babbled with steadily advancing incoherence; mostly it was about boxing, about the warrior spirit, about the self-discipline, the abstinence, the tunnel vision. Nathan said, *Sure, Right, Dead on*, a few times, but his thoughts were with Lisa: how she thought of herself as the big city girl, the woman of the nineties; but he had seen her crying alone before, he had seen her helpless.

They ended up in a rock club. An English band was trying to break America by playing a small eclectic club. All they were doing was breaking a small eclectic club: but they weren't bad, loud guitars, strident beat. Nathan went up and danced by himself. Brian went to follow, but collapsed onto his knees; it took him several minutes to pull himself back onto his chair. *Fuck*, he mumbled into his beer; he took a mouthful, tried to swallow, couldn't, spat it back into his glass. He repeated the process several times. Then he knocked the glass over and it rolled off and shattered on the concrete floor; the band had just finished a song, the applause was small and eclectic; the bouncers heard the glass break and hurried across. They picked Brian up by the hair and set about throwing him out. Nathan rushed across bawling at

293

them. They grabbed him and chucked them both out, landing on their arses on the sidewalk, screaming and cursing back at the bouncers, safe from their vitriol behind slammed steel doors; then they fell into hysterics and rolled about as theatre-goers in big fur coats picked their way through.

Nathan closed his eyes outside the rock club, and opened them lying on his makeshift bed in Brian's apartment; and he was only half as legless as Brian.

The noise that woke him was Brian clattering about the kitchen, attempting to pacify a rumbling stomach. He appeared eventually at the door, showed him something that looked like the two heels of a loaf surrounding a layer of asphalt. Nathan respectfully declined; or told him to fuck off; by the time it was said it was forgotten and by the time the first bite was taken, he was asleep.

Hours later he was lost in a dream of sex with Lisa, great thumping sex the like of which they had only occasionally enjoyed. In bed with Lisa, sex had been languorous, romantic, and all the more erotic for it, but this dream was sweatily vibrant, animalistic, thrusting with scant regard for her pleasure; and her bucking against him with no regard for his; it was fast sexy lust. And yet . . . he was coaxed slowly into consciousness, the thick-headed with drink kind of awareness which teeters on the knife edge of sleep . . . there was perfume . . . familiar . . . warm . . . comforting . . . Nathan's head lolled back on the pillow; his hand moved slowly, naturally to his groin; it ruffled her hair. He breathed deeply and for a moment he was content and happy and convinced it was Lisa. Then slowly, slowly he remembered who else wore that perfume, and the disgust he had felt for her use and abuse of his body, but that didn't matter now; this wasn't examination under the cold light of day. He tangled his hands tightly in Lucy's hair and held her mouth even firmer upon his manhood, urging her on through the darkness, building the rhythm, forcing the pace, moving his hips against her; she half gagging but not for an instant relaxing her grip. The half-remembered argument filtered once again through the pleasure: of being used; of sperm being extracted with an extraordinarily cool Calvinistic methodism; of the absence of love, lust or even slight regard. But it didn't matter, because the pleasure taps were turned on to maximum and he no longer cared who was down there. That wasn't the point. The point was achieving orgasm.

He came.

As he fell back, laugh-groaning with pleasure, the light was abruptly switched on. He opened his eyes, blinked.

From the doorway, Lucy said: 'So what are you boys up to?'

Brian dropped Nathan's penis from his mouth and gulped loudly. He wiped a hand across his lips. 'Sorry,' he said, drunk-bashfully.

Nathan reared back on the bed as if he had been bitten by a snake. His hands engulfed his crotch. He stared at Brian, then at Lucy, befuddled momentarily by the facts, willing himself out of the dream. But it was no dream, and Lucy was laughing from the doorway.

She gave him a little shrug and smiled. 'Nathan, the desire for good skin runs in our family,' and she turned back to her room.

Brian sidled back on his ass, sensing that all was not well. Nathan, recovered enough to let his instincts take over, stuck a bare foot into Brian's face, shattering his nose. The blood began to pump as Brian let out an anguished scream. He rolled over onto his back, clutching his nose. Nathan reared up over him, burning with anger, then stopped momentarily to pull on his underpants. Lucy appeared in her doorway again. Nathan kicked Brian in the face with his other foot.

'Stop it!' Lucy yelled.

Nathan reached down and pulled Brian up by the hair. Brian's hands shot up to protect his scalp, but he couldn't do anything. Nathan started to drag him across the room.

'Get off him!' Lucy yelled, racing across the room.

As he dragged him, one-handed, Nathan punched him in the face.

Lucy slapped Nathan across the back of the head.

Nathan backhanded her and she fell back, dabbing at her split lip. Then he started to bang Brian's head against the wall.

Lucy was suddenly on his back, her legs wrapped round him, beating him about the face. Her fingers tried to plough into his skin, but she had bitten her nails to the quick; she tried to push them into his eyes. Nathan lurched forward, tossing Lucy over his shoulders. She crashed off the wall. She lay still. Beside her brother. Who also lay still.

Nathan stood above them, shaking.

He kicked Brian again.

'Oh Jesus,' he said, aloud. He half-knelt to see if they were okay, then he straightened again, revolted. He lowered his underpants, checked his penis for signs of . . . something. 'Oh Jesus,' he said again.

He hurried into the bathroom. He stood under the shower. He scrubbed and he scrubbed and he scrubbed.

When he emerged, Lucy was standing in the bathroom doorway. The first thing he noticed was the kitchen knife in her hand. Then the thin fissure leading off her eyebrow and the blood that dripped down the side of her face.

'He raped me,' said Nathan.

'I think he's dead,' said Lucy.

'Good,' said Nathan.

'You thought it was me, didn't you?'

'But it wasn't.'

'What difference does it make? If I hadn't switched the light on he would have finished you off and you wouldn't have been any wiser. It's only rape because he's a man.'

Nathan shuddered at the thought of it.

She began to finger the wound above her eyebrow. 'You've killed my brother. We took you in off the streets, gave you a home, money, our love . . .'

'The love I appreciated. The oral sex was stepping over the border of acceptable etiquette.'

Nathan moved towards Lucy. She backed up, pointing the knife at him. He passed her slowly, the point of the knife an inch from his stomach.

He crossed the lounge. Brian was still lying against the wall, but he had curled himself into a ball and was softly moaning to himself. His eyes blinked. There was a considerable amount of blood about his face. Nathan knelt beside him.

'You okay?' he asked.

'Sure,' said Brian.

'Damn,' said Nathan, and thumped him on the nose again.

Lucy let out a scream and came tearing across the room, knife behind her now, ready for the swing. Nathan moved sharply left, allowed her momentum to bring her level then tripped her and she plunged forward, clattering off the wall again. She slid down it like a cartoon character.

Brian, sobbing into the blood, turned his head slightly. 'You won't tell anyone in work, will you?' he whispered.

Nathan shook his head in disgust. 'Who could I tell?' he spat.

23

John Smedlin gave it one last big sniff, then wiped his nose and pressed the button to admit Michael Tate.

'Michael,' he said, 'good to see you again.'

Tate slouched across the office, removed a gnarled Kleenex from his tracksuit pocket and wiped down the leather seat. He rolled up the tissue in a ball and threw it behind him, then sat down.

'I'm not even going to comment,' Smedlin said.

Tate shrugged. They began twenty minutes of small talk. Sport. Business. Tate talked about his plans for the Empire, about his plans for Eastern Europe. Smedlin made a few notes. Eventually Tate said, 'Okay, hit me with it.'

'Hit you with what?'

'Today's penetrating analysis.'

'Ah, yes. Your meetings with Senator Broole . . .'

Tate raised a hand. 'Let me guess. It's not that Broole is increasingly coming into line with my own political views, it's not that he sees the need to retain the current status quo in the health industry, it's because I see him as a father substitute.'

Smedlin shook his head. 'Do you think I also have to reduce everything to those terms, Michael?'

'You mean he's not?'

'*He's* not. Broole's what I'd call your uncle figure. When an uncle calls he doesn't call to discipline you, to chastise you; he wants to be your friend, he agrees with everything you say, he tells you what he thinks you want to hear, he tries to impress you, he puts up with your tantrums.'

'And why would my uncle do that?'

'Because he wants to wheedle his way into a position of power. He wants to throw your father out of his own house by showing that he's in some way unfit to look after you. And he can do that through you. By wooing you away, by being mister nice guy.'

'And if I follow your line of thought, what you're suggesting is that yes, I have a father figure, but it's not Senator Broole, it's . . .'

'President Keneally. Exactly.'

'But he's . . . a cunt.'

Smedlin raised an eyebrow. 'It takes one to know one, Michael.'

Tate smiled at that. 'My dad the president.'

'Think about what a father is, Michael. He educates. He disciplines. He scolds. None of it's very pleasant at the time, but you emerge a better, stronger person, and you realize that your father really does love you.'

'Ah. So that's what that look he gives me means. I always thought it was loathing, but it must be loving.' He sat for several moments with his chin dropped down towards his chest. Smedlin could see Tate's eyes darting about under those hooded lids, this way thataway, this way thataway, that way thisaway, that way thisaway. When he finally looked up that grin had slipped and his eyes were suddenly cold. 'They've got to you, haven't they?'

'What?'

'Keneally's people. They've bought you up. They want you to convince me to support him.'

'Don't be ridiculous.'

'Don't *you* be ridiculous. You've made a fortune treating loons, now you want to piss it all away by making it free?'

'That's not what he's suggesting. It's giving those who can't afford it—'

'Those who can't afford it should be left to rot.' Tate was on his feet. His eyes were blazing. 'You don't understand how the world's changing, John. Everything's disappearing. I don't give a damn about fucking pandas, but I do give a damn about the human race surviving. I'm telling you, in twenty years there's not going to be enough food, enough fuel, enough anything to support us. *I'm* working on plans that can help us survive. *He's* working on plans that will kill us. I want less health care. I want fewer people. He wants more health care. More people. It won't work.'

'Y'know, those are pretty unorthodox views, Michael. You go public with them you—'

'I have no intention of going public with them. I'm not a fool.'

'Nevertheless, what you're basically saying is, *kill America's poor.*'

'No I'm not. I wouldn't confine it to America. Listen, I'm taking a step back from day-to-day living, I'm looking at history to be, the future of the world. There isn't enough room, there aren't enough resources. We need space, and we need to conserve energy. Keneally is supposed to be the most important man on the planet, but he's diametrically opposed to everything I believe in.'

'So you are going to vote with Broole.'

Tate shrugged. '*Everyone* is going to vote with Broole.'

'You don't think maybe there are some senators out there with the balls to stand up to you?'

'Remember Iowa?'

'What're you gonna do, Michael, pull the plug on the whole of America?'

Tate nodded. He pulled at a lip. 'I've thought about it,' he said. 'You know it, I know it, I have the power to destroy every computer in America, one word from me and everything crashes. *I am* the supreme being.'

'There's only one thing I can say to that, Michael.'

'What?' Tate snapped.

'You'll need another appointment. Is Friday okay?'

'Friday's fine.'

24

George Burley rose early, did his exercises, shaved, bathed. He dressed in a pair of black canvas jeans, a white shirt, yellow tiger print tie and dull red zipped jacket. He spent a little longer than usual on perfecting his hair. On this of all days he had to look his best. Then he spent ten minutes cleaning as many surfaces as he could find likely to harbour fingerprints. When he was satisfied he packed his few belongings into a suitcase, which he left by the door ready for collection on his return. Then he lifted his make-up bag, gun, and computer and left the hotel.

He preferred not to order breakfast on room service or eat in the fake gentility of the restaurant, choosing instead the anonymity of a busy diner. He ate scrambled eggs, ham, hash browns and drank thick black coffee, favouring the left side of his mouth. He wasn't nervous at all. He glanced about him at the crowded restaurant. Most didn't have time to sit and eat; they ordered their bagels and ate on the hoof; those who did manage to sit down wolfed their breakfasts into them like, well, wolves. As George sipped his coffee he wondered how many would remember him sitting there, serene and supremely confident, when in years to come they were asked where they were when Keneally was shot. They would have no reason to remember him specifically, of course, for George had every intention of carrying out the deed and returning to his normal life, but if by chance he was caught and his picture flashed, how many would remember him, what he ate, his calm demeanour, his courtesy to customers and staff, his dollar tip? How could they possibly know that he was about to enter history? He smiled at the thought, then nodded as the waiter offered him a coffee refill. As he left the tip, four quarters, he examined the coins for a moment: one day his face might be on them. Perhaps in the next century there would be no dimes or quarters, there'd be Burleys. *Buddy, can you spare a Burley? For a Fistful of Burleys*. It was Burley credible. George's shoulders shuddered as he tried to keep his laughter at bay.

As he crossed the Circle and skirted the edge of Central Park lithe young things in lycra raced past him on roller blades. He barely noticed. He was focused. On Clark Fuller. On his mission.

Fuller had an apartment on Central Park West. Evidently the Reuters man enjoyed some wealth. George disliked him even more for it. During the night he had reconsidered his Top Ten: he sneaked Fuller in at number ten, thus displacing Rap Music. But it wouldn't be for long.

A security guard tarted up in a mock-Edwardian uniform admitted him to the building and buzzed Fuller. George stepped out on the seventh floor then found apartment 3D. As the chain went back on the door George patted the pistol in his pocket. The silencer would make things a lot more convenient.

A girl, seven, eight, ponytailed, big smile, looked up at him. 'Hi-ya,' she said, 'are you daddy's friend?'

George smiled. 'Yes ma'am,' he said.

She nodded, then stepped back from the door. 'Daddy says to come on in, he'll be out in a mo-mo.'

George stepped into the apartment. It was bright, airy, there was a huge television set, the carpets smelt new, there was a graduation photograph of Fuller on the wall, then one of him receiving an award. There were several paintings too: modern, but not so modern as to defy logical explanation. The furniture was dark, a mix of leather and mahogany, but welcoming with it, soft, without too many sharp edges; child-friendly. Everything about the apartment spoke of quality and value, of heart and soul. George's first instinct was to douse it in petrol and set fire to it.

'Do you want some coffee?' the girl asked.

'Why thank you,' said George, 'that would be nice.'

'No trouble. How would you like it?'

'White,' said George.

She turned away, then swung back and stuck out a tiny hand. 'My name's Annie.'

'Little Orphan Annie?' George asked, clasping the little black fingers in his hand.

Annie giggled. 'Course not,' she said and skipped away.

'Course not,' George repeated.

Clark Fuller appeared from a doorway, fixing his tie. He nodded across at George, gave him the faintest of smiles. 'Sorry,' he said, 'I'm running a bit late.'

'Perfectly understandable,' said George. 'I didn't know you had a kid.'

'No reason why you should.'

George shrugged. 'Is there a Mrs Fuller?'

'Was.'

'Divorced?'

'Dead.'

'I'm sorry.'

'So am I.'

'What happened, if you don't mind me asking?'

'Cancer.'

'Oh, that's terrible.'

'Yes, it is.'

George shook his head for a few moments. 'I'm really sorry,' he said.

'Yeah, well.'

'You raise the girl yourself?'

'I do my best.' Fuller, still not happy with the tie, positioned himself in front of a mirror. 'Did, uh, you bring the money?'

'Yes, of course.' George produced an envelope from his jacket pocket. He tapped it against his fingers. 'I wanted to go over with you some of the questions I'm interested in you putting to the President.'

'If I have the chance.'

'Yes, of course.'

Fuller took the envelope and folded it into his back pocket without examining the contents. George liked that – the trust. The reporter's failure to discover the neat collection of dollar-sized newspaper cuttings served only to temporarily postpone his imminent demise.

'You'd better zip through them,' said Fuller. 'I'm running late. I've to drop Annie off at school, then get to the Empire State.'

'Of course.' George rubbed his hands together, then arched an eyebrow. 'Are you driving? Maybe I could tell you on the way. I need a ride downtown anyhow.'

A look of annoyance flashed across Fuller's face. He caught George's eyes in the mirror.

'I'm sorry,' said George. 'I'm sure you prefer to say goodbye to your daughter alone.'

Fuller shook his head. 'No. It's okay.'

Annie emerged from the kitchen carrying a cup of coffee. She handed it to George who thanked her. He took a quick sip. 'Woah!' he said, 'best I ever tasted.'

She giggled and ran back into the kitchen. She reappeared in a moment with her satchel. 'Ready now,' she said.

Fuller smiled round from the mirror. 'Okay, kid,' he said, 'let's hit the road.'

George set the three-quarters-full cup down. It *was* nice.

As they went down in the lift to the basement car park George said: 'Nice apartment. I didn't realize Reuters paid so well.'

'They don't. I work hard.'

The car was good too, a big black sedan. George got into the back with Annie. He helped her belt up.

'Strange, this,' said George, as they sat in traffic. 'Anyone walking past, looks like you're my driver.'

Their eyes met in the mirror again. 'Sure,' said Fuller.

George shrugged. 'Guess that's just the way things is.'

Annie twittered quite happily beside him for five minutes until Fuller pulled up outside a dull grey building flanked by expensive-looking clothes shops. Parents with kids clustered about the doorway. George read a brass nameplate: The Petard School.

Annie leaned across, straining against the belt, to give George a little kiss goodbye. He turned slightly so that she missed his lips. Fuller slipped out of the driver's seat and opened Annie's door. He unclipped her and she raised her arms for him to lift her out. He shook his head. She screwed up her nose and shuffled herself along the seat until her legs hung out, then with a little jump she landed on the sidewalk. Fuller knelt beside her.

'He has stinky breath,' Annie whispered in his ear.

'Shhh now,' said Fuller. 'Kiss for daddy?' he said.

Her eyes were already on the other kids. She brushed his cheek with her lips and ran on. 'Byeeeee!' she called.

Fuller smiled happily after her for a moment, then crossed behind the vehicle and got back in behind the wheel. 'Do you want to move up front,' he asked, 'or are you happy perpetuating this myth about me being your driver?'

'I'm quite comfortable here, thanks,' said George.

Fuller pulled out into the traffic again.

'She get any hassle? The kid,' George asked suddenly.

'What kind of hassle?'

'Y' know, because of her colour. That looks like a pretty expensive school. I imagine most of the pupils are white.'

A cool edge slipped onto Fuller's voice. George loved it. *The slow burn.* 'It strikes me,' Fuller said, his head darting about, looking for a gap in the traffic, 'that you come from a society unused to the thought of black men in positions of wealth and power. That you are perhaps a little unsettled by it.'

'Lord no,' said George. 'Not unsettled. Depressed, maybe.'

'Excuse me?'

'I said I'm depressed by the state of society. You must be as well.'

'Sometimes,' Fuller said, after a moment. He kept one hand on the wheel as he patted his pocket, then removed a packet of cigarettes. He removed one expertly with the same hand, and slipped it into his mouth. He waved the packet at George.

'No thanks.'

Fuller threw the packet on the passenger seat and extracted the cigarette lighter from the dash.

George leaned forward. 'You're going straight to the Empire.'

Fuller nodded, puffed.

'You must feel pretty good, being the only reporter invited.'

Fuller shrugged.

'You have a pass or something, or is your face your passport?'

The reporter shook his head. 'Not in this day and age. That how it is down south?' He reached into his top pocket and produced a photo-ID. His eyes darted from the road to the plastic card, then he stuck it back in his pocket.

'Sometimes.'

Fuller glanced at his watch. 'Cutting it a bit fine,' he said. 'Where can I drop you?'

George waved vaguely. 'Oh anywhere round here. You haven't forgotten my questions?'

Deadpan. 'How could I?' Fuller went for a gap, made it, horns blasting him. He glanced back at George. 'Well, shoot.'

George smiled at that. 'Okay now,' he said. 'I want you to get to the heart of Keneally's policies on the race issue. I want to know what he's going to do about violence in the inner cities, about the epidemic use of crack, heroin and all other narcotics by the black underclasses, I want to know what he's going to do about immigration. I want to know how he's going to preserve the purity of the race.'

Fuller pulled the car over sharply to the left as horns blasted again, then threw it into a parking space. He switched off the ignition, sat for a few moments tapping the steering wheel, then turned. 'What?' he said.

'Didn't you hear?'

'I heard, sure. I'm just not sure I believe it. I thought you ran a computer magazine.'

'I do.'

'And?'

They stared at each other.

Eventually George shrugged. 'Hey, even computer wimps

have political views. I have a Southern readership, they happen to hate niggers. Can't help that. You offended, Clark?'

Fuller shook his head warily. George loved it. Hit 'em hard, then apologize. Confuse. 'No offence intended.'

'I'm not sure I'd feel comfortable asking those kinda questions.'

'Why not? Surely they're more pertinent, coming from a *brother.*'

'A . . .? Man, what decade are you from?'

'I'm sorry if my poor Southern way of speechifying ain't up to Noo Yawk standards. Phrase the questions whatever way you want. Jive talk it. Rap it. Just get me the answers.'

Fuller drummed his fingers on the wheel. 'I'm not very happy about this,' he said. 'This isn't what we agreed.' He lit another cigarette. 'The chances are I won't get to ask him anything anyway, but if I do have the opportunity, I'm damn sure not going to ask him how he feels about preserving the purity of the Aryan race.'

'Aryan? Who mentioned Aryan?'

'You said—'

'I said *the race*, I didn't say Aryan . . .'

'You meant . . .'

'Don't tell me what I meant, boy.'

Fuller thumped the steering wheel. 'God dammit,' he shouted, 'you are deliberately—'

'Have you got insurance, Clark?'

His brow crinkled. 'What?'

'Life insurance, y'know, 'case something happens to you. What happens to the little girl?'

'Sure I got insurance. What are you on to now . . .?'

George drew the gun. 'I'd like to say I'm sorry, Clark.'

Fuller's eyes widened. Then his jaw dropped. 'What . . .?' he asked limply.

'I'd like to say I'm sorry, but I'd be telling a lie.'

'I don't understand what's going on.'

'C'mon, Clark, you're a smart man. Where you going today?'

'You know where . . .' He stopped. His head turned a little. 'Jesus, you wouldn't . . . but . . .'

'Hey, *I am Clark Fuller*. I know, pigmentation problem! But not insurmountable. However, I'm glad the girl's provided for, she seems a sweet little piccaninny.'

Clark had sucked one of his lips into his mouth. When he let it go there were teeth marks on it. 'You're . . . not . . . sane . . .' he said.

George laughed. 'Of course I am. You think a madman could pull this off?'

Fuller nodded, then grabbed for the door handle. Quick. Not quick enough. Before he could open it George had fired twice. The reporter slumped forward. He gave a low groan, like a subtle orgasm. At least one of the bullets passed clean through him. It ricocheted off the radio button, switching it on. Something rap enveloped the car.

George replaced the weapon in his jacket, but remained in the back for several minutes until the gurgling from the front had stopped. Fuller was lying over the wheel, head resting on his arms. He might just as well have been asleep. The mess on the window was minimal. When he had satisfied himself that there were no inquisitive passers-by George reached forward and carefully pulled the body back against the driver's seat. The eyes were open. George closed them. He reached into Fuller's top pocket and removed the presidential ID, then the wallet from his inside pocket.

He examined them both. He was pleased to see that the presidential ID photo was slightly fuzzy. He flicked through the wallet. Two pictures of Annie, one of his late wife – a good-looker, albeit with the usual drawbacks – an Amex card, two tickets to *Phantom of the Opera*, a press card and driving licence, both with much clearer photos of the deceased, and assorted credit card receipts.

George closed the wallet and placed it in his own pocket. He reached forward again and removed the envelope of newspaper clippings from Fuller's back pocket. He looked at his watch and nodded. Everything was going according to plan.

25

Leonard Maltman had his bag of doughnuts searched on the way into the Empire State Building on the morning of the President's visit. Pawed and squeezed. *President killed by exploding doughnut.*

'Christ,' he said to the sunglassed android on the door, 'are things that bad?'

'If Christ came along, we'd search him too.'

'Christ.'

Leonard was not a happy man. Neither were his staff. Most of them had gathered in the canteen prior to their shifts starting. The security process which goes with any presidential visit had been clearly explained to them, and they'd understood and accepted the theory of it, but the reality was a little different. The Secret Service had breezed in and taken complete control. There was no room for argument. There wasn't even room for small talk. There was a steely silence, an unveiled threat. Leonard began to feel positively ecstatic about getting a few words out of the guard in the lobby. The sooner they could get this day over the better.

He'd barely sat down in his office, was starting to shake his head at the fingerprints in his favourite doughnut, when an impressive-looking man walked in. He was in his fifties. Trim. Confident. Good-looking. Leonard disliked him immediately.

'Fred Troy,' said Fred Troy, extending a hand. 'FBI.'

'Leonard Maltman, head of security.'

Tight grips, both sides.

'Sit down, Leonard,' said Troy. 'You don't mind if I call you Leonard?'

'Everyone else does. Fred.'

Troy didn't much like that. He remained standing. He leaned on the table. His eyes bored into Leonard's. 'Okay,' he snapped, 'now that we've established cordial relations, do you mind telling me what the fuck all your people are doing hanging about the canteen? Don't they know the President's coming?'

'Of course they—'

'Well get them out there!'

'Their shifts don't start until—'

'Shifts! Jesus Christ, man, this is the President we're talking about.' Troy pulled out a chair and sat. 'You ever in the army, Leonard?'

'I was in the NY—'

'In the army the first thing you learn is to secure your base camp and your avenues of approach and supply. This we have done. The President will get here safely and he will ascend to the 86th floor safely. That floor, and above, is sealed off. He is as safe as we can make him. Below that I'm not so sure. I wanted to close the god-damn building down, but they wouldn't have it.'

'There's ten thousand people work here, Fred.'

'My point exactly, and every last one of them a potential

killer. We've searched them on the way in this morning, but that's purely for show. It's their offices that worry me. What they might have stock-piled there.'

'Well now, I wouldn't say that—'

'Leonard, do you remember when the IRA tried to kill Maggie Thatcher in England?'

'Vaguely, I don't really—'

'They planted the bomb in her hotel eight months before she stayed. Eight months!'

'Fred, the President's visit has only been on the agenda for a few wee—'

'You're missing the point, Leonard. I want your guys out there. Checking every office. Every shop. Every god-damn orifice they can find.'

'They won't know what to look for, they're not trained—'

'Jesus Christ, are they security guards or monkeys? They're looking for suspicious-looking men with guns! Foreigners with large amounts of high explosive! I want bodies out there sweating blood!'

'You do realize there are over six hundred and fifty tenants in this building. Fred, there's seventy-three elevators alone.'

'I know these facts.'

Leonard let out a long sigh of resignation. 'Do you want to tell them?' he said weakly.

'No.'

'I thought not.'

Troy stood. He extended his hand again. 'Good doing business with you, Leonard. You're coming up top later?'

'If I can spare the time, sure.'

'What about the two prize pigs?'

'The . . .?'

'Two of your guards, selected for duty on the eighty-sixth.'

'Of course. Sam and Brian.'

'I want to have a word with them.'

'They're not here yet.'

'Don't tell me, their shifts haven't started yet.'

Leonard nodded.

'Jesus Christ,' said Troy, wheeling away.

Leonard slumped back down behind his desk. He peered into his bag of doughnuts. When he looked up, Troy's head had reappeared in the doorway.

'I want those offices searched,' he said, growling the last word into a spit, 'now!'

Up top, Fred Troy slipped a quarter into the binoculars and surveyed the city below. 'New York, New York, so great they named it twice,' he said.

'Don't seem so great to me.'

Troy pulled back from the binoculars and gave Mark Benedict, Michael Tate's right-hand man, a cold look. 'You strike me as a miserable son-of-a-bitch,' he growled. 'Would that be right, Mark?'

'Yes, sir, I'm one of life's pessimists.'

'And how does that sit with Michael Tate's yo-ho-ho philosophy?'

'Uncomfortably, Mr Troy.'

'But he employs you because he likes to see all sides of the equation.'

'No, Mr Tate pretty much knows all sides of every equation.'

'So what's your secret, your wonderful personality or your sharp silk suits?'

'A bit of both, maybe. And the fact that he's trusted me since we were in kindergarten.'

Troy nodded. 'I see. You were networking even then.'

Benedict smiled. 'The early bird gets the worm.'

'You must be very close to him.'

'You could say that.'

'So knock this one on the head, Mark. Is it true he masturbates twice every morning before work? Is that true or just some hippy bullshit?'

'No, that's pretty much true. Reckons he won't think about sex all day that way; gets in the way of making money, sex.'

'Jesus. And you're his right-hand man.'

'Not under those particular circumstances.'

Troy turned back to the binoculars. The money had run out. He couldn't find another quarter. Benedict flipped him one. 'A loan,' he said.

'Talking of worms and early birds, where's yours?'

'Michael will be here shortly.'

'Before the President, I trust.'

'That is the protocol,' said Benedict, 'for the moment.' He pulled up his collar against the wind. 'It's a lonely old place, this,' he said.

Troy didn't respond. There were a dozen Secret Service agents patrolling the 86th floor observatory. A platform was being hammered into place by two maintenance workers and a Magiform public relations team was setting up a state-of-the-art PA system. Thirty chairs had been arranged before the podium, ten in a semicircle and ten in single column running left and right. It really was a ridiculous place to hold a presentation.

Troy stepped back from the binoculars. 'I'm always jittery in places like this. Advised the man against it. No back door.'

'You should have a parachute on stand-by, just in case.'

Troy laughed. 'It was considered.'

Benedict waved a hand vaguely over the ledge. 'Did you see the demonstration forming up outside? Hastings Bandana and the Moravian Army of Christ.'

'Yeah. I know. We're keeping an eye on it.'

Benedict nodded. 'I was handed a recruitment leaflet on the way in. Looks cool.'

Troy raised an eyebrow. 'You're considering it?'

'I've been a right-hand man all my life. You can't tell me that being at the right hand of Christ isn't a promotion. Besides, Michael bankrolls it.'

'He ....?'

'For tax. He gets a kick out of being the main benefactor of an organization dedicated to the eradication of the Aryan race. Besides, he likes to cover all options.'

'You mean he wants to continue the computer franchise if by some miracle they do come to power?' Benedict nodded. 'Won't being white hinder his chances of that?'

'He's prepared to change,' Benedict said.

26

Leonard, like any great general in difficult times, rose to the occasion. His performance was inspirational, his words soared, his sense of loyalty, patriotism and concern for the good health of the President filled his men with pride and fervour and they filed out of the canteen happy to get out there and do good.

'Sure, Leonard,' said Bobby Tangetta from the back of the canteen, 'in your dreams.'

In truth it had not gone that well. He had tried to be inspirational. He had tried to imbue them with a sense of pride. They just weren't interested. They yawned through it. They wanted to know about bonuses. They wanted to know if they had the right under company or union law to kick the fuck out of any Secret Service men who gave them a hard time. But, at least they got on with it. They filed out of the canteen with their sneery faces and carping mouths, but they'd agreed a loose strategy and they'd do their best to follow it. Leonard knew, his men knew, even Fred Troy knew that the search would be no more than superficial and couldn't hope to cover all of the many offices in the building. That wasn't the point. The point was that it was done and seen to be done. It was all about the assigning of blame if something did go wrong. The concern was not for the safety of the President. It was for the protection of jobs in the unlikely event of a catastrophe.

As the troops left, Nathan and Sam appeared out of the elevator together. Leonard, sipping a cup of coffee, looked from one to the other.

'Two of the Three Stooges,' he said. 'Where's Brian?'

Nathan shook his head. 'Brian won't be in today. He's not well.'

Leonard rolled his eyes. 'Oh great. Just fucking great. Nothing trivial, I hope.'

Nathan shrugged. 'I saw him last night. He didn't look well. He sends his apologies.'

'Fucking big of him.' Leonard drained the paper cup, squashed it, dropped it. 'Right, you two; into my office.'

They followed him in. Leonard squeezed in behind his desk. He lifted his bag of doughnuts and peered into it. Then he closed it again. 'I think there's part of a fingernail stuck in my doughnut. Sometimes I hate this fucking job.'

Sam tapped a finger on the edge of the desk. 'I'm still meeting the President, aren't I?'

Leonard tutted. 'Sam, you were *never* meeting the President. You're not even guarding him. You're up there in a purely decorative capacity. Stand there. Shut up. Stay in the background.' Leonard jutted a finger out at Nathan. 'As for you, you're going up too.'

'But I—'

'But nothing. Brian hasn't turned in. If you think I'm organizing another fucking lottery you're mistaken.' Leonard pulled open a drawer. He rifled for a few moments, then produced two badges which he tossed across the table. 'I won't tell if you won't tell.'

Nathan picked one up. It read BRIAN HOUSTON, *Empire Security*. 'Are you sure this is okay? If I'm rumbled, they'll probably shoot me.'

'If you're rumbled, they can shoot me. Take my word for it, Nathan, you'll be fine.'

'But . . . I mean, Jesus, I haven't been vetted or anything. What if I turn out to be some mad Irish terrorist?'

'Believe me,' said Leonard, 'I know a mad Irish terrorist when I see one.'

Nathan shrugged. 'Whatever you say.'

They turned for the door. Leonard called after them. 'Hey, Nathan, did you ever think that day you saved me in the park, you'd end up spending the morning with the President of the United States?'

'Of course I didn't fucking think that,' Nathan said.

27

The presidential motorcade left for the Empire State Building at 10 AM. The President, apart from the 200 Secret Service agents, the 32 NYPD motorcycle outriders, his 60 staff and 15 limousines, felt completely alone. He alternated between flicking through his speech and staring morosely out of the window. He didn't acknowledge the gawpers and wavers. They wouldn't mind. They would see that studied concentration and realize that he was contemplating the Chinese civil war or the Ugandan famine. His triumph at the United Nations the previous evening had dominated the news. He was hot. Then he was cold. He called Tara.

Tara and Slovenski were sharing a limousine en route to Dulles airport, which was thirty minutes from the White House. Tara had spent several hours under a hairdryer already that morning. Slo had spent several hours under his quilt, thinking hard. She wore sunglasses, though the sun seemed reluctant to peek through the ominous grey ceiling.

She was on fire. She was going to have him. She was going to have a baby. A son for the President. She wasn't even going to wait for Ireland. She was going to have him on the plane. The mile-high club.

Slo held the receiver aloft. 'It's for you. The President.'

Tara shook her head. 'I'm not here.'

Slo pressed the receiver to his chest. 'I can't say you're not here, Tara. For God's sake, he knows we're travelling together.'

'Tell him I have a migraine.'

Slo set the receiver down on her lap. 'You tell him.'

Her face snarled up. 'Thanks,' she barked. She removed her sunglasses, then picked up the phone. 'Darling,' she said, smiling sarcastically at Slo, 'how are you?'

'Uhm,' said the President, and that struck her as so down, so unlike the man she knew, that her attitude changed instantly.

'What's the matter?' she purred.

Slovenski was so surprised by the change that his mouth dropped open. It allowed the sex fantasy that had been building up all morning to escape. He'd known that he was crazy to let it build like that, but he was helpless. All that huffing and puffing and downright nastiness couldn't disguise the fact that the woman was still in love. He shook his head. His jaw waved about.

He picked up the other phone. He called his wife. The kids were screaming. 'I'm sorry about last night,' he lied. 'It couldn't be helped. So much work.'

'I know, honey. Are you okay? I do miss you, y'know.'

'I miss you too.'

'I just feel . . .' said the President, '. . . alone.'

'You're never alone,' Tara whispered. 'I'm always with you. You know that.'

'Are you?' said the President. 'It doesn't always feel like that.'

'We might fight. But it's you and me against the world, kid.'

'I need a hug.'

'I'm giving you one right now.'

'It's not the same.'

'We need a holiday,' said Slo.

'You've been so busy.'

'I know. I wish you could come to Ireland too. I hear it's lovely.'

'Doesn't it always rain?'

'Would you mind? To be away from it all?'

'No, I wouldn't mind.'

'Slo will look after you, won't he?' asked the President.

Tara glanced across at Slo. Slo glanced back. They locked eyes. The sex fantasy shot right back up Slovenski's nose.

'Of course he will,' she said. 'I'm in very capable hands.'

Slo turned away so that she wouldn't see him turning red. She chatted away to her husband quite happily, but her eyes were glued to Slovenski's crimson ears.

Ten minutes later the presidential motorcade ground to a halt. The roads in central Manhattan were benefiting from the President's hugely unpopular road improvement bill, but all the kicking and screaming by his people up ahead couldn't change the fact that traffic was down to single file, nor that a truck had jack-knifed while taking a corner too fast. An apologetic Secret Service agent tapped on the President's window. As it wound down he said, 'We're gridlocked, Mr President.'

'That's okay,' said the President, 'don't worry about it.'

He was happier now. Speaking to Tara had done him the world of good. He wasn't really alone. It just felt like it. He would just fly straight to Ireland after the Empire

State and make love to her. It wasn't as if there was no precedent for it, there was *always* an Irish problem to be solved.

'How're we doing for time?' the President asked.

His driver glanced at his watch. 'We've half an hour. But I'm sure they'll wait.'

The President doubted it. Tate would get the ball rolling and turn it into a political snub. He looked out of the window. The Secret Service team had formed a tight circle about his car. He leaned forward so that he could get a better look at the street. People were beginning to congregate around the motorcade. He could see now that they were stopped outside Macy's. He had an idea.

He opened the limousine door and climbed out. It was a few moments before the Secret Service agents realized that he was among them, and then only because the onlookers let out a roar.

'Mr President, I really would suggest that the best place for you is in the car.'

'I'm sure you would,' said the President, 'but I'm going shopping.'

He led the way. The agents, panic-stricken, quickly formed a raggedy wedge about him as he mounted the sidewalk and proceeded into Macy's, waving and shaking hands as he went. A security guard looked up as he led the procession through the doors.

Keneally walked straight up to him. 'Lingerie?' he asked.

The security guard stared at him.

'Lingerie department?'

The security guard opened his mouth, but nothing would come out.

'Never mind,' said the President and marched on.

He came to a halt in front of a store directory. He nodded

down the list of floors and departments. 'Lingerie,' he said quietly. On he went.

Secret Service agents, speaking excitedly into their sleeves, began to fan out.

The President found the escalator and began to ascend. Secret Service agents scrambled up the stairs to secure the next floor before his arrival.

On the third floor a young girl, name badge in place, glanced at him as he came off the escalator, then walked on. Then stopped.

'Lingerie?' said the President.

'Marjorie,' said Marjorie.

'Never mind,' said the President.

He marched on. He spied the lingerie department. He stopped. The agents stopped. 'Please wait here,' he said.

'Mr President, I cannot allow . . .' the lead agent began, but stopped when he saw the jaunty smile slip from the President's face.

'The First Lady's lingerie,' said the President, 'is the First Lady's business.'

'Absolutely,' said the agent. He spread his arms. The agents, still crowding off the escalator, came to a halt.

'Thank you,' the President said crisply. 'I won't be long.'

Kathleen Horne had worked in the lingerie department for twenty-five years. What she didn't know about lingerie wasn't worth knowing. In fact, a lot of what she did know about lingerie wasn't worth knowing. But hey.

'Help you, sir?' She was well used to men pawing their way through her lingerie. An average day turned up half a dozen perverts. She smiled and crossed to the man with the good hair and the smart suit. It was too early to bracket him.

'Hi,' he said, smiling broadly.

They looked at each other for several moments. The President grinned while he waited for the penny to drop. It didn't. Suddenly flustered, suddenly missing Tara, Slo, and aware of the Secret Service agents still hovering anxiously by the escalators, he mumbled, 'Under . . . wear . . . for . . . my . . . wife . . .'

'And do you have any idea what type of lingerie you want to buy for your wife?'

The President shook his head. 'What do you have?'

Kathleen pursed her lips. 'This morning we have special prices on ring bras, underwired camisole bras, trousseau basques, briefs and garters, convertible padded underwired bras, deep-line strapless bras, underwired bodyshapers, super-stretch thong-briefs, underwired lace bras, garter belts, lace thongs, embroidered bras, cotton bras, satin bras . . .'

'I'm looking for something . . .'

'Sexy . . . yes, sir . . . cup size?'

'Excuse me?'

'Cup size?'

'I'm sorry . . .'

'How big are her breasts?'

'Oh . . .' The President thought for a moment. He looked at the massed ranks of bras hanging about him like body warmers for skeletons. He raised his hands, spread them. 'About this size,' he said.

She escorted him to her sales desk. 'You just bring this right back if it doesn't fit,' she said as she began to wrap the black lace bodysuit they had picked together after ten minutes of head-shaking and hand-measuring. 'You really should find out your good wife's proportions.'

'I will.'

'Cash or credit card?'

He opened his mouth, then he stopped. He patted his pockets. A mildly panicked look crossed his face. 'I'm sorry,' he said, 'I don't seem to . . .'

Kathleen tutted. *Pervert*. He'd disguised it well. One of the better ones. 'Okay, buster,' she growled, pulling herself up to her full figure, 'you just get the hell out of my store.'

The President tried his back pocket. 'There's some here, some . . .'

'Scram, you sick son-of-a-bitch!'

'I'm telling you . . . I have . . .'

Kathleen pressed the security button. The alarm wasn't much more than a higher-pitched telephone ring, but it was different enough to bring the security guys running. They'd have him out on the sidewalk in seconds.

She looked towards the escalator and was quite surprised to see nearly fifty men in dark suits and sunglasses hurrying towards them.

'Good God Almighty,' she said.

Clutching the Macy's bag, the President climbed into the back of the limousine. The visibly relieved Secret Service agents made sure he was secure and then fanned out about the car again. 'What about the gridlock?' he said to the driver.

'Gridlock's fine,' he replied. 'We're causing the problem now.'

'Okay, let's go. How late are we?'

The driver shrugged. 'We called ahead. Delayed by affairs of state.'

The President nodded. *Affairs*. He had never considered having an affair. Not even in the darkest moments with Tara. He slipped his hand into the Macy's bag. He felt the material. Fifteen years of marriage and he'd never bought his wife underwear. He tutted. Things would have to change.

The President waved at the crowds as the sirens started up and the motorcade got under way again. Still clutching the underwear, he asked the driver his name.

'Morgan, Mr President, William Morgan.'

'Been with us long, William?'

'Five years, Mr President.'

'Married?'

'Yes, sir, married twenty-five years.'

'Happily married, William?'

'Yes, sir. Very happily married.'

'William, do you know your wife's cup size?'

'Sir?'

'Do you know what cup size her brassiere is?'

Morgan caught the President's eye in the mirror. 'Can't say that I do, Mr President.'

'Well make sure that you find out. It's the sort of thing a husband should know.'

'Very well, Mr President.'

It was the sort of thing Graham Slovenski was about to find out.

28

There was a definite buzz about the Empire State Building in the minutes leading up to the arrival of the President of the United States. Everyone felt it: from the Empire security staff checking the hundreds of offices to the Moravian Army of Christ, pinned back on the sidewalk by three lines of New York's finest, from the ponytailed Magiform executives sipping cocktails and admiring the view from the 86th to Michael Tate himself, relaxing over a complex computer program in the management offices on the floor below. You could hate Keneally for myriad reasons, but he was still the President of the United States.

Even George Burley felt a buzz, although that had more to do with his pleasure at successfully negotiating the tight security surrounding the President and making it to the 86th floor and his date with destiny. With the right ID you could get anywhere. He had arrived early, long before the VIPs. He felt confident, looked good, the only real hiccup had been with the third and last of the security checks before getting into the elevator for the observation floor. One supercilious son-of-a-bitch Secret Service agent had closely examined his photograph, but George had every confidence in his make-up and his acting, and sure, how could he begrudge the man being suspicious of a black guy anyway, especially with that Moravian rabble screaming at everything white that moved below. If fate was ever to lend a hand, it lent it then. The guard read out Clark Fuller's name as he checked it off his list and this old guy turned at the sound of it: Sam McClintock. Although highly trained secret agents weren't ever going to let someone near the President on the okay of a lowly security guard, it was just the final confirmation the agent needed that George was kosher. *Kosher*. George nearly gagged at the thought of it.

They rode up together, Sam working the buttons, of course, George clutching his computer, his fingers tingling, his head throbbing. He passed Sam the envelope of dollar-sized newspaper cuttings he had retrieved from Clark Fuller.

'I think this should more than compensate you for your trouble, Sam,' George said.

Sam nodded. 'It's nice to find someone interested in what I have to say. Been here all my life. Met every president since . . .'

'Are you meeting him today, Sam?'

Sam laughed. 'Not officially, no. But I have my ways.' He put the envelope inside his jacket. George smiled benevolently at him.

When they reached the 86th Sam gave George a guided tour. He was content to nod along beside the old man while familiarizing himself with the layout and counting the number of ponytails he wanted to throw over the edge. What was it with computer companies that so many of their experts felt the need to grow girl-length hair?

Sam took him into the Empire State Deli. It wasn't much more than a concession stand. Sam ordered two coffees.

George lifted two straws from a box and began to drum absentmindedly on the counter.

'You're looking mighty fine today, Marilu,' Sam said. And she was.

'Not every day the President comes visiting,' Marilu said. 'That'll be two dollars.'

Sam raised his eyebrows. 'Hey, Marilu, since when did you charge me for coffee?'

'I can't go out giving free coffee, today of all days. I'd get fired. 'Less you want a cocktail, they're free to guests.'

Sam checked his pockets, but he'd left his wallet in his locker. 'I'm sorry, Marilu, but I don't . . .' then he trailed off. What was he thinking? He'd an envelope packed with cash in his jacket. He pulled it out.

George, who'd been counting secret agents through the glass, glanced back just as Sam tore open the envelope. In a flash he was across and had grabbed Sam by the arm. 'Don't you dare!' he scolded.

Sam, surprised, pulled away. 'What the . . .?'

'That money's for you! These coffees are on me!'

With a flourish George produced a roll from his trouser pocket and counted off three dollar bills. He passed them across to Marilu.

'I insist. Expense accounts are a wonderful thing, Sam.'

'If you say so,' Sam grumbled, slipping the envelope back inside his jacket.

As they went back outside Nathan appeared from the elevator and sauntered across. Sam gave him a long, appraising look. His face was grey. He looked like he had three-week-old teabags stuck under his eyes, which were noticeably bloodshot. His hair was greasy, dank. His uniform didn't seem to fit.

'How's the form?' Nathan asked. He looked at George, then nodded at his lapel.

'Nice rose,' he said.

George looked down at the brilliant red rose. 'Thanks,' he said.

Sam, who was no oil painting himself, just nodded, then thumbed at George. 'This is Clark Fuller, he's writing a piece about me for . . . well who for, Clark?'

'Just about everyone. *Time, Miami Herald*, London *Times.*' George held out his hand.

'Nathan Jones,' said Nathan Jones.

'Not Brian Houston?' asked George.

Nathan looked perplexed for a moment, then followed George's gaze down to the name badge on his chest.

Nathan laughed. 'Officially, yeah. Bit of a mix-up. Don't let on, eh?'

George smiled. 'Won't tell a soul.'

Nathan walked on. Every time he thought of Brian Houston and what he had done, he came out in a cold sweat. Nathan had nothing against homosexuals, but he'd be damned if he was going to let them interfere with his private parts. He folded his arms on the wall and stared out over New York. What if Brian had a disease? What if Lisa found out? Where was Lisa? Who was she with? What was she doing with him? Would she do *that* with a complete stranger?

Someone giggled behind him. He turned. Two young fellas, maybe his age, in smart suits, were looking at him. They slurped from cocktail glasses containing a dark blue liquid. They were already drunk.

'Hey, nice uniform,' one, bespectacled, said, and giggled again.

Nathan curled up a lip. 'Nice ponytail, arsehole,' he spat and pushed himself off the wall. He entered the concession stand with the sound of renewed splutter-giggles in his ears. Marilu smiled across.

'Get you anything, *Brian*?'

'So the word is out, is it?'

Marilu shrugged. 'Coffee, tea or me?'

Nathan ignored her. He nodded down at a tray of glasses filled with the blue liquid. 'What's the piss they're drinking out there?'

'Cocktail, some description. Brought it up from down below. For the guests. Be *my* guest.'

'Have you tried it?'

'Had a sip. Quite a kick. Don't let Leonard catch you, he was up earlier breathing fire.'

'Don't you worry about Leonard.'

Nathan lifted a glass, sniffed it. It smelt . . . *blue*. He took a sip. It didn't taste of anything, really. He drained the glass, then took two more. 'For Sam,' he said, 'and the other bloke.'

Marilu shrugged again. 'I didn't give you them, if anyone asks.'

Nathan nodded and returned to his position by the wall. The drunks had moved on. He placed one glass on the wall, then drained the other. Then he lifted the second and emptied it as well. He returned to the concession stand.

'Marilu,' he said, 'those eejits just sent the drinks flying. Do you mind if I take some more?'

'Help yourself, Nathan.' She beamed.

Nathan took one in each hand, then balanced a third between the two. Outside Sam and Clark Fuller were just completing their fourth circuit of the observation floor. Nathan noticed the familiar glazed expression in Fuller's eyes. He needed rescuing.

'Hey, old man, celebratory drink.' He offered a glass to Sam, who took it, then examined it disdainfully. George refused his. He preferred to keep his mind unclouded by alcohol.

333

'What is it?' Sam asked.

Nathan shrugged and drained his glass. 'It's blue,' he said, setting the glass down and cupping his hands round the drink George had refused.

Sam took a sip. Then spat it out. 'I'm not drinking that. It's poison.'

'It's rocket fuel,' Nathan laughed, and relieved Sam of his glass. He walked on. Sam saw him stagger slightly as he turned.

Leonard Maltman saw it too as he stepped out of the elevator with Fred Troy. Nathan smiled stupidly.

'I'm just helping to hand these out,' he blurted.

Troy looked him up and down. He didn't like what he saw.

'This is Brian Houston, Fred, y'know . . . prize pig.'

Troy nodded sullenly. He jabbed a finger at Nathan. 'Lose the glasses, kid. If I see you with another drop you'll be down that shaft quicker than spit.'

Leonard gave Nathan a filthy look. The prodigal son gone bad.

Nathan looked at the ground. 'Sorry,' he mumbled, 'I'll take them back.' He turned for the concession stand. As he entered he drained one of the glasses. As he approached the counter he emptied the second. He set them both down.

'You okay, Nath?' Marilu asked.

Nathan swayed. 'I'm young,' he said, 'and I'm in love.'

'Aw,' said Marilu.

'Except she's run off and I don't know where to find her.'

'Aw, Nath.'

Nathan shook his head. He gave a sad little shrug. 'She never even came to see me here. She would have been proud.'

Marilu bit her lip. He looked like he was about to cry. *And so am I.*

334

She wanted to go round and hug him, but just as she made her move the elevators disgorged the biggest wave of visitors yet. As they streamed into the concession she lost sight of him.

He made his way to the men's toilets. He knew now that he was drunk. That he shouldn't have fired back so many drinks. He was a beer man, generally. Cocktails were for women and gays . . . *God*, he thought, *one moment of forced passion with Brian and I start drinking cocktails*. He ran the cold tap, splashed his face. He staggered up to the urinals. He was about to pee when the door opened. A man stepped up to the next urinal. Nathan froze. Bad enough not being able to pee . . . but what if *he can sense that I've recently had a homosexual experience . . . maybe he's followed me in with the express purpose of* . . . Nathan looked to his left.

'Uuuuuugh,' he began, grasping for the name, 'aren't you . . . what's it . . . money bags . . . Donald Trump.'

Trump, and it was Trump, didn't look up. 'I'm sorry, no autographs.'

Nathan looked closer, to see whether he was smiling or not. He couldn't decide; it was one of those faces that seemed to have a perpetual smirk on it.

Nathan put a hand up to hold himself steady against the toilet wall. Trump was pissing away. 'I've never been able to pee in front of other men,' Nathan said.

'Really,' said Trump.

'Give me a thousand dollars,' Nathan said, 'and I'll be your friend for life.'

Trump stepped back, zipped up. 'I can buy friends for less than that,' he said. He walked off.

Nathan finally had his pee. He didn't feel much better for it. He returned to the washbasin and splashed some more water. He looked at himself in the mirror. *I know I look rough, but do I look homosexual?* He bent to the sink again, drank from the cold tap.

'You're a fucking faggot.'

He looked up, saw Sid standing in one of the cubicle doorways. 'Christ,' said Nathan.

'Christ,' said Michael Tate, stepping out of his office, 'never wore a fucking tie.'

'We don't know that for sure. Just because it's not mentioned doesn't mean . . .' Mark Benedict stooped to help his friend and employer complete the knot. 'It's just one of those things, Michael, everyone has to do it.'

'And the fact that I have more money than Keneally and as much power, and the fact that this is my party, shouldn't it mean that I can get away without wearing a tie?'

'No, we must observe protocol.'

'Why?'

'Because that's the protocol.'

'You mean the reason we have protocol is because it's the protocol. To have protocol.'

'That's about it.'

Tate tutted. 'I knew there was a reason I was trying to change the world.'

He ran his hand along the back of his neck. It felt strange: the tie, and the lack of a ponytail. He'd cut it off that morning. His barber had wanted to hold onto it so that he could auction it for charity. Tate had nailed that one right away. It would go right down the toilet.

Keneally's people were everywhere. But not in the little management office. In there it was just Keneally and Tate; Keneally behind the desk, *his* desk, and Tate on a chair facing him, like he was being interviewed.

'Like the hair,' Keneally said.

'Or lack of.'

They smiled at each other, but they might as well have snarled.

'Where do we stand, Michael? On you know what.'

Tate shrugged. 'I don't think my position has changed.'

'You're going to keep me waiting, right up to the vote.'

'I told you then and I'm telling you now. I just haven't made my mind up.'

'Michael, you're the richest man in the world. You make your mind up ten thousand times a day. And I remember Iowa.'

'Hey,' Tate shrugged again, 'I was a kid then. Now I'm, y'know, more of statesman kind of thing. Okay? I see the big picture. Believe me, you'll be the first to know.'

'Before Senator Broole?'

'Before Senator Broole.'

'All I'm trying to do is make everyone's lives a little easier.'

'I understand that.'

'Do you think it's right that people should die because they can't afford proper health care?'

'It's not as simple as that, Mr President.'

'But it is, Michael.' He stood up. 'Okay. It's up to you. Let's get this shit over with.'

Tate stood and opened the door. 'Okay. Thanks for coming.'

'The pleasure's all mine.' Then Keneally stopped, and held the door. Their faces were only a foot apart. 'I know you've made your decision already. And I'm allowing you your little bit of fun keeping everyone waiting. But I'm telling you, if this goes against me, I'll really fuck you over.'

Tate smiled. 'You can try.'

Up top an earnest PR woman was urging the ponytailed and sober-suited alike into their seats. A few meandered lazily over, others stood their ground, yakking, drinking, but then one caught sight of Benedict and Tate stepping out of the elevator and there was a sudden setting down of cocktails and a rush for seats.

Fred Troy met them as they emerged beside the concession stand and began to walk between the rows of chairs. 'He's on his way up,' he said, his voice quiet but authoritative, 'and everything's on schedule.'

'What about the Moravian Army of Christ?' Benedict asked.

'Less of an army, more of a rabble, but all the more worrying for that.'

As Tate stepped up to the podium a hush settled on the small audience, the only sound was of the cool wind whistling through the PA system and somebody throwing up in the men's toilets. Tate, speaking without notes, rambled for five minutes in a highpitched little squeal. He spoke on the uniqueness of Magiform, then thanked his staff, 'without whom all of this would have been possible'. It got a laugh. Then, following a signal from the back he straightened up and, unconsciously adopting a deeper, movie-trailer voice, spoke slowly into the microphone.

'Ladies and gentlemen, the President of the United States.'

29

Sam massaged Nathan's neck as he was sick.

'Will you stop massaging my fucking neck?' Nathan
pleaded groggily. He threw up again. 'Oh God,' he moaned.
'I'm never drinking again.'

Sam shook his head. 'You should stick to normal drinks.'

'Thanks. I'll bear that in mind.' He drank from the tap.
Gargled. Spat. 'You're missing the President.'

'I'm missing the President's speech. It's a different thing
entirely.' Nathan stood up from the wash-hand basin. He
staggered.

Sam held on to his shirt. Nathan steadied himself against
the ceramics. 'C'mon, let's get some coffee.'

'Oh God,' said Nathan.

Sam took his arm. 'You're gonna have to walk by yourself.
Those Secret Service guys see you staggering about, they
won't let you past.'

Nathan pulled his arm away. He took a deep breath. Pulled
his head up. Shoulders back. 'Okay,' he said, 'let's go.'

Sam opened the door and they walked out onto the observation platform. It was difficult to tell with all the sunglasses

what kind of looks the Secret Service guys gave them, but they weren't stopped.

Fred Troy, standing to the left of the President, watched Sam and Nathan enter the concession stand, then returned to scanning the audience. He'd read the President's speech, so he knew there was only a couple of minutes to go, and so far, so good. He prided himself on running a slick operation. It was still a bad location: the back-door scenario still worried him. He'd a helicopter circling, bristling with guns, but it couldn't get too close without drowning out the speech. At least the audience was docile. Half-drunk, probably. The absence of reporters jostling for position was also a plus; it wasn't that they themselves were a danger, but the press-pack turning on itself was a distraction which protestors had taken advantage of in the past. There was only one reporter this time. Clark Fuller sat in the front row, a portable computer on his lap. Troy wondered what Fuller had done to wangle this particular gig: he wasn't a familiar face at the White House or on the road. He *almost* looked dapper. Sharp suit, set off nicely by a rose in the lapel, black shoes with an army shine. He spoilt it by drumming on his teeth with a striped plastic straw.

Michael Tate smiled benevolently at his audience. He had enjoyed seeing the surprised looks of his employees when he'd appeared *sans* ponytail. By the end of the day word would have spread from coast to coast. By the weekend he doubted if there'd be one left in the entire company. Ties would suddenly appear, too. He pondered over whether to remove his tie as a symbolic gesture at the end of the President's speech; it would be a signal to his people that although a certain amount of compromise was inevitable, he remained essentially a free spirit. He was aware that the other guests, the industrialists, the stock market guys, were studying him; he could see in their faces the odd mixture of awe and contempt which he had become so familiar with. Awe at the achievements, contempt at the way he looked.

George Burley could barely hear the President's speech for the blood rushing through his brain. It felt like he was in a wind tunnel. Or being sucked down the plughole in a bath. Everything he hated about life was standing a few metres in front of him. He drank in the pink skin, the warm smile, the sparkling eyes, the earnest delivery, the succulent intonation. *Oh, he looks so cute*. This man had not only helped destroy the greatest nation on God's earth, but had conspired, directly or indirectly, to destroy George himself. No wonder he was number one on his death list. He had the list up on the screen before him, although he made sure it was in small enough type so that the hippy beside him couldn't read it.

George drummed the national anthem on his teeth. Then he set the straw down on his computer. He pulled up the lapel on his jacket and smelt the rose. He breathed it deep. Nature's goodness. Then he turned the lapel forward until the stem of the rose and three venom-dipped thorns were exposed.

Keeping his eyes glued to the President, carefully, carefully, George snapped off one thorn and held it in the palm of his hand. Then he picked up the straw and began to tap out the national anthem once again.

Nathan leaned against the concession stand and nodded vaguely as Sam asked him for the second time whether he wanted coffee. He felt that the gravitational pull of the sun on his head was beginning to lessen; it was now spinning only three or four times a second. He wanted Lisa. He wanted her to hold his head, to *stop* his head; to tell him everything would be all right. He wanted to be in bed next to her, he wanted to cry and say what a fool he'd been, drinking so much, and that it really wouldn't happen again, and for her to reassure him and say, okay, love, it's okay. He broke out in a pre-vomit sweat, battled not to let it happen, not here, not right in front of the President. *The President, even more powerful than Oprah. Would he help? Would he help a vomit-stained Irishman find his lost love?*

'Not so well, is he?' said Marilu as she poured.

'He's okay,' said Sam.

'Don't want him being sick in here if the President drops by for coffee.'

'He's okay, Marilu.'

'He don't look it.'

'Well he is,' Sam snapped.

'You okay, Nath?' Marilu asked.

'Been better,' said Nathan.

'He's okay,' Sam snapped.

'Okay, mister, I hear you.' Marilu pushed the cups across the counter. 'Two dollars.'

Sam rolled his eyes. He patted his pockets again. No money – then for the second time he remembered the money Fuller had given him. He removed the envelope. He tapped it against his hand. The money was for Mary. He only needed two dollars, but once he was into it he knew it would rapidly disappear.

'That's two dollars,' Marilu repeated.

'I'm not deaf,' Sam shot back. He opened the envelope and pulled out the notes. It was a few moments before it actually registered that what he held in his hands was not several thousand dollars but worthless newspaper. He counted two off and put them on the counter. He looked at them. Marilu looked at them. Nathan raised one fatigued eyebrow. Sam flicked through the rest of the sheets, he spread them out in his hands like a deck of cards; he shook his head. He looked up at Marilu, then at Nathan, his eyes large with disbelief, fright. He let out a low groan. Then he threw the paper in the air. As it began to flutter down around them, Sam turned quickly.

'Sam?' Nathan stumbled after him. 'Sam? What's going . . .'

'Fuck him,' Sam growled. His face was red. The shrapnel in his head caught his mood and began to throb. Secret Service agents turned as Sam appeared suddenly in the doorway to the concessions stand, peering myopically into the crowd.

The President scanned the audience one last time; he always tried to make eye contact with as many people as possible. It was amazing how much it reduced animosity. 'Thank you,' he said, and they stood to applaud.

As George stood he carefully slid the thorn into the end of the straw. He gingerly placed the straw in his mouth. He mimicked clapping along with the rest of them: he took aim. He was barely three metres away. It was harder to miss.

The President made eye contact.

George drew his breath.

'You fuck!' Sam screamed.

As the President, surprised, shifted left, Fuller shot.

Fred Troy, stung, slapped his own face.

'You fuck!' Sam screamed again and began to charge towards the front. The audience, panicked, pushed left, right, back and front, began falling over seats to get out of the way of the madman. They couldn't see that he had no gun, that he was a harmless old man; they saw a madman flailing towards them. They saw, they ran. Secret Service agents threw themselves in Sam's path even as they fumbled for their guns. Sam disappeared under a pile of bodies.

Michael Tate dived to the right. Fred Troy, his own weapon out now, bundled the President out of the way. In seconds the President had disappeared under a protective scrum. Nathan stood helpless in the concession doorway as Sam struggled through the melee on hands and knees, but was then felled by a pistol butt. His head cracked off the cement with a sickening thud.

A Secret Service agent thrust Nathan back as he rushed forward to help. Nathan threw up his fists, but a gun to his temple stopped him.

'Stay right where you are, mister!' the agent yelled, sweat breaking on his brow, his upper lip trembling.

In seconds every orifice of Sam's body had been searched. An agent spoke into his cufflinks. 'Suspect is clean,' he said.

Fred Troy, bringing all his experience to bear, had the situation assessed in seconds. He stepped up to the microphone. He raised his hands. 'Please, everyone, the President is safe.' He glanced down at the President, just beginning to emerge from beneath the suit scrum, looking crumpled and flustered. 'There's no need to panic. If you could all just make your way to the elevators while we get the situation under control.'

Michael Tate rose slowly, brushing himself off. He looked to see if anyone had noticed his dive. He was the richest, maybe the most important man in the world, but nobody had thought to protect him in that moment of crisis. Not even Mark Benedict. *He* was slowly raising himself from beneath a chair. So much for loyalty.

The guests didn't wait for a second invitation to leave. The Magiform team moved as one for the elevators, jostled all the way by the industrialists. They all had too much to lose by dying.

Tate moved off the platform and down to where the

assassin lay. The Secret Service agents stood about him, bristling. Their shoulders were further back, their chins jutted out. They'd done their stuff, they'd protected the President. Boy were they good. Tate pushed through. Benedict appeared at his elbow. They peered at the bleeding man in the Empire State security uniform.

'I thought I told you to get rid of that old fuck?' Tate spat.

Benedict's face was white. 'The order was given.'

Then the President was there, looking at Sam. 'Does anyone?'

Leonard Maltman poked a toe at Sam. 'He's an employee. An ex-employee. He was retiring today. I'm sorry, Mr President. He was a little senile; we thought it would be nice to let him meet you on his final day. The excitement of it must have pushed him over the edge.'

The President managed a smile. 'No harm done,' he said. 'And if anything it proves just how well prepared my security staff are.' He turned and nodded round the gathered agents. 'It's good to know I'm in safe hands.'

Fred Troy, sticking close, said: 'Let's get you out of here.'

'Nonsense,' the President laughed. 'I've had my scare for today. Let's get some coffee now the official part's over. How about it, folks?'

The Secret Service agents smiled at their Man. A job well done. Let's celebrate, but never, *ever*, off duty.

The President turned and led them into the concession. The agents, Leonard, Tate, Benedict, all followed.

George lingered. What a guy, he thought, what a leader. A Secret Service agent touched his arm.

'Can I show you to the elevator?' he asked.

'No thanks,' said George. He fished out his press card.

Nathan, his heart galloping, his legs shaking, knelt beside Sam. As he touched the old man's head, Sam gave a little cough, his eyes fluttered. 'Sam, are you okay?' Nathan whispered. There was no response. The eyes closed again. A little trickle of blood appeared from his nose. 'Has somebody called a doctor?'

A Secret Service agent shook his head.

'Well do you think you could?' Nathan snapped. He cradled the old man's head in his lap. 'I think he's dying.'

The agent spoke into his cufflinks. Then he put a hand on Nathan's shoulder. 'Perhaps you should go to the elevator. We'll look after him.'

Nathan slapped the hand away. 'Will you fuck,' he spat.

George followed the crowd into the concession stand. Nobody paid any attention to the newspaper cuttings scattered on the floor. Not giving Sam real money had been an act of reckless bravado. But he remained undetected. He had two more thorns left. And he had perhaps twenty minutes before Fred Troy died and a fresh wave of panic set in. If he remained calm and took his time, perhaps all was not yet lost.

Nathan took off his jacket and gently laid Sam's head on it. The old guy was breathing. 'You'll be fine,' Nathan whispered. He sat back. He hated this. Hated it all. Every little aspect of his life had gone wrong; it seemed like every thing he touched ended up bruised and battered or covered in sick. He knew that if he threw himself over the side of the Empire *right this instant* he would not only kill himself, but whoever he landed on as well, and that that death would in turn cause misery, heartbreak, bankruptcy, a political crisis and revolution in a small African state, thousands would die, maybe millions. That was the Nathan effect. Lisa was lucky to get away with just her heart broken. Who was he kidding? Her heart wasn't broken. It was made of diamond. It wasn't even scratched. There were two glasses by his elbow. *Never drinking again.* Of course he was. Who was he kidding? Sure, he could blame the worst moments in his life on it, but he could also look back fondly on the best. Just the two drinks. To settle him. So that he wouldn't think about the Secret Service agents and their hard, cold stares. He lifted one, drained the blue liquid. He lifted the other, emptied it. He looked at the solitary agent. 'Why don't you go and get some coffee with the President?' He nodded down at Sam. 'I don't think he's going to do a runner.'

The agent stood where he was.

Ten minutes passed. Still no medic.

Inside, George, a cup of coffee in one hand, the straw jutting out of his top pocket, roved around the President as he laughed and joked with his agents, never quite getting a clear view. He looked at Fred Troy: his face was white, beads of sweat stood out in his brow. *Not long now.*

The President set down his cup. He thanked Marilu. A huge smile split her face.

'Time to move, I think,' he said. A dozen coffee cups were rapidly put down. George cursed under his breath.

The elevator doors opened and a man in a white coat emerged. He carried a leather bag. As the presidential party began to leave the concession he stood to one side, speaking briefly to Fred Troy as he passed. Then he crossed to where Sam was lying. Nathan stood, swayed.

'About fucking time,' Nathan said.

The man ignored him. He knelt beside Sam. He opened his bag, took something out.

Nathan sneered down at him. 'Where's the stretcher?'

The man looked up at the other agent. 'What stretcher?'

The agent grinned. The man in the white coat lifted Sam's hand.

For a moment Nathan didn't understand. Then, suddenly, through the recharged alcohol, it clicked. He was not a doctor at all. He was taking Sam's fingerprints.

The temper broke on him.

Nathan lashed out. His DM boot caught the fingerprinter on the side of the head and he rolled backwards. Surprised, the agent stepped forward with hands upstretched to pacify him. He did not expect the whirling dervish that was Nathan Jones. Once, twice, thrice. Into the stomach, into the head, into the groin. The agent reeled back, collapsed over the already upset chairs. Nathan was on him. He clattered a chair on him. The fingerprinter, struggling to his feet, reached inside his jacket. A chair hit him on the head as well. He sprawled back. A gun tumbled from his hand. Nathan was on him, banging his head off the cement.

'You just don't care! You just don't fucking care!' Nathan screamed.

Marilu appeared in the concession doorway. 'Nathan! Nathan, don't! Please!'

'Fuck off!' he screamed.

He lifted the gun. He looked desperately about him. Marilu saw madness in his eyes; she let out a little scream and dashed back into the concession. Nathan waved the gun about. He didn't know what to do. His breathing was heavy, his ears rang. He could hear Sid singing. He saw Coolidge's dead head. He felt sick, the alcohol racing up his throat; he clamped his mouth shut, gagged. He saw Brian's face. The disgust coursed through him. Jesus, he had attacked the Secret Service. He saw Lisa's face close, *close*, then it zipped away until it was a pin-prick and then was gone. And he knew she was gone, gone for ever, because if ever there had been a remote chance to ask the President to help him it had disappeared the moment he had attacked the Secret

Service. It was not merely an assault. It was his ticket out of America, and he would never return. Never be allowed to return. His only chance, his only tiny, tiny chance was to get out *now*, run away, run for ever, *get out of this fucking building before they clap me in irons*. Get downstairs, melt into the crowd, somehow find her, find that beautiful face. He rubbed desperately at his forehead. *Run away, run away*. He stuck the gun in his jacket pocket. Behind him the fingerprinter moaned and began to raise himself. *Now, before they raise the alarm*. For *Lisa*.

Nathan tried desperately to control his breathing. As he passed the concession stand he saw Marilu peeking out at him, her eyes level with the counter.

He rounded the corner to the elevators. A phalanx of Secret Service agents stood there. And the President of the United States. Nathan groaned. He couldn't just turn away. He had to keep going. To keep calm. Make good his escape. Disappear. Blend in.

The President turned, smiled. 'Hello there,' he said.

Nathan opened his mouth, but nothing came out.

The President was used to this. 'Worked here long?' he asked. 'Seems to me like a mighty fine place to work. How's the old guy?'

Nathan glanced behind him. All the horror came back. Old Sam lying there, dying there, ignored. 'He needs a medic,' said Nathan. His voice was light, wispy.

'I'll make sure one is sent up,' said the President.

The elevator door opened. Bobby Tangetta grinned out. His eyes fastened on the President.

The presidential party boarded. Five sets of sunglasses bore down on Nathan. He shivered. He felt like he was facing a firing squad.

'Afraid we're out of room here, son,' said the President.

He smiled again. They weren't out of room. There was plenty of room. They just didn't want *him*. Because he was just an Empire guard. And he was gaunt. And red-faced. And his eyes were staring and he smelt of vomit. Nathan smiled back.

'Goin' down,' said Bobby Tangetta.

Nathan stepped closer to the elevator. 'Mr President?'

'Uhuh?'

'Could I shake your hand, Mr President?'

The President looked along the Secret Service line. Only one moved, raising a hand to his ear, listening. *The fingerprinter*. It was no use. It was all over.

The President took a step forward and extended his hand.

Nathan grasped it firmly. They grinned at each other.

Then Nathan pulled hard and the President came shooting out of the elevator. In one fluid moment Nathan had the gun out and pressed into the President's throat.

'Don't move a fucking inch!' Nathan yelled.

The Secret Service agents froze mid-movement. Not an inch. Not a millimetre. Their job was to give their lives to save the President. Not to have the President killed saving the President.

'Nath—' Bobby Tangetta began.

'Shut the fuck up!'

'Nathan . . . don't do this . . .'

'Shut it, Bobby, just fucking shut it. Now push the button. Push the fucking button!'

Bobby pushed the button. The doors closed. The elevator began to descend.

Then there were just the two of them standing in the cool breeze by the elevator on the 86th floor of the Empire State Building. Lonely, bad-tempered Nathan Jones and his hostage, Michael Keneally, President of the United States.

THE JESUS RODRIGUEZ STORY

Here is Jesus Rodriguez aged thirteen, not long over the border, trying to fly from the roof of his school.

The teacher is a kind man, but there is a limit to his patience and this is the third time this week he has tried to talk Jesus down from the roof.

'Jesus, what is it with you and flying? You're not a bird, y'know.'

'I am a bird, I am an eagle, strong and proud,' says Jesus, but the teacher hardly knows Spanish.

He calls Jesus' father, who works here as a janitor. 'Mr Rodriguez, this can't go on. What is it, this obsession with birds?'

'Mr Grover, we come from a remote village. In that village there is much poverty, little hope. The people are very superstitious. Thirteen years ago a great eagle soared above the village, for several days it swooped and hunted, and the people knew that it was an omen, but not whether it was good or bad. On the night that Jesus was born a great storm blew up and many homes were destroyed, but when the morning came, the eagle was found dead outside our house. Ever since it has been said that Jesus has the soul of that eagle, and that he will do great things. That is why he stands on top of your school, wanting to fly.'

Mr Grover spits in the sandpit. 'And you believe this, Mr Rodriguez?'

'No, sir, I think it's the greatest crock of shit. But Jesus, now, he believes it with all his soul. What am I to do?'

'Get him down.'

Jesus sticks his beak in the air, sniffs the wind. Then he spreads his wings and flies.

Straight to the ground. He is taken to hospital suffering from a broken leg and two broken arms.

Here is the Rodriguez family migrating east. Jesus is fifteen now, a strong boy, good-looking. Not many feathers. He is never in school for more than a few months before they move on. Work is not hard to come by, but good work is. Mr Rodriguez is an ambitious man, but not as ambitious as his wife; they have plans. So has Jesus.

Mrs Rodriguez is a beautiful woman. She has not put on weight like so many in her village. She would like to work on the perfume counter of a New York department store. Mr Rodriguez, he has tried night school, but they move so much he doesn't take any exams. He still works as a janitor, one term here, one term closer to the Big Apple.

Jesus, he comes home one day with a bruised face. At first he is reluctant to tell his father; he is ashamed. But eventually he gives in. 'They attacked me because I'm a Mexican,' says Jesus.

'You sure wasn't because you a bird?'

Jesus shrugs. 'They attack me 'cause I'm a Mexican bird.'

Mr Rodriguez has a quick temper, he's heard enough, heard enough for too long. He snaps, he slaps Jesus' face. Not hard, but hard enough. 'Leave me alone, janitor!' cries Jesus.

'Oh yeah, Mr Bird, and you're so great. You ain't no eagle; you're a fucken' gooney bird.'

'Just you wait!' Jesus spits. 'One day I'll show you!'

'Yeah, yeah, that'll be the day, Mr Gooney Bird, as the late great Mr Buddy Holly used to say.'

Yeah, Jesus has ambitions.

Comes the day, Jesus Rodriguez flies the nest. He's lived in Queens for four years. Studied hard. He knows what he wants to be. Mr Rodriguez, he's working as a janitor still, but a better class of janitor, he's in the New York Academy of the Performing Arts. Yeah, where Fame was made. For his interview he did a routine with his wash bucket that just tickled them. Even got a mop-on part in an Entertainment Tonight documentary. Mrs Rodriguez, she not so well. Her feet are bad. Varicose veins. She never did get to the perfume department. She works in a pet store.

Jesus goes to the USAF recruiting office. He shows them his qualifications, they're impressed.

'Why you want to be a pilot, son?'

'Wanna fly like a bird.'

'Do you want to defend America?'

'Sure do.'

'You have a criminal record? You a drug addict? Crack dealer? Ever done time?'

'No, sir, I'm a good All-American boy, wants to fly.'

'Okay, son, you come over here. Let's do some rudimentaries. Can you read the top line of that chart?'

'What chart?'

'The eye-test chart. Beside the picture of President Clinton.'

'What picture of President Clinton?'

'Do you wear glasses, son?'

'No, sir.'

'Contacts?'

'No, sir.'

'You ever consider wearing one or the other?'

'No, sir, I have the sight of an eagle.'

'Son, whatever eagle you got the sight of, he's a myopic son-of-a-bitch.'

Jesus Rodriguez, he's depressed. Only thing in life he wants to do, he can't do 'cause his eyesight's failing. Sure, he gets glasses, great glasses too, see a mile, but they ain't gonna get him into the USAF. Jesus, he ain't flying nowhere.

One thing Jesus knows for sure, he ain't gonna end up like his father, he ain't going to no janitor school. He ain't dumb, that's for sure. He gets a job. He works for the government as a clerk, sitting behind a desk, checking forms. But this sure as hell ain't for him. He is a caged bird, restless, dangerous.

Now there ain't many Jesus can talk to about being an eagle, that's for sure. Took enough beatings to prove that one. These days though, he's getting on okay, and there's a girl in the office takes a shine to him. Lindsey, now she's a country girl like him, 'cept he's a country boy, anyhow, they get talking one day about this and that and they get on just fine. They start taking lunch together, then they go to see a movie or two and they're really good friends. Then, hey, one night they get to kissin' and next thing you know, last of the red-hot lovers.

Jesus' father, he's pleased at this development, thinks his boy will grow outta this eagle shit, but man, he's in for a surprise. Lindsey, she starts talking like an eagle too!

Jesus, he's never been happier. Lindsey moves in with him. They build a little love nest. Come Christmas he buys her an engagement ring. She's bought him something too, but won't tell him. She drives out to the mountains, up to a house she's rented for the weekend.

Jesus, his dream's coming true.

They soar together!

This is heaven! This is magic! High above the rolling pine! The eagle and his mate, together!

Why didn't he think of it before? He loves her more and more. She has not only given him the gift of love, but the gift of flight.

Later she tells him that her brother used to do some hang gliding; she should have thought of it sooner; she was a little scared that he would hate the idea, dismiss it as artificial; but no, whoah! He's the happiest little man on God's earth.

Every weekend they can they're up to the mountains. Not to the house, they can't afford that, but they buy a small van, fly all day, drive home or sleep in the back, whatever they feel like.

Soon, though, it isn't enough. They need to fly every day, they can't stand the waiting until the weekend. They are caged birds, and caged birds do not prosper.

On a Monday evening they leave the office as normal. The van is parked nearby. In the back they change into their flight gear, then they lift their guitar cases and make their way to the Montrose Hotel, just a couple of blocks. They have a drink in the bar, a couple of rock 'n' rollers discussing music, then, part of the furniture, they make their way to the top floor. From there, once they're sure no one is watching, they hit the stairs and reach the roof. Up there, smiling at the breeze, they unpack their hang gliders.

They are nervous, of course, but pumped full of adrenalin. They are a new breed now – city eagles. Adapt and survive.

Jesus, he takes off first, disappearing into the dark. Lindsey waits, anxious, scared, ready to run, when suddenly she sees him flashing through the night. He is safe! He is majestic!

Soon she joins him. The winds are awkward, channelled, competing, but the eagles are young and strong and bright and soon they begin to master them. They chase each other through the skyscrapers, love birds, loving every moment.

Oh, how they love to fly. Too much, perhaps. Soon it is two nights a week, then three, four, five . . . Jesus Rodriguez and his now wife

Lindsey still go to the country, but increasingly not . . . there is some-thing new and challenging about the city. In the mountains it was the freedom, the space that exhilarated them, here it is the lack of space, the danger, the launch into the unknown, the swirl of strange, poisonous air, the thrill of observation. They have seen it all, floating past those windows: the movie stars at play, the boardroom at war, drug deals going down; they see sex, sex, sex in all its many forms, they see love and romance, hate and betrayal. Occasionally someone sees them too, a late-night drinker on a balcony, a couple dreaming on the stars, they see a shadowy form swoosh past, and they think maybe they've imagined it, and then the second follows soon after and maybe this time it waves over.

More and more, Lindsey is not herself. At work colleagues notice she is lifeless, listless, but hey, she's newly wed, give her time, she'll settle down. Jesus, being so close, doesn't notice, not for a while anyhow. Then she starts to take time off work, days, weeks, Jesus can't help but notice. She lives only for the sky. Jesus, he's a natural-born eagle, but he knows this can't go on; they both need the money to live in the city, they need to live in the city to enjoy their secret passion.

This goes on for some months. Lindsey is hardly talking now. Finally Jesus, who is not a man for confrontation, he confronts her. He tells her how much he loves her and how much he loves flying with her, but something is wrong and she better tell him pretty quick. At first she won't tell him, but he keeps at her for days and finally in the midst of a shouting match she lets slip what has been worrying her. They have been trying for children, but each month, nothing. She is broody, restless, she cannot wait. She goes to see her doctor, she sends her to another doctor, and she tells her she cannot have children. She is barren. They don't ever actually say barren, that's an old-fashioned kind of a word, but that's as sure as hell what they mean.

This hits her hard. Hits any woman hard. Any woman wants kids, that is. She sinks into a deep, deep depression by day; at night she comes alive, soaring higher, farther, closer, lower. Jesus follows where he can, he is an eagle and braver than all birds, but where Lindsey goes is not brave, it is foolhardy. He talks to her, he reasons, he shouts, he cries, but she will not listen. It is all that she has now.

'You have me!' says Jesus, and she softens a little and they make love. But it is a temporary respite. The next night she is a shadow across the neon of Times Square, she lands briefly on the TV tower tip of the Empire State Building, she rockets towards Washington Square. Jesus watches helplessly as she careers towards the ground, only catching the wind at the tops of the trees and climbing slowly back. He is scared for her.

On Christmas Day they go to his parents' apartment. Mrs Rodriguez, she keeps it well, but it's not big enough for her, it's not in the right area, she doesn't like the neighbours, pretty much all the neighbours don't like her. Her ambitions have long since withered into idle daydreams. Mr Rodriguez, he's happy enough at Fame, he don't mind the apartment so much, hell it's better than Mexico ever was. He's pleased that his son turned out good, making good money working for the government. He thinks his son is a real high-flyer. He's not wrong.

'That woman of yours,' he says to Jesus as they share a cigar on the stoop, 'she ain't too happy. I only met her five minutes ago, I can tell she's not happy.'

Jesus shrugs. 'I tried everything. What more can I do?'

'What more can you do,' agrees Mr Rodriguez. Like most fathers and sons, they get on better when they don't have to share the same roof.

'What do you do when momma is upset?' asks Jesus.

'Well,' says Mr Rodriguez, passing the cigar, 'in the old days I used to sit her down and we'd talk it through. That worked fine

357

for a while, then after that while I started to notice that it wasn't working fine no more. So I decided on a new strategy. Now when she starts to complain, I smack her with my hand, here, like this, across the side of the face.'

'And that stops her,' says Jesus.

'No, but it makes me feel a lot happier,' says Mr Rodriguez.

'Happy Christmas, pop,' says Jesus.

'Happy Christmas, son,' says Mr Rodriguez.

Jesus appreciates his father's advice, but figures it's not appropriate in this instance. He takes his wife on vacation to Mexico, to show her where he grew up.

This isn't much of a vacation. The village, it has mostly dried up and blown away. A couple of folks, they remember Jesus. 'Some good luck you were!' they shout and throw stones. One hits Lindsey on the head. This doesn't help her much.

Easter comes. The warmer nights, they fly until dawn. Lindsey has given up work completely now, during the day she stays at home. Jesus doesn't really know what she does.

One day he's in the canteen eating his lunch, reading his paper, when he senses things going quiet all around him. When he looks up he sees a police officer crossing the room towards him.

'Jesus Rodriguez?' the policeman asks, removing his hat.

'Yes, sir,' says Jesus, looking from hat to policeman to hat. Jesus knows it is a rare form of respect for a policeman to take his cap off to a Mexican.

'Mr Rodriguez . . .'

'Mr Rodriguez is my father. I am Jesus Rodriguez.'

'Jesus Rodriguez, I have some bad news for you. Your wife, Lindsey Rodriguez – well sir, we found her body an hour ago. She . . . well sir, she fell off the roof of a hotel downtown. She seems to have killed herself.'

Jesus remains calm. He nods his head slowly, chases rice around his plate. 'Was there anything near the body?'

'Like a note? No, sir.'

'Like a hang glider.'

'Uhm, no, sir.'

'Thank you for telling me, officer, it's an awful thing to have to do.'

'You get used to it.' He replaces his cap. 'Sir, do you know of any reason why your wife might have done this?'

'She wanted to fly,' says Jesus, and it is the truth.

Later, at the hospital, the doctors are very pleasant. One takes him aside. 'It was all very quick. Once she hit the ground.'

'Yes,' says Jesus. 'I can see she would have enjoyed it right up to that point.'

'The baby as well,' says the doctor, and Jesus' chill blood turns to ice. 'I'd say eleven weeks pregnant. It's a terrible truth, some women, they just can't cope with being pregnant.'

Jesus does not return to work. He stays in his apartment. He does not eat. He watches television. He does not fly.

His father comes to visit. He stays for several weeks. He talks, he makes food for Jesus, he tries to make everything as comfortable as possible, but there is no wresting Jesus from his morbid reverie.

He watches talk shows. He has always known that there are a lot of sick people about, but it takes talk shows for him to see them real close. Up there, in the sky, he has seen them too, in their towering ghettos and penthouse suites. But television – they're in your home. He watches and he grows to hate humans.

Jesus has lost his job now. The rent is due. Jesus is wasting away. His father can't get in any more, he bangs the door, but Jesus ignores him. One time Mr Rodriguez sends round the police, just to make sure he's still alive. Jesus is polite to the police, but he doesn't let them in.

One day he is watching Oprah. *Now Jesus has never been one to pay much attention to politics, even less since he was turned down for the USAF. But he always makes sure to watch* Oprah, *she seems less plastic than the others – this day the President is on, President Keneally. Jesus is tempted to switch off but leaves it on; he spends ten minutes throwing pieces of the lining of his chair at the screen. There isn't much foam rubber left, he's been doing it an awful lot. It sits around him like orange snow.*

He's hardly even listening, but then, gradually, the calm, reassuring voice, the confident yet caring voice, it starts to seep through. For a little he listens, still throwing the odd ball of foam, then he stops even that. The President is talking about crime in the cities and how everyone must help to defeat it; if everyone does just a little bit, then a little bit will add up to a big bit, and if we put all the big bits together, then maybe we'll get sorted out and our children will be able to walk the streets without being shot or stabbed or sexually assaulted.

By the end of the broadcast Jesus is crying.

He cries himself to sleep. When he wakes in the morning the sunlight is streaming through the window, illuminating the framed photo of Lindsey he keeps by the bed.

It is a sign.

He will help to reduce crime. He will patrol the skies. He will report. He will apprehend. He will deter.

When Jesus gets up he calls his father and tells him everything is all right again. Then he makes eggs and ham.

The ham is bad.

III

SIEGE AND DESTROY

III

1

Alexis Mascara's performance the previous evening was, everyone agreed, her best yet. Polished, professional, warm, loving, witty, and all achieved without over-indulgence in alcohol. Where before there had been a sense of desperation about the act, a need to please, now she seemed relaxed: she still went over the top, but not so far that anyone was worried that she might not be able to drag herself out of the abyss on the other side. There was a light in her eyes, and it shone on Lisa. Lisa looked pretty chipper too.

After the show Alexis became Alex very quickly. Lisa watched approvingly as he transformed himself. They didn't linger over drinks, but walked hand in hand back to the Elephant Strides. They entered Lisa's room; he entered Lisa.

'This is wonderful,' she said later. 'It's like someone's put me on a drip which just relaxes every bone in my body.'

'Call me a drip again and I'll scratch your eyes out,' Alex purred.

They slept together, spooned up, and woke to the sound of gulls. They ate breakfast on the way down to the harbour. The beach wasn't much to write home about, so for a couple of bucks a young fella took them half a mile across the harbour to a small island where the sand was white and fine and the sea shallow and safe. They swam, they kissed, they ran along the sand, chased, wrestled, tumbled, laughed, kissed again. Quite sickening really, but hey, young love.

The boat returned for them at noon and putted lazily across to the harbour. They ate lobster salad in a restaurant along the main strip and then wandered hand in hand back towards the Governor Bradford.

'I'm glad I stayed,' Lisa said.

'I'm glad you're glad you stayed. I'm glad you stayed.'

'I'm glad that you're glad that I'm glad I stayed.'

'I'm glad that—'

'Put a sock in it.'

'How unhygienic.'

She tweaked his bum. He skipped forward a step, laughing. Lisa glanced on up the street, tutted. 'Shit,' she said. 'Looks like our idea of a quiet romantic drink is off the menu.'

Alex looked up towards the Governor. 'Flaming buggery,' he said. There was a crowd gathered about the swing doors. 'I heard there were three busloads of queens due in from New York, but I didn't think that was until next week.'

'Maybe they came early.'

'They usually do.'

'Do you want to try somewhere else?'

Alex shook his head. 'Alexis Mascara can always get a table,' she said petulantly.

As they approached the doors it became clear that this was no royal gathering. Alex recognized most of them from about the town. Residents, shopkeepers, summer rentals. They were gathered about the doorway because the bar was full: not just tables-taken full, but every standing space as well. Everyone was watching the big TV hanging above the bar.

Alexis and Lisa pressed against the crowd in the doorway, but there was no getting through; everyone was peering into the gloom, trying to catch a glimpse of the screen between the bobbing tip-toed customers within.

'What's going on?' Alex asked. 'Wall Street crashed or something?'

A big guy from the t-shirt shop three doors down spoke without turning round. 'Somebody's shot the President.'

The girl beside him, bouncing up and down because she wasn't tall enough to benefit from tip-toes, turned quickly. 'He has not been shot!'

'Not officially, maybe. They just haven't announced it.'

'Oh my God,' Lisa said.

'Jesus,' said Alex.

He wasn't *their* President, but he might as well have been.

'He's being held hostage,' said the girl. 'Some nut with a gun. There's four or five of them.'

'Nuts with guns?' Lisa asked.

'Hostages.'

'Jesus,' said Alex, 'how'd he manage that?'

The girl shook her head. 'I don't know. I'm trying to hear. There's too many people. I'm half hearing.'

'Blessed are the cheesemakers,' said Alex. He grabbed Lisa's hand. 'C'mon. We can go in by the kitchens.'

He led her round to the back of the bar. The door was open, the kitchen deserted. They hurried through to the bar and pushed and squeezed their way as close to the TV as they could.

'What's happening?' Alex whispered to no one in particular.

'Shhhhhh,' said everyone.

A female reporter was speaking to camera. She had the wide adrenalin-pumped eyes of someone required to talk at length while armed only with the very minimum of information. She had a naturally high-pitched voice, but she was doing her very best to make it sound sombre. The caption beneath her said *Katey Gettis, Channel 9 News Live.*

'. . . no, Martin, the President arrived at a little after 11 AM for a private meeting with Michael Tate of Magiform and was then scheduled to give a short speech on the observation floor . . . that's the eighty-sixth . . . of the Empire State Building.'

'Oh my God,' said Lisa. She squeezed Alex's hand tight.

'What?' he whispered.

She shook her head. Her mouth was suddenly dry.

'After that the facts are a little sketchy. What we do know is that a gun was produced, one source has said it was a disgruntled employee, possibly by a security guard at the Empire and that the President was taken hostage. At the time of the incident there was also a clash between police and members of the Moravian Army of Christ who were protesting outside. At this stage we have no way of telling if the two events are connected. There have of course been medical teams on stand-by throughout, but as we saw here on Channel Nine about twenty minutes ago what appeared to be a body was brought out of the Empire and taken away by ambulance. However, the President's staff are insisting that the President has not been harmed and that negotiations are ongoing with the . . . the . . . man.'

Her eyes flitted briefly away from the camera.

'Katey, what's the mood on the ground there?'

'Frank, since we broke the news here on Channel Nine people have been flocking to the area. There are thousands. Every office, every shop . . . you just can't move for people. The mood is obviously one of deep, deep shock and concern for the safety of the President. They are asking how something like this could happen, particularly in the light of previous assassination attempts on the President.'

'Though we can't say that this is yet an assassination attempt.'

'No . . . no . . . of course . . . we should make it clear that the President has not yet been shot . . . has not been shot and that his people seem very confident of getting him out of there alive.'

A hand reached a slip of paper across to her. She scanned it quickly. 'I have . . . just this moment . . . a list of the people who remain on the eighty-sixth floor with the President . . .'

'This is from . . .?'

She peered at the list, then off camera. 'I don't know who . . . yes, it's from the management office at the Empire State Building, which is working in tandem with the FBI, the Secret Service and of course the New York Police Department . . . to try and bring this situation to a satisfactory . . . the list, ahm, of course doesn't state who the hostage taker is . . . he . . . indeed *she* might be one of these names . . . at this moment in time we can only guess . . . those names are . . . Sam McClintock, security guard, Brian Houston, security guard, Marilu Henner, who works in the concession stand . . . Clark Fuller, a Reuters reporter and two Secret Service agents.'

'Oh thank God,' Lisa whispered.

'He's a dead man,' said an ibex-faced man in front of Alex.

'Who?' Alex asked. 'The President or the gunman?'

'Both,' said the man sourly.

'Oh my God,' said a stout woman in a baker's apron. 'He was such a beautiful man.'

'Oh sweet Jesus, I never thought I'd see two Presidents killed in my lifetime.'

'He's not dead yet,' Alex said.

'He's dead meat,' said the man in front.

'You're such an optimist,' said Alex.

'Realist, bozo. He's not gonna walk away from this. Somebody wants to get him that badly, he's not going to let him walk away.'

'On the contrary,' said Alex, 'if he just wanted to kill him he'd have done it by now. Holding him hostage suggests demands of some sort. Political. Financial. Religious. All three maybe.'

'He has killed him. They took the body out.' The man shook his head. 'They're not releasing it until they can settle Wall Street.'

'Bollocks,' said Alex. 'You can't possibly know that.'

'Whaddya know anyway, y'Limey bastard?' the ibex shouted.

'Shhhhh,' went the crowd about them.

'Please,' said Lisa, 'let's get out of here.'

Alex looked at her: at her paleness, at her suddenly sad eyes, at the little furrows on her brow, like a child's picture of gentle waves on a sea. 'Are you all right, kid?'

Lisa shook her head. 'I don't feel so good.'

He took her hand again and they pushed their way back to the kitchens. 'You shouldn't let it get to you, love,' Alex said. 'You've got to remember, this is America. They turn every little drama into a crisis.'

2

It was warm, despite the air conditioning, so there was justification for a button undone. Maybe two. But certainly not *three*. Tara smiled at the thought of it, at catching Slo's eyes darting to her basque as they chinked glasses; the smile widened as she bent for a refill, then looked up suddenly and caught him staring down the front of her top. He was red, of course, but he was keen; they were alone; they were going to do it. And she would have a beautiful little baby.

'Can you just repeat that, please?' said Captain Phillips.

Air Force One was out over the Atlantic when the news reached the crew. Despite the several million dollars' worth of complicated communications equipment on board the news was broken by the First Lady's personal hairdresser, who had taken advantage of the fact that her employer was closeted in a private meeting with the White House Chief of Staff to make use of the President's private phone to call her husband, a Washington fitness guru, who happened to be watching CNN when news of the hostage drama broke. The hairdresser had no intention of breaking the news to the First Lady. She was paid to fluff up hair, not to make historic announcements. She hurried immediately to the cabin.

'Is that a serious "repeat that",' she asked, 'or do you just not believe what you're hearing?'

'I just don't believe what I'm hearing.'

'Well I swear to God it's the truth.'

The captain looked at his crew. Then he thumbed back down the aircraft. 'What're they doing?' he asked.

'They're having cocktails.'

'It's midday.'

'Not in Ireland.'

He chewed at a lip. 'Who's going to tell her?'

'Rank has certain privileges.'

'Like giving orders?'

'Like taking responsibility.'

'I thought you might say that.' He cupped his face in his hands. 'Maybe we should wait until we have it officially,' he said through his fingers. 'No point in causing a panic.' His crew shook their heads. 'Or maybe we shouldn't. She wouldn't forgive us if we didn't tell her. We'd never fly again.' He made a decision. He deared his throat. 'Okay. Let's do it.'

Captain Phillips handed control to his co-pilot. He brushed down his uniform. He gargled with mouthwash. He fixed his hair and took a deep breath. He knocked on the door to the presidential suite. There was laughter from within. Graham Slovenski, flush-faced, opened the door. He had a glass in his hand. His tie was undone. The captain could see the First Lady reclining on a leather chaise-longue. Her legs were folded under her; a pair of black high heels were toppled on the floor.

'Uhuh?' said Slovenski.

'Mr Slovenski, sir,' the captain began. The First Lady smiled across. 'I have some news for the First Lady. Mrs Keneally. Uhm.'

Slovenski glanced back. He smiled. These past two hours had transformed his life. In the car to the airport she had opened her eyes and looked at him in a way that no woman had ever looked at him before. Miranda had looked at him as a wife and mother; with *love*. But Tara could see into his soul, and it made a new man of him. Where before he had fumbled awkwardly in his dealings with her he was suddenly fluent and intimate, where before he had felt small and worthless and as relaxed as a man going to the electric chair, now he was tall and imposing and warm. He had never felt so at home with a woman. Sure, it was still a chess match, sure, it might yet end in a stalemate, but what a match it was. They were grandmasters. They were still moving strategically about the board, but there was a shared goal: not necessarily checkmating the king, but forging a unique new union. The where and when didn't matter; the fact of the matter was that their union was as inevitable as the sun rising and the moon throwing its light on young lovers everywhere.

Tara unfolded her legs. She smiled again at Slo. *He's funny when he's drunk*, she thought. She had to remember not to get him so drunk that he couldn't perform.

She nodded wearily at the pilot. 'Yes, captain, of course. Come in. Let me guess: the President sends his love. Ireland has sunk into the sea. There is life in outer space.' She grinned again at Slovenski and raised her glass. 'Something trivial, I'll bet.'

'I'm afraid not.' The captain drew himself up. 'At least, I thought I'd better tell you. We, uh, heard something over the radio, concerning the President. There's no other way for me to tell you than straight out, ma'am. The President is being held hostage by a gunman at the top of the Empire

State Building. About thirty minutes ago. He has not been harmed. Nevertheless . . .'

The colour drained from Tara's face. It pretty much drained from Slo's, too.

Tara rose from the seat. She clasped her hands in front of her. The tip of her tongue appeared and she licked her bottom lip. 'Very well. Thank you, captain. Please turn the plane about and take us to New York.'

'Yes, ma'am.'

'Let's not waste any time.'

'No, ma'am.'

God she's regal, thought Slovenski.

'And captain?'

'Ma'am?'

'Will you send some coffee through,' she said, 'for Mr Slovenski?'

The White House Chief of Staff felt himself shrink to about three centimetres. *Regal?* He stared at her. The blood pounded in his head. *Ice Queen.*

'Forget the coffee,' Slo snapped. 'Get someone to get me a litre of iced water.'

'Very well, Mr Slovenski.'

The captain hurried away. Slovenski glared across at the First Lady. 'I'm not drunk,' he said.

Tara shrugged. 'Then do something. My husband is in danger.'

'And you never were.'

'What?'

'Nothing.' Slovenski padded out of the suite. Outside, word had already spread through the travelling circus that was accompanying the First Lady to Northern Ireland. Everyone looked at him. 'Please remain calm,' he said bluntly, 'we're turning round.'

His first call was to Vice-President Santos. The VP, attending the Chinese peace talks in Thailand, knew even less than he did. 'I'm going straight to the airport, Slo, but I'm the best part of a day away. The chain of command gets pretty fudgy at times like this anyway. You're the man for now, Slo. The Chinks send their best wishes. That'll cheer him up.'

The chain of command wasn't *fudgy* at all. Slo didn't doubt that Santos was secretly relieved to be so far abroad: this was a game of high risks; better for some not to play at all. The iced water arrived. He gulped all of it down. Tara watched him. He watched her distorted face through the bottom of the flask. *That's how she is, distorted.*

In the next hour he made thirty phone calls. He was abrupt, abrasive. He was power.

The most important thing was not the President. That was out of his control. His fate was in the hands of experts. The machinery for dealing with such a crisis was already in place and, he trusted, well oiled. The most important thing was the country and its stability. It was showing confidence and authority at a time of crisis. It was reassuring the American people and democracies the world over; it was safeguarding the economy, ensuring that the nation remained safe, alert, prepared. It was uniting the government in a common cause, eliminating in-fighting and preventing panic. It was ensuring that whatever happened, whatever the outcome, he came out of it smelling of roses.

'You've always been a great friend to Michael,' Tara said. She had a litre of iced water by then as well. She was drinking it steadily from a paper cup. He noticed her hands shaking. *How could I have been such a fool?* Slo shrugged. 'I mean it. He doesn't have many friends. Not real friends. He talks to you. He bares his soul, doesn't he?'

He shrugged again.

'See? A real friend wouldn't say anything. Slo, he's going to die, isn't he?'

Slo rested the telephone receiver on his shoulder. 'Not if we can help it, Tara.'

'That's the kind of thing you tell the press. Tell me the truth. He's going to die.'

Her eyes were soft now. Close to tears. Although it was a moment of crisis, he was beginning to think that she was a little bit schizo. Either that or he was a seriously bad judge of women. He nodded slowly. 'I think you have to prepare yourself for that possibility.'

He called Fred Troy at the Empire State. As he waited for a response, the First Lady began to cry. He watched the tears drip down her face. Saw her shoulders shake. He wanted to . . . he flung open the door. Three members of her fashion team were yakking outside. He motioned them towards him with an impatient wave. 'See to her,' he snapped. They hurried past. An unfamiliar voice came on the line.

'Get me Troy.'

'I'm afraid that's not possible right now.'

'Make it possible. Now.'

'Who is this?'

'This is Graham Slovenski. Chief of—'

'Mr Slovenski, sir, I'm sorry, I didn't recognize—'

'Get me Troy.'

'Mr Troy is dead, sir.'

'Good God. The gunman . . .?'

'No sir, he appears to have suffered a heart attack.'

'Good God. So who's in charge?'

'Yes, sir. Me, sir. For the moment.'

'And who the hell are you?'

'Morton, sir, James Morton. FBI Assistant Director. New York office.'

'Yes of course, Morton. What's happening? Be brief. Cut the bull.'

'Everything is under control.'

'You mean the President has been released?'

'No, sir. Not yet, sir.'

'Well that doesn't sound like it's under control, does it? How many gunmen?'

'We haven't been able to establish that yet, sir.'

'Have any demands been made?'

'Not yet, sir.'

'So what the hell is going on Morton? You're telling me nothing.'

'At present we are manoeuvring towards a negotiation situation, sir.'

'And what the hell does that mean?'

'Well, sir, it means . . . well, sir, we're waiting for someone to answer the phone.'

Slovenski took a deep breath. 'I'll be there just as soon as I can.'

3

'Who released the list? Who released the fucking list?'

James Morton, Assistant Director and head of the largest and busiest FBI field office in the country, wasn't a happy man. He prowled about the Empire State's management offices pointing a finger at everything and everyone. He had heard of organized chaos. This was unorganized chaos.

'Too many people! Too many fucking people! Get them out of here!' He grabbed FBI Agent Mulder. 'You. I saw you with the lists. At the photocopier! How did the fucking press get hold of them!'

'Don't know, sir. I gave them all to you.'

'You're a liar, Mulder. Get outta here. I'll have you transferred to the darkest corner of Quantico, your mother'll think you've been abducted by aliens. Now move it.'

'Yes, sir.'

'Doyle! Where's Doyle?'

Doyle, one of three SACs under Morton, and the only one not currently on vacation, hovered behind Morton. He removed his sunglasses. 'Here, sir.'

Morton turned. 'Commandeer an office. Have the phone

on the eighty-sixth connected exclusively to that office. I want direct lines to the White House and Quantico. I want whoever's in charge of Empire State security in that office. I want to know where the fucking Hostage Rescue Team is, and why the fuck it isn't here. I want the critical incident negotiating team, get me a behavioural scientist, the logistics team, I want the media relations squad, I want a plane up there with thermal image equipment, and I want some coffee. Call my wife, cancel lunch. And clear this floor, there are too many people here who don't need to be here. And get that little fuck Michael Tate out of here. He's annoying me.'

Why don't you just pass the whole buck, Doyle thought. 'Yes sir. What about the press?'

'Shoot them.'

'Yes, sir.'

Doyle hurried away. Morton looked up at the ceiling. Up there, the President. When he looked back Michael Tate was being frogmarched under protest out of the management suite.

The lines were set up in thirty minutes. People began to arrive, their faces suffused with panic. This was the big one.

'Any word from above?' Morton snapped.

'No, sir, no response,' said Agent Blake.

'Keep trying.'

'Doyle!'

'Sir?'

'Hit the switchboard! I don't want any bullshit calls from politicians! No one below the rank of Slovenski and VP Santos gets through, okay?'

'The First Lady's waiting on line three!'

'Refer her to counselling . . .'

'Sir?'

'Reassure her, Doyle! You! Fat man! In my office!'

Leonard Maltman was sitting on a desk looking miserable. He reluctantly pushed himself up. 'Everything was going so well,' he whined.

'Yes, right up to the point where the President got taken hostage, right under your nose! What the hell kind of an operation do you run here anyway?'

'Those were your agents up there!'

'They weren't my agents shooting the President!'

'He hasn't been shot!'

'We don't know that, god-damn it! Just were the hell do you think you're going to get another job on this planet with this on your CV?'

Leonard pulled out a chair and flopped down into it. 'I might ask you the same question.'

Morton ignored him. As many senior security officials from the Secret Service, CIA, NYPD as could be mustered in such a short time were already waiting in the office, Experts in sound, vision, weather, psychology, psychiatry, news management, stress management and catering stood nervously waiting for direction.

Morton rapped on the table with an empty Diet Coke can. It took a couple of minutes for everyone to come to order. 'Ladies and gentlemen,' he began, 'you may regard this as possibly the greatest crisis in American history. As the defining moment in all of our lives. What we do in the next few hours, perhaps days, could change the future of the world. That said, I don't want to over-dramatize the situation. We have a siege situation and we must treat it as we treat all siege situations. Our priority is to get the hostage out alive. We must work as a cohesive unit, we must combine our areas of expertise with the aim of securing the President's release. That said, this is not a democracy.' He prodded his own chest. 'The buck stops here. My motto is this: No bullshit! Give it to me straight!'

He hadn't expected an enthusiastic response. They all had their own agendas. They murmured, they nodded. He banged the table again. 'Okay,' he said, 'let's find out what's going on up there. Sound?'

'We have a problem on sound. There's too many TV and radio stations broadcasting from the Communications Transmission Centre. They're playing havoc with our equipment. We're working on it.'

'Great. Good start. Shut them down. Pictures.'

'Problem there, too. Pretty much the same as the audio. Ordinarily we would have parabolic microphones and fibre optic cables in place by now to broadcast closed-circuit pictures and sound to the command centre, but there's so much interference we're having trouble getting anything useful. We have the thermal imager on a helicopter, and from the movements we can tell the President is still alive. Of the others, only one remains on the ground, can't tell whether dead or alive. One man is sticking close to the President, that's our gunman. He's one of two in Empire State uniform.'

Morton looked at his list. 'Okay. That's McClintock and Houston. What do we have on them, Doyle?'

Doyle lit a cigarette. Inhaled deeply. 'McClintock's an old guy.' Exhaled. 'Went off the rails this morning, took a run at the President. Secret Service agents used the required force to stop him. As far as we're aware he was in no state after that to take the President hostage. The agents with the President when he was, uh, taken, have identified Houston as the gunman.'

'But it suggests a conspiracy?'

Doyle nodded. 'Looks that way.'

Morton nodded at Leonard Maltman, who was staring at the floor. 'What about them? What would they have against the President?'

Leonard gave a little shrug. 'I don't know.'

'They're annoyed about something.'

'Sam . . . Sam McClintock – Michael Tate wanted him sacked. The rest of the guys threatened to strike. We agreed to keep him on until after he'd met the President.'

'Okay, so he might have a grudge. What about Houston, what's his beef?'

Leonard chewed on a lip.

'C'mon Leonard, we're all friends here. It may not seem important to you, but every little detail could be vital. How he works, who his friends are, disciplinary record, hobbies, political beliefs, what he has for lunch, for godsake. We have people here can build a psychiatric profile based on what way he ties his shoes and knots his tie.'

'Well,' Leonard began ponderously, 'the little detail I had in mind, uh, was this. Uhm, that's not Brian Houston up there.'

'Well, who the fuck is it, then?'

'His name's Nathan Jones.'

Half a dozen experts began to flick through their lists of Empire State employees. They soon turned blank faces towards Leonard.

'You better tell us a little more, Leonard.'

'Brian Houston called in sick this morning. I asked Nathan to take his place.'

'You didn't think to inform anyone?'

'I didn't think it would make much difference.'

'You didn't think at all. We don't appear to have any record of this Nathan Jones.'

'No. You wouldn't. He only joined us a few days ago.'

'You mean he wasn't vetted by our people?'

Leonard shook his head. 'I guess not. We're behind in our paperwork.'

'So *we* have nothing on him. You'll have interview notes. Job application form. Home address.'

'I have his address. Not much else. Look, it's not as bad as you think.'

'Isn't it?'

'I mean, he saved my life. I was attacked in the park. He fought off a couple of muggers.'

'So he has a violent streak.'

'No! I was grateful. I got him a job. He seemed okay to me.'

'He seemed okay. Brilliant. He could be anyone.'

Leonard shrugged helplessly. 'I guess so.'

'What is he, black? Wasn't Nathan Jones a Motown song?'

'Supremes,' said Doyle, 'after Diana Ross left.'

'No, he's not black. He's white. He's Irish. Northern Irish.'

Morton rolled his eyes. 'Great!' Hands on hips, he practically spat into Leonard's face. 'You've managed to slip an Irish terrorist in to kidnap the President! Y'know, Leonard, if this was Japan, you'd have committed suicide by now, because you're one major league fuck-up.' Morton nodded at Doyle. 'Contact Scotland Yard. The Northern Irish Police, Interpol, see what they have. Contact every Irish support group in town. Pick up everyone who lives within a block of him. We need to know.'

'On it.' Doyle left the room.

'Leonard?'

'Yeah?'

'Will you get outta my fucking sight?'

'Absolutely.' Leonard heaved himself up out of the chair and turned for the door. Then he stopped. 'Y'know, I was only trying to help him. He seemed like a good kid.'

'Sure, Leonard. So was Lee Harvey.' He shook his head, then waved a finger to stop the departing security chief. 'Just one thing, all that stuff about suicide, I didn't mean it.'

Leonard nodded weakly. 'Okay.'

'At least not until you've gone through the floor plans and access routes with our boys. Then you just go on out and blow your fucking head off. Clear?'

Leonard nodded sullenly. He closed the door behind him.

'Stupid fat fuck,' Morton barked. He turned to the assembled experts. 'Where does that leave us?'

'It's better if he's a terrorist. He'll have an agenda. Demands. Better that than an out and out psycho.'

'What if he's both?'

'Well, then we're really fucked.'

The door opened. Morton swivelled, ready to abuse.

An agent poked his head in. 'Sir, the elevator's coming down from the eighty-sixth.'

4

As the elevator came to a halt, forty-four guns were trained upon the doors. Hearts slowed or sped, according to temperament. Sweat broke. Shivers shivered. Fingers pressed lightly on M16 assault rifles, Heckler and Koch submachine guns. Morton thrust his pistol out before him.

The only sound was the whirr of old machinery. It seemed like an eternity before the cage settled and the doors ground slowly open: but instead of figures within, there were vague outlines camouflaged by the security grille.

'Hold steady!' Morton hissed.

The grille was pulled back. There was a long moment when fingers tensed on triggers, an extended pause between sight, recognition and the message reaching the brain.

The two Secret Service agents assaulted by Nathan Jones were pressed back against the rear of the elevator. They knew better than to make any sudden movement. They looked nervously out at the firing squad. One, in a white coat, had a bent and bloody nose; the other had one eye closed. Both had damp stains on their shoulders.

A collective sigh of relief was followed by nervous laughter.

Agents hurried forward to help the two former hostages out of the elevator.

Morton turned quickly. 'Bring them to my office. Immediately.'

He handed them paper cups of water as the office filled again. As the specialists took their seats, readied their pens and files, Morton looked closely at the agents' faces. 'Any major damage?' he asked quietly.

Agents Calhoon and Mowbray shook their heads.

'Pride, sir,' Mowbray whispered.

Morton nodded. 'Pride can be restored.' He drew back from them, rapped on the table as he had before with an empty Diet Coke can. 'Okay, folks, some more first-hand information. I'll ask the obvious ones, then you can form an orderly queue for your specialist subjects. Okay, gentlemen, how is the President?'

'The President seems fine, sir,' said Calhoon.

'And what of the gunman?'

'He didn't say much, sir,' said Calhoon.

'He has demands?'

'No, sir.'

'He gave you a message?'

'No, sir, he just told us to get into the elevator.'

'And what did you do?'

'We got into the elevator.'

'Did you ask him if he had any demands? Or if he wanted to say anything?'

'No, sir.'

'Why in hell's name not?'

'He said he would blow our heads off if we said a word,' said Mowbray.

'So we didn't say a word,' added Calhoon.

Morton sat on the edge of the desk. He rubbed at his front

teeth with a finger. They began to squeak: He stopped. 'What do you make of him?'

Mowbray looked sheepishly across at Calhoon, who nodded back. 'Sir, he overpowered us, disarmed me. Then he took the President off five Secret Service agents. I'd say he came from an army background, probably special forces. He's good, very good.'

'We're no pushovers,' said Calhoon.

'He's Irish,' said Mowbray, 'he may be a terrorist.'

Morton nodded. 'Yeah. We'd kind of come to that conclusion. What has he been saying to the President?'

Calhoon looked at Mowbray. Mowbray gave a little nod. 'We couldn't say, sir.'

'Whaddya mean you couldn't say? Did he keep the President away from you?'

'No, sir, the President was right there in front of us,' said Mowbray.

Morton rolled his eyes. 'He didn't make you *promise*, did he?'

'No, sir, it's not as simple as that.'

'Of course it is. Tell me.'

Calhoon took a deep breath. 'The fact of the matter is, sir, that Houston ordered the reporter . . .'

'Clark Fuller.'

'Yes, sir, Clark Fuller, sir, to place . . . well, sir, ice cream cones in our ears.'

Morton stood from the desk. 'Run that one past me again.'

'Well, sir, he ordered . . .'

'God-damn it, I heard you!' Morton threw his arms up in the air. 'What sort of a sick son-of-a-bitch is this?'

'I don't know, sir. I couldn't hear a thing, sir. All I know, he was laughing a lot.'

Morton shook his head. He looked around the crowded

office. 'By God,' he said, 'you'll be analysing this one for years.' He turned back to Mowbray. 'He's on drugs, isn't he?'

'I don't know, sir.'

'Two of my top agents have ice cream cones in their ears, and they don't think the perpetrator is on drugs?'

'I don't know, sir. He seemed to be enjoying himself.'

'There was a certain detachment from reality,' said Calhoon, 'but I wasn't convinced that it was drug related.'

'Okay, okay.' Morton perched himself on the edge of the desk again. 'What about the old guy. The security guard. Does he appear to be working in tandem with Jones?'

'Jones, sir?' asked Calhoon.

'I'm sorry. Yes, Nathan Jones is his real name. For now.'

'For most of the time the old guy . . . Sam? . . . was unconscious. Jones certainly seemed to be concerned for his wellbeing, of course we did everything in our power to look after the old guy, both prior to and during this incident. Jones didn't seem to appreciate it. The old guy came round near the end, but no, sir, I wouldn't say that he seemed part of it.'

'Did he try to talk him out of it?'

'I don't know, sir, I had ice—'

'Yes. Okay. I know. The reporter, then, Fuller. How did he seem?'

'Calm. Very calm.'

Morton shook his head. 'Course he's calm. He's sitting on the story of the century. God-damn him. There's a woman there too. Marilu Henner. What about her?'

'She stayed behind the concession stand,' said Calhoon. 'She provided the ice cream cones. She looked scared.'

'I'm sure she did. Okay, I'll throw it open to the floor, then we'll get these good men some medical treatment. Oh, and one thing. I wouldn't go telling anyone about the ice cream cones. It does not reflect well on the service.'

Mowbray and Calhoon nodded, then looked nervously up at the assembly.

'Shoot,' said Morton, and immediately regretted it. 'You know what I mean.'

'Did Jones make any reference to Northern Ireland?'

'No, sir,' said Calhoon.

'Were his eyes glazed, were there any facial tics?'

'Not that we saw, sir.'

'You say he disarmed you. Did he appear to be carrying any other weapon?'

'Not that we could see, sir,' said Mowbray.

'*We*, Agent Mowbray? Have you discussed this?'

'No, sir, but I think we saw pretty much the same.'

'Did he appear excited? Nervous? Emotional?'

'Yes, sir.'

'Which?'

'All three, sir. But then I think most of us were.'

'Did he appear to want to harm the President, as opposed to wanting to take him hostage?'

'I couldn't say, sir,' said Calhoon.

'Was he wearing any religious emblems? A cross? Rosary beads?'

'Not that I noticed, sir.'

'Tattoos?'

'His arms were not uncovered, sir.'

'Agent Mowbray, would you say that the ice cream cones were placed in your ears to embarrass you, or placed with force, to cause you pain?'

'To stop me hearing, sir.'

'But did you form the impression that you were prevented from hearing something of importance?'

'No, sir.'

'There didn't appear to be any intense discussion taking place?'

'No, sir.'

'Did Jones appear to have any form of communication equipment with him? A radio? A mobile phone?'

'Not that we could see, sir,' said Mowbray.

It went on, and on, and on. Eventually Morton tapped the Diet Coke can on the desk. Half of them were busy scribbling. He looked at his watch. When he spoke, his voice was already tired and raspy. 'Gentlemen,' he said, 'we have some decisions to make. Let's get down to it.'

5

As the siege slipped into its fifth hour, America ground to a halt.

In Washington, those members of the government who couldn't directly benefit by scheming in the President's absence, gathered around TV screens. The Supreme Court adjourned indefinitely. In Detroit the production lines slowed, then stopped. In hospitals surgeons replaced hearts with one eye on the pulsing muscle, one on developments at the Empire; meals weren't delivered to patients who weren't in their beds. Whole schools gathered in assembly halls. Factories, shops, offices closed. Diners waited in restaurants to be served; waited, waited. The subways thundered, empty, ghostly. Traffic became gridlocked. As word was passed along the Miami beaches tourists hurried back to their hotels. In Birmingham, Alabama, a cheer went up from the White Armed Resistance and a hundred similar organizations, though they'd no idea that one of their own was involved. In the same city Grace Burley settled herself in front of her TV for the duration, marshmallows and gin by her side. In Manhattan, little Annie Fuller began to cry outside the Petard

School. Her daddy was *never* late. A teacher, locking up, found her and took her back inside. 'It's okay, your dada will be here soon,' she assured the orphan. Lisa and Alex walked by the harbour in Provincetown. Something gnawed at Lisa, and for once it wasn't Alex.

It was time for the Feebies to come into their own. For the NYPD to wipe out thirty years of bad press. And it was time for the bad press to prove that their freedom was worth preserving, to prove that they could outgun the networks, for the networks to prove that they could outgun cable, and for all three to revel in a sudden revival in advertising. This was bigger than OJ. Bigger than Nuremberg. The Linbergh case by comparison was a mere soundbite, a throwaway paragraph. The feeding frenzy had begun. There was so much money on the table, the table wasn't big enough.

As the foot soldiers of the FBI/Secret Service/CIA/NYPD amalgam were about to hit the road – or the sidewalk, because the roads were gridlocked – they were treated to the increasingly familiar picture of AD James Morton blowing his top. He came thundering out of his office, face red, eyes blazing.

'Who released his name!' he screamed. 'Who released his fucking name?'

Everyone looked at the ground.

'Leaking like a fucking Vietnamese boat . . . people, boat-thing . . . Jesus Christ! Nathan Jones, Nathan Jones, Nathan Jones all over the fucking radio! Who gave you permission! When I get to the bottom of this you'll all be . . . oh, fuck you all!' He turned back to his office and slammed the door.

Suitably inspired, they began to fan out across the city.

Of course, not everyone was on the ball. Lucy Houston was fixing lunch for her brother when the door to their apartment was taken off its hinges. The SWAT team had her on the ground and begging for mercy before she could scream. Brian, lying in bed quietly moaning to himself, hoped maybe that the rumpus was a crowd of his colleagues from the Empire come to cheer him up; he trusted Nathan hadn't said anything about the little incident. Then *his* door came off its hinges and they were taking aim all around him.

The SWAT team had something to prove. Made up of volunteers from other FBI squads – Violent Crimes, Task Force, Special Operations Group – and rigorously trained, it was nevertheless not considered rigorously trained enough to handle anything as important as a hostage rescue. It was destined always to play second fiddle to the Hostage Rescue Team. So it was feeling pretty mean at this important juncture in modern American history, some of which manifested itself in slaps about the head for Brian Houston as he was dragged into the lounge. He saw Lucy, cuffed, being restrained by two female cops. The apartment was being torn apart. For a few moments Brian forgot his bruises.

'Don't, please!' he pleaded. 'I'll tell you, I'll tell you. Don't wreck the place.' He was houseproud.

The searchers stopped, surprised.

Brian hung his head. 'In the video cabinet,' he said dejectedly, 'third row. Frazier v Foreman.'

They raised their guns again and advanced on the video cabinet. One reached carefully up and pointed to the tape.

Brian nodded. 'Inside,' he said.

The agent shook his head. 'I ain't opening that, damn thing'll explode in my face.'

'Open it, Frank, he's not going to booby-trap his own apartment.'

'Says who?'

'C'mon, Frank, open the damn thing.'

'Yeah, sure, blow my fuckin' hand off.'

'C'mon, Frank, don't be such a big baby.'

'Fuck you, man, I'd like to have a big baby one day. You want it, you open it.'

'You closest, man.'

The agent in charge shook his head. He pushed Brian into the arms of another agent. 'Fuck it,' he barked, 'you want something done round here you do it yourself.' He stepped up to the cabinet and removed the video box. He weighed it in his hands for a few moments. He nodded almost imperceptibly. *Much lighter than a videotape should be. Heavy enough for Semtex. Too light for homemade.* He looked round at his team. They watched, grimfaced. The President was waiting. He opened the box.

He turned and glared at Brian. 'What the fuck are you playing at?'

'I'm sorry,' said Brian.

The captain angled the box so that everyone could see. 'Fucking coke,' he said, and tipped the contents. A white cloud quickly blanketed the carpet. 'But . . .' Brian began.

The agent in charge stabbed a finger into Brian's chest. 'You know why we're here?'

'Narcotics,' Brian said wearily.

The captain shook his head. 'We don't give a flying fuck about the drugs. We want to know why you didn't go to work this morning.'

'Well . . .' Brian fumbled, 'I didn't think it was that serious to take . . .' He glanced across at Lucy, who looked perplexed. 'What's happened?'

'You are aware that as we speak President Keneally is being held hostage at the top of the Empire State Building by somebody using your name?'

'Oh God.'

'You do know Nathan Jones?'

'Oh God.'

'Are you involved in a conspiracy with Nathan Jones to kidnap the—'

'Oh my God, no!'

'What happened to your face, Brian?'

He looked back to Lucy. She gave a slight shake of her head. 'He beat me up. Jones. Nathan Jones beat me up. Nearly killed me. That's why I'm off work. I'd no idea . . .'

'Why'd he beat you up, Brian? A falling-out between conspirators?'

'No, God, no! He . . . I'd rather not . . .'

The agent in charge grabbed a handful of pyjama and floppy skin. 'Brian, you're not in a position to *rather not* anything. The President is being held hostage and you're the only link we have at the moment. Talk, god-dammit.'

Brian nodded. 'Of course. Oh God I . . . he tried to . . . well he tried to perform a sexual act on me, officer, I refused . . . he went mad, he nearly killed me . . . my sister can back me up . . .'

The captain turned. 'He tried to do this while you were present?'

Lucy shook her head. 'I heard the rumpus from my room. When I came out Nathan was attacking him. I tried to stop him, he hit me too. He's mad. He's a psycho. If he's got the President, God help the President.'

It took five minutes to secure the apartment and get back downstairs. As they were marching Brian and Lucy across the sidewalk a TV news crew came rushing up.

'This is Brian Houston! This is Brian Houston!' the reporter shouted. A tiny Chinese cameraman pushed forward. 'Channel Three reporting live from Brooklyn! This is Brian Houston!' shouted the reporter.

The SWAT team pushed the crew away as Brian and Lucy were helped into the back of an unmarked van. Unperturbed, the cameraman began to jump up and down trying to get his shot.

'Is it true you're Nathan Jones' lover?' the reporter shouted.

'No!' Lucy and Brian shouted at the same time.

James Morton held his head and thumped his desk in tandem. 'Some cock-sucker's got him? Jesus Christ, that's all we need.' Doyle grinned morbidly. Morton could feel his hair turning grey. By the time this was over he'd be an albino. That or he'd be on a slab with Fred Troy. 'Any word on Troy?'

'Still waiting.'

'Okay, what about Jones? Irish militia or gay militia?'

Doyle shrugged. 'Both, maybe. Jones vacated his last known address in the Village a few days ago. Guy downstairs says he split up with his girlfriend. She threw him out, then took off herself.'

'So he swings both ways.'

'Seems it. No idea where Jones has gone, but he reckoned the girl was heading for Cape Cod. She told him, made him swear not to tell the boyfriend. The ex-boyfriend.'

'Find her. Now. What'd the guy say about *him*?'

'Quiet, bit of a drinker, been some fights in the apartment in recent weeks.'

'Did he leave anything behind? Photo would be helpful.'
'Nothing. All personal effects removed.'

'What about the Irish angle?'

'Nothing yet. New York's a blank. Scotland Yard, Interpol have nothing on him. The Northern Irish police say he's not a known player, but they're trawling. They have a lot of files to get through.'

'Don't they have an information database?'

'I'm not sure if they have computers. They're getting back to me.'

In the corner of the office Agent Kipriskie was on the direct line to the 86th floor. Morton turned to him. 'Anything?'

Kipriskie shook his head.

Doyle looked at the ceiling. 'What the hell are they doing up there?'

'That's what the whole world wants to know,' said Morton.

6

Arnie Mead was snarled up in the traffic on Columbus Avenue. It was hot and sticky and some bastard had stolen his radio. He slammed his horn for five minutes, just to tell everyone who didn't already know that he was stuck in the gridlock. Arnie sold shoes, but the boss had let him go early, along with everyone else, because nobody was interested in shoes this day. Go home, watch it on TV. Like it was some big fucking soap. It annoyed Arnie, though not enough to turn down the afternoon off. He didn't give two cents for the President. It annoyed him because the boss wouldn't consider giving him five minutes off to watch the World Series or to go see a doctor when his back was aching working in *his* fucking shop, or if he did he'd have to make up the time. Sometimes Arnie felt like taking one of the boss's elegantly appointed shoes and sticking it right up his ass.

Arnie climbed out of the car. Nothing moving, as far as the eye could see. He leaned through the door again and pumped the horn a few more times. He was thirsty. There was a 7-Eleven about three blocks down, but he wasn't risking it. He'd come back and his tyres would be gone. Arnie removed his tie and unbuttoned his shirt collar. The shirt was stuck to him. He spat on the road.

Okay, so I'm slightly interested. There was a black guy listening to the whole damn drama in a sedan by the side of the road; Arnie could just make out the rapid thud of urgent voices through the closed window, but not enough to make any sense. He rapped the window.

'Hey, buster,' he said, 'drop the window, let's hear what's going down.'

The guy ignored him. His eyes were closed, pretending to sleep.

Arnie knocked harder. 'C'mon, open up. Let's hear.'

Nothing. Arnie knocked again. It began to annoy him. Fair enough if the guy didn't want to let him share his radio, but completely ignoring him, pretending not to hear him, shoot, that was bad manners. Manners and Arnie were not normally intimate acquaintances, but right then it seemed pretty important to him. 'You're not fooling anyone, deadbeat. A simple *no* would suffice.'

Arnie was beginning to lose it. He slammed his door shut. A guy in front got out of his car and stretched. He looked back at Arnie. 'What's the hassle?' he said.

'No hassle, just this son-of-a-bitch won't let me hear about Keneally on his radio.'

'Hey, no worries. It's on here, man, c'mon up. Looks like half the world's heading downtown.'

'That's not the point,' Arnie snapped, 'the point is that this son-of-a-bitch won't even acknowledge me.'

The driver stepped forward and peered through the sedan's front window. 'Hey, let the dude sleep if he wants to.'

'He ain't sleeping. He's faking it.'

'Leave him be, man. He ain't doin' you no harm.'

'He's annoying me.' Arnie slapped the window. No

response. 'Let's say I just turn his radio off and see how long he keeps his eyes shut?'

Arnie grabbed the door handle.

'Don't do it, man,' said the driver. 'He's within his rights to shoot you if you open that door. Maybe that's what he's waitin' for.'

'Baloney,' said Arnie, and pulled the door open.

Clark Fuller fell sideways. His seatbelt prevented him from flopping to the ground. He hung, half in, half out, the last vestiges of his blood dripping onto the asphalt.

'See,' said the driver, 'told you you should have left him. Now you gonna be up to ya ass in paperwork.'

Not a million miles away Chief of Staff Graham Slovenski and the First Lady, their respective staffs, Secret Service agents and police escort were caught in the gridlock just on the downtown side of the Lincoln tunnel. Traffic cops were making valiant efforts to clear the way, but the cavalcade was only able to make slight headway.

Tara slumped in the back of the limousine staring morosely out of the window. *While I was trying to be unfaithful to my husband, somebody was trying to kill him.* People were beginning to gather on the sidewalk, watching. They knew where she was going and why. They shook their heads, they pointed, they put their heads together and whispered.

Tara slapped the back of the driver's seat. 'Can't we do anything?' she shouted.

The driver glanced back. 'Doin' everything we can, ma'am,' he said.

Slo was on the phone to the Empire. He was having trouble hearing. 'What is that god-damn noise?' he demanded.

'Helicopters,' shouted James Morton, 'circling above us.'

'Well how's that going to help the situation?' Slovenski asked.

'It's not, sir, must be hellishly loud up there.'

'Well why don't you move them back?'

'We're trying, sir, but they're not ours. TV news crews. We try to move them back they'll have us in court. Our people are talking to their people.'

'Good God, damn it, man, this is a national emergency. Get them moved back or I'll call up some fighters and have them blasted out of the skies. Hear me?'

'Yes, sir.'

'Now what the hell else is happening? Has the gunman contacted us?'

'Nothing yet, sir. We have established something more on his background: name's Nathan Jones, he's Northern Irish. He survived a terrorist ambush there some years ago, but suffered something of a mental breakdown sometime later. He entered the United States eight months ago. We, uh, also believe him to be a militant bisexual with a tendency to violence.'

Slo shook his head. Tara noticed; her brow furrowed and she peered across at Slo. 'What?' she said.

He put a finger to his lips. 'Tell me more,' he said.

'We have evidence that he carried out a homosexual assault last night in Brooklyn. We also have video testimony that he was involved in an assault following a bondage session with a young lady the previous evening in the Chelsea Hotel.'

'What do you mean by video testimony?'

'Uh, sir, we recorded it off the TV. Hotel manager was bought up by Channel Three. We haven't been able to get near the girl yet, sir.'

'Jesus Christ, what is the world coming to?'

'I know, sir.'

'You don't know damn all! First it's helicopters, now it's reporters buying up witnesses. This is the god-damn President of the United States we're talking about. Get out there and sort it out. Break every law in the god-damn book, just sort it all out.'

Slovenski slammed down the phone.

'What is it?' Tara demanded.

Slo ran a hand through his hair. They looked at each other. Her eyes seemed darker now, the light in them burned low. 'Nothing to worry about. They're just compiling some information on this guy, Nathan Jones.'

'Tell me all about him.'

'I'd rather not.'

'Tell me. Don't sugar it.'

'Tara, what's the point? You'll only worry.'

'And I'm not worrying now? Tell me.'

Slo shrugged. 'Okay, so your husband is being held hostage by a gay Irish bondage freak with a history of violence. Is that sugar free enough?'

Tara bit at a quivering lip. 'Slo the great diplomat,' she whispered.

'You asked, I told you.'

Slo lifted the phone again. Tara opened her door. He replaced the phone. She climbed out. He followed.

'What do you think you're doing?'

'Getting out of here,' she snapped. Secret Service agents quickly formed up around her. There came a smattering of applause from the onlookers. Tara forced a smile, a little wave. Then she marched forward. Slo followed.

'Tara, will you get back in the car?'

'And sit here all day? My husband's in trouble, I have to go to him.'

'You're going to *walk*?'

Tara shook her head. 'Of course not.' She approached the closest police outrider. He was staring moodily out at the growing crowd; he turned suddenly at Tara's tap on his shoulder.

'Move up,' she said.

'I'm sorry . . .?'

'Move up, gimme room.'

He was more than a little frightened by the sight of the First Lady in her bottle-green skirt and jacket. He looked about him for support. The Secret Service agents hung back, unsure; the police outriders looked at each other, looking for a lead from the agents.

Tara slapped the back of his leather jacket. He shuffled forward. She hitched up her skirt and straddled the leather seat.

'More!' She slapped him again. He slipped forward another few inches. She pointed at herself. 'Me. You. Motorcycle. Sidewalk. Empire State Building. Let's go.'

'But I—'

'Go!'

With a despairing look at his colleagues the outrider revved his bike, then moved smoothly towards the sidewalk. The crowd, momentarily stunned to silence, hurried to make space. Then as the outrider finally gunned the bike up, somebody clapped, then somebody else, and somebody else, until it Mexican waved its way around all of the people standing there.

Slo watched, mesmerized. *Sex on wheels*, was his first thought. Admiration for her flooded through him. He would have to remember that he was finished with her now and for all time. That her charms were ethereal, schizophrenic.

The closest agent turned helplessly to him. 'Sir?'

'Sir?' he shot back, then mellowed instantly. 'The First

Lady has a point, son,' he said kindly. 'Too much standing on ceremony, not enough getting things done. Let's get on these god-damn bikes and head for the Empire.'

As they manoeuvred towards the Empire, Michael Tate manoeuvred towards a nervous breakdown. He spent an hour screaming at everyone and anyone he could find. The gist of it was: 'They threw me out of *my* fucking building! They can't do this, this is America!', but they could and they had and they would continue to keep him away from it.

Mark Benedict, as he had spent his life, tried to keep him calm and eventually a kind of angry resignation settled on his employer: fifteen minutes of quiet fuming, then an outburst, then forty minutes, then an outburst, the peaceful periods gradually lengthening. After a few hours Tate asked to be left alone in his suite. They had commandeered the top three floors of an expensive hotel. Benedict was relieved; the whole country was going to hell and someone had to keep an eye on the business.

When he was alone Tate opened a can of Mountain Dew, flipped on the TV, and phoned Smedlin on the coast. He got the answerphone, so he called him at home.

At first Smedlin didn't recognize the voice, thought maybe it was one of his loons. Then he laughed at *that* word and remembered who did use it.

'Michael, sorry. Kinda early.' He touched his face. His head throbbed. During the night he'd had a nosebleed. The pillow-case was stained red, dry and crumbling now. The TV glowed in the corner.

'Am I disturbing you?'

'Michael, you always disturb me. Now what's so important that you have to call me in the—'

'Mr Smedlin, they done gone and kidnapped my daddy.'

Smedlin deared his throat. 'What?'

'They've kidnapped the President.'

'I know. I'm watching it. And in your building.'

'My *erection*. My daddy, my erection, and some loons.'

'And how do you feel about it?'

'They threw me out of my own building.'

'You gotta expect that, Michael.'

'I don't *gotta* expect nothing. They *threw* me out. Like the trash.'

'They're panicked, you gotta—'

'I don't *gotta* anything. Don't they realize that with one button I could just close New York down?'

'I'm sure in the cold light of day they might regret treating you this way, Michael, but you gotta understand . . .'

'Will you stop saying *gotta*? Gotta, gotta, gotta. That's all you can fucking say.'

'Michael?'

'What?'

'I gotta go.' His nose had started to bleed again.

There was silence for a while from the other end, and then: 'I was right about the loons, wasn't I?'

'You were.' He pinched the top of it, angled his head back. 'And they're going to kill him. You will be guilty of patricide.'

There was a silence at the end of the line. And then: 'What do you mean? For patricide *I'd* have to kill him, and even then he'd have to be my *real* father.'

'Your building. Your employees. Your father. You're killing him, Michael. Simple as that.' The blood was really starting to flow. 'Do you not think you could do something to help him?'

'*Help*? He's my enemy. He's diametrically opposed to everything I stand for.'

'But he's the President of the United States of America. And we're *Americans*. Isn't that important to you, Michael?'

'I'm not so sure I'm an American any more. I have doubts.'

'Believe me, Michael, you're an American, you can't help it.'

'But if I bought Africa, or part of it, I'd be an African, wouldn't I?'

'Goodnight, Michael,' Smedlin said. He put the phone down and went to find a towel.

Tate sat, stunned. No one had *ever* put the phone down on him before.

7

They spent the late afternoon walking along an empty Commercial Street. Alex was anxious to watch the drama unfold on TV, Lisa anxious to miss it. They looked in shop windows. The shops were shut.

'What's got into you, girl?' Alex asked as they walked. He had his hands on her shoulders, massaging. 'Ooooh, so tense.'

'It's Nathan. I'm worried.'

'Listen, kid, he might work there, but so do thousands of others.'

'They said there was a body brought out. I have this terrible feeling.'

'You're such a pessimist. I'm not even going to mention being left out in the cold while you worry about an ex-boyfriend.'

'I'm sorry, I . . .'

'Is he really an ex?'

'Yes. Of course he is. But you still worry. You still care.'

'You still love.'

'Stop putting things in my mouth.'

'It's the thought of putting things in your mouth that keeps me interested.'

She slapped him. It was a laughy slap and they chased each other along the deserted street for a hundred yards. Then she suddenly stopped and the blues were back on her again. 'You're dying to watch it, aren't you?'

'Well, y'know, it's one of those moments. First moon landing. England winning the World Cup. Kermit and Miss Piggy having a snog.'

She took his hand. 'Elephant Strides. Not a crowded pub.'

'That's okay, luv. Snuggle up in bed, if you want.'

She smiled sweetly.

Alex had plenty of drink stashed in his room. He filled an ice bucket in the kitchen, they stripped off and drank each other's health lying on the bed. The Empire was on screen, but after a while he moved his hands onto her breasts. She giggled.

'What?'

'Nothing. Hah. Only I never used to have any feelings in my boobs. But that . . . well, c'mere and let me explain.'

She folded her arms about him and they kissed long and soft. She could feel him hard against her; she reached down, began to massage him. She opened her eyes to watch him. She kissed the back of his neck. Her eyes flitted to the TV screen.

She screamed.

'Oh Jesus Christ! Oh no! Oh sweet Jesus Christ, no!'

Alex shot backwards. 'What . . .?'

Her mouth worked, but then nothing came. She pointed at the screen.

Alex looked. A photograph of a battered and bleeding young man. Police around him. Being led down a corridor. 'Lisa . . .?'

Her arms flailed before her. 'Turn the sound up! Turn the sound up!'

He tumbled across the bed and grabbed the control off the locker. In his hurry he missed the sound and flicked the channel. She screamed at him. He flicked it back.

'It's okay, it's okay . . .!'

'It's not okay! Look!'

He found the volume; Lisa had four fingers in her mouth.

'. . . the picture, in a special edition of the New York *Daily News*, purports to show Nathan Jones, the man thought to be responsible for the kidnapping of President Keneally, shortly after being arrested by police at the Chelsea Hotel in Manhattan on sexual assault charges two days ago – incredibly Jones escaped from police custody.'

'Oh my God, oh my God,' cried Lisa. He bundled her into his arms. She shivered against him. 'It's him. It's him. He's done it. He's done it. Alex, for Christ's sake, it's him. It's Nathan. He's going to die!'

'Lisa . . .'

'He's flipped! He's flipped because I threw him out! Oh my God, it's all my fault! He's kidnapped the President of the United States because I got fed up with him. If I'd given him another chance he'd still be alive!'

'He's still alive!'

'He's not! He's a dead man!'

'. . . police sources say that Jones, of Northern Irish origin, is a bisexual with a history of violent assaults on both men and women . . .'

'Oh my God!'

Gradually, with the drink and the repetitive nature of the broadcasts, she calmed down. They remained naked. He did his best not to get an erection, but it was a losing battle.

'I'm sorry, luv,' he said, shy with her for the first time at the inappropriateness of it. 'It's involuntary.'

She hugged him. 'It doesn't matter. It's lovely.' And they hugged again and began to move against each other and then they made love. Slow, beautiful love and for half an hour she managed to block out every thought of Nathan; but when she came to her climax, and it was spent, the fear came flooding back, even worse than before. She clung to him, suddenly cold, and whispered: 'That's the last time we'll make love.'

He lifted her chin. 'I don't intend to let you go.'

She laughed sadly. 'Alex, Alex, don't you see that it's all over now? That it can never be the same again?'

'Hey, so you have a famous ex . . .'

She grabbed his hand, squeezed it hard. Her eyes, beginning to drip tears, bored into him. 'Alex, please, listen to me. My boyfriend has kidnapped the President of the United States. He may well kill him. He will probably be killed himself. People will want to know who he is. What caused him to do what he did. They will want to know about me. They will pursue me until they have wrung every column inch, every mile of videotape out of me. They will photograph me. They will photograph you. They will come to your gigs. They will say this man in a dress is the man Lisa left Nathan for. This man in a dress is the reason why our President was killed. And someone, somewhere will blame you and will want to kill you. And kill me. Don't you understand? This is the end.'

Alex looked a little surprised. 'You're being a bit dramatic, aren't you, girl?'

Lisa shook her head vehemently. 'I'm underplaying it, Alex. It'll probably be worse.'

'God,' said Alex.

'I know.'

They sat quietly, lost in their own thoughts, for several minutes. Alex forced a smile. 'So I might lose my gig for the Provincetown lesbians for a while. Wow, heartbroken.'

'Alex, it's not as simple as that.'

'I know, luv.' He bent across, kissed her brow. 'What are we going to do?'

She gave a little incredulous laugh. '*We* aren't going to do anything.'

He looked crestfallen. He opened his mouth; she put a hushing finger against it.

'It's the truth, Alex, you know it. *I* can run. I can try to hide. But they will get me eventually. But if we end *us* here, *now*, at least your life continues as before. There's no need to get involved.'

He smiled, but it was a smile to cover up a tear. 'Lisa, luv, who are you to talk to me about need? Don't you know what *I* need?'

She shook her head warily.

He sucked on his lower lip. 'You bitch. You're going to make me say it.'

'Alex, don't . . .'

'I *need* you . . .'

'Oh God.' She looked down at the bed. There was a long silence. When she looked up there was a glint in her eye. 'Alex, you are a gem.'

'I'm only a gem so long as you promise that we're not running back to New York so that you can team up with Nathan again.'

She took his hand. 'Absolutely not. It's the last thing on my mind. I loved him, Alex, but I'm not going to let him take me with him. That's over. He's over.'

8

Eventually a calm settled upon the management offices: after Morton's tirade, Slovenski's squall, the First Lady's rant and everyone else's blushes. Blame was assigned everywhere. Blame was denied everywhere. For a while it seemed as if there wasn't a President in peril at all, merely his employees trying to justify their continued existence.

By now, despite Morton's orders, everything was beginning to crowd up. In addition to the presidential party and attendant security there was Slovenski and Tara's crew, a succession of New York's leading lights and now a steady dribble arriving in hot-foot from Washington. There were experts in more fields than anyone could keep track of. The jabber of advice and opinion was deafening.

'It's like fucking feeding time at the zoo,' Slovenski said, adding to the uproar. 'We're going to have to get this sorted out.'

Morton nodded. 'We have a tried and tested crisis management programme, it just seems to have gone out the window because the President's involved.'

Slovenski, his anger spent, nodded. 'I want you to gather

in this room everyone you need to see this thing through. I will then see to it that you are not disturbed.'

'I have them already. They just keep getting interfered with.'

'Not any more.'

Morton thumbed behind him. 'What about the First Lady?'

She was sitting with Kipriskie by the phone. Slo nodded solemnly. 'She knows the President better than anyone else. Might be no bad thing to have her on hand.'

'Not if she's going to blow up like before.'

'Okay. I'll have a word. You give me a list of the rest and we'll organize it.'

'There are more experienced men than me, Mr Slovenski. This isn't going to go down well.'

Slovenski smiled. 'Yes, I know there are. But one, I know your background. You're trained for this as much as any man, and you've the practical experience – in Colombia and Beirut, wasn't it?'

Morton nodded, impressed. 'Yes, sir.'

'Two, do you think any of those brass-heavy fucks actually want this gig? They want to be around, they want to give their advice and to be seen to give their advice, but they don't want the responsibility.' He pressed a finger into Morton's chest. 'It's down to you. If the President dies, it's all your fault.'

'As simple as that?'

'As simple as that.' He moved his hand up to Morton's shoulder, gave it a little squeeze. 'Now, go get organized. There have been enough histrionics, let's set about getting the President home.'

'Yes, sir.'

Slovenski turned to Tara. He took her arm and led her across to a quieter part of the office.

'Bad news?' she asked, warily.

411

He shook his head. 'No. No news is good news. We're just trying to get organized. We're pulling a small team of experts together, throwing everyone else out.'

'I'm not going anywhere.'

'That's okay. We need you to stay. But we don't need you to disrupt. We don't need you to throw a tantrum when you don't get your own way . . .'

'Tantrum!'

'See?'

'Slo!'

'Quiet. I mean it. You hold your tongue and you can stay. Disrupt and we throw you to the wolves outside. And you wouldn't like that. You saw what it's like, it's New Year's Eve out there. What is it they say, give the public what they want and they'll turn out for it . . .?'

'That's hardly fair.'

'Life's hardly fair. Do we have a deal?'

She nodded slowly. 'Is that really what you think of me, Slo? Tantrums and disruption? Really?'

He avoided her eyes. 'Sometimes,' he said.

Morton sat down at his desk to work out his team. He knew from sad past experience that you could have too many experts: a plethora of contradictory advice was no good to anyone. On a scientific project, sure, the more the merrier, like Apollo 13, bringing that baby home, but not for this. Better to go with a few; build a tight little unit, shut out outside interference, mix in experience, instinct and luck, battle through to a successful conclusion.

It was daunting.

He looked at his list. His name first, of course. Doyle, his assistant, a buffer between him and those external forces. Then Slovenski. He had the power to get things done. He would be difficult to work with. He would want to run things in spite of himself. Then James Cameron, an analyst with the investigative support unit of the FBI's behavioural science department; Morton had already decided that Cameron should double up as the chief negotiator. He'd sat in on the earlier meeting. He hadn't said much, but what he said made perfect sense. Next he wrote *Hostage Rescue Team commander Martin Dillon*. Morton had worked with him before: there had been a hostage situation at La Guardia which had been successfully resolved – three hostages freed, three Algerian terrorists shot dead. If ever it came to an armed solution, Dillon was the kind of man to lead from the front.

Before he realized it, Morton had written *Fred Troy*.

He scribbled it out.

What would Fred have done?

He shook his head. It didn't matter. Fred was dead and gone and his years of expertise with him.

Morton called home. 'I'm going to be late home,' he told his wife.

'I know. Doylie called.'

'Of course. I forgot. He's efficient.'

'And so are you.'

'Thanks. Andrea, I have the world on my shoulders.'

'A good job they're broad shoulders.'

'What if this doesn't work out?'

'Then come home.'

'Simple as that.'

'Simple as that.'

'How's Rory?'

'He's watching TV.'

'The siege?'

'*The Simpsons*. You know what he's like.'

'One day he'll regret it.'

'I doubt it.'

They were silent for a few moments. 'Who do you love?' Morton asked quietly.

'Oh, Mum and Dad.'

'Anyone else?'

'Well, Rory, of course. My brother Tom. Uncle Marty.'

'No one else?'

'Gee, let me think. The President, of course.'

'Of course.'

'And you. Goes without saying. Is it really horrible there?'

'No. It's okay. Don't worry. You're right, at the end of the day, no matter what happens, I'm not the one in danger. I'll come home whether he lives or dies.'

'Just do your best. You always do.'

'But is my best good enough?'

'It has been so far.'

Doyle brought in a copy of the *Daily News*. 'You'll want to see this,' he said.

Morton looked up from his desk. 'No I won't. I haven't time.'

'I think you have.' Doyle laid the paper in front of him. 'That's our man.'

Morton took a long look at Jones. He was only a kid. Mad, despairing eyes: but then *he* would have mad despairing eyes if *he* was dragged half naked out of a hotel by police in the early hours of the morning. 'Okay. Get some copies.'

'You took that well,' said Doyle.

Morton shrugged. 'Nothing surprises me. Besides, knowing what he looks like isn't going to do us much good.' He tapped his skull. 'It's what he has in here that matters.'

'Or hasn't,' said Doyle.

'Or hasn't,' agreed Morton.

414

'Coffee?' asked Doyle.

'Sure.'

He fetched two cups from the now relatively quiet outer office. There were only about a hundred and fifty experts scrambling to set up their equipment. Morton sat back from his desk and stretched. He took a sip. Bitter. He put it to one side.

'What about Jones's girlfriend?'

'She's a stripper. Or was. Joint on Times Square.'

'I thought they were all closed down.'

'Most of them are. A few are fighting the zoning laws. She worked in a place called Star World. Described as a nice kid, wouldn't go too far with the johns.'

'Sure. The whore with a heart of gold. But she's gone to Cape Cod.'

'Took off a few days ago. Maybe got wind of what he was planning. Every cop in the area's looking for her.'

'You have a picture of her as well?'

'Expecting one in the next few minutes. British passport guys have one. She's Northern Irish, too. Entered at the same time as Nathan.'

'Bonnie and Clyde. What about the old guy? The octogenarian accomplice. Sam McClintock?'

'Lives alone. Bit of a drinker. Wife's senile, in and out of a coma, lives in a nursing home.'

'Who pays for that?'

'Has some insurance. But not enough. And the fees just went up. Sam wasn't a happy man. Guy down there says he was going to speak to the President about it.'

'Well, he tried.'

'But did he speak to Nathan Jones about it, and are they partners in crime?'

'That, Mr Doyle, is the three-billion-dollar question.'

9

Sam was in the park. Mary was pushing his chair. It was a summer's morning. Their poodle, Trixie, jumped playfully as they walked.

'This is a dream, isn't it?' said Sam.

Mary, humming to herself, her hair pushed back in a bun, her skirt long, her blouse brilliant white, didn't seem to hear.

'I know it's a dream,' said Sam, 'it's a beautiful warm day, but I'm cold.'

They were approaching a bandstand. Couples sat on the grass, picnicking. When they got closer he could see that they were watching Sinatra, young Sinatra. He was singing 'Blue Skies'.

'This is a dream,' Sam said again.

'What makes you say that, love?'

'Because we've never had a poodle, and if we ever had, I wouldn't have called it fucking Trixie.'

The fog began to lift from his mind, as if sweet Liberty had blown it away. He was on his back. His head hurt. The old familiar hurt, sure, but something more too, something bruisy. He shivered. Somebody was holding his hand. He forced his eyes open: they fluttered, closed, fluttered, open. He focused – blue skies, sure enough, the Empire breeze. He had fallen. At work. He had embarrassed himself. This time they would let him go for sure. Yeah, somebody holding his hand, saying *Coming round, old fella*? like he was Jim Reeves' dog. He focused.

'How're you feeling?'

'Shitty,' said Sam, then added: 'Mr President.'

The President, on his knees, squeezed Sam's hand again, then softly set it down on the old man's chest. 'Just take it easy, we'll get you sorted out soon.' He turned. Marilu had grown in confidence somewhat in the preceding hours, but she hadn't yet ventured beyond the door of the concession stand. 'Could you get him a cup of coffee or tea, something hot anyway, Marilu?'

'Yes sir, right away.'

Sam tried to turn. He groaned, settled back the way he was. 'I'm sorry. Did I fall? I feel like I've been run over by a truck.'

'Sure, you fell.'

'God,' said Sam, 'how embarrassing. Did I disrupt everything? Good of you to see how I was. Y'know, I met all your predecessors. One time or another, they all came up here.'

'So I'm told, Sam.'

Marilu appeared in the doorway with a cup of coffee. The President waved her across. She stepped reluctantly out onto the platform, giving Nathan a wide berth as she crossed to the old man.

The President helped Sam into a sitting position. He groaned again, but it didn't feel as bad as the last time. He cupped his hands around the tea and sipped. 'Mary will be worried,' he said.

'Don't worry,' said the President, 'we'll let her know.'

Sam smiled. He looked around the anxious faces. At the President, smiling benignly; at big-eyed Marilu, warm-faced, worried; Nathan, wan, drained; beside him a coloured guy he didn't recognize, sucking on a straw.

'It's nice to know people worry,' said Sam. 'But you needn't concern yourselves unduly. There's life in the old dog yet.'

As Sam drifted off to sleep again Marilu, flushed with the success of her venture out into the fresh air, took orders for drinks. The President wanted coffee, Fuller tea, and Nathan drank orange juice. He held the gun rigid against his side. The breeze had grown in strength during the afternoon, but he was swaying far beyond anything that would induce.

Thus far Nathan hadn't spoken much. Most of it was drunken babble and variations of *Shut the fuck up*. George had loved the stunt with the ice cream cones. Magnificent. He had shoved them in extra hard. Then Nathan had ordered the agents to the elevator. That was okay by George, the fewer the better.

Nathan had paced. He had waved the gun. He had glared and stamped his feet. He had smashed the postcard rack in the concession stand. He had toppled the pyramid of plastic Empire State Buildings, then knocked the constantly ringing telephone off its hook. He had approached the cocktail table, debated with himself whether to indulge, then gave a little cry and kicked it over. Glasses smashed everywhere. Then he had made the President kneel for nearly an hour with the pistol in his mouth while the helicopters circled ever closer.

Nathan had a lot on his mind.

George Burley had bitten holes in his cheeks, he was so desperate to laugh. He couldn't have dreamt this one up in a million years. Killing the President with a straw was one thing, getting someone else to do it for you was something else entirely. It had always been his firm intention to escape, but he hadn't let planning his getaway weigh unduly on his mind. Getting the job done was the main thing. Now this stupid little boy, with just a little encouragement, would do it for him. Luck was running with him; he'd worried for a while after that nigger farmer had destroyed his car that it wouldn't be with him, but since then everything had fallen nicely into place. Luck and the tactical brain of a master terrorist would see him through . . . no, not terrorist, freedom fighter. No – not freedom fighter, patriot. He wasn't doing this for himself or his family – well he was doing it for both, but not primarily for himself and his family – he was doing it for his country. He was doing it for America. He was sad in some ways that this boy was going to complete the job for him: the fame would be his, the short-lived notoriety, the long-lived legend. Burley National Holiday was no more. It would be Nathan Jones Day.

He wondered what it was that had driven the wimpy security guard to such extreme action. How excellent it would be if they shared a motive! And how perfect if it was for opposite reasons, too! Perhaps he was doing it to protest at the miserable treatment blacks received from the government. Or because he was a communist or a homosexual. Looking at him, his scrawny frame, the hunted, wasted look, George figured it was for none of these things. It was because he was one of life's losers, and he just wanted to make his mark. He'd seen *Butch Cassidy* once too often, revelled in *Dog Day Afternoon*. If he could time it properly, George thought he might blow a poisoned thorn into Nathan's neck as well, providing the little shit had already blasted the President.

George switched his computer on. He could relax now

that the helicopters had disappeared. He began typing as he saw Nathan approach. He hadn't got much more than *he seems so young and proud* on screen before Nathan was nudging the gun into his forehead.

'What the fuck are you doing?' he said, his voice slurred, reading the line, as intended. Nathan was fighting to get his diction back.

'I didn't think you'd mind if I kept a record. That's why you let me stay, isn't it?'

Nathan nodded vaguely.

'Do you mind if I ask you questions as we go along?'

'Don't mind,' said Nathan. 'But not now. Not yet.'

'That's okay. I'll just observe. I appreciate the opportunity.'

Nathan tapped the gun barrel on George's shoulder. 'You can be Boswell to my Dr Johnson.'

George nodded. *What's he talking about? Boswell? Charlie's Angels?* 'It could be useful at the trial too,' he said, 'to have a record.'

'As if,' said Nathan.

Marilu began to tidy up the concession stand. George typed. Nathan stood over the President, the gun pressed into his temple. 'You don't seem so tall, on your knees,' said Nathan.

The President didn't know whether to smile. He gave a little nod, just enough to register appreciation, not enough to jerk the gun into blowing the top of his head off.

'We must talk,' said the President.

'We must,' said Nathan.

'People will be worried.'

'I think that's a bit of an understatement.'

'Not just about me. About you.'

'I think the balance will probably shift in your favour.'

'Do you want to tell me why you're doing this?'

'No.'

'Do you intend to kill me?'

'Not if I get what I'm looking for.'

'What are you looking for?'

'I have no idea.'

'Will you let the others go?'

'Nope.'

'Let the woman go, at least.'

'Commendable, I'm sure, but politically incorrect. I should keep her until last, for the sake of equality. If I told you I was going to pull this trigger in ten seconds, what would your last thoughts be?'

'I probably wouldn't be able to concentrate for counting backwards.'

Nathan smiled.

The President could feel the barrel shaking against his temple. Nathan's eyes were red-rimmed, half-closed.

'Okay, if I asked you to write something down before I blew your head off. What would you write? Your epitaph.'

'I don't know. Nothing profound. That I loved my wife.'

'Really? That's nice. That's really nice. What was it like having the barrel of a gun in your mouth?'

'I've had more enjoyable experiences.'

Nathan removed the gun from the President's head, then placed the barrel in his own mouth. His finger curled about the trigger. 'It's noth vera pleasanth,' he said. For five long seconds they held each other's eyes. Nathan's finger began to squeeze the trigger.

The President wanted to say, *don't do it*, but he couldn't.

Nathan closed his eyes, pictured Lisa, and squeezed harder.

Then the phone rang.

Marilu, having replaced the receiver without first asking, now stared at it, as if it had somehow betrayed her.

'Do you want I should get it?' she asked.

Nathan removed the barrel from his mouth.

'Sure,' he said.

Marilu lifted the receiver. 'Empire State Concession Stand,' she said.

George sniggered over the top of his computer.

Marilu held the receiver out. 'It's for you,' she said to Nathan.

Nathan nodded his head slowly. The gun returned to that rigid position down his left side. He stepped across to the phone: Marilu dropped it into his hand as if it was hot, or he was.

'Yup,' said Nathan.

'Nathan Jones. Hello. This is James Cameron. I work for the Federal Bureau of Investigation. How are you this afternoon?'

'I'm fine and dandy,' said Nathan.

'And how is the President?'

'He's fine and dandy too.'

'Nathan, do you want to tell me why you've done this?'

'For a bit of crack,' said Nathan, and put the phone down.

10

'*For a bit of crack.*'

James Cameron turned his thin-lipped, chicken-beaked face pensively towards the rest of the team. His voice carried just a trace of his first ten years in Glasgow. 'This spells trouble,' he said with quiet authority.

Morton drummed a pencil on the table. 'The words bad and worse come to mind.'

'It makes an expedient military solution mandatory,' said Captain Martin Dillon. He looked at his watch. It was a little after 5 PM. 'We already have the plan, let's get swinging.'

Slo nodded. 'Martin, he's on crack, what's he thinking, how's he likely to react?'

'I doubt if he's *on* it, probably coming off. A crack rush doesn't last very long. If he was on it when he took the President and he's on a downer now, well, he's starting to get ratty. Very ratty. Progressively more irrational. Violence goes hand in hand with crack deprivation if you're an addict. If he's pleading for crack, I'd say things are degenerating pretty badly up there.'

'But do we risk sending people in?'

'I would.'

'It's the President.'

'I know. I still would.'

Morton pointed his pencil at Cameron. 'You agree things are degenerating?'

'Yeah, of course they are. He's already irrational, but the paranoia will be growing with every minute that passes. He'll still be aware of who he has up there. If there's violence to be handed out he'll probably go for the most vulnerable first, the woman or the reporter. He'll have enough of a grip on reality not to want to harm the President just yet. In that sense we still have time to negotiate, if the President is our main priority.'

Morton nodded slowly. 'Well of course he is. But this request for crack, it's not all he's after. That's a buffer until he issues his real demands, right?'

'Almost certainly. There are easier ways to get crack than kidnapping the President.'

'So by giving him some crack, we'd certainly be buying time. Keeping him happy.'

'Sure,' said Dillon, 'keep the psychos happy, give them some crack.'

'We need time,' said Morton. 'I'm not going to botch a raid and lose the President because we rushed things.'

Slo nodded. 'Okay, point taken. But we can't give him crack. That's a no-no.'

Morton looked at Cameron. 'James?'

'It would settle him. He'd be high, but not as dangerous.'

Dillon shook his head vigorously. 'Eighty per cent of violent crime in New York is drug related. It's a fallacy to say we'd be buying ourselves time by supplying him with crack. And I can't condone giving anyone crack.'

'Not even to save the President?'

'That's not the point!' said Cameron.

'That is the point! The safety of the President is our number one priority!'

'But it isn't buying him any safety! Listen to me! It' won't work!'

Slovenski raised a placatory hand. 'I don't know crack very well. Is it the equivalent to buying an alcoholic a drink to pacify him?'

'No,' spat Dillon, 'it's not. It's the equivalent of buying a pyromaniac a box of matches to pacify him.'

'Okay.' Slo turned to Morton. 'From a public relations point of view, we'd be playing with fire.'

'Who gives a fuck about public relations?' Dillon growled.

'We all do,' said Slo. 'And we all should. Remember, the President has very strong views on both dealing with terrorists and dealing with the drug problem. We'd be compromising both to supply this guy. Even if we got him out, the damage would be irreparable.'

'What are we more concerned about, getting him out or winning the next election?' Morton asked. 'We're not talking about a ten-million-dollar deal here, we're talking about a couple of rocks to keep the guy happy until we can get Martin's guys in there to kill the bastard.'

Slo shook his head. 'In a way it would be better if he was asking for a ten-million-dollar deal here. People would see that he couldn't possibly smoke that amount, nor would he have any realistic chance of getting away with it. But there's something sordid about giving him just a few rocks. It makes it all seem so petty. It's just not right, James.'

'So what do you suggest? He's asked for crack, with the veiled threat that he will harm someone if he doesn't get it.'

'But there was no *actual* threat,' said Slo.

'Subliminally there was,' said Cameron.

'Subliminally fuck,' said Dillon, 'that was a threat. The whole fucking exercise is one long threat. He needs to be taken out.'

'Okay,' said Morton, 'take us through your plan again.'

Dillon stood. He crossed around the back of Morton's desk to where a floor plan of the Empire State Building was pinned to the wall, with a detailed plan of the 86th floor beside it. He reached across and lifted Morton's pencil.

'This,' he said gravely, 'is hardly the invasion of Normandy. It sounds simple enough, but it requires efficiency, timing, ruthlessness and a little bit of luck.'

He looked up as the door opened. Doyle entered, followed by the First Lady. They both carried cups of coffee. Doyle, realizing that something was going on, stopped immediately; Tara bundled into the back of him, spilling her coffee.

'Oh for God's sake,' she said, shaking the hot drops from her fingers, 'will you watch . . .'

Doyle nodded at Morton. 'Do you want us to wait . . .?'

Morton waved them in. 'You should both be aware of what's going down.'

Doyle let Tara pass, then closed the door. As he took a seat he said, 'I have some news on—'

Morton held up a hand. 'Later,' he said. 'Okay, Martin, proceed.'

'Thank you.' He glanced at his watch. 'It's going to be dark in the next thirty minutes or so. The observation floor is well lit at night, but if there are no further developments, we can presume that Jones will move his hostages into the concession area. To seek cover at night, it's the natural thing to do.'

'To a crack addict?' asked Slo.

'Yes, even to a crack addict. If you've ever been in the Port Authority station at night you'll know what I mean.

From there he will still have a view of the elevators, but a restricted view of the rest of the floor.' He raised the pencil to the map. 'From our floor, here, we can send a team up the outside of the building and over onto the eighty-sixth.'

'You can do that without making a noise?' Slo asked.

'I'll have them wear sneakers,' Dillon snapped.

Slo spread his hands apologetically. 'Of course,' he said. 'The lights on the eighty-sixth can be controlled from down here. Once we are in position around the two access doors to the concession stand, we hit the lights, throw in some stun grenades, then our men with night vision go in and rescue the President.'

'Our men with night vision?' said Tara. 'I take it this doesn't refer to police officers with a particular fondness for carrots.'

Everyone looked at her.

'Sorry,' she said, 'if I'm not *au fait* with the technicalities . . .'

'Did you ever see *The Silence of the Lambs*, Tara?' Slo asked.

'Sure.'

'At the end when the killer is chasing Jodie Foster round the darkened basement, he can see everything, she can see nothing. He was wearing night vision goggles.'

Tara nodded. She fixed her eyes on Dillon. 'Didn't Jodie Foster kill him, despite the *night vision goggles*?'

'That's hardly the point,' said Dillon.

'Isn't it?' said Tara. 'The point is to get my husband out alive, not to start a gun battle in the dark, night vision or no night vision.'

'Tara,' Slo said sympathetically, 'we have to do something, and we have to do it quickly. We have a crack addict up there and he could blow up on us at any time.'

'Since when was he a crack addict?'

'Oh.' Slo glanced about the table. 'You were out. We spoke to him. Just a few minutes ago. He answered the phone.'

'Well thanks for letting me know. How is my husband?'

'He's fine,' said Morton.

'And dandy,' added Cameron quietly.

Tara looked daggers at the both of them. 'What is going on? What did he say?'

'We asked him how the President was,' said Slo, 'and he said he was fine and dandy. We asked him why he had done this, and he said he had done it, and I quote, *for a bit of crack*. That was the extent of it. He hung up.'

Tara bit at a lip. She gave a slight shake of her head.

'It'll be okay, Tara,' Slo said quietly.

'Do any of you sad fucks know what a bit of crack is?' she asked in a cool, steely voice.

'Oh, I think we all know what a bit of crack is,' Dillon said haughtily.

'For your information,' Tara shot back, '*a bit of crack* is a Northern Irish expression for having a good time, a bit of fun. This has nothing to do with crack cocaine.' She nodded at Slovenski. 'I thought you did your research before visiting foreign countries, Slo?'

'Well . . . I . . .'

'Oh for God's sake,' said Morton. He took his pencil back off Dillon. He drummed it on the table. Then he snapped it in two. 'You sure about this?'

Tara nodded. 'Check it out if you want.'

Morton looked up the table to Cameron. 'How does that change things? For the better?'

Cameron shook his head. 'Doing it for fun? Doing it straight and clean? A cool, calculating psychotic. Give me the crack addict any day.'

They lapsed into silence for a few moments. Then Dillon tapped the map with his knuckles. 'I still say we go for it. Nothing has changed on that front.'

Morton looked about the table. 'What do we all say?' he asked.

11

Nathan hadn't always had a bad temper. But since that day in the cold and dark and blood outside Crossmaheart something had clicked; the fear, the horror had prompted some chemical imbalance; you didn't want to be around Nathan Jones when he lost his temper.

If he'd been American he might have been sent to anger classes, taught how to deal with it, to get it out of his system, but as it was his dad, no slouch in the temper department himself, had tried to quell it by slapping his son about the face and telling him to grow up. This hadn't much helped, but over the years Nathan had learned to accept his temper, accept the consequences of it, and to live with it. Now he realized, with the night closing in, it would be the death of him.

The dull ache of creeping sobriety echoed through his bones. He took a deep breath of the warm night air, allowed himself a few moments to enjoy the twinkling view, then turned to contemplate his prisoners and his future.

Clearly, there was no turning back. He couldn't just apologize and hope they'd understand. At the very least he was looking at an extremely long prison sentence. Most probably he was looking at death, either at the hands of the police, the public or a fellow inmate.

He examined the gun. He had never fired one in his life. Never even held one, or wanted to. It felt heavier than it looked. With some difficulty and a little nervousness he removed the magazine and counted the bullets. Eight.

They watched him do this and he knew that any one of them, even Marilu, could have attacked him then and overwhelmed him. His legs were tired. His arms throbbed. There were little spears of pain in his eyes.

The President sat straight-backed against the concession stand counter. He was doing some sort of breathing exercise. Fuller was fiddling with his computer. Marilu stood wearily behind the counter, waiting to serve. They'd carried Sam inside between them; he slept on the floor, his head on a folded coat. He was breathing easily, healing in the best possible way.

Nathan tapped the President's knee with the gun. 'What's that, yoga?' Nathan asked.

The President shook his head. 'Just breathing exercises. I used to have panic attacks as a kid, this was the best way to deal with them.'

'You having a panic attack now?'

'No, but I can see how it might happen. I'm taking preventative action.'

'Preventative action.' Nathan rolled the words about in his mouth. 'Pre-vent-a-tive ack*chun*,' he said. He held up the gun. 'Where do you stand on the gun thing, Mr President?'

'Officially I'd like to see a reduction in the number and calibre of guns available to American citizens.'

'I'll bet you would.'

'Unofficially I'd like to see the right to bear arms removed from the constitution.'

'So why don't you make your unofficial stance official?'

'Because I'd be out of office before I could suggest it. Americans like their guns, and that's a fact.'

'Be a lot less psychos running about with guns if you did.'

'Yes, there would. But it's not going to happen. Not in my lifetime.'

'Maybe it would take something to prompt a change in public opinion.'

'Maybe.'

'Anything come to mind?'

The President managed a tight smile. 'Is that what this is about, gun control?'

Nathan shook his head. 'Not necessarily. It's not necessarily about anything. But it can be.' He turned the gun in his hand. 'It's not my gun. I stole it off one of your Secret Service agents. You know why I did that, Mr President?'

Keneally shook his head.

'I did that because they weren't giving old Sam here any medical treatment. They beat him up, then they let him lie there. Does that sound fair to you?'

'No, I . . .'

'No, it doesn't seem fair to me either. There's this old guy, worked here for fifty years, about to get thrown out of his job, he has a bit of a fit for God knows what reason and what happens? Instead of being looked after, because you're here, he gets beaten up. Does that seem fair?' Before the President could answer, he prodded him with the gun. The temper was starting to grow on him again, like a hammer pounding at his brain. 'Does it?' he spat, despite himself.

'No it doesn't. These agents can be over . . .'

'And that really got to me. It really did, and I snapped. That's it. I snapped. Simple as that. And here we are.'

'Nothing serious has happened yet, Nathan, if we could all just go home now . . .'

Nathan laughed. 'Aye. Catch yourself on. What're you going to do, give me a presidential pardon and that'll be the end of it? What would you say, that it was an accident, a misunderstanding?'

'I could . . .'

'Under duress! You could promise me all the tea in China and it wouldn't be worth shite.'

'There are witnesses . . .'

'They're under duress as well!'

'There are ways, Nathan, there are always—'

'I don't want ways!' He waved the gun above his head in frustration. 'Jesus Christ!' he shouted. 'You know I'm dead! I'm a corpse! Look at me! Smell me! I'm starting to go off!'

George looked up from his computer. 'If you're going to rant, could you rant a bit more slowly? I'm having trouble keeping up.'

Nathan stared at him for a moment, the gun flexed involuntarily in his hand. Then he let out a great laugh. 'Ah now,' he said to the President, 'there's a man with confidence in me. Hey, Boswell, that saying about not shooting the messenger, you know it's shite? Back home the messengers used to get shot all the time.'

George nodded. 'One or two s's in messenger?' he asked.

Nathan looked down at the President. 'Now there's a man will keep us sane,' he said.

The President nodded. 'Back home, you say. Where was that?'

'Do you not recognize the accent?'

'Scotland, is it?'

'Ireland. Northern Ireland. That little corner of Ireland that will be forever British, until they decide they can't afford it any more and sell it down the Swannee.'

'Is that what this is about, Northern Ireland?'

Nathan thought for a moment. 'No,' he said, 'but it could be.'

'My wife was on her way to Northern Ireland this morning.' His brow furrowed: he tried to remember why she was going there, besides getting away from him. Slo had told him as well. It was . . . it was . . . it was . . . 'She's handing over grants from the International Fund for Ireland.'

Nathan nodded.

'That's an American initiative,' said the President, on a roll. 'It's been going for some time.'

'Yes, I know, you've been patronizing us for many years now. Still, better than a poke in the eye with a blunt stick. What do you think would happen if I said I wanted the Irish Republic to renounce all claim to the northern counties in exchange for your life?'

The President shook his head. 'No country would accept international blackmail like that.'

'Not officially they wouldn't, but they all do it on the sly. Jesus, you lot have been bankrolling Ireland for years. Use whatever secret political channels you have. Say to them, hey, listen Paddy, the good life's over unless you give the North up, we're cutting the strings unless you leave the poor Protestants be. You could do that, couldn't you? Then I could let you go, and you could let me go like you said you could, and we'd all live happily ever after, not a soul hurt, and some even saved in Ireland.'

'Well,' the President began, 'we could certainly look at . . .'

Nathan started to giggle. 'I'm only joking, y'know, I don't give a fuck about Ireland. I don't give a fuck about politics. That's why I'm here, in the land of the free, where I don't have to worry about all that shite.' Nathan scratched at his head with the gun barrel. 'And look what I've done with my freedom. Stuck up a pole with the President, staring at death.'

'Y'know,' George said, 'you're quite a pessimist.'

Nathan turned from the President and strode across to the reporter. 'And what the fuck would you know about it?'

George shrugged. 'I don't know anything. I'm just saying, re-reading this, you come over as a bit of a pessimist.'

'And how the fuck do you expect me to feel! I've kidnapped the fucking President of the United States!'

'Okay, okay, I realize that, I know, I'm sorry.' He looked down at his screen.

'Some people have no comprehension!' Nathan shouted.

'All I'm saying is that if I were in your situation, as hopeless and as black as it may seem, if death were such a huge certainty . . .'

Nathan waved the gun at him. 'You *are* in that situation, mate.'

'I know, I know, but *I* don't have the deadly weapon. What I'm saying, is that if I was in your situation, in control, and let's face it, in control of the most powerful man in the world, I'd want to have a bit of fun.'

'Fun?'

'Okay, well not fun, exactly. But my say. Get things off my chest. Make an impression. Let the world know why I'm here, what I believe in, what I want. That's all I'm saying. There's not many get this kind of opportunity.'

The President glanced over. 'Exactly whose side are you on?' he asked.

George shrugged. 'I'm on nobody's side. I just report what happens. There's just not much happening.'

The President shook his head. 'Some of us like it that way,' he said.

12

Alex was getting them something to eat at the corner store when the cops came in. He was wearing a silk dressing-gown and slippers. He'd picked up some salami, cheese, a French loaf, was just approaching the counter when the cop pulled out a sheet of paper and showed it to the owner.

'You seen this girl before? Anywhere local? In here?'

The owner, Billy Ballard, a reformed New York queen Alex had known for years, studied the picture, then slowly shook his head. He glanced up at the cop, then at Alex, who averted his eyes *suspiciously* in spite of himself.

'Cute-lookin' kid, what she do?'

'I'm afraid I can't tell you that, sir. You're sure you haven't seen her?'

Billy shook his head. 'Not in this life.'

The cops thanked him and turned from the counter. Alex stepped back to let them pass. The lead cop thrust the picture at Alex as well. 'What about you?'

Alex tried to stop his hand from shaking as he took the sheet. It was Lisa, okay, looking about five years younger and with a seriously dodgy hairstyle. But Lisa.

He shook his head and camped it up: 'Sorry, I don't remember *girls*.'

The cop snapped the picture off him and they left without thanking him.

Alex put the groceries on the counter. 'Cops today just have no manners,' he said.

'But nice butts. Still, Alex, tell *me* all about your *girl* friend.'

'What *girl* . . .'

'Alex! It's me! I saw you together! What's she done?'

Alex put his money on the counter. 'Nothing. Much. Thanks for . . .'

'My pleasure. As always.'

Alex smiled and left the store. Outside the cops were in their patrol car. Alex slipped past in the dark without looking. When he got to the corner and looked up towards the Elephant Strides, he could see the neon lights of another cop car at the end of the road.

Lisa was just getting dressed when he came thundering into the room. He dropped the groceries unceremoniously on the floor. The TV was still switched on, there was a case packed on her bed.

'You look as white as a ghost,' Lisa said.

'There's cops at the end of the road. There's cops in the store. There's cops everywhere.'

Lisa nodded. 'I was thinking, it was pretty stupid to pay for my bus ticket here by credit card. Of course I wasn't to know at the time. It's not the sort of thing you think about when you're running away from your boyfriend, how should I pay . . .'

'Lisa! There's cops at the end of the road!'

'I know!'

'What are we going to do?'

'I don't know!'

She slumped down on the bed beside her case. She rested her hand on it, pulled at the straps. 'I'm tired of being on the run already, and I haven't run anywhere.'

He crossed to her, knelt at the edge of the bed. 'Answer me one question.'

'Do I have time?'

'Do you want to give yourself up, or do you want to run? With me.'

She looked him in the eye. 'I want to run with you.'

They tried to leave the Elephant Strides by the back stairs. They were just crossing the yard when they saw the cop. The houses in the area were so chaotically built that the back porches of half the buildings led onto the front porches of others. The cop was standing in the yard across from the Elephant Strides, illuminated by the weak light of a single bulb attached to the rear wall of the guest house, scratching his head. He was plainly confused by the lack of cohesion to the lay-out, trying to decide where to approach next, or if he'd already been there. Alex pulled Lisa back in behind the cover of a storm-wrecked wooden fence and shushed her lips; then pointed at the cop.

Lisa's eyes widened. 'They *are* everywhere,' she whispered.

The cop stepped off the porch and approached the front door of the Mulberry Pie. Keeping close to the fence, Alex led Lisa towards the Elephant Strides back door. As they entered, the kitchen door began to open. They froze.

Jamie Blair, the owner, smiled across. 'Kids, howsa ya doin'?'

Alex and Lisa smiled inanely back at him.

'Taking your case for a walk?'

Alex tapped it. 'Out buying drugs. Three million worth.'

He walked across the kitchen and out into the hall. 'Don't tell a soul, okay?' he called back.

'I'll tell everyone!' Jamie laughed after him.

'You do that!' Alex called back.

They returned to Lisa's room. She hurried across to the window and peered out. There was a cop car about twelve doors down on one side, further away on the other.

'What're we going to do now?' Lisa asked.

13

Marilu had practically left her shell behind. The phone was off the hook again, so she didn't need to answer it every ten seconds with a curt: *No, Mr Jones is in a meeting right now, I'll have him call you right back.* So she served hot-dogs and chips and soda and it would all have been quite pleasant if they weren't all about to die.

Nathan paced, though never so far from the President that he couldn't turn and plug him at the first hint of danger. He was drinking plenty of orange juice, but his mouth remained resolutely dry. Eating the hot-dog was like chewing wood, the onions slithered down his throat like Peruvian tree slugs. Still – one thing, they weren't going to have to bargain for food. They'd enough to keep them going until the end of the month. The cholesterol would probably get them before the FBI.

'Do you want that I should turn this on?' Marilu asked from behind the counter. Nathan turned. She was holding a miniature television set. 'I'm not really supposed to have it, but we all need our fix once in a while.'

'Sure, stick it on,' said Nathan. 'Let's see how the world turns.'

440

'Mightn't be such a good idea,' said George. 'You know what reporters are like.'

Nathan shrugged. 'Well if I don't like what I hear, I'll take it out on you, Boswell, seeing as you're their official representative.'

Every channel – talk, talk, talk.

'I guess it's a big story,' said the President.

'Will you stop flicking the channels and settle on one?' Nathan said.

'I'm just trying to find the best reception, Nathan,' Marilu snapped. 'You think you can do better y'self, you do it.'

Nathan shook his head. 'Just pick one, Marilu, please.'

Marilu settled on ABC News. On screen a grey-haired, supertanned presenter was interviewing a fleshy-faced man in a red bow tie. The caption, which remained in place throughout, read *Abel Dershowitz, News Analyst.*

'Turn the volume up,' said Nathan, 'but not so loud that we can't hear the sound of approaching death.'

Marilu turned the little knob carefully until Nathan nodded.

'. . . what's happening,' Abel Dershowitz was saying, 'is that we are in the process of creating a boogey man for the twenty-first century. It has only been a handful of hours since this started, but already, thanks to the speed of modern communications and the genuine concern of the American people, we've been able to build up a profile of Nathan Jones which has horrified both the media and the ordinary man in the street. He represents everything every decent, white-collar, blue-collar American despises: he's Bundy, Manson, he's Mi Lai, he's OJ, he's Michael Jackson. Set against that we have an American President who has set about improving the standard of living, cutting taxes, he's made America strong again both at home and abroad, and he has such personal charisma: it's the classic showdown, good versus evil.'

'Bundy was in a sit-com, wasn't he?' Nathan asked.

Marilu said, '*Married with Children*?'

'So what the fuck is he on about? Is he calling me a comedian or what?'

'You can be called worse things,' said George, 'like a psychopathic mass killer.'

'I've heard of Mi Lai,' said Nathan. 'I haven't killed anyone. Where does Michael Jackson come into it? What right have they . . .?'

'Free country, Nathan . . .' said George, 'and you do have that freedom to reply.'

'Shhhh,' said Nathan.

'. . . yes, of course,' said the anchor, 'he does seem to be carrying some remarkable personal baggage.'

'More than enough for one person to be dealing with. His bisexuality will pull him one way, his love of inflicting sexual pain on women another, the break-up of his romance with Lisa Mateer in another direction . . .'

'And we have a picture of Lisa . . . currently being sought by police . . .'

Nathan's mouth dropped open. There she was. His Lisa. A photo. Younger than he remembered. Beautiful, beautiful, beautiful. So beautiful that tears welled up and for a moment he forget what they'd said.

He rubbed his gun hand across his face, but not before the President had noticed. 'Oh God,' said Nathan. Then he snapped back in. 'What the fuck are they talking about? Bisexual? Inflicting pain . . . Jesus Christ, what are they trying to say?'

'They're not trying,' said George, 'they're saying it. Is this true, Nathan? Do you turn both ways?'

'Jesus-fuck no!'

'Are you in denial?'

Nathan brought the gun up suddenly. 'Are you?' he demanded.

George didn't look unduly worried. 'I've nothing to hide, Nathan.'

Nathan turned away, drawn back to the screen.

'. . . we have a grade A student who goes off the rails after surviving a gun battle in his native Northern Ireland. British police tell us he has had several convictions for damaging property. Now, despite what we've heard over the years, terrorism aside, that part of Ireland is really quite . . . shall we say unsophisticated. Nathan Jones comes to New York and is seduced by it . . . he immediately faces a number of problems: battling with his repressed bisexuality, enjoying the liberties of New York on the one hand, being weighed down by terrible guilt with the other; how does he deal with it? It manifests itself at first in sexual violence towards women, which is fine for a while, but very soon it isn't enough, he needs to do something more. This is where serial killers quite often come from, and who is to say it wouldn't have led Nathan Jones down that path . . . but for the opportunity which presented itself to him this morning at the Empire State Building.'

Nathan was mesmerized. His mouth moved. Nothing came out.

'Yes, and that really was an appalling lapse in security. What will be the fall-out from that, Alan?'

'Well obviously, Bob, heads will roll. One is, or was, FBI Assistant Director Fred Troy who was on special assignment with the President, charged with his personal safety . . .'

'Who of course died at the scene this morning from a suspected heart attack.' Bob turned to camera. 'If you've just joined us, we had a dramatic update on the Fred Troy story just a few minutes ago. Ken, can we roll that one again, please?'

'I am not bisexual,' Nathan said flatly.

The caption read, *Larry Bond, Empire State Building*. Larry was black and sweltering in a heavy brown coat. He read breathily from a clipboard. 'My source inside the Empire State says that Fred Troy, the FBI agent who we saw being removed by stretcher from the scene this morning and who was later pronounced dead on arrival at hospital, did not, and I repeat, did not, die of a heart attack as suspected, but that some sort of toxin, some sort of poison has been found in his body. It may be that Nathan Jones has claimed his first victim.'

'Jesus Christ,' said Nathan Jones, the Empire Poisoner.

The President looked up at him. 'Is this true?'

'Is what true?' Nathan spat. 'That I'm bisexual?'

'Your sexuality is your own concern. That you're a killer. A poisoner.'

'Jesus Christ, do I look like a poisoner?'

'There's no answer to that,' said George.

Nathan spun. He wedged the gun into George's mouth. A tooth broke. 'You are on seriously dodgy ground, Boswell. There are times and places for smart fucking comments, and this is not one of them.'

Nathan removed the gun. He turned to the President. 'I've never harmed anyone.'

'I'm only calling it as I see it,' George said. He picked a sliver of tooth from his mouth and examined it.

'Just shut the fuck up!' Nathan yelled. 'How can they be allowed to do this? Every damn bit of it is made up, every damn thing . . .'

'What about the girl?' the President asked. 'Lisa.'

'Yes, Lisa. Lisa. That's true. They got something right.'

'You've just split up with her.'

'Lisa. Yes.'

'And is that who they're talking about, about the sexual violence towards women?'

'Good God, no! Never in a million years!'

'With someone else, then?'

'No! No! No!'

'They've got their facts wrong,' said George. 'Let's get your denial down here properly, then. The long and the short of it is, you deny everything. Apart from kidnapping the President, you've done nothing wrong.'

'I don't like your . . . *intonation*.'

'I try not to intonate at all. I'm an impartial—'

'Cut the fucking crap. You've been winding me up right from the start, Boswell. Just you do your observing and leave the interpretation to someone else . . .'

'Like those guys on the TV. Nathan, I'm not trying to be smart here, but if you want this official record to be accurate you better start spelling out . . .'

'I don't give a fuck about the official record!'

'Well who do you give a fuck about?'

'Lisa!'

They were all quiet then, for a few moments. They watched the TV. There was a commercial running for an insurance company.

For the first time the President reached out. Carefully, no sudden moves, he softly touched Nathan's arm. The gun, in Nathan's other hand, held steady on the President's face. 'Is that what this is all about, Nathan?' he asked, his voice calm, reassuring, concerned. 'Splitting up with your girlfriend?'

Nathan looked to the screen. He glanced out into the darkness. He did his best to pack his voice with disdain. 'You think I'd do this over a *girl*?'

14

They had a street plan, they had a list of guest houses and their owners courtesy of the Provincetown Tourism Department, and they had enthusiasm. This was the big one. It wasn't quite being up in the Empire with the President, or catching Lee Harvey, but it was right up there with getting the gun off Jack Ruby.

Officer Peter Cornwall had called at thirty-six addresses, his partner, Officer John Ardagh, at thirty-eight; there were hundreds more to go. It was the height of the season, the population was up tenfold, and half of them were faggots. Officer Cornwall hid his distaste for faggots pretty well; had to, really, as Officer Ardagh was one. *A faggot.*

They drank coffee. Cornwall looked up the street. Another cop car cruised past the intersection. Every cop in the state must have descended on the little town.

'She's close,' Officer Ardagh said. 'I can feel it in my water.'

Cornwall rolled his eyes. *Feel it in my water.* He longed to serve in a town where he could give his partner a hug and everyone wouldn't presume they were *doin' it.*

As he rolled down his window to throw out the empty coffee cup, Cornwall smiled up at the woman squeezing through the narrow gap between the car and the picket fence. Then he hastily tried to withdraw the smile when he saw that she had *stubble*.

'God-damn it,' he began, and Officer Ardagh looked at him, so he stopped and said: 'God-damn it, it's warm.'

After a moment Cornwall realized that the shadow of the *woman* had not passed. He stuck his head out at her and angled it up.

'Ma'am?' he asked, half gagging on it.

'Why you bustin' our balls?'

'Pardon me, ma'am?'

'I said,' and she slapped her hand down hard on the roof of the squadcar, 'why you bustin' our balls?'

Cornwall gave his partner a confused look, and then began to open the door. He got it a foot wide, then the *person* slammed it shut on him, whacking his shoulder with it as it closed.

'Jesus!'

'*Jesus*,' said Ardagh.

Cornwall turned to his partner, then followed his gaze. The street was suddenly filling up. They were coming from all directions. Women. Caked in make-up. Big hair. Loud clothes. Anger etched in lipstick. *Men*.

A rock clattered off the hood.

'What the fuck . . .' Cornwall exclaimed, raising his hands to shield his face.

A squeal came from outside. 'Leave Alex alone!'

'Leave Alex alone!' was taken up by a dozen voices.

Another rock bounced off the hood, ricocheted off the window.

Cornwall lifted the radio; his head nodded along, counting. 'Base, this is Car Eleven, we need some assistance. We're at Monument Road.'

'Help on the way, Car Eleven. What's the nature of your problem?'

Cornwall took a deep breath. 'We're being attacked by twenty-three screaming queens,' he said solemnly. He didn't hear a thing in response, but he *knew* they were laughing.

Alex and Lisa stood by the bedroom window and watched as cops began to appear from the back alleys to try and quell the mini-riot. The number of queens had swelled to somewhere close to fifty. They now had hold of the squadcar and were rocking it back and forth; Cornwall and Ardagh remained inside; the newly arrived cops were beating at the queens with their nightsticks, but they weren't getting anywhere. The call went out for even more assistance.

Lisa gripped his arm. 'Alex, all this from one phone call?'

Alex shrugged. 'The old girl network. They may be the biggest bitches on earth, but when one of their own gets threatened, they act as one.'

'But it's a bit over the top, all because . . .'

'Hey, they love their entertainers. And if the cops get away with searching every boarding house in Provincetown for a queen without a green card, what'll they try next? I'm taking advantage of a little persecution complex.'

Lisa smiled. 'This is one crazy country.'

Alex nodded and picked up her case again. 'Let's go.'

They turned for the door, then back at the sound of a metallic crash and a cheer from outside. They hurried to the window. Outside, the cop car had been turned over. Cornwall and Ardagh remained inside and upside down; in the street light, as far as Lisa could tell, they looked very scared indeed.

They ran for several hundred yards between the houses, using alleys, traversing gardens, jumping hedges. Half a dozen people said hello, waved; it was that kind of town.

Breathless, Lisa pulled at Alex's arm. He stopped. 'Are we running *somewhere*, or just running?'

'Somewhere,' said Alex, and started again.

Another half-mile until they emerged from the rear of the houses onto the main road out of town. They stopped for a moment, waited until the traffic cleared, then entered a wood which ran along the opposite side. Then they stopped for a rest.

'Well,' she said wearily, 'that was exciting for the first hundred yards. Now I'm wrecked.'

Alex nodded solemnly. 'I know. My plan to walk undetected to the West Coast may not work after all.' Then he smiled and lifted her chin. 'Don't worry, kid, okay?'

She nodded. 'I'm not spending the next six months living *here* either.'

He smiled. 'I have it sussed.'

'You . . .'

He put a finger to her lips. 'I'll be back in ten minutes.'

'Alex, don't . . .'

But he was gone back across the road and she was left in the moonlit dark with just the crackle of broken twigs, which she knew meant huge savage beasts were coming to get her.

After twenty minutes there was still no sign of him. With each minute Lisa sank lower and lower until by the time a car pulled to a halt twenty yards away she was cowering on the wood's mossy floor. Its lights flashed above her; her lips tasted the tinder leaves.

She tried to hold her breath, but it was impossible; she could hardly catch it let alone hold it. Then the lights dimmed. *Why am I hiding like a criminal? I've done nothing. I have every right to stand up and say, leave me alone.* For the first time in her life she considered claiming allegiance to the country of her birth. *You can't do this to a British citizen! Just wait till the Queen hears about this.*

Her eyes were closed and her teeth were clenched. The engine was gunned once, then the car door opened, closed. The engine was still running. Footsteps. *One set.* And a voice like a snake's hiss: 'Lisa!'

She opened her eyes, raised her head. 'Alex?' she said softly.

He called again. She jumped up and ran through the trees towards him. In a few moments she was out onto the road. 'You were gone for ever,' she panted, hugging him.

He kissed her swiftly, then unhooked her arms and bundled her into the passenger seat before the next car came along. In thirty seconds they were on their way.

'Sorry,' he said, eyes on the mirror. 'Took me longer than I thought.' Then he slapped the steering wheel. 'Whatchoo think, eh?'

She didn't need to look. 'Perfect,' she said. 'Where'd you get it?'

He smiled proudly. 'Down the road. Elbowed in the side window, then hot-wired it. It wasn't an entirely wasted youth, y'know?'

'You *stole* it?'

They looked at each other in the dark for several moments until a car with its lights on full-beam distracted his attention. Then they began to laugh. A stolen car really was the least of their problems.

15

Sparks were flying, literally. Blow-torches were employed to speed the removal of windows on all four sides of the management floor. Martin Dillon's elite team of fifty special agents, with three back-up SWAT units, readied itself. Dillon went over the plan with his men time and again, though there wasn't much to go over. They chewed gum, their square jaws marching in rhythm; their eyes spoke of steely resolve, or would have if they could have been seen behind their night vision goggles.

Tara was white. Christmas skin, Slo thought, as he watched her hug herself. She stood behind the welders, shifting her weight nervously from foot to foot. She turned as he approached. He handed her a cup of coffee. She thanked him and cupped her hands about it. She didn't attempt to drink it. She was caffeined to the eyebrows. She nodded at the windows: 'What happens if they fall off?'

'The windows?'

'The FBI. Eighty-six floors is a long way down.'

'Not if you have a parachute.'

'They have parachutes?'

'They have everything, Tara. The only thing they have to worry about is landing down below and being torn apart by souvenir hunters.'

She managed a weak smile. 'I heard about Fred Troy. It's a bad sign, isn't it?'

Slo shrugged.

'It shows he's prepared to kill.'

'I think we took that for granted. I know it's ridiculous saying don't worry, but try not to worry too much. I'm assured they're very good.'

She nodded vaguely. 'If you say so, Slo.'

'They are, Tara. They're the best. They don't leave things to chance. They know exactly where Jones is, where he's standing, what angle he's holding his gun at; they know where the President is, where the other hostages are, they know what's being said, Cameron's with them, listening, he can judge how Jones is, assess if his mental state deteriorates. They'll be ready to go in a few minutes, but they can hold on for hours. When the time's right they'll go in and they'll save the President.'

'Will they kill him, this Nathan Jones?'

'Not unless they have to. They will certainly shoot him. But there are a lot of questions need answering. We don't want the same farrago as happened with Lee Harvey. Conspiracy this, conspiracy that. Nearly forty years ago and still the talk of the town. It quietens down from time to time, and then some fool like Oliver Stone comes along and opens it all up again. So this time, we wing Jones, he answers every fucking question on God's earth, then we lock him up for ever.'

Tara set her cup down. She stepped across to where one of the workmen had just removed a window frame. She peered down into the neon night. 'It just seems to me that

most sieges go on for a number of days. There are negotiations, there are demands, there are compromises, there are
ultimatums.'

'And there are aircraft that explode on the runway, killing
everyone.'

'It just seems terribly rushed. It has only been a few hours.'

'Tara, I think you're underestimating how important your
husband is to this country, how important it is that we get
him out alive and soon. Imagine you're not his wife, and I
imagine you have over the past few days . . .'

'What's that supposed to mean?'

'Well you've hardly been bosom buddies . . .'

'We've been fine.'

'You've been at war, Tara.'

'The President and I have merely been undertaking official
engagements in different parts of the world, our marriage is
as sound as—'

'Tara, please, cut the PR bullshit. It's *me*, I *know*. What was
all of that on the plane about?'

'All of what?' They glared at each other for several
moments. She looked away. 'You don't know as much as
you think.'

He sighed, shook his head. 'Listen,' he said softly, 'let's
not get into this. Imagine you're not his wife, just for a
moment, take away the emotion, the sentiment. Try to
remember what this country was like back in the seventies.
Remember when Nixon resigned? Our self-esteem nose-
dived. We had no pride. The world laughed at us. It took us
years to recover. Think what would happen if something
happened to Keneally. The whole country could just fall
apart, descend into anarchy.'

'But why do people keep trying to kill him?'

'That's just what happens to high achievers. Think of when

you were in school. Think of the cheer-leader who looked a million bucks, got all the guys, had a really warm, modest personality, passed all her exams as well. You'd admire her, you'd die to be just like her. But one little bit of you wanted to punch her in the face for being so god-damn perfect. Am I wrong?'

'Slo, I was that cheer-leader.'

'You're missing my point. You can admire, you can worship someone, but a little bit of you can also hate that person for being so good.'

She hated herself. She was still thinking: *baby*. That they could find an empty office in the Empire and make love there and then she'd be pregnant with a lovely little baby ready to announce the news as soon as the President was released. 'Sometimes, when I look at you, I try to see into your mind. Do you know that?'

Slo held her eyes. He nodded slowly. 'I can't say I'm unaware of it. Do you succeed?'

'Sometimes, I think.'

'And what do you see?'

'Oh, I think you know.'

Slo averted his gaze to the neon below.

'Do you want to know something terrible, Slo?'

He shrugged. He didn't really.

'Earlier I imagined being at Michael's funeral. The state funeral. I was doing my Jackie thing, being resolute and strong, looking beautiful in black, winning the nation's heart.'

'It's natural, Tara. You can't help but look at the worst scenario.'

'But that's just it. I was *enjoying* it. I was enjoying being the centre of attention. Is that natural, Slo?'

'Tara, you're under pressure, you don't know what's going

to happen, it's natural for your mind to wander at a time like this.'

'But Slo, I think about it all the time.'

Slo sucked on a lip. One of his own. 'Then I'd see a shrink,' he said.

Morton was staring at the plan of the 86th floor when Doyle appeared in the office doorway. He stood nodding for a few seconds until his boss turned to him and said: 'What?'

'Yeah,' Doyle replied, 'I always get nervous before I attempt to save the President's life, too.'

'How do you know I'm nervous?'

'The pencil behind each ear. It's a dead giveaway.'

Morton reached up. He retrieved one pencil, left the other. 'Yeah, well,' he said, rolling it onto the desk. 'What's happening?'

'I thought you might want to listen in. That reporter guy, Fuller, he's not taking any shit from Jones.'

'What's the point in that?'

Doyle shrugged. 'He has *attitude*. He'll get himself shot.'

'One less reporter, is that a crime? What does Cameron think?'

'He has a big smile on his face. He's enjoying this. He likes to see how people react under pressure.'

'And how's our man bearing up?'

'He's doing okay. Retaining his presidential dignity.'

Morton gave a sad little laugh. 'What else can he do? If he broke down and cried for mercy a tape of it would be on air before his tears hit the ground, and that would be the end of it, he'd be out of office in days. Better to have his head blown off than be pitied for the rest of his life. Nobody wants a yellow dog in the White House.'

Cameron appeared at Doyle's elbow. 'What's this about yellow dogs in the White House?'

'You have acute hearing, Cameron,' said Morton. 'I hear you're having fun.'

'More fun than those up top. There's some pretty heated talk going down, the eye in the sky says Fuller just got smacked. Mightn't be a bad time to send in the troops.'

'I thought you wanted to wait until the early hours? Isn't that when they're supposed to be at their lowest ebb?'

'Ideally, sure, but if he's started hurting people, the whole thing could blow up in just a few seconds. I'd have a crack at him now, before things deteriorate much further.'

'We don't want to do anything too hasty,' said Morton.

'James, this is one occasion when the saying better late than never doesn't apply. I think we should get them out now.'

'Get *him* out,' said Morton, *'he's* our priority.'

'Whatever. Dillon's ready to go.'

'I get the feeling Dillon's always ready to go.' Morton sucked in. He took a long look at the plan of the 86th floor. He reached for his top button, buttoned it, then fixed the knot in his tie. 'Okay,' he said, 'let's go and wave them off and then pray to God that this all works out. Maybe we'll be home in time for *Letterman.'*

16

The Eagle soars amongst the skyscrapers. It is The Day of the Jackal, The Planet of the Apes, The Three Musketeers, *it is a legend in the making. Jesus Rodriguez will not even require a gun, he will rely on the weapon of surprise, the stab of his rapier wit, he will subjugate by intelligence, captivate by charm, eliminate by subliminal suggestion. He is master of the skies, an eagle amongst the pigeons. In the morning he will be front-page news.*

He certainly will.

They were all uneasy. Their talk had ceased. The phone no longer rang. It was still warm, but they shivered. Marilu had cleaned and cleaned and cleaned until there was nothing in her concession stand left to clean, unless she washed the hot-dogs. The glass was swept up, the Empire models were back in their pyramid, she could have opened up shop there and then.

Nathan, hollow-eyed, felt pain in every sinew: the nagging pain of stress and fatigue, the weight of the world on narrow, bony shoulders. Sam was up, shuffling along outside the concession stand, thinking he was still on duty and wondering at the lack of visitors. The President was doing his breathing exercises, when he wasn't being pleasant and caring and presidential.

George closed the lid on his computer. 'This,' he said to Nathan, 'is the lull before the storm.'

Unconsciously Nathan had edged closer to the President. 'And what would you know about it?'

'Quite a lot, if you want to know. I did some siege training when I was in the Marines.'

'Oh God,' Nathan mocked, 'the Marines. Does that mean you're going to do a *Die Hard* kind of a thing on me now?'

'I'm only trying to give you the benefit of my experience. I take it you've never been in this kind of situation before.'

'It's been several months.'

'So you'll be thinking that this is quite an easy place to protect. You can see the elevators from here. There are two entrances to the concession stand which you can cover, and you're so close to the President you can take his pulse without moving.'

'Yeah, it's an okay situation.'

'No it's not. It's poor. It's very poor. This whole floor is too big for one man to guard. They'll be over the walls and through those doors before you have time to blink. There'll be so much noise, so many distractions you won't even think about shooting. But they will. You will die. So might the President. Probably all of us.'

'So?'

'You're not ready to die, Nathan.'

'What?'

'You heard. The President heard.'

Nathan pointed his gun at the President. 'What did you hear?'

'I heard the man say you weren't ready to die. I don't think you are either.'

'Am I missing something here? Did I stumble into the analytical half-hour? Who the fuck do either of you think you are to tell me what I'm feeling?'

'Because,' said the President, 'I'm the President and I do it all the time.'

'And I'm the reporter, and I can read you like a book.'

Nathan laughed. 'Did you two work this up while I was on the phone? Do you know double acts don't work with two straight men?'

'If I were you,' George said, 'I'd move us out of here. Take the elevator to the 102nd floor. It's tiny. You'd be virtually unassailable up there. One elevator, a set of stairs.'

'You seem very familiar with the lay-out.'

'I did my research. I always do. I like to familiarize myself with unfamiliar territory.'

'What a Marine. And what a godsend.'

'I'm only telling you what I think. It's up to you what you do.'

'I know it is.' Nathan eyed the perimeter wall warily, then glanced towards the stairs. 'So what's it to you if this thing ends early?' he asked Clark. 'It wouldn't be the money you're going to make, would it? The fact that the longer it goes on, the more you stand to make?'

George gave a little shrug. 'Money's not everything. Only about ninety-eight per cent.'

The President wasn't impressed. 'He wants the glory.'

'There's a Clash song,' said Nathan. '"Death or Glory". You know it?'

They both shook their heads.

'*Death or glory, just another story*', he sang. They looked at him. 'I'm not making any dramatic point,' he said. 'I just felt like singing.'

'I'm glad you're so relaxed,' said George. 'Please don't stand beside me when they come over that wall.'

'Nor me,' said the President.

There was a moment when they all looked at each other, three sides of a triangle united only by geography, resignation and testosterone. Then they began to laugh, loud, pounding, hysterical. Down below James Cameron shook his head and wondered where the joke was, and then how, even if it was the best joke in the world, they could laugh at all.

'Fuck me pink and call me Rose,' he whispered, pulling the earphones off. 'They're bonding.'

The Eagle came in from the east, tracking the Queens Midtown tunnel, then the UN building, the Chrysler and Grand Central before fixing his sights on the Empire. The air was warm, but it gusted awkwardly between the skyscrapers forcing Jesus to bank sharply; the engine needed all the physical help he could give it. But he was The Eagle, the king of the skies, and he would not be frustrated by his old friend Nature. The engine coughed, spluttered, he dropped twenty feet, then it rallied and he soared again. Soon he would land, soon he would dispense The Eagle's justice.

The phone rang. Marilu reached for it.

'It's beginning,' said George. 'They'll get you talking. You won't notice.'

The President looked to the windows.

Nathan looked from the phone to George, to the President.

'It's for you,' said Marilu.

Nathan looked at the receiver. He knew that Fuller was right. It would be easier to make a stand on the 102nd. He should have gone there straight away. But did he want to make a stand at all? Surely it would be easier just to stay where he was, let them kill him, then it would all be over. There was no hope. There was no future. *No future*. Sid had sung that in the backing vocals of 'God Save the Queen' and he'd been right.

'Hang up,' said Nathan, 'hang up now.'

He looked at Fuller. If the reporter was right about the 102nd, maybe he was right about other things as well: about the need to set the record straight on the bisexual thing, the sexual assault thing, to let people know that he wasn't a twenty-first-century boogey man at all but just an Irish boy with a broken heart. And he could tell the world, he would never have a better opportunity to appeal to Lisa to come home to him. He had never been able to tell her what he thought of her, not properly; as things stood he would die without ever telling her, without even seeing her; his last memory would be a old snapshot on a TV screen. He wanted to hold her one last time. To smell her hair. To feel her bum. To kiss her lips. He could do that. How could they turn that down in exchange for the life of the President?

'Okay,' said Morton, 'it's time.'

Dillon nodded. There was a thin line of sweat on his upper lip. He pulled down his night vision glasses and stepped up to the nearest window. He turned, surveyed the management floor. Dozens of agents and politicos stood pensively watching the HRT unit preparing to depart.

'Good luck,' said Morton.

Dillon nodded. He held his hand up. He spoke into his radio. 'Okay,' he said with cool authority, 'let's go get the President.'

Slo, in the doorway to Morton's office, found himself holding Tara's hand. It felt surprisingly small and cool. He squeezed it. She pressed herself into the angle of his arm and shoulder. He moved his hand down her arm to hold her there.

'It'll be okay,' he said.

Their heads appeared at windows all around the Empire. Then their upper torsos, leaning out, shooting sky-hooks up to the 86th, waiting, then pulling, making sure their lines were secure against the perimeter safety fence above. An eighty per cent strike rate: better than average. Those that missed tried again and succeeded. Then they were out, their black forms slithering upwards like spiders on a web.

Above them, suddenly, the lights on the 86th floor went out.

Continue came the command.

Eye in the sky: 'Sir, something just crossed the radar screen.'

'Well what the fuck is it?'

'I don't know! A fucking big bird!'

Within a minute of easing out of their windows, the first hands grasped the perimeter safety fence. With their heads still below the wall, they began to cut through the mesh. They worked quickly and efficiently. Hand through, shoulder through, head, then a tumble forward and crouching on the observation floor, Koch submachine gun ready, night vision on. Ten, twenty, thirty, forty, fifty men over the top, lying low on four sides of the 86th floor.

They eased towards the darkened concession stand. The first raider, on one knee, peered around the door.

'Something's moving,' he whispered.

'Okay, okay,' Dillon breathed into his mike. 'Stun grenades are go.'

As The Eagle zipped round from the east, centring his sights on the 86th floor, he hit another pocket of air which rattled the frame of the hang glider and forced another cough from the engine. Jesus zeroed in on his target. At first he thought the light was playing tricks, he could see movement on the side of the building, like giant ants. Then he knew what it was – but he would not be beaten. Before they could scale the wall he would have landed deftly on the observation deck and ordered the terrorist to give himself up. He would save the President. He could see figures moving inside the glass building on the 86th. He veered right, figuring to come at it from the other side to give him more time to land in safety and get ready for combat. As he did so he hit another sudden gust and the engine finally died. He cursed as the glider went into freefall, but he would not be beaten. It was too heavy now, it couldn't support him and the useless engine, but it would give him enough lift still to hit his target. He worked at the supports, angling them to channel the air in the right direction. It was a struggle, his arms weren't so strong since he'd switched to mechanical propulsion. He should have trusted in nature all along. As he fought to bring it back on course, he looked to the 86th for guidance. But it had disappeared. The strip lighting, the gaudy concession stand illuminations, all had disappeared into the night.

He was losing height now. It was time to land, to take his chance on the vague shadow that was the observation floor. Luck had always shone on him. The engine had failed so that he would have a silent approach. The lights had gone out to mask that approach in darkness. He would prevail.

The first stun grenades bounced across the tiled floor of the concession stand. Somewhere within they heard the anxious yelp of a scared woman, then came the flash and thump of shockwaves. They counted to five and darted through each door, searching for the shocked and stricken victims, searching for the President.

From nowhere there was a shout: *'I am coming to save you, Mr President!'*

And all hell broke loose.

There was a deafening crash.

They dived for cover as what looked like a giant bird came crashing through the roof of the concession stand. One man let loose with his Koch as he jumped.

Screams rang out as shattered glass ripped through uniforms.

Sparks flew as the flying machine hit the ground; the engine ruptured as Jesus was thrown through the counter, gasoline spraying, then igniting with a great *whoosh*.

Suddenly, the 86th floor was alight.

The world, watching from below, above, left, right, north, south, east and west, held its breath.

17

'Oh my God!'

With the screams of humans burning echoing through his brain, Cameron threw down his earphones and dashed across to where Morton and the rest of the team were craning their necks out of the windows. As sophisticated surveillance went, it wasn't very sophisticated, but it was the natural reaction; all the data was there before them, all the sonics, all the infra-red, everything the satellite could tell them, but there was no substitute for sticking their heads out the window.

'Oh my God!' Tara yelled again as the flames licked out over the edge of the 86th. If Slo hadn't been holding onto her, she might have fallen to her death below.

'He has explosives!' yelled Morton. 'Jesus Christ! He's blown up the President! Why didn't we know this! Why in God's name didn't we know this!'

'We did a scan!' came a panicked voice from behind. 'We did a scan! Nothing, nothing!'

Morton screamed into his microphone. 'Martin! Martin! Can you hear me! Martin! What's going on! What's happened to the President! Oh my God, it's the end, we've lost him!'

There was no response.
There was static.

Nathan and the President had just reached the stairs leading to the tiny 102nd observation floor as the explosion rocked the 86th. The blast threw them through the swing doors and crushed them against the wall. For a long moment Nathan fought for breath, gained it, then waited for the shots that would kill him. The violence and recklessness of the assault had surprised him. It had sure as hell surprised the President too. He lay helpless, gasping, his breathing technique blown out of him.

Nathan shook himself back to reality. He was alive. He still had the gun. He stuck his face against the fireproof glass panel in the swing doors. The 86th was glowing. He couldn't see anyone moving in the half-light. He hadn't been able to switch the lights on the stairs off with the rest of them; now it was no bad thing. He hurried across to the President, got hold of a lapel and heaved at him. 'C'mon,' he rasped, 'it's not over yet.'

The President rose shakily to his feet. For the first time Nathan saw fear clearly etched on his face. *Welcome to the club*, he thought, then pushed him towards the stairs.

The swing door suddenly swung. Nathan spun round as a black-uniformed figure wearing some sort of goggles stumbled through; the uniform was in tatters, there was blood seeping through. He held onto the wall for support. Nathan raised his gun, tried to be quiet, but the President tripped on a step and gave a little yell as he fell forward. The man glanced up, raised his weapon. Nathan closed his eyes and squeezed the trigger. The force of the shot threw his arm back at him.

There was no response. When Nathan dared to look the

man was rolling on the ground, clutching his leg, moaning quietly.

'Sorry,' Nathan whispered. He turned and helped the President up. 'Let's go,' he said.

'What about the others . . .' the President began.

'They're free. Or dead. Forget them. They're not what this is about.' He gave the President a little push. *He* had no idea what it was about. They began to ascend.

George was momentarily panicked. Everything had been going so well up to that point. He had talked Nathan into moving to less exposed ground, he had suggested switching off the lights to disrupt any invasion. Perhaps he'd been too keen. Nathan had sent him to the far end of the concession stand to switch the lights off. The stand had been plunged into complete blackness and he'd had to feel his way across to them – except they'd already moved on. He cursed himself for being so stupid – why should Nathan wait for him? It was the President Nathan had to be concerned about getting to higher ground, not him or Marilu or the old guy.

He was three-quarters of the way across the stand when he saw a shadow at the window, blotting out the stars for an instant, and he knew the attack was under way. He clattered into the table full of miniature Empire States, cursed, then the first stun grenade exploded. He had trained with stun grenades – well, he'd attended half a class on their use and misuse – so he half-knew what to expect; it was the half he didn't know that flattened him. Winded, he lay where he was for a few moments, then rolled sideways to get against the wall for when the shooting started: but instead hell descended. There was an almighty shattering, a crash, then an explosion. A sheet of flame shot over his head. George scampered for the door. As he flung himself through it, burning pillars seemed to move themselves out of the way for him: it was a few seconds before he heard them scream.

George landed on the cool-tiled floor, breathing hard. The screaming stopped abruptly. All he could hear now was the crackle of fire. He tried to think rationally: the explosion had been loud, but not so devastating that it would take out every single person assigned to free the President; something, somewhere had obviously gone wrong in a very bad way. Whoever was out there was probably just as surprised as he was: they were watching, waiting, regrouping, trying to decide what to do; probably in a blind panic, probably convinced that the President had died in that explosion, nobody wanting to be first to find out, to be irrecoverably associated with it, blamed even. George at least had the advantage of knowing where the President was going.

He rose carefully to his knees, then sprang up and raced for the swing doors. He peered through the glass panel. The stairs were well lit, and empty. He pushed through, tripping immediately over the policeman on the floor.

The policeman turned a tear-streaked face towards George; one hand clamped his leg, the other snaked out to his gun. He raised it, then seemed to recognize George.

'It's okay,' he said, grimacing, 'keep down until the back-up teams arrive. You're safe now, Mr Fuller.' He set the gun down again.

'I know,' said George, 'it's a pity you're not.' He flashed out an Oxford boot which sent the agent's head shooting back against the wall. Concussed, he tried to reach for his gun – one of three he could see – but George was on him; he locked his arms about the policeman's head, then gave a sudden twist to the right. The neck snapped.

George wiped the gun, then dropped it on top of the agent's body. He ripped the night vision goggles from his head, thought of bringing them with him, then threw them to one side. He wouldn't need them. He ran his hands up and down the policeman's body, searching for other, smaller weapons. There was nothing of any use until he came to the bullet-proof jacket. Nathan surely wouldn't object to a reporter wanting to protect himself . . . even if he did, the worst he would do would be to demand it himself. Time was running out. His hands ripped at the body armour . . . when it came away it felt strange, too loose, too bulky, *what's all this cord?* And then he knew, and he knew God was with him. That big white guy in the clouds was cheering him on. A fucking parachute! That was worth taking another twenty seconds over. *And pass it off as a bullet-proof jacket!*

Sam screamed as the B-52 bomber struck the 86th floor. The force of the impact threw him to the ground. He beat at his head as the flames licked about him. 'Dad!' he screamed. 'Dad!'

Men all around him were burning.

He was dying. He would never live his life. He would never grow up. He would never see Mary again . . .

Mary . . . God, God, God . . . in the midst of it all, the mayhem, the death, the dark pierced only by leaping flames, Sam came back.

He remembered the President talking.

Nathan being sick.

Buying him a coffee . . . the money, the fake money, the reporter trying to rip him off . . . what then? Caught in another firestorm on top of the Empire State Building. His bones were so sore. But why? . . . He struggled to his knees, coughing against the thick black smoke . . . he crawled towards the stairs . . . he'd make it down all eighty-five sets of steps if he had to, and he had to. He had a sudden urge to see Mary. Right that instant.

There was no point in chancing the elevators; get stuck in one of those and he'd be boiled to death. The dark was no problem to him. He knew every inch of the 86th. As the smoke began to thin he forced himself up into a crouched run and hurried towards the swing doors. He took a deep breath as he pushed through them into the light. A man stood with his back to him, struggling to fit something around his torso.

'You'd better get moving,' Sam rasped. 'Hit the stairs, now!'

The man turned. Sam stopped. 'You . . .' he raised his hands, wiggled his fingers as if grasping for . . . it came, it came back . . . 'You bastard, you . . .'

He flung himself at Fuller, whose arms had become stuck in the arms of his coat as he tried to wedge in the parachute so that it wouldn't be noticeable.

The old man and the nut cannoned off the wall. George tripped over the outstretched dead leg of the policeman and the pair of them toppled over. George landed on top, knocking what little wind there was out of Sam. George rolled off, finally pulling his arms free as he rose to his feet. As Sam began to struggle to his feet George pulled the gun from his jacket and shot the old man twice in the chest.

Sam continued his upward movement, a look of utter surprise on his face. He forced himself erect, then began to pat his chest with his hands. He looked hopelessly towards Fuller, then something caught his attention and he turned to the stairs.

A figure was slowly rounding the bend. George looked too, swinging his gun round.

A smile, so warm, so, so, warm, sprang onto Sam's face.

Mary was coming towards him, her arms outstretched, her eyes dancing with life.

18

They were prisoners. To have asked the bus to stop would only have drawn attention to themselves. They might as well have stood up and said, *hey, look, it's us, stars of TV and radio, America's most wanted, bar one.*

The Trailways bus was comfortably appointed, which made their experience all the more excruciating: suffering on a soft seat, with the air conditioning just perfect. Having the bus equipped with a sound system which enabled every passenger, curious or not, to enjoy every breath of what was happening at the Empire was just another little extra Lisa and Alex hadn't bargained for when they'd ditched the car at Providence, Rhode Island, and headed north again for Boston. They weren't convinced that their backtracking would fool anyone, but it was *something*. Lisa wore a baseball cap pulled down tight over her ears, masking her auburn hair almost completely, but not quite. She promised Alex she would have it cut and dyed as soon as they reached Boston. Or the place after that. As darkness fell and events unfolded at the Empire it seemed increasingly to Lisa, clamped to Alex's arm, her face buried in his chest, that they weren't en route to Boston at all, but on the road to nowhere. Except they weren't Talking Heads, they were mute with fear.

The bus was three-quarters full. The air was clean and cool and thick with the anxious intensity of forty disparate people glued to a television screen. Events at the Empire seemed so stage-managed. Highs, lows, dramatic pauses, deceptive normalities, eyewitness accounts, then sudden flurries of activity. All that and a mounting sense of national paranoia. It reminded Lisa of the stories she had read of Orson Welles's radio broadcast of *The War of the Worlds*. Across America panic was setting in; but it would be a miracle if a group of actors claimed responsibility for this one.

The worst moment, when her blood froze, when America froze, came as a reporter was dully relating the progress, or lack of progress, in the negotiations with Nathan Jones. He had managed to gain access to the Empire State's management floor and had been, under the instructions of his editor, seeking to reassure the nation of the competence of the team brought together to secure the President's release. He had not been allowed to report that the raid was taking place for fear of Nathan being tipped off, and had done an admirable job of keeping his excitement in check as he watched the Hostage Rescue Team slip out of the windows while continuing with his deadpan commentary. But then the explosion had occurred and his voice slipped away to be replaced by the uproar of dozens of calm and collected experts freaking out. In catering terms, confident American fudge cake had become a frightened, wobbling jelly.

Lisa cried gently against Alex's chest; her eyes clenched tight. Others on the bus were crying as well, but none of them cried for the departed soul of Nathan Jones.

'The world turns on such silly decisions,' Lisa whispered. 'Splitting up like that, causing all this.'

'Shhh,' Alex breathed into her ear, 'stop blaming yourself. It's not your fault. It's not.'

'But if I'd stayed with him . . .'

'Shut it, kiddo. You did the right thing. You know you did. It's easy to look back and say what if, but you made the right decision at the time, and it's still the right decision: you can't take responsibility for what other people do.'

They did not speak for another ninety minutes. The road, largely empty of traffic, flashed by. She watched the lights of the houses, thought of Nathan and how they'd spent all those weeks watching Woody Allen play his clarinet in that pub in Manhattan. And Woody wouldn't even remember meeting him, the funny wee Irish man at the urinals at Michael's Pub.

'Ladies and gentlemen, we're going over to the Empire State Building where Graham Slovenski, White House Chief of Staff, is about to make a statement. Ahm, here he comes now.'

The driver pulled the bus off the road. He switched off the engine and sat with his hands folded beneath his chin in prayer. Nobody complained. Dread flushed through Lisa like a nuclear-powered enema.

His voice was hoarse, drained of emotion. Lisa could hear the crack of a thousand flashguns as he came forward to speak.

'I am going to read a short statement. Please listen carefully, uhm, I won't be taking questions afterwards.' He took a deep breath, sucking in the fears of the entire population. 'Earlier this evening the decision was taken after due discussion at cabinet level and after taking on board all available advice, to end the siege of the Empire State Building by force. This was implemented by an FBI Hostage Rescue Team. As you know the President has long pursued a policy of non-negotiation with terrorists and the decision was taken to abide by this policy. Surveillance of the 86th floor where the President was being held suggested that this operation could be carried out with the minimum of risk to the President.'

He took another deep breath. His voice faltered slightly over the first few words. 'Just over two hours ago the operation began. It was progressing according to schedule when a motorized hang glider, whose late pilot remains unidentified, avoided aerial surveillance and crashed into the 86th floor, causing an explosion which has resulted in the deaths of several members of the HRT team and at least one of the hostages. This naturally threw the operation into some disarray and in the confusion the terrorist, together with the President, was able to relocate to the 102nd floor of the Empire State Building, which is another, smaller, observation floor. We understand at this time that the President has not been injured. I repeat, the President has not been injured. We are now attempting to re-open lines of communication with the 102nd floor. Let us all pray to God for a satisfactory outcome. Thank you very much.'

There came a barrage of questions, flowing out of the radio speakers like massive waves crashing on a beach of glass.

'Oh thank God,' Lisa said aloud.

The other passengers gave a round of applause. Lisa hadn't quite meant it like that.

Slovenski and his bodyguards hurried back into the Empire and took the elevator to the 85th. His face was white, his throat was dry, his head was pounding.

Morton met him at the door. 'Okay,' said Slo, 'now gimme the truth.'

'Seven dead from the HRT unit,' Morton said grimly.

'What about Dillon?'

'He has serious burns, but he'll live. He won't live down what happened, though.'

Slo nodded. As they crossed to Morton's office Slo could see Tara lying across three chairs, fast asleep. Morton opened the door, ushered him in.

'Two hostages dead, too,' said Morton, taking a seat. Slo perched on the edge of the desk. 'The woman, Marilu Henner, the smoke got her. Sam McClintock, the old guy – well, once the explosion occurred some of the HRTs seem to have opened up. McClintock got caught in the crossfire.'

'And now they're on the 102nd floor.'

'Yeah. Nathan Jones, the President and probably the reporter too.'

'*Probably?* Jesus.' Slo shook his head. 'Why did no one think to block that avenue of escape?'

Morton shook his head. 'Now that it has happened, it was pretty obvious. It's easy to be wise after the fact,' he added, weakly.

'We are required to be wise before the fact, Mr Morton,' Slo snapped. 'Why was it not considered relevant? We had the best brains in the business working on this one, why did someone not think of something as elementary as a flight of god-damn fucking steps?'

'It's not that it wasn't thought of, sir, it was thought of and discounted.'

'And why was that?'

'Because we had them exactly where we wanted them. Right slam bang in the middle of the concession stand. It was a simple matter of surrounding, assaulting, liberating. But they threw a spanner in the works.'

Slo nodded slowly. 'The hang glider.'

'No, sir, we don't know yet where the hang glider comes

in the scheme of things. All we know is that the pilot is dead. Jones and the President had moved before the glider hit.'

'You knew they'd moved?'

'No, we know now they'd moved.'

'And why didn't you know then?'

'Well, sir, they switched the lights off.'

'And with all the sophisticated equipment we have, we couldn't follow them in the dark?'

'It just took us by surprise. The operation was in progress. Our guys were in the act of climbing over the wall when the lights went out. They escaped with seconds to spare.'

'You're telling me that the most powerful military machine in the world, the mightiest nation on God's earth, was outfoxed by someone switching some god-damn lights off?'

'Yes, sir.'

'Mr Morton?'

'Sir?'

'You can take the next press conference.'

19

By the time George reached the 101st, he was a little purple about the gills. He blamed this lack of fitness on his failure to train since he was forced onto the road after bombing his own house; the tautness had been lost, the muscle tone had slipped, the finely tuned rhythms of his body had gone awry. Those who knew him best might have queried whether George enjoyed any of these attributes in the first place.

George came to a halt as he reached the bend leading to the 102nd floor. He took many, many deep breaths, waiting until his heart had stopped racing, then cautiously peered round. The steps were clear. He called softly: 'Nathan Jones . . . Mr President?'

The response was swift. He almost didn't recognize Nathan's gravelled voice. 'Anyone comes round the corner, I shoot the President. I mean it.' The voice echoed around the stairwell. 'I have the gun in his mouth right now. Just stay away. Leave us be.'

George stayed pressed to the wall. 'Nathan . . . it's me, Clark Fuller. The reporter.'

There was silence for a few moments. Then: 'What do you want, Clark?'

'I want to come up.'

'Clark, you're free, go and sell your story.'

'The story's not over. It's not worth anything unless I stay to the end.'

'What you mean is it's not worth as much, 'less you stay to the end.'

'That too. Can I come up? You still need your Bosley, don't you?'

'Boswell. Boswell, Clark, for God's sake. Where did you study journalism, Clark?'

'Columbia,' said George, impressing himself.

'Columbia the fucking coke capital or the university?'

'The university.'

'And you don't know your Bosley from your Boswell. Fuck, George, come on up, it's just my luck to get a fucking ignorant reporter to get my fucking waste of a life down on paper. Come on up, George, for the final countdown.'

George pushed himself off the wall and cautiously began to mount the steps. Gradually Nathan and the President came into view. The gun *was* in the President's mouth. George was half-inclined to make a sudden move and see if the little Irish shit was scared into blowing the President's head off.

But no, not yet.

He came to the top of the steps, his hands raised. The 102nd floor, entirely enclosed, was certainly small. *Claustrophobic.* He already knew the views were breathtaking, but without the fresh air they somehow lacked reality. He could just as well have been on a stage with the breathtaking scenery painted onto a backdrop.

'Sure you got no one with you, Clark?'

478

'All by myself. Didn't see anyone alive down there to bring with me.'

Nathan took the gun from the President's mouth and moved to the edge of the stairs. He peered down. He waved George in. Then he put the gun to his back. He felt something soft. 'How is it, Clark, that you suddenly look like the Michelin Man?'

'There's a lot of dead people down there, Nathan. I took the liberty of relieving one of his bullet-proof jacket.'

'That's most enterprising of you.' He turned George round, opened his coat and slipped a hand into the back of it. He pulled forward a roll of thin material. 'Doesn't look like it could stop a bullet,' said Nathan, who couldn't have told a bullet-proof jacket from an electric blanket.

'They make them remarkably thin these days,' said George, 'or so I'm told. I would hope not to find out how effective they are.'

Nathan nodded. 'Tell me, Clark,' he asked, 'did you ever see the end of *Butch Cassidy and the Sundance Kid*?'

Nathan asked for silence, and he got it. An hour's worth of silence so silent it was noisy. The silence, the depth of it, drowned out everything. It sapped thought. It sucked in air and spat it out stale. It settled like tonne-weights on overburdened shoulders, it throbbed through veins and dragged at eyes. Sleep was equidistantly the closest and furthest things from their minds.

Nathan couldn't think straight. He thought circular. Everything kept coming round and round and round, but there was no path shooting away, suggesting what course of action to take. Or rather there was not one, but hundreds of them, and all contradictory.

One thing was clear to him: the reporter had his head

screwed on. He had predicted the attack and advised on the retreat; where he could have run for it and possibly given vital information to whatever security services were lurking out there, he had chosen instead to stick with him, at a not inconsiderable risk to himself. Nathan knew his own limitations: the anger, the occasional bursts of irrationality, the emotion. He was not going to survive this, he knew, but if he was to go out with his head held high, with dignity, he was going to have to pay heed to the reporter's impartial advice.

Nathan looked at Keneally, lying back now on the cold tiled floor, his hands clasped behind his head. He was disappointed in the President. He had expected him to talk more, to use his celebrated skills of diplomacy, to talk Nathan out of it. God knows, if he'd been any good at it he could have had Nathan surrendered and contrite within a couple of hours; but he had chosen not to become involved; his was almost an abstract presence, there to be bullied and threatened.

'What do you think?' Nathan said, prodding the President's outstretched leg with his foot. 'Will they storm up the stairs, guns blazing, like they did below?'

The President raised himself onto an elbow. 'I don't know what they're going to do, but you may know that I subscribe to a policy of not negotiating with terrorists.'

'I'm not a terrorist,' said Nathan.

'You're terrorizing me,' said the President.

'By accident,' said Nathan.

'If this happened by accident, Nathan, give it up now. Before one of us gets killed.'

'Before you get killed, you mean.'

'No, I don't. I don't want any of us to die. I just want us all to walk out of here. To walk out of here, back to our loved ones.'

Nathan shook his head. 'Well that's a big help. The reason I'm here is because I can't walk back to her.'

'Well then, let's find her. Where is she?'

'Lost in America.'

'We can find her, Nathan.'

Nathan turned to George. 'What happened to your computer, Boswell?'

'Lost it in the firestorm. But don't worry,' he said, tapping the side of his head, 'it's all up here.'

'Tell me what you make of it. Do I seem like a terrorist to you?'

'You seem like a patsy.'

'Meaning?'

'You're the fall guy. You've been set up, consciously or unconsciously, by brainwashing, mind control, hypnotism, something, you've been manoeuvred into this position by outside forces.'

'Clark, I'm here because my girlfriend dropped me and I have a bad temper.'

'You think you are. No doubt Lee Harvey thought he was acting alone. Didn't you see *JFK*? Nathan, there are forces at work here which are bigger than all of us, bigger than the President. Do you not think it strange that the President was allowed to carry out an engagement in such a remote location? Do you not think it strange that you were able to get so close to him that you could put a gun to his head? Is it not strange that an attempt to free the President should involve so much firepower that it reduces an entire floor to ashes? Make no mistake, my friend, you have been propelled into this position, no matter what your heart is telling you.'

Nathan turned to the President. 'Is he talking a lot of shite, or what?'

'I would say,' the President intoned quietly, with all the

gravity of a state of the union speech, 'that Mr Fuller subscribes to the theory that there is a conspiracy behind everything in life. It sells papers, I have no doubt that it will sell many books. But it's not right.' His eyes flicked to George. 'Incidentally, who was it, Mr Fuller, that taught you at Columbia? I have several friends in the journalism faculty there.'

'And now,' said George, 'he's going to try and start undermining my credibility as a reporter. Don't listen to him, Nathan. The facts speak for themselves. He just doesn't want to listen. But deep down he knows it's right: there *is* a conspiracy, and that conspiracy is to have the President killed and someone else placed in power; you *are* the patsy.'

Nathan held the bridge of his nose. He had a pain there. He was thirsty, but there was nothing to drink. He closed his eyes. He saw Lisa, in bed, by herself.

'Nathan?' said George.

'What?'

'The old guy, Sam. Before I ran for the stairs, I found his body.'

'Jesus Christ.' Nathan shook his head violently.

'He wasn't near the explosion. I thought maybe the smoke had got him. I tried to give him the kiss of life.'

'Oh God,' said Nathan.

'But it was no use. It wasn't the smoke. He'd been shot. Twice. Nathan, don't you see? They don't want any of us to come out of this alive.'

20

They moved wearily in the grey dawn, dewed FBI agents and police officers removing bodies, hauling tangled metal, sweeping bitter ash. There had been no word from on high for many hours.

On the 102nd floor Nathan, the Irish bisexual terrorist sadist, George Burley, the Southern gent with the penchant for murder, and Michael Keneally, the President of the United States but currently least powerful man in the world, slept. It just came upon them in the early hours when their talk had dulled. Their minds could take no more; they had pulled down the shutters. Their aching limbs had called a time-out. The surviving members of the HRT could just have walked up those stairs and removed Nathan's gun, freed the President and Clark Fuller. Heck, a reasonably well-drilled troop of Scouts could have done it.

But down below, everyone was scared.

There was no respite for them. They moved in a depressed shuffle; their eyes loomed out of cavernous sockets; they ate, but they ate cardboard, they drank, but they drank rusty water. They had messed up, and they had messed up bad.

'This is meant to be happening to *him*,' Cameron said to Morton as they stepped over a mound of ash on their third circuit of the 86th floor, 'getting depressed in the early hours of the morning. Now *he's* supposed to be at his most fallible. But everything's reversed.'

'Cameron, if you're trying to motivate me, you're not doing it very well.'

Morton stopped, peered out over the scorched wall. Down below, traffic was still gridlocked. Those who trusted their fellow New Yorkers simply locked their cars and went home. Those who didn't slept in them or huddled on the sidewalks awaiting developments either at the Empire or in traffic management. The last police estimate Morton had heard was that there were thirty thousand people on the streets in the Empire State area. Over a hundred concession stands had moved in to help feed them. There had been three shootings, one of them fatal, a rape and countless reports of petty theft amongst those maintaining the vigil. Central Park had been transformed into a giant heliport to cope with the influx of news teams from the world's media. T-shirts were already available in a bewildering variety of styles and bearing a range of slogans that ran from *We Love Michael Keneally to Shoot the Bastard.*

'Right now,' said Cameron, 'he holds all the cards. He has the President in a nice enclosed space. He's pissed because we mounted our attack. He's tired. If he wasn't paranoid to start with, he certainly is now.'

'So what do we do?'

'We give it until dawn. Then we call him. We cut a couple of very large slices of humble pie and we choke on them. Then we ask him what he wants.'

'And what about not negotiating with terrorists?'

'Forget it. Give him what he wants. Within reason.'

'What's within reason?'

'I have no idea.'

Morton rolled his eyes, then nodded across to the other side of the burnt-out concession stand to where Graham Slovenski stood by himself, looking out over the city. 'We have problems, but at the end of all this we can go home. There's a man will have to carry the can.'

'That's a pretty damn big can.'

'His choice. I suppose you have to admire him for taking it on. There's a hell of a lot to lose.'

'And a hell of a lot to gain.'

'Tell me all about it. I just got a million-dollar offer for my version of the siege.'

'Jesus. What'd you say?'

'Whaddya think I said? Call my agent.'

On the West Coast, John Smedlin got a call from a lowly secretary at Magiform informing him that his contract with the company had been terminated.

Smedlin didn't have a contract, but he thanked the secretary nevertheless, then called Tate on his mobile number.

'Michael,' he said, 'what's going on?'

'Fuck you, Smedlin, and your progeny,' Tate said.

'Michael . . .'

'Do you mind not bothering me, Smedlin. I'm busy. I have a girlfriend now. I don't need you.'

'No you don't. And yes you do.'

'Are you calling me a liar?'

'I'm calling you a disturbed fantasist, Michael. If she's there, put her on. Come on, Michael, put her on.'

'I didn't say she was here.'

'Uhuh.'

'I don't need you, Smedlin. You're sick. You've been filling my head with sick ideas for too fucking long.'

There was silence. A lengthy silence.

Eventually he said, 'Mr Smedlin?'

'What?'

'I thought you'd gone.'

'No. I'm still here.'

'You hung up on me before. I didn't like that.'

'It wasn't intentional. I had a nosebleed.'

'Are you okay now?'

'No. No I'm not okay. I've been thinking.'

'What about?'

'About what an asshole you are.'

'Pardon me?'

'You heard. You're an asshole. A tiny little asshole.'

'I'm the most powerful—'

'Asshole in the world.'

'What right have you to—'

'And I don't want you to ever phone me again.'

'*You* phoned *me*!'

'See! You'll twist anything. You're paranoid, Michael. You need help.'

'That's why I come to you!'

'No. No you don't. Not any more. I've had enough. I'm retiring. Listen. Listen to this. This is the sound of me retiring. I've had twenty years of creeps like you talking your bullshit, and I've had it up to here. Goodbye, Michael. Good luck. The world's a crazy place, and you're just the man to run it.'

Smedlin put the phone down. Then he checked his wallet. Then he went out to try and score some more coke.

Graham Slovenski heard something crack. It was a few moments before he realized it was the plastic casing on his mobile phone. A thin sliver fell to the ground. He kicked it away. There was a smear of blood on his hand. *Relax.* He switched the phone to the other hand. 'You still there?' he barked.

'Yes, Slo, I'm just thinking. Trying to.' Vice-President Santos had flown direct to Washington. 'God-damn it, I can't stand the thought of the whole world laughing at us again. Jimmy Carter Syndrome. At least that was fucking Iran, thousands of miles from home. This isn't just on our doorstep, it's up the stairs and down the hall and right into our bedroom. This guy Nathan Jones is wearing our slippers. He's sipping our hot chocolate. He's warming his hands on my wife.'

'So what do you suggest?'

'I have every faith in you, Slo. So does the cabinet.'

'I'm offering my resignation.'

'It won't be accepted.'

'The whole operation was a fuck-up. Somebody has to go.'

'The only reason it was a fuck-up was because of that fucking birdman. Otherwise we'd have Keneally free. Nobody has to go.'

'I resign, you come and take over.'

'Not on your life. I'm needed here. You stay where you are . . .'

'And take the flak.'

'Slo, it's a dirty job. But somebody has to do it. That's politics.'

'That's bullshit.'

'Politics is bullshit, Slo, you know that.'

'You think you're going to bullshit your way right into the White House, don't you?'

'Slo, c'mon. You're tired. We're all tired. The country's come to a standstill, we don't get it up and running soon there'll be anarchy in the streets.'

'And at the end of the day, that's my responsibility as well.

Thanks a bunch.' Slo clicked off, then he smashed the phone against the wall. As the remains hit the ground, he kicked them.

'You okay, Slo?'

He turned, rolled his eyes. 'Sorry, Tara. Chief of Staff loses his grip.'

She touched his arm. 'You're only human.'

'Am I?' He thumbed upstairs. *'They're* only human. *They're* at risk. *We're* just playing games.'

She touched both arms. 'Slo, c'mon. I'm the one should be suicidal. It's my husband. My future.'

Slo nodded slowly. As his temper subsided, lust raced up to replace it. She was holding him. *God-damn lust at a time like this.*

'Slo, I've been listening to this Nathan Jones talking.'

'Yeah, depressing, isn't it?'

'You think so? I've never heard a man talk about a woman the way he does. He's *so* in love.'

He looked at her beautiful face. 'Tara. There are two types of love. The love you have for your wife, your husband, nice normal ordinary love.' He shook his head and looked beyond her, out over New York. 'Then you have the kind of love that makes you want to go out and kidnap the President of the United States. Obsessional love. Paranoid love. Schizoid love. Love for which there are no rules. Love for which you would do anything.'

'God.' She was *still* holding him. 'Have you ever felt like that about a woman, Slo?' she asked.

He looked back into her eyes. 'Have you ever felt like that about a man?'

She nodded slowly, her eyes glued to his. He could feel a tremendous warmth washing over him. From the heart. From the soul. God he could . . .

'I love Michael so much.'

And all that warmth shot out the end of his nose and out over Manhattan.

As Cameron returned to the management floor to see if the bug squad had managed to wire up the 102nd yet, Morton crossed to the stairs leading up to the President. Nearly forty police officers stood, sat, lay, guns pointed. Morton shook his head.

Doyle appeared at his elbow. 'Do you want to eat before I tell you about Fred Troy?' he asked, offering a hot-dog.

'Put like that, what can I say?' He took it anyway; his fingers closed about the bun for a little warmth. Then they opened again. 'Thanks,' he said, 'for the cold hot-dog.'

Doyle shrugged. 'I had to get someone to go out to get it. It's madness down there.'

'And it's a sea of tranquillity up here. Okay. Tell me about Fred. The poison.'

'Yeah. The poison that killed him has been identified as the venom from a Nigerian slipper snake.'

Morton nodded slowly. 'Yeah,' he said, 'I thought it might be that.'

'The Nigerian slipper snake is one of the most deadly snakes known to man.'

'You are joking, aren't you?'

'No, sir. It's one of the most dead—'

'A *slipper* snake?'

'Yes, sir. I think it's an anglicization of a Nigerian—'

'What're you saying, Doyle, that there's a fucking snake on the loose up here as well?' He cast doubtful eyes about the management floor. 'Or that Fred was at the zoo yesterday?'

'No, sir. There was no snakebite on his body. The pathologist found a small puncture mark on Fred's cheek, but it was more like a pin-prick than a bite. It looks like someone used a pin, or a dart or something to poison him.'

'What do you mean, *someone*? You mean Nathan Jones.'

'Well, sir, that's the obvious conclusion.'

'Doyle, I see that shifty look on you. Tell me what you're thinking.'

'Well sir, according to the experts . . .'

'There are experts on Nigerian slipper snakes?'

'Yes, sir, there are. Quite a few. And the leader in that field is a Dr Martina Crawford. She's normally based in Nigeria, but for the past six . . . sorry, sir. She told me that the poison takes between twenty and twenty-five minutes to work.'

'So?'

'Well, sir, according to what I've been able to work out, that *would* make it possible for Nathan Jones to have administered the poison. He was close enough to Fred Troy right after the old guy made that run at the President. But the fact is, there's nothing whatsoever in his background to suggest this level of sophistication. He seems to lack a plan. There have been no demands. It strikes me that he could be up there by accident.'

'You almost sound sympathetic, Doyle.'

'No. Of course not. But . . . the snake. I don't know, it doesn't feel like *him*. Extracting snake venom requires a certain amount of skill, administering it that little bit more. It's not the sort of thing you do in a blind panic.'

Morton nodded slowly. 'Y'know Doyle, I think I agree with you. Where does one come by a Nigerian slipper snake anyway?'

'There are strict import restrictions. Those that do get through go either to zoos or specialist stores. Licences are required. There are two stores in New York that specialize. I have agents on their way there now. It'll take a while, sir, with the gridlock.'

Morton turned and looked at the sharpshooters, unblinking, then at the steps leading to the 102nd. 'If you're suggesting there's someone else involved, then he must have been up there from the start. And he's already escaped.'

'Possibly.'

'But nothing yet suggests that there is a conspiracy . . .'

'No, sir. Even the birdman, he was just a Queens nut, far as we can work out he was trying to save the President.'

'So we could be looking at two independent attempts on the President, presuming that someone wouldn't go to all the trouble of extracting venom from a Nigerian slipper snake just to kill Fred Troy.'

Doyle nodded. They looked at each other gloomily for several moments. Morton's throat was dry from the acrid residue of the fire. He closed his eyes, rubbed at them, absentmindedly threw the hot-dog into a bin.

'You any good at math, Doyle?'

Doyle shrugged. 'So-so.'

'Tell me, then, what are the chances of two men coming to a decision to assassinate the President on exactly the same day, at exactly the same place, and at exactly the same time?'

'Slim to none.'

'And what are the chances of those two bastards doing it on my fucking shift?'

Morton gave a great hacking cough-laugh, then smiled grimly at Doyle. 'Get hold of the videotape Magiform's people shot of the President. Have it examined minutely for anything out of the ordinary. Then get everyone who was up here at the time checked out again – including the Secret Service. I want the entire shift changed. If it's one of our own guys involved, I don't want to give him a second chance.'

'You really think it could be?'

'Doyle, a Nigerian slipper snake? Nothing would surprise me.'

21

Cody Rutteger, *New York Newsday*'s assistant metro editor, was in the john enjoying a rare break from his desk when he was paged. He wasn't about to hurry to another editorial meeting. He dried his face and hands, relit his cigar and examined himself in the mirror. He needed a shave. It would only take five minutes, he could manage it, no sweat, before he dragged himself back to the newsroom. Hell, he'd been there for twenty-four hours straight, been through three special editions already, so they couldn't complain, even if it was the story of the century.

Matt Kelleger, his young metro assistant, stuck his head through the door. 'Hey, Cody, call for you. Personal.'

Yeah, sure, personal calls were rarely that, they were merely a way of by-passing a zealous telephonist. *But it might be the call that breaks the story of the century.* Cody cursed, flung the half-smoked stogie into the urinal and hurried back up the corridor. He was a small man, given to unkempt receding hair and one of the few in his profession still fond of the booze.

'Rutteger,' he said, lifting the receiver and slipping in behind his desk.

'Cody? Eric Harleson.'

'Eric, long time, my friend.' Eric? Eric? Eric? He tapped Eric Harleson into his computer. It was up in an instant. Assistant DA in Denver. They'd helped each other out on the Maesterling serial killings way back when Cody was still allowed out of the office. 'How's Colorado treating you?'

'Fine, as ever. No guesses what you're working on.'

'You got it. Hectic ain't the word.'

'What's the latest?'

Damn it if he's phoning me for information. 'Not much happening this morning . . . Jeez what time is it?' Cody cursed under his breath. He'd left his watch in the john.

'Be a little after nine where you are.'

'God it feels like . . . well, you know all about all-night sessions. So, to what do I owe the pleasure?'

'Cody, I've been watching some of the coverage of this and one of the interviews on CNN kinda caught my attention.'

Cody reached into a drawer and removed a notepad and pen. He cupped the receiver between his ear and shoulder and wrote down the ADA's name, the date and the time. 'Uhuh,' he said.

'Yeah, I mean, it's probably nothing, but they ran a piece on a guy named Brian Houston, he . . .'

'Houston, sure, the guy Nathan Jones tried to suck off.'

'Yeah, well, he kinda looked familiar to me . . . no, he didn't, but the name rang a bell, so did the whole scenario. I checked back on our files and I think he's the guy. About six years ago we had a guy of the same name, Brian Houston, come through here, he was due to face about twelve sex charges. Used to get young guys drunk, bring them back to

494

his apartment, wait till they fell asleep, then attempt to have oral sex with them. It was never gay guys, always straights. I remember him because it seemed to me it wasn't the sex act that interested him, but the getting beaten up afterwards. He left town before we could get him into court, but I guess that's him in New York.'

Cody was writing as fast as he could. 'Okay,' he said.

'It just got me thinking about all the hysteria that's building up over this guy Jones. Y'know, if he's not guilty of this, maybe he's not guilty of some of the other stuff. I mean, he's up there holding the President, but maybe he's just not the sick pervert some people are saying he is.'

'You're an Assistant DA, why not just tell the FBI?'

'I already have. But I know the Feebies. It'll get buried in a report somewhere and not surface until there's a Congressional enquiry in about twenty years. I thought tipping you off might mean it gets public a little sooner. You're about the only reporter I ever got on with, Cody. Only one I know ever kept his word.'

'Well, thanks.'

'Of course, the main thing is he's holding the President, but I just felt bound to set the record straight.'

'Okay, Eric, consider it straightened. Every little bit helps us paint the picture. I appreciate the call. I'll buy you a drink next time I'm in Denver.'

'Make that two and you have a deal.'

Cody hung up, then read through his notes again. Did it make any difference what way the sucking went?

He crossed to the water filter and got himself a paper cupful. He drained it in one, then filled another and crossed back to his desk. For the importance of the story, the news-room was deceptively quiet. Many hadn't made it into work because of the gridlock and were either working from home or pounding the streets. *Shit.* Cody remembered the editorial meeting. He hurried back to the john and picked up his watch. When he entered the editor-in-chief's office there were fifteen senior members of staff already gathered about a large table. They were very quiet.

Cody coughed. 'Sorry I'm late, I . . .'

'Shhhhhh!'

Cody followed the direction of the Shhhhh! to editor-in-chief Tony Bradman, and from him to the TV screen set high in the corner behind him. White House Chief of Staff Graham Slovenski was about to address the press. Cody slipped into his seat, then tipped foreign editor Mark Goodyear's elbow. 'What's happening?' he whispered.

'Why don't you listen and find out?' Goodyear hissed.

'Thanks,' said Cody.

He was itching for a cigar now, but it wasn't allowed. He focused on Slovenski. On his paleness, on his sweaty brow and tangled hair, on the undone top shirt button. It became clear in a few moments that Cody hadn't missed anything; everybody was just holding their breath, waiting for the latest instalment.

Slovenski raised his eyes from the papers he held in his hand and looked out over the assembled international press corps, and beyond them to the tens of thousands of ordinary citizens waiting expectantly.

'I have a short statement to make. Once again I regret, ladies and gentlemen, that it is not possible to take questions afterwards. We are at a very delicate moment in our negotiations and the sooner we can get on with those the better. Uhm-hum . . .' He cleared his throat, a stagey clearance designed to alert everyone to the fact that the real business was about to start. 'We have this morning,' he began, his voice adopting the same dull monotone, 'spoken to the

President. He has assured us that he is well, and also of the continued good health of the other surviving hostage, Clark Fuller. He has appealed for calm and for patience until this whole episode is concluded. We have also spoken to Nathan Jones, who is holding the President and Mr Fuller hostage. He has now asked us to fulfil two requests in exchange for the release of the hostages. These are the delivery of ten million dollars in unmarked single dollar notes to the 102nd floor of the Empire State Building, and the opportunity to broadcast live to the nation. The cabinet will meet shortly to discuss the options open to it. Mr Jones has given us a deadline of noon today to respond to his demands. Thank you.'

Slovenski had been swallowed up by his security men and was back inside the Empire before the tidal wave of the reporters' howled questions could envelop him.

'Godshit,' editor-in-chief Bradman shouted, pounding his left fist into his right palm, 'it's time we got into cable in a big way. Can we do another special before twelve, and is there any point?'

There was an immediate explosion of voices from around the table. The consensus was yes, they could do it, and no, there was no point. Nobody was buying papers, they were watching it on TV.

Bradman nodded down the table. 'Cody, this is official. I'm lifting the smoking ban. Now give us the benefit of your opinion.'

Cody smiled. He had one lit in seconds. 'We have a duty to publish. We have a mountain of material. Let's just do it.'

Bradman nodded. 'I tend to agree. What angle on his demands?'

Cody puffed out. They waited. He'd been at *Newsday* since before most of them could write. 'The way I see it, they're going to capitulate. Fuck the ban on negotiations. They'll deliver the cash. Why not? What's he gonna do with it? He sure as hell ain't going anywhere. And what's the harm in letting him broadcast – what can he say? As we know, certain newspapers let themselves down agreeing to print the Unabomber's philosophy a few years back, now it's TV's turn to swallow its morals and improve those viewing figures at the same time.'

There was general agreement about the table. They got down to the nitty gritty of page lay-outs and headings and advertisers jockeying for position. As the meeting broke up Cody threw the end of his cigar to the floor and stepped on it. Bradman remained at his desk, studying a file of notes. He walked up to him. 'Tony, I thought you should know about something.' Bradman looked up, gave a short nod. Cody told him about Brian Houston.

Bradman nodded again. 'So?' he said.

'All the world loves a villain who isn't too much of a villain. They hate OJ, but love Ollie North. They hate Michael Jackson, but love Patty Hearst. What if Nathan Jones turns out not to be so bad? Everyone has him next to the antichrist at the moment. What if we took a different tack?'

Bradman's eyes narrowed speculatively. 'Like what?'

'Like here's a guy come to America full of hope, been used and abused since he arrived, breaks down under the pressure, does something incredibly daring. Nathan Jones represents the breakdown of contemporary American society.'

Bradman shook his head. 'Cody, I pretty much go with the antichrist theory.'

'But what if I could prove it was wrong? Whatever happened to innocent until proven guilty, anyway?'

'Everyone's guilty, Cody, it's just the degree of guilt that concerns us. Besides, the bottom line is, he *has* kidnapped the President. There's no getting round that. You show me how to get round that, I'll change my mind.'

Cody was already fumbling for another cigar as he turned for the door. 'Yeah, well,' he said, his voice heavy with resignation, 'maybe I'm just tired. Maybe I just look for the good in people.'

'In the wrong business for that, Cody. You're mellowing with old age.'

22

As Nathan replaced the phone the President said, 'Now it's official, you're a criminal. You're a terrorist.'

'What the fuck are you talking about?' said Nathan.

'Demanding money. Before you gave me all that bull about losing your girlfriend. I had a certain sympathy for you. Now that's all gone out the window.'

'As you will, if you don't shut your cakehole.'

Despite this, Nathan smiled. He felt better for the sleep, relieved to wake up and not be dead. Shocked to wake up and find the gun at his feet. Surprised to wake up and find the others asleep as well. It was a warm new day, the sun was bright, the view was breathtaking, all he had to worry about was his impending death.

Fuller was still asleep, curled up on the floor in his trench coat and bullet-proof vest. He snored the easy snore of a relaxed man.

Nathan stuck the gun into the waistband of his trousers and went to peer out over the city. 'You don't know what I have in mind, Mr President. Maybe you should wait and find out.'

'I'm getting tired of waiting.'

Nathan looked round at him. It was the first hint of rebelliousness the President had exhibited since the whole affair began. 'My,' said Nathan, 'who got out of the wrong side of the bed this morning?'

'I'm tired and I'm sore and I want to get on with my life.'

'Yeah, pretty much what I'm feeling.'

'Addressing the nation I understand, Nathan, not the money. How do you expect to get away with it? A helicopter? A bus? A Ferrari? Haven't you seen any movies, Nathan? It doesn't work. They'll kill you.'

'No, sir, they'll kill you. Didn't you take on board what Clark was saying? There's a conspiracy to kill you, and I am the unwilling conduit of that conspiracy.'

'That's bullshit, Nathan. I am the President of the United States. I know the people I work with. They haven't the sophistication, the cunning or the intelligence to come up with a conspiracy, they have enough trouble doing their day jobs badly.'

'You know what happened downstairs.'

'That just reinforces what I say. They fucked up. They're panicked. They're scared. The most powerful nation on God's earth is being held to ransom by a punk with a pistol. It's not conspiracy, Nathan, it's hysteria.'

George was in the jungle surrounded by natives. They wore leopard-skin loincloths and lions'-teeth necklaces. They carried spears which they beat against their shields and sang in a tongue he did not recognize. George wore a baggy white nightshirt over snakeskin boxer shorts and pink puppy-dog slippers. He carried a rolled-up copy of *Computer Generations* which he waved threateningly at the natives as they edged closer. 'I haven't got the nipple!' screamed George. 'I haven't got the nipple!'

'He hasn't got the nipple,' said the President.

'Apparently not,' said Nathan.

George blinked into daylight. They were above him, closing in. He rolled instinctively to one side, protecting his face and groin.

'Hey, Clark, relax,' said Nathan. 'You were having a nightmare.'

'Not that you'll notice the difference,' added the President.

Nathan looked at *him* again. There *was* a difference. He would have to be watched more carefully. The earlier reticence had now given way to an edgy belligerence; the President had spent the first day of the siege weighing up his options, analysing the protagonists and now he had come to some conclusion. It wasn't one he would care to share, but Nathan had the feeling it would become increasingly apparent the longer the siege wore on.

The President, for his part, looked more closely at Clark Fuller as he rubbed at his eyes. 'I can't believe I fell asleep,' said George. 'God. What'd I miss?'

'Nathan has asked for ten million dollars and a chance to address the nation.'

George looked at Nathan and smiled. 'Excellent. What was the response?'

'They're thinking about it.'

George looked to the President. 'But what will it be?'

'I would like to think they'll continue with their policy of non-negotiation. But the reality is that they'll talk. I don't know what the hell happened downstairs, but they're not going to try it again. It's not about saving the President any more, it's about saving their own skins. They'll do anything to get me out alive.'

'I stick to the theory that they'll do anything to get you out dead,' said George.

The President shook his head. 'You're a regular Angel of Death, Clark, do you know that?'

'I call it as I see it, Mr President.'

'Tell me something, Clark.'

'Anything.'

'I don't wish to be overly personal, but I notice you share something in common with Michael Jackson. The singer.'

George looked from the President to Nathan and back. 'What are you talking about?' he said.

'That skin disease. The involuntary whitening. You're starting to flake, Clark.'

The President's words struck through him like a spear. He fought to control his initial response: to kill them both, right now. He raised a hand to his face, dabbed carefully at his skin. It felt okay. The old Jew had assured him the make-up was good for a week.

'Just about the eyes, Clark,' said the President.

Nathan looked closer. 'He's right,' he said.

'Clark,' the President said gravely, 'you can tell us the truth.'

'What're you talking about?' George snapped.

The President's eyes bore into him. 'I think you know.'

George flexed his fingers. He was a *ninja*. He could kill Nathan with his bare hands in seconds, then take his time with the President. If he needed to. He sucked on his lower lip. For the moment, he decided, he would use the power of his intellect to handle this delicate situation. It would be just as much fun. If that failed, well, so be it. George shook his head warily at the President. 'I think you should spell it out, Mr President, because we're obviously not on the same wavelength.'

'Clark,' the President said, 'you've gone in for that skin whitening treatment, haven't you? You want to be a white man.'

George pulled himself up off the ground. He stuck a finger out at the President. 'That's bullshit.'

'I see the evidence before me.'

George shook his head. 'For a President, you're not very sensitive or even diplomatic.' He turned his head, sniffed up as if he was fighting back tears; he was, in a way – tears of laughter. He allowed his face to crumple, his voice to shake. 'You were right the first time, apart from the fact that what you said was dripping with sarcasm.' He avoided eye contact. He stared at the ground. 'I can't sing, I can't dance and I don't have much of an interest in children, but Michael Jackson and I do share something, and it's a pigmentation problem. It's triggered by stress. This, you might appreciate, is a stressful situation. So thanks very much for pointing it out and making me feel bad.'

'I don't believe you,' said the President, 'any more than I believe Jackson. You want to be white.'

Suddenly he was up and eye-balling the President. 'I'm not going to stand here and let you run me or my race down!'

The President shook his head. 'Clark, if I don't know which race you belong to, how can I run it down?'

Nathan fingered the handle of the gun. He didn't like this. *He* was the one who was supposed to be temperamental, he was the one who was supposed to be falling to pieces, but now his hostages were bickering it out and ignoring him completely.

He turned abruptly and crossed to the phone, the solitary modern appliance, indeed the only piece of furniture on the 102nd. When he lifted the receiver, there was somebody waiting at the other end.

'Hi,' said Nathan, 'is that room service?'

The President and Clark looked round.

At the other end James Cameron said, 'Nathan. We haven't had time to. . . .'

'I have another demand,' said Nathan.

'Of course,' said Cameron.

'Since you saw fit to blow up the Empire State Deli down below, we're a little short of food and drink up here.'

'I'll have someone bring it right up,' said Cameron.

'I think not. You'll put it in the lift. I don't want another soul so much as peeking round the corner. I don't want it drugged or poisoned, either. Anything I eat, the President eats. I start to feel even slightly sleepy, I shoot the President. Understood?'

'Understood. What can I get you?'

Nathan lowered the receiver. 'What do you want to eat?'

The President shrugged. 'Whatever,' he said.

'Clark?'

'Chicken,' said George, drawing on his new-found cultural heritage, 'and sweetcorn.'

'Chicken and sweetcorn for three,' Nathan said to Cameron.

'It might take some time,' said Cameron. 'It's bedlam out there.'

'I'm sure you'll find a way,' Nathan said. He hung up and turned to his hostages. 'Now,' he said quietly, 'let's restore a little order round here.' He withdrew his gun. 'This is the gun. You are my hostages. Gun. Hostages. Hostages. Gun. Hostages bad – gun shoots them. Hostages good – chicken and sweetcorn and freedom. Now try and relax. Let's not make this any more unpleasant than it has to be.'

George sat down again. 'Okay,' he said. He smiled wearily at the President. 'I never was very good in the mornings.'

The President turned away. He walked across to one of the windows and looked out over the city.

'Be careful,' said Nathan, 'someone might shoot you.'

The President shook his head, but didn't look round. 'Oh I doubt it,' he said quietly.

23

Information wouldn't break the siege, but it would give them an angle on it where no other angles existed. They had simply run out of original things to say to Nathan Jones; they reassured him that everything was well, that there was no problem getting the $10m together; they didn't tell him that the real problem lay with getting it to the Empire State through the gridlock. It would take an army of trustworthy men to ease through the jampacked crowds, and an army of trustworthy men was difficult to find. Setting up the live broadcast was not a problem either; the whole world was clamouring for it.

Morton paced, raged, thumped, sulked. While Cameron tried to build a relationship with a man who was by turns chatty and monosyllabic, Morton demanded information; Slovenski demanded information from Morton, and Tara demanded information from Slovenski. Nobody knew anything, but they all sensed that somebody did, that somebody knew something, but wasn't telling.

The taciturn owner of a Reptiles R Us in Washington DC *did* know something but wasn't prepared to say, that is until threatened with a check of his import licences for the last eight years, and only then did he admit selling a Nigerian slipper snake the previous week, to a guy staying in a Georgetown motel. He didn't think it strange that someone in a hotel should buy a snake. He catered for all types of deviant sexual behaviour. The FBI agent showed him a picture of Nathan Jones – but no, that wasn't the guy. He couldn't furnish a description of the guy – but he could provide pictures from his security video.

A lazy mortuary attendant, he knew something too, but didn't know that he knew it, not for a while, anyway. A black guy getting plugged on the day the President got kidnapped – well, he wasn't top of the agenda. Clark Fuller's body lay stuck in traffic for thirty hours. End of that time he was starting to smell so bad that the morgue crew had to bundle him onto a stretcher and carry him half a mile along the sidewalk until they got back to base. Then they shoved him in a fridge and got back to the television. Nobody had claimed the body, so there was no rush, but eventually they got round to taking his prints. And whaddya know, he has a record. One conviction, eight years previously; Clark Fuller had been covering a political rally and had refused to clear a sidewalk when politely asked to by a patrolman; the cop had then taken his nightstick out and politely beaten Clark up, before charging him with assaulting a police officer.

And then there was Cody Rutteger, out on the streets for the first time in years; at least he *knew* he knew something, he just needed verification. The veteran newsman had a gut feeling, and it wasn't just his diet of cigars and coffee: he'd spent six hours loitering in a doorway across the street from Amie Kellerman's house, and then once she clunked into view, five minutes persuading her to tell him about one of her clients. Her picture and phone number were in that week's issue of *Screw*, so she wasn't hard to trace once the manager of the Chelsea had put him in the right direction. She was wearing stilettos, a leather miniskirt and a blond wig. She was happy to cough up the information for fifty bucks; it was easier than most of the other things she had to cough up in a night's work.

'Sure, I remember the guy. So what?' she yawned. 'I did him.' She laughed. 'By accident. Poor kid. Case of bad timing, got more than he bargained for. Had to go yelling for the cops.' She looked at his photo and tutted. 'So what's he done, robbed a bank?'

Cody thought that was *pretty damn funny*. Then he got back to the office and everyone was laughing even harder at a whisper that'd come in over the wires from the West Coast. A psychotherapist had walked into the *Los Angeles Times* with a sack full of audio tapes.

'It's Michael Tate,' his assistant, Matt Kelleger, said breathlessly. 'They've only listened to the first half-dozen, but so far he's called the President a cunt and bragged about what he's going to do once he comes to power. We're talking *conspiracy* here.'

24

Lisa decided against the demure approach. There was nothing to be gained by lurking in the background looking suspicious. She flounced up to the reception desk and booked their room with a chatty confidence. They registered under the name of Mr and Mrs J. T. MacRandall, with a home address in Glasgow, Scotland. No one could have guessed that as she signed the registration card with a flourish her insides were churning like a big churny thing in a giant dairy.

Alex, in contrast, lingered behind her like a wayward shadow. He was looking a little pale. While the clerk checked his computer for a room, Lisa glanced back at him, gave him a supportive smile. She could see that the significance of what was happening was finally getting through. On the bus, on the radio, it could have been happening to someone else, it was just talk, shooting out into the ether, gone for ever. Getting off the bus at South Station he'd seen Lisa staring out at him from a special edition of the *Boston Globe*, and it had stopped him in his tracks. Lisa, head down, baseball cap pulled tight, had forced him to walk on.

The Boston Park Plaza was extremely expensive, but they had decided on the hide in plain sight routine. Whoever was looking for them, and they assumed everyone was, they'd be looking in dark hiding places, under stones, not in a hotel that boasted of itself as the late President Clinton's favourite. The clerk asked for her credit card. She told him she'd pay cash when they checked out. He looked at her as if she was from another planet. 'I don't use plastic,' she said, 'it's non-recyclable.'

It wasn't that they were broke. There was a stash of cash in her bag. Thousands. All of it taken from sweaty-pawed males in dark sex-stinking cubicles. The clerk shrugged and passed across a key. He would leave it to others to chase up the money when it became due. What with rock stars and writers, you never could tell these days who had money and who was bullshitting.

Upstairs, Alex flopped down on the bed. Lisa went to the mini-bar and got them both drinks. Then she lay down beside him, propping herself up on one elbow, and sipped at her vodka and ice.

Alex turned strained eyes to her. 'Go on,' he said.

'Go on what?'

'Turn the telly on. Let's see what's happening. And if it turns out to be an elaborate *Candid Camera, I'll* kill the fucker.'

Lisa pulled herself up to her knees. 'You're sure you don't mind?'

Alex shook his head. Lisa reached across to the side of the bed for the controls. There were forty-six channels on the set. Forty-four of them were covering the siege at the Empire State. *Scooby Doo*, with presidential update subtitles, and *Mork and Mindy* were the alternatives. On screen one hundred men in fawn uniforms, each carrying bags containing $100,000 in used dollar bills, were being shepherded through the throng outside the Empire by three hundred National Guardsmen in khaki.

Lisa tutted. 'It's not like him. He was never into money.'

'People change. It's like old girlfriends. They drop you, then next time you see them they're with somebody they always told you they hated. D'ya know what I mean?'

'Sort of.'

'Your Nathan, never fussed about money, asks for ten million dollars. The quiet, shy, retiring type, now he's the most famous person in the world.'

'Infamous. But point taken.'

Abruptly Alex turned on the bed and pulled himself up to his knees. He finished his whiskey and Coke in one, then reached over and pulled up his travelling bag. 'Okay girl, it's time.'

'It's . . .?'

He held up a pair of scissors, then placed them on the bed. He fished further, then produced a bottle of dye.

Which was a mistake.

They weren't in the eye of *the* hurricane, but they were in the eye of *a* hurricane. Because they were intent on their own survival, they were not fully aware of the extent to which the fever was gripping the nation. They expected that some portion of the combined strength of the internal and external security services of the United States would be turned to tracking them down; some of the more enthusiastic sections of the press would be after them as well. What they had not counted on was the interest from other sources: from every unlicensed sleuth, every drink-sodden barfly that'd ever imagined himself to be Columbo or every truck driver who'd ever pictured himself as Petrocelli. Or every chambermaid who'd ever imagined herself on *Murder She Wrote*.

Maria Gonzales Conquistador Benitez, forty-two, a loyal and trusted hotel employee of thirteen years' standing and twice that sitting down, knew instinctively that something was not right about the couple in Suite 406. It wasn't just the trashiness of their clothing or their studied brashness; she was used to that. It wasn't even the furtiveness she detected hiding beneath the brashness; she'd seen that a hundred times in cheating couples. It was their *aura*.

Maria Gonzales Conquistador Benitez was big on auras. Her mother, God rest her soul, had been big on auras, too, and had taught her how to read them. She knew when a person was up to no good. She knew when she saw this Mrs J. T. MacRandall that she was not only dishonest, but scared. It was in the eyes, in the way she turned sideways and half hid her face with a fake shield of a fake yawn when Maria Gonzales Conquistador Benitez came to turn back the bed. And the way her husband hurriedly switched off the TV when she entered the room. And the way he bustled to give her a tip before she'd even reached the bed. Someone that anxious to impress a chambermaid had something more than infidelity to hide.

Downstairs, on her break, Maria Gonzales Conquistador Benitez studied the latest edition of the *Boston Globe*. It was pretty much the same as the edition she'd bought two hours before, save for the addition of two photographs. One of the kidnapper Nathan Jones; one of his estranged girlfriend Lisa Mateer. She blocked off the hair and studied the girl's face. Could it be? The basic bone structure was the same, but the overall shape was different; smaller, more defined in print. There was no way of telling how old the photograph was.

Later, when she had checked downstairs that the MacRandalls had gone out for the evening, she let herself into Suite 406. She knew within seconds that she was right to be suspicious. Neither husband nor wife had bothered to unpack. Even the most uncouth lady guests hung up their dresses so that they didn't crease, but their cases stood locked by the door.

They had drunk from the mini-bar, but the glasses were washed and dried. How many people did that for themselves? None. She hit paydirt in the bathroom. In the pedal bin she discovered copious amounts of shorn hair and an empty bottle of hair dye. She held up a bunch of the hair, then let it go, watched with a big smile on her face as it fell back into the bin.

She looked at her reflection in the mirror.

'Aha!' she said.

They had dinner, after a fashion, sitting on a bench on Boston Common. Sandwiches: two pieces of balsa wood with chalk in the middle. And a little birdshit mayonnaise.

'I'm not paranoid,' said Lisa. 'Everyone's looking at me.'

'Of course they are. You're a beautiful woman.'

'I can run, but I can't hide.'

'Many hands make light work.'

'This is stupid. I'm putting off the inevitable. I should give myself up.'

She threw her sandwich into the garbage utility beside behind the bench. 'But I haven't fucking done anything.'

Alex shrugged. 'So do it. Enter the limelight. The end of one life, the start of another. You might enjoy it.'

'I like this life. I like you.'

'I like you too. Given time, like a few weeks, I might even love you.'

Lisa gave him a sad little smile. 'I don't think we have weeks.'

'Then let's enjoy what we can.'

'What would you suggest?'

'A good healthy screw.'

'Okay.'

Alex was turning the keycard over in his fingers with nervous anticipation when the elevator doors opened. Lisa had her right hand on his right buttock, inside his trousers. They stepped out of the elevator, turned right, stopped. Their suite was at the end of the corridor. Outside it stood a hotel maid and a police officer. The maid was gesticulating with some considerable animation. The policeman was nodding his head. Then he lifted his radio and began to speak into it.

Lisa and Alex stepped back into the elevator.

'Looks like the screw will have to wait,' Alex said.

'Uhuh,' said Lisa.

Alex thought the chances of his making love to her ever again were about level with those of the President emerging from the Empire State Building unscathed.

25

Nathan was still picking sweetcorn from his teeth when Clark Fuller sidled up to him. The President, standing staring out over the city on the far side of the observation floor, had now spent several hours lost in his own thoughts. Monosyllabic seemed too large a word for the breadth of his conversation.

'He's a worried man,' George said.

Nathan nodded. 'So he should be.'

'I don't mean about this, I mean about the conspiracy. He's the sort of guy will deny something, then go away and think about it for a while, and then come back with a completely different viewpoint. Like Bush and his taxes.'

Nathan shook his head slowly. 'Clark, I don't wish to be offensive, but you really are talking shite. I don't mind you thinking it, but talking it is really starting to annoy me.'

And you're really starting to annoy me. George looked at his watch. It was getting on for 7 PM. He had not expected it to continue this long. He had expected either to be dead or starting out on a new life before this; but here he was thirty-six hours into a siege and the only real progress had been in the deterioration of his make-up. He was going to have to step up the subtle yet precise psychological warfare he had been waging since the beginning of the siege. George had attended a couple of classes in subtle yet precise psychological warfare.

'Sorry,' George said. 'I'm not trying to annoy you.'

'Forget it,' Nathan said. 'I'm a little edgy. God knows why.'

George smiled. 'Well, maybe it'll all be over soon. If it's any help, I think you're handling this very well. When I write my book I'll say you were calm and authoritative throughout. People may try to paint you as a lunatic, but I will say otherwise.'

Nathan nodded. 'Very decent of you.'

'Addressing the nation, a master stroke.'

'You think so?'

'I couldn't have thought of better myself. If I had any reason to think along those lines.'

'Well, y'know.'

'Do you know what you're going to say?'

Nathan shrugged. 'I've a vague idea. What do you think I should say?'

'Oh, now it wouldn't be my place to suggest anything. It's not my platform; I'm sure if I wanted to strike my message home to the hearts of the American people, maybe change the way an entire nation thinks of itself, I'm sure I'd do it very differently. I couldn't burden you with my ill-thought-out ideas.'

Nathan handed George a can of Diet Coke. 'Here,' he said, 'eat, drink and be merry, for tomorrow we may die.'

George smiled. 'I hope not.'

Nathan shrugged. 'I'd be interested to hear what you think I should say.'

'I'm sure you wouldn't.'

'I would, really.'

'I doubt it.'

'No, I really would.'

'Oh, I don't think so.'

'Oh for fuck's sake, Clark! Tell me what you think. It's what you came over for!'

'I did not!'

Nathan took a deep breath. 'Okay, okay, leave it.' He looked at the President, who looked back and then away. He studied George for a few moments. 'Make up,' he said quietly.

George froze. His response was a panicked, 'It's not.'

'What?' said Nathan.

'It's not, no way. It's an hereditary disease.'

'What?' Nathan asked, perplexed. 'Being argumentative with people?'

'What?'

'What are you talking about, Clark? I said go and make up with the President. I'm sure he didn't mean to embarrass you over your skin condition.'

'Oh,' said George, then shook his head. 'I'd rather let sleeping dogs lie.'

'You mean you want to paint a negative picture of the President in your book.'

George smiled. 'You must have a very poor opinion of reporters.'

'I have a very poor opinion of everyone.'

George nodded. 'I'm sure you must have.'

'You'll be sure to write that I never meant to harm anyone. That I wasn't a terrorist or a bisexual or a sado-masochist. That I just found myself in a situation and I tried to make the best of it. You'll write that, won't you?'

'If you want.'

'Not if I want. If you want. Tell it as you see it.'

'Okay.'

518

'How do you see it, Clark? How do you see me?'

'Honestly?'

'Honestly.'

'I think you're an American hero. You're only an ordinary little man, but you saw what was wrong with this country and you determined to put it right. The little man has no say in government any more; no say in law; no freedom and too much freedom, both at the same time. He has no recourse, nobody listens, nobody cares. You took up the challenge, I think you've done the bravest thing in history, and now you have the opportunity to tell it like it is. You can change America for ever. More people will listen to you than ever listened to the President. This is JFK's funeral, landing on the moon and OJ driving through LA all rolled into one.'

Nathan shook his head. 'And this from someone who hasn't thought about it. C'mon, Clark, what would you say, if you had the opportunity to address the nation?'

'You're determined to find out.'

'I respect you, Clark. You obviously care about America.'

'I do. Very deeply.'

'Is that rare in a black man? I'm Irish, I've hardly ever even spoken to a black man, but I grew up with the impression that they all hated white people.'

George was laughing his head off, but inside, way down in his soul. He lifted the straw from his pocket and tapped it against his teeth. 'I think they do. Y'see, you have your middle-class, successful blacks, who hate the whites because no matter how talented they are they're never going to be *as* successful. Then you have your black underclass, who are the dregs of society. Ill-educated, unemployed, drug-ridden, murderers, draining the nation of its resources with every moment of their scabrous existence. They surely hate the whites. The whites gave them freedom after the Civil War, and they choked on it then, and they're choking on it now. They haven't the temperament or the inclination to better themselves. They'd be better off shipped back to Africa and forced to fend for themselves.'

'So you're a bit of a liberal,' said Nathan. 'That's strong talk from a white, let alone a black.'

'I'm a realist. That is how it is.'

'And you've got to be cruel to be kind.'

'Yup.'

'And you think I should tell the nation this?'

'It would be a start.'

'You don't think there'd be some sort of uprising if I did?'

'Maybe it would be better if there was. Something has to change. This nation is going down the tubes. You can't walk the streets any more for the drugs and the violence. You can't chat to a girl without being worried about catching Aids, you can't even be sure that she's a girl at all.'

'And you can't go to your job without being kidnapped and being forced to suck a gun at the top of the Empire State Building for a couple of days.'

'You're different.'

'You think so? Or am I only different because I'm the one making you suck the gun?'

'You are different. You see what's going on. You had the guts to do what every American thinks of doing, but is too scared to do.'

Behind them the phone rang. Nathan set his can down and crossed to it.

'Cameron,' said Nathan, 'how are you?'

'I'm fine. I just called to say that the money has now safely arrived in the building. Do you want us to bring it right up the stairs to you? There's about a hundred bags.'

'Oh I think not. You just put it in the lift and send it up. *Sans* guards. We'll haul it out this end.'

'Nathan, the elevator'll only take a few bags at a time. It could take hours.'

'So?'

'Well, I just thought . . .'

'Hey, look on the bright side, it'll give you more time to plan another raid like the one below.'

'I've already apologized for that, Nathan.'

'But apology not accepted. You tried to kill me.'

'Nathan, we—'

'What about the broadcast?'

'It takes a little time. We'll need to send some equipment up. Microphones, satellite dish, mixing desk, a couple of sound men, a producer.'

'No people, thank you. You'll send up one microphone in the lift, with no wires attached, or strings for that matter.'

'No, we need . . .'

'A radio mike. Madonna sings into one at her gigs. I've seen her back home. It allows her to dance. I'm not intending to dance, but I'd like a radio mike.'

'Okay.'

'And remember. I have people out there. Monitoring. If you think you can fool me into broadcasting to two men and a wee lad, you're sadly mistaken.'

'We wouldn't do that.'

'I'll say.'

Nathan put the phone down. He looked at George. 'Y'know,' he said, 'I've never performed in public before. I was in a nativity play at school, once. I played a shepherd. The teacher asked me to stop singing because I was putting everyone else off.'

'It will be nerve-racking,' said George.

'I didn't think I was singing badly,' said Nathan.

26

As the first bags of money were loaded into the elevator for the 102nd floor of the Empire State Building, James Morton felt sick to the stomach.

It was a nausea born of hunger, fear, panic, dehydration and the weight of billions of expectant people's hopes lying heavy on his muscular but not *that* muscular shoulders. The money itself didn't worry him. Nathan Jones wasn't going anywhere with it. It was the sheer frustration, born of helplessness, fermented by an accidental cataclysm and nurtured by the gnawing truth that he was no longer in control of the situation. If ever he had been. The future, or lack of it, frightened him. It wasn't that he was worried about suffering from post-traumatic stress disorder. The Agency had a fine and effective PTSD employee assistance programme. It was getting on to it. There would be hundreds clamouring for it, he knew, and 48 hours before all of them would rather have gone mad than see an EAP officer. It was too much.

Long ago, in another life, Morton had been an accountancy graduate. Then he was headhunted by the FBI. Being bored to death now sounded quite lovely to him.

He thought of Troy, and what he would have done: probably he wouldn't have taken the bullshit. He would have said it's not my responsibility and passed it on to some higher office; to the Director of the FBI, to the NYPD, the military. He would have said, *you out-rank me, earn your money*. But he wasn't Troy, he didn't have the guts. He had accepted the burden while the others had run for cover. Slovenski was in the same boat; there were others more powerful than him, but he had stayed to see it through.

Doyle touched his arm. 'What I could do with that lot,' he said, nodding at the money.

Morton nodded vaguely. 'Right now, I'd prefer a bath and a massage.'

Doyle grinned. 'I'm sure our adoring public would appreciate *that*. Maybe this will help.' He handed Morton an envelope.

Morton pulled out a black-and-white photograph. It was blurred, grainy. It showed a white man, tall with curly hair, standing at a shop counter. There were some glass tanks on either side of him and behind, with the top of someone else's head in the foreground.

'The snake shop,' said Morton.

'Reptile shop in Georgetown, Washington. A few days ago. As far as we can judge the only Nigerian slipper snake sold in this country in the past month was sold to this man.'

'It's not Nathan Jones.'

'No.'

'And who's to say the man we're after didn't always have a slipper snake anyway?'

'Nothing, until you hear this: the FBI have matched the pic. His name's George Burley. From Birmingham, Alabama.'

'Alabama. Fuck.'

Doyle nodded. 'Ex-Klan. Ex-everything. Possibly a little too right-wing for the Klan.'

'George Burley.' Morton rubbed at his eyes. 'George Burley. Where do I know that name from?'

'*Oprah*.'

'*Oprah?*'

'*Oprah*. Remember the President got the crank call? Fred blew a fuse.'

'Ah. Right. Sure. Didn't the FBI . . .?'

'Yeah. They had him, then they lost him. He killed one of their agents, escaped from hospital. Called Oprah, been outta sight since. Until this.' He tapped the back of the photo. 'He was on a mission to kill the President when the FBI stopped him. We can only presume that he still is.'

They stepped into the elevator to return to the management floor. 'So what's the connection between him and Nathan Jones?' Morton asked.

'None, so far as anyone can establish.'

'Not even a thread?'

Doyle shook his head. 'We've scanned the PR tape of the President's address. There's no George Burley there. Everyone who attended the event has been accounted for.'

'So it's our worst fear. A conspiracy. Sam McClintock, Nathan Jones and this George Burley. Two accounted for and he's still on the loose.'

'That's how it looks. And then there's Michael Tate to consider. Virulently anti-Keneally, it emerges, it's his building, his employees. He's been threatening all sorts of things. Genocide. Wants to pull the plug on America's computers. At least there's a firm connection between him and Jones. A conspiracy. At last.'

'It just gets deeper and deeper. Okay. Have him picked up as well. Release the photo.'

'It's already out there.'

The elevator came to a halt as Morton snapped, 'What the hell do you mean? I didn't give—'

'The snake shop guy. Someone let slip Burley was connected to the President. He had a copy of the security video. He sold it to Barbara Walters for a hundred thousand dollars.'

Morton threw his head back. He faked a yell, then gave a big sigh. 'Maybe we should get Barbara fucking Walters in here to negotiate with Nathan Jones.'

'She already asked. I didn't want to bother you with it.'

'Good God. Have these people no—'

'No,' said Doyle. 'They haven't.'

They strode into the management offices together. Morton glared about him. He'd given orders that the numbers allowed access to the floor be strictly controlled; but it looked to him that its population had doubled. His orders were being ignored, or he was being overruled, or they were beginning to reproduce themselves.

As he hurried through the chaos to the presumed sanctity of his private office, he caught someone waving at him. He stopped, nodded over.

'Who's that?' he said quietly.

'Mervyn Paul. He's been analysing the video.'

Morton nodded and led Doyle across the floor. Paul sat hunched before a desk groaning with double video recorders hooked up to a PC monitor and a sound desk.

'Mervyn,' said Morton, 'what's the story?'

'Thought you might want to see this.'

He pointed at the screen. The picture was paused on the President addressing the audience on the 86th floor. Behind the President stood Fred Troy. His eyes were alert, enquiring, frozen; frozen as he was now, down in the morgue, all cut up by probing scalpels; hollow; a husk. Morton wondered suddenly if anyone had been detailed to inform Fred's wife, Fred's *widow*, that he was dead. Often he didn't come home for weeks on end because of his commitments with the President. He knew Martha was quite happy leading an independent life; she was a reader, a thinker, a solitary woman; he'd been there for dinner; there had been no television in their house. What if she didn't know? What if Fred was due home right about now after a 48-hour shift and even as they stood looking at his frozen features she was preparing a meal for him? In all of the chaos since the siege had begun, who would have thought to tell her anything? She was peeling potatoes while a pathologist peeled back the top of Fred's skull in order to dissect his brain. She was grating carrots while . . .

'Mr Morton, sir?'

Morton shook himself. 'What?'

'You want me to roll it?'

'Yes. Of course.'

'I've slowed the tape right down.' He hit the pause button, then used a pencil to tap the screen. The President's voice was slow, mournful, ghostly. Then there was another voice, lower in volume, but harsher, guttural. 'That's the old guy, Sam McClintock, about to make his attempt on the President. The President looks up and . . . there!' He jabbed the pause button again. 'Look at Mr Troy react; his head jolts to the left, opposite to where McClintock is . . . just a couple of frames on . . . Troy's hand comes up, touches his neck. He's been hit by something. That's where he was poisoned.'

Morton nodded solemnly. 'Any way of telling where Nathan Jones was at that precise moment?'

Paul sucked on a lip. 'Sure . . . as McClintock advanced on the President the PR video camera panned round to him . . .

here he is . . . there's our guys cutting him down . . . and there . . . just let me freeze it again . . . there . . . in the doorway of the concession stand, that's Nathan Jones.'

Morton studied Jones's face as best he could. He was looking towards McClintock; there were the beginnings of an angry scowl on his face. 'He doesn't look like someone who's just tried to kill the President with a poisoned dart.'

Paul shook his head. 'The dart missed the President, but it still came pretty close. Some sort of mechanism would have been required to shoot the dart, and something small at that. I dare say someone would have noticed a six-foot blowpipe. So whoever fired it would have had to be very close to the President. I'd say Jones is way out of range.'

Morton looked to Doyle. 'What do you think?'

Doyle nodded. 'I agree. It wasn't Jones.'

Morton nodded. 'Fair enough. Thanks, Paul, good work. Let's see if you can find who did shoot that dart then.'

'Yes, sir.' He grinned broadly and turned back to his equipment.

Morton hurried back to his office.

'It brings us back to Burley, doesn't it?' Doyle said, following behind.

'Looks like it.'

'But how did he get in? And how did he get out?'

'How did who get in?' said Tara Holmes-Boyce, First Lady. 'How did who get out?'

She sat behind Morton's desk reading a copy of the *National Enquirer*.

Morton stopped in the doorway. 'No one,' he said bluntly.

'No one got in, or no one got out?'

'Both.' Morton shook his head. 'Neither. I'm sorry, we need some privacy to go over some things, do you mind?'

Tara pushed her seat back and stood. 'I require you to

keep me up to date on what is going on. That is my husband up there. He is the President of the United States.'

'I know that, ma'am.'

'I've been reading that aliens quite regularly kidnap American citizens and perform scientific experiments on them before returning them to earth. Do you think aliens could be responsible for the kidnap of my husband?'

'Nothing would surprise me, Tara.'

Tara nodded her head slowly, then moved from behind the desk. She strode imperiously across the room. Morton stepped back out of the office to let her pass.

She stopped, and the look she gave him could have defoliated evergreens. 'Never address me as Tara again, do you understand?'

27

George's arms were sore from hard work; but his throat was dry from something else: *greedy gulch throat* it was called in the Old West.

Between him and the President they'd already made twenty-five staggers from the elevator to the top of the stairs where Nathan, gun hanging loosely from his left hand, directed the building of a wall. They were the most expensive defensive sandbags in the history of the world.

George had laughed – inwardly, of course – when Nathan had swallowed his bait and gone for the money. So crass. So predictable. So sad. As the bags had slowly begun to arrive George hadn't felt in the least affected by it; they were just brown sacks, they could just as well have been filled with old newspapers or dead kittens. But then the President had stumbled and one had fallen and the money had spilt out of it and suddenly the money wasn't some remote idea, something intangible; it was lying there on the ground in front of him. He bent and picked up a bundle; he smelt it; his eyes closed. He wondered if he would be stretching things too far to hope to succeed in killing the

President, then Nathan Jones, and finally make a clean getaway with a couple of million dollars.

'Smell good, eh, Clark?' Nathan asked.

George opened his eyes. 'Be a fool to deny it.'

'A taste of things to come, what with your book and everything.'

George shrugged and threw the money back into the sack. 'At least that will be honest money,' he said.

'My,' said Nathan, 'what moral fibre.'

George stifled a scowl and went to lift the next bag.

'In all the movies about sieges,' said the President, running an arm across his sweaty brow, 'they never show anyone taking a leak.'

'You need to pee?' Nathan asked. 'You peed downstairs. I had to watch.'

'Nathan, that was yesterday.'

'So?' Nathan waved his gun. 'Pee in the corner.'

'I can't pee in the corner; we have to live here.'

'So stand on the money bags and pee down the steps.'

'I can't do that. It's indoors. I'm the President of the United States.'

'What would you suggest? I give you permission to take the lift down below, as long as you give your word of honour to return?'

The President shrugged. 'I have to pee.'

George pulled another bag onto the wall, then collapsed onto it, breathing hard. It wasn't weakness, of course; it was fatigue caused by sleep deprivation and dehydration. 'I gotta pee too,' he wheezed.

Nathan looked from one to the other. 'Okay,' he said, 'simple enough.' He lifted his gun and pointed it at the windows opposite the stairs.

'Don't!'

Nathan stopped, glared. The President suddenly looked a little flushed.

'What?'

'Please, don't shoot the windows out.'

'Why on earth not?'

'Because it will cause panic down below. You never know what sort of reaction there'll be.'

'Save your bullets,' said George, 'you might need them. By my estimate you only have five left.'

'Yeah. Four for you,' Nathan snapped, 'one for his nibs.' He crossed to the window and peered out. If he'd known how to quantify it, he would have appreciated the eighty-mile view; if he'd been aware of the geography of that panorama, he'd have recognized New Jersey, then Pennsylvania, Connecticut and Massachusetts. But he didn't. He saw a vast landscape that he had never dared to explore, and now never would. He gave a little shake of his head. Then he smashed the closest window with the butt of his gun.

'There you go,' he said to the President, 'piss-hole.'

The President didn't move.

Nathan smiled. He nodded at George. 'What about you, Clark? You need to pee or are you going to bottle your water and sell it off come the liberation?'

'I don't think I could hold on that long,' said George.

Nathan smashed another window. He waved the gun back at them. 'C'mon then, don't be shy.' He smashed a third window. 'May as well join in. Boys that pee together, stay together.'

George heaved himself up off the bags and approached his window first. He unzipped. The President watched for a moment, then quickly followed. Then Nathan, holding the pistol in one hand, pulled his zipper down and carefully pointed his penis through the hole in the glass.

In a few moments the three of them were pissing over New York.

'This would make some photo for your book, Clark,' said the President. It was the first time he'd spoken directly to George in quite a while.

'Wouldn't it just,' said George.

'They see this much steam from down below,' said the President, 'there'll be just as big a panic.'

Suddenly, Nathan was laughing. His forehead pressed against the higher pane of glass, his body shook as he sprayed out into the air.

'What's so funny?' said George, smiling.

'Nothing,' Nathan managed to squeeze out through the whoops of laughter. How could he tell them that this was the first time he had ever been able to pee in front of other men? *What a time to become proficient.*

The President began to laugh as well. 'This is ridiculous,' he groaned.

Even murderous George. He let out a great sigh as the relief enveloped him, then dissolved into giggles. 'I've been dying for this for thirty-six hours,' he said.

'God,' said the President, 'I thought I was going to explode.'

'Never mind you,' said Nathan breathlessly. 'I can feel the pee draining out of my brain.'

George's shoulders began to shake up and down. 'Which would make you a pee-brain,' he said.

'God-dammit,' cackled the President, 'the reporter made a joke.' And his own shoulders began to go.

'Jesus Christ!' yelled Nathan.

The President froze; Nathan whirled, his gun pointed, his penis dribbling, as the elevator doors opened. George pissed away quite happily.

But it was no assault. It wasn't even more money. It was

a set of earphones and a radio mike. It was time for Nathan Jones to address the world.

Cameron asked twice if Nathan had a copy of his speech, or wanted a stenographer to take it down for him. Twice Nathan told him to get lost. He asked for thirty minutes to compose himself Cameron told him it would be at least that long before the broadcasters were on line.

'How many stations am I on?' Nathan asked.

'It would be easier to list the ones you're not on, Nathan. The whole world is listening. To give you a small example; there's a simultaneous translation going out in Nigeria.'

'Really?'

'You know Nigeria?'

'Know of it.'

'The home of the Nigerian slipper snake.'

'Figures,' said Nathan.

'You know the Nigerian slipper snake?'

'Should I?'

'You tell me.'

'Cameron. Is it you or me that's getting things out of perspective here? Why are we talking about fucking snakes?'

'No reason. Small talk. Being friendly.'

'There's no need for us to be friendly. There's only a need for you to be efficient.'

Nathan slipped off the earphones and began to pace around the observation floor.

In Boston, in a crowded bar, with FBI agents stopping cars outside and searching neighbouring buildings, Lisa and Alex ordered drinks and wheedled their way through the throng until they sat in front of a large television screen.

In Birmingham, Alabama, Grace Burley dozed before her

television, a bottle of gin spilt on the floor and a giant pack of marshmallows upturned in her lap.

In Brooklyn, Leonard Maltman, suspended on full pay, opened a beer and cursed Nathan Jones for the hundredth time that day.

In the McDade Funeral Home, owned by the same company as the Cedar Nursing Home and only a block away, but mercifully out of sight of each other, the bodies of Sam McClintock and his wife Mary lay side by side. Amongst the wreaths was one from the estate of Frank Sinatra.

At *New York Newsday* Cody Rutteger lit a cigar and blew smoke into the back of foreign editor Mark Goodyear's head. On screen was the Empire; there was some very solemn commentary rolling out of the speakers; then the coverage flipped to an expensive mid-town hotel where a heavily armed FBI SWAT team was dragging Michael Tate into custody.

In their apartment, Brian and Lucy Houston lay in bed together. Their things were packed in the hall. They would leave to seek out a new city where Brian wasn't known as soon as the fate of the President was decided.

On the management floor Tara leaned back against Chief of Staff Graham Slovenski. They were watching TV as well. She had a throbbing headache. Slo had a throbbing hard-on.

On the 86th the FBI marksmen continued their vigil. James Morton paced, spat, paced, spat. Doyle followed a step behind, trying to second-guess where his boss would spit next.

On the 102nd Nathan began to smash more windows.

There came a remote sound from his earphones. He pulled them back on again. 'What?' he said.

'What's going on? We can hear . . .'

'We just need some air,' Nathan snapped. 'We just need some fucking air.'

'Okay! Okay!' said Cameron. 'Just take it easy. We're just about ready to go down here. Are you all right?'

'I'm all right.'

'Have you any idea at all how long you're going to talk?'

'No,' said Nathan.

'Okay, that's all right. That's cool. Could I ask you one thing?'

'Shoot.'

Cameron swallowed. 'There may be children listening. Could we keep it clean?'

'I'm not a fucking comedian,' Nathan snapped.

Yes you fucking are, thought George.

28

The world held its breath. Nathan took his. And then he launched into 'I'd Like to Teach the World to Sing'. His voice was clear and strong, at least in his own head. The first verse was an uncomfortable surprise. The second a tuneless embarrassment. The third had half the world's population reaching for their volume controls. When he finally stopped, Nathan smiled at the President, then Clark. Sweat cascaded down his brow. His head looked like it had picked up a puncture. 'I always wanted to do that,' he said.

He wiped an arm across his forehead. He gave a panicked little laugh. 'Ahm, is a record contract out of the question?' He giggled. Stopped himself. Coughed. 'What do you think, I release the President in exchange for a record contract? Sorry. I'm only joking. I know this is no time for jokes, but there you go, my timing never was great. So. Here goes. I know there are a lot of you listening out there. Ahm, if you're parents and your children are listening, hey, don't worry, I'm not going to say anything that's going to offend them. Okay. Right. I've given this a lot of thought. Not *that* much thought, but, y'know, a fair bit. First off, I have to nail a few things on the head. I've been listening to some of the coverage of this . . . situation, and some of the things that have been said haven't been nice. Number one, I am not a bisexual. I've nothing against bisexuals, I just want it made clear that I'm not one. Call me old-fashioned. Number two, I have never voluntarily been involved in bondage or any of that weird sex stuff . . . sorry, kids! . . . I'm just an ordinary guy in an extraordinary situation. Three, I've never hit a woman before, no way, not me. Four, I never meant to harm the President, the fact that he's here just . . . well it just happened. But he's fine, he's hale and hearty . . .' Nathan walked quickly across to the President. He threw an arm round his shoulders. '. . . in fact he's right here beside me . . . say hello, Mr President.'

The President bent into Nathan's radio mike. 'Uh . . . hello,' he said.

'Mr President, could you tell our listeners how you've been treated since the siege began?'

'I've been well treated. I'm in good health and good spirits.'

'Have you any message for the people out there?'

'Just not to worry, to stay calm, everything will turn out okay.'

'What about your wife?'

'I miss her. I love her. This will be harder for her than me.'

'Do you want to say anything about me?'

The President paused, then raised his hand slowly to the mike. His fingers curled around it, blocking the transmission. Nathan raised his gun until it stuck into the President's belly. The President lifted his head and whispered into Nathan's ear. 'I'd like to tell them that you're a god-damn son-of-a-bitch, that I hope the next SWAT team blows your fucking head off.' Nathan's eyes widened in surprise. 'But I won't.'

He dropped his hand from the mike. He bent back to it. 'We're all in a very fraught situation here, and I'm sure everyone out there's picturing a crazed gunman holding me hostage. But I've got to say that Nathan Jones really isn't as bad as he's been painted. To me, and through no fault of his own, he illustrates exactly how the younger generation feels in America. It's frustrated by unemployment, by drugs, by peer pressure, by lack of education; it lacks the morals and convictions of previous generations, it lacks guidance, it lacks national figures it can look up to and be inspired by . . . all of this I see in Nathan Jones.'

Nathan stepped back. 'Woh!' he said, 'right off the top of his head. Thank you, Mr President. Of course I'm not American, but point taken. I also have with me Mr Clark Fuller, a reporter who by chance seems to have stumbled upon the biggest story of his career. Clark's a thoughtful man, like the President, he has many and varied opinions on what is wrong with America today. Haven't you, Clark?'

George bent to the mike. 'Yes, I—'

'Thank you, Clark, but three of us pontificating would be a bit much. Presidents make speeches, kidnappers make demands, reporters report. I'm sure we'll read all about it one day.' Nathan spun away. He crossed to the shattered windows. 'I'm looking out over New York, I'm looking out over America, I'm speaking to the world. You'll want to know who I am and what I want.' Nathan stopped, licked his lips. He scuffed his shoes over the shards of broken glass. He took another deep breath. 'My name is Nathan Jones. I come from Crossmaheart in Northern Ireland. I've never hurt a fly. And I've kidnapped the President of the United States by mistake. Forgive me. I'm not an angel. I have a bad temper. There are reasons why I lost my temper the other day, but they don't seem that important now. What is important is that I'm here now, with the President, and no matter how long I live, might be five minutes, might be fifty years, I will never have an opportunity like this. When I decided I wanted to speak to the world, a lot of ideas went through my mind about the subjects I could address. Drugs. The environment. Race. Immigration. The Irish situation. Nuclear testing. Life in outer space. All of them, none of them. I thought hard. I tried to decide which one I really cared about.'

There came a sound, to *them*, like a million soldier ants gnawing at a tree: Nathan scratching his head too close to the mike. He looked at the President: he may have spoken publicly as the thoughtful patriarch, but his face, his eyes, spoke of a steadily growing condescension; Nathan wondered where he had gone wrong, why the change from quiet diplomat to studied hatred. He turned to Clark: the look wasn't greatly different; something else too – jealousy, perhaps?

Nathan closed his eyes. 'And at the end of the day it isn't any of these things. I don't have demands, I have a request. I don't want to speak to ten billion people. I want to speak to one. There is a girl out there, somewhere, who I love very much. I'm just a stupid, shy, angry fool; I was never able to tell her that I loved her. I always meant to. I sometimes tried to, but it always came out all wrong.' He stopped, because what had happened wasn't meant to happen. He'd battled against it. He'd even sung, his voice so level, so fine, but now there was no control: his voice was breaking. If *they* could have seen, they would have seen a tear. He sniffed up. He didn't want to lose it now. He was a wreck anyway, but he didn't want to be a sad gibbering one. 'She left me. She left me all alone and I love her so much and I've no idea where on God's earth she is. But I need her. I need her so much that it hurts. That, really, is what all this is about. It's for beautiful Lisa who I loved and lost. All I really want is to tell her that, tell her to her face. Can you help me? Please? Can you find her? Just so that I can hold her hand and tell her and then I'll let your President go and you can shoot me or hang me or whatever you want. Is that okay?' There was a long pause. Then: 'That's all I have to say. Thanks very much.'

He took off the radio mike and threw it through one of the shattered windows. He was soaked through. He turned to the President, who nodded his head slowly. 'I'm not looking for approval,' said Nathan.

'I'm not giving it,' said the President.

Nathan nodded at scowling Clark. 'What's wrong with you? Never been in love?'

'Sure,' said George, 'just never felt the need to shout it all over the airwaves.'

Nathan shrugged. 'I said what I wanted to say.'

Clark shook his head sadly. 'You had such an opportunity. You blew it.'

'I didn't blow anything.' He thought about that for a moment. 'Despite what you might hear.'

George wasn't satisfied. 'You could have been history. Now you're just a soap opera. Imagine Neil Armstrong setting foot on the moon for the first time. One small step . . . imagine if he'd just babbled into the mike, "Gertrude, I love you so much!" or whatever the fuck you call his wife. Or if General MacArthur had said: "Well I'm going now and there's a possibility I might return at some point if we can just get enough troops together and a decent invasion plan." Do you see what I'm driving at?'

Nathan glanced at the President, then back to Clark. The reporter was becoming more upset. He'd removed a straw from his jacket pocket, and was rolling it between two fingers. 'There's no need to take it so personally, Clark,' Nathan said.

'I just hate wasted opportunities!'

'I don't think it was.'

'You had the whole world in your hands!'

'That's another song.' Nathan grinned. He nodded at the President. 'What'd you think of the singing, anyhow?'

'Novel,' said the President.

'Childish,' said George. He had the straw in his mouth now, flicking it this way and that with the tips of his teeth.

'Clark, I thought you were here to observe and report?'

George ignored him. It was no time for talk. He manoeuvred the straw left, then right, deciding which one was annoying him most, which one might benefit least from a few more seconds of life.

The President.

No matter how annoying Nathan Jones was, no matter how much of a disappointment, he must always remember that his primary purpose here was to assassinate the President of the United States. Look after him first, then finish off the loser after that.

The President wasn't even looking at him. He was watching Nathan Jones. He was only three feet away. He was a dead man.

'Clark, I'm talking to you,' Nathan said, and snapped the straw out of George's mouth.

George made a reflex grab for it, a slow reflex grab in keeping with his training. Nathan slapped the arm away with his gun hand. 'Watch it now, Clark, don't do anything too soap opera on me now.'

'You fucking . . .' George began.

'What's wrong, Clark?' Nathan laughed, swinging the gun before the reporter's face. 'Is it your favourite straw?'

George licked at a lip. He counted to ten, real quick. He gave a little shrug. 'Sorry,' he said, his voice calmer than an iced lake. 'You surprised me.'

The phone rang. It was Cameron.

'That was very eloquent,' he said, 'very emotional.'

'Really,' said Nathan.

'We're all of us very affected, Nathan. We've all been in love.'

Nathan gave it a few moments to sink in. 'Cut the shite talking, Cameron. I don't want to hear this phone ringing again until you've found her and you're telling me she's coming up in the elevator, okay?'

'Okay,' said Cameron.

As Nathan talked, Lisa hugged Alex. She tried to stop the tears rolling down her cheeks, but she was helpless. His shirt was soaked. He didn't say a word. He knew when to keep quiet and she loved him for it. *Nathan! Why hadn't he said something? Told me instead of the world.* But she knew that if he had, she probably wouldn't have believed him.

29

FBI Agent Wallace Hardy was five months short of retirement and he wasn't about to go giving himself a heart attack chasing shadows through downtown Boston. No, he intended giving himself a heart attack throwing back some cool beers, a couple of hamburgers and maybe a quart of ice cream. Some of those old ideals they'd drilled into him at Quantico were starting to wear off. Sure, he'd been down for a refresher shoot 'em up to Hogan's Alley only three months before, so he could turn it on when he had to, but with his clock ticking away nicely he was doing his best to ensure that he wouldn't have to.

The Black Rose, right next to Faneuil Hall, was a large, busy Irish pub he frequented from time to time. It specialized in Guinness and traditional music and he enjoyed the bawdy atmosphere. After enough beers he sometimes managed to fool himself into thinking he was as young as the rest of them again: ripping the ass outta life. Falling down drunk as a kid was fun, doing it as an old timer was sad. He watched them at play and he was jealous. Sometimes he watched them at play and he was in love. Usually both.

He sipped his Bud, sitting at the bar. When he'd come in Nathan Jones had been speaking on the TV; he caught the tail end of it; Jones's voice, high, cracking with emotion, had almost yanked a tear from him. All that shit about love. Hardy's wife had died a year before; it brought it all back. When the anchor's dull, monotone voice, completely at odds with his bright, fake-tanned face, had cut in, the bar exploded with noise as hundreds chose to ignore him and began to dissect this latest instalment themselves. He'd wondered how Jones would go down in an Irish bar, whether there'd be support for him or hatred. The Irish, he knew, were fiercely patriotic to more than one country.

The barman said, 'He's not that bad, y'know.'

'Don't be taken in,' said Hardy. 'He knows what he's doing.'

'Imagine being that taken with a girl,' said the barman, one of the few in the establishment who was actually Irish. 'God love him. Been there. Been dropped like that.'

'And who'd you kidnap?' Hardy asked.

'No one. Gave her dog a fuckin' good fuckin' though.'

He laughed and went to answer another order down the bar. Another laugh, from behind, drew his attention. As he turned, an errant elbow caught a glass, it toppled, rolled, smashed on the floor. A girl giggled, then bent to pick up the shards. Hardy strained for a glimpse of breast, then reddened as the guy with her caught his eye. The guy stood, staggered a little; Hardy feared for a moment that he was coming to cause trouble, but he merely reached across to the girl and pulled her arm away.

'Watch it, luv,' he said. 'You'll cut yourself.'

The girl giggled again. 'Maybe I should,' she said, holding up an ugly-looking sliver. 'Maybe we should cut each other. Become blood brothers. Or sisters. Or . . . whatever the hell it is?'

'Blood lovers.'

'Blovers,' said the girl. She was inebriated. So was he. Hardy grinned and returned to his drink.

Another barman crossed the floor and began to sweep up the glass. The guy at the table apologized, then tipped him. The barman returned a few minutes later with a heavily laden tray.

They raised their glasses. 'To us,' said the guy.

'To us,' said the girl. They clinked, they drank, they set down. They lifted two more. Hardy looked at the glasses. They looked like doubles. In such a hurry, yet they'd so much time.

'To Nathan Jones,' said the guy.

'Fuck 'im,' said the girl.

'To what he's done for us.'

'Fuck all squared in a box.'

They clinked, they downed. They lifted two more.

'How much cash do we have left?' said the girl.

The guy shrugged. 'About thirty dollars.'

'Will that cover the drinks?'

He shrugged again. 'Does it matter?'

'It matters.'

'From here on in, you buy the drinks, girl. You own the bar. You own the fucking brewery. You're made.'

'And so could you be.'

The guy shook his head. 'Darlin',' he said, 'I want to make it under my own steam. Y'know, maybe ten years from now you'll be cruising down Broadway in your limo and you'll see this tired old drag queen staggering out of some tacky club. Spare a thought. 'Cause I'll have pushed her there, I'll be up on stage belting 'em out like the star I am.'

The girl smiled sweetly. 'I'll never forget you,' she said.

'Yeah, you will.'

'Honest. Cross my heart and hope to die.'

'Don't say that.'

He raised his glass. 'To President Keneally, the only man that could come between us.'

'To President Keneally.'

They clinked and drank.

'What are you going to wear?' he asked.

'What for?'

'The cover of *Time*.'

'Wise up.'

'I'm serious. Or *Playboy*. Or *Guns and Ammo*.'

'Get a life.'

'I've a wee number picked out for myself already. That pink sequined one I do "Michelle" in. I'll be lying across a bed, smiling demurely at the camera. *Vanity Fair* it'll be, and the caption'll be: *Alexis Mascara, Lisa's lover: he helped clean up her vomit.*'

She squealed and slapped at his hand. He giggled. Then they both drank.

Hardy unfolded his wallet and pulled out the photostat of the girl some of his colleagues had been busting a gut to find. He hunched his shoulders up, dragged his thick arms in so that no one would see what he was unfolding. He studied it, then nonchalantly turned in his seat again to study the girl. Anyone sober might have noticed, but the couple at the table behind him were too far gone. His eyes bored into her for a minute and a half, then he turned back to the photostat. Face the same, different hair. Dyed hair. He nodded his head slowly. He refolded the picture and replaced it in his wallet. He took a sip of his beer. Then he pushed himself up out of his seat, and with a sweat just beginning to break across his brow, he walked to the end of the bar and lifted the pay-phone. He called his office.

He'd been around long enough to know not to wait for instructions. He told them, he put the phone down. They'd tell him to leave things alone until they could get a squad down. A squad to take the glory. They'd tell him, don't under any circumstances approach because they are probably part of the conspiracy. They are probably armed and highly dangerous. Leave them alone. Back-up will be there in seconds.

No way. This was his.

He walked back up the bar. When he was six feet away from them he drew his gun.

'Lisa,' he said quietly.

Lisa looked round.

'Freeze – FBI!'

They both looked up. They didn't look at all surprised.

'And about fucking time too,' said the guy.

Chairs screeched as drinkers all around them shot back. A few women screamed. A man as well.

Lisa managed a nervous smile. 'We just wanted to enjoy a last blow-out before things got heavy,' she said.

Nostrils flared, sweat streaming, Hardy's gun veered from one to the other. They were his. His breaths came in rapid, shallow puffs, like an eleven-year-old smoking for the first time. 'Don't move a fucking muscle!' he bellowed.

The bar was silent but for the booming voice of the anchor. The girl looked behind Hardy to the screen. She began to smile. 'I don't believe I'm seeing this,' the anchor said, 'but I sure wish I was down there. It's raining money in Manhattan, folks. Nathan Jones is throwing millions of dollars off the top of the Empire State Building.'

Alex shook his head. 'Well maybe he's not such a bad chap after all,' he said. 'Let's you and me have a last drink, luv – this guy doesn't look like he takes prisoners.'

Alex reached for a glass.

'I said don't move a fucking muscle!' Hardy growled. Despite the training, the years and years of training, his hand was shaking. There was sweat in his eyes. He tried to blink the saltiness away, but it only made it worse.

'Listen, mate,' said Alex, 'I've done nothing wrong. I'm about to lose the woman I love, so don't get your knickers in a twist just 'cos we wanna have a last drink together, okay?'

The guy reached for his drink.

Hardy pulled the trigger.

Alex jerked back.

Lisa screamed.

'Don't move! Don't move! Don't move!' Hardy screamed.

Lisa screamed on and on and on, but she didn't move. She stared at Alex and she screamed, but she didn't move an inch.

Hardy kept the gun on her as he skirted the table; he pushed the toppled chair out of the way and slowly sank to his knees. He searched the body for a weapon; then he searched for a pulse.

He found neither. He raised himself. He kept the gun trained on her chest.

'FBI,' he said. 'FBI.'

30

It had been raining money for over fifteen minutes.

James Morton, like half his agents, had a hand stuck out of one of the management-floor windows. He grabbed a few dollars as they passed, brought them in, scowled at them, then threw them out again.

He glared at Doyle at the next window. 'Careful you don't fall out,' he said.

Doyle took the hint and pushed himself back off the window frame. 'Not a sight you see every day,' he said lamely.

Morton slumped back behind his desk. Doyle took a seat as well. 'What's the word from below?' Morton asked.

'A big word. Pandemonium.'

'Figures,' said Morton. His helplessness had reached a new peak. Or trough. Every step of the way Nathan Jones had outwitted him. This latest episode with the money was, he had to admit, brilliant. There was no better way to a New Yorker's heart than through his wallet. None of them were going to get rich, the breeze would see to that, but the act of doing it was enough. That and professing true love from the top of the Empire State. Inspired. Out there now, across every state of the nation, there were some twelve thousand special agents looking for Nathan's ex-lover; and countless millions of patriots. Morton nodded across the room to where Slovenski was making notes on a big yellow legal pad, oblivious to it all. 'What do you reckon, Doyle: analysing the situation, or last will and testament?'

'If he's analysed the situation, it'll be his last will and testament.'

Morton nodded. 'Maybe he could do me one, too.' He dropped his head into his hands. 'Between the raid upstairs and this Robin Hood stunt, Nathan Jones is gonna be responsible for more deaths this year than Harlem's finest.'

He looked up at a cough from the doorway. 'Not now,' he said.

Agent Kipriskie took a step forward. 'Sir, there's a cop here thinks he has something for you.'

Morton sighed. 'Find out what it is, Kipriskie, I can't be bothered sifting every shitty thing comes this way.'

'Will only speak to you directly, sir.'

Morton dropped his hands from his face. 'God-damn it, Kipriskie, make him tell you . . .'

Officer Linster McCreedy popped his head over Kipriskie's shoulder. 'You should really hear this first hand, sir.'

Morton rolled his eyes at Doyle. A glory hunter. Didn't trust the chain of command.

'As if we haven't enough to contend with,' he said. 'Okay, you got thirty seconds, officer. What've you got?'

McCreedy stepped into the room. When he started to talk it came out in a torrent. Morton had to raise his hand. 'Okay, okay,' he said, 'you have the full minute. Take your time.'

McCreedy took a deep breath. He looked anxiously from Morton to Doyle, and then noticed Slovenski for the first time. 'Oh,' he said.

Slovenski, looking up now, smiled and said, 'Never mind me, officer.'

McCreedy nodded. Then he told them about the body in the car.

'So?' said Doyle.

'So, we ran the prints.'

'So?' said Doyle.

'So the guy in the car's called Clark Fuller. I think we all know who he is. Twenty minutes ago I had the body positively identified by Reuters' New York bureau chief.'

What little colour there was drained quickly from Morton's face. He looked grimly across at Slovenski. 'Fuck,' he said, 'you know what this means?'

Slovenski nodded. 'Apart from the fact that Reuters will have it all over the world by now and we are once again the last fucking people to know? Yes of course I fucking know. There's another killer up there.'

Morton turned to Doyle. 'Get Cameron in here.'

Doyle nodded, stood.

'Thanks very much, officer, you've done great work. Now, if you'll . . .'

'I'm not finished yet.'

'Well I'm afraid I haven't . . .'

Doyle paused by the door. 'What is it?' he asked.

McCreedy turned to him. 'I turned up another report.'

Morton's tongue darted out, wet his lips. *It never rains but it pours dollars.* 'Officer?'

'I just have this instinct for things, sir. Something crossed my mind, and I just wasn't able to shake it.' He nodded between the three of them, looking for encouragement. *A pat on the head*.

'Go on,' said Slovenski.

'Sir, a couple of days ago a white male walked into a theatrical shop off Columbus Circle. Meril Steiner's Review. Old guy owns it, seventy years in showbiz. The white male asks Meril to help him with his make-up. Said he was doing Shakespeare, needed to black up for a part. Far as we know, Meril doesn't get many customers, so he spends most of the afternoon turning this guy black. Meril turns his back for one moment, this guy robs the shop then half kills Meril for his trouble.'

Morton pinched the end of his nose. 'And you think maybe . . .'

'I took a walk up there. I showed him a picture of Clark Fuller from *Newsday*. He'd seen it before, said it was the same picture the guy asked him to use as a basis for the make-up. It was a thorough job. He's a pro.'

'If he's such a pro, how do you know he's just not trying to cash in on all the hoopla?'

'Sir, Meril didn't even know the President had been kidnapped. He doesn't believe in TV or radio; he's a theatre man.'

Morton turned to Doyle. 'I think we know where this is leading. Get a picture of George Burley up to this Meril Steiner, get a positive ID.'

'Then what?'

'Then we'll start to panic.'

Along the corridor they were deleting their front pages and hastily redesigning. He'd been right all along.

'Cody,' said Tony Bradman, 'you got that smug, self-satisfied look on your face. I ain't seen that since Sugar Ray came out of retirement to beat Hagler.'

'And I don't even have a thousand bucks riding on this one. Maybe I should have.'

Bradman had one hand clamped on Cody's shoulder, the other hovered with a lighter, ready to light Cody's stogie. 'Houston was good, the prostitute was better. With this much Woodstock and Winebarrel brought down Nixon. I should've gone with you. Now it's raining money and he's brought romance back to the world. Let's go big with it, Cody, real big. He's Robin Hood *and* Kevin Costner; he's Romeo and Juliet, Donny and Marie. He's . . .'

From the doorway a sub-editor said: 'This just came in from Reuters. Clark Fuller's body has been found in a car on Columbus Avenue. Whoever's up there with the President sure as hell isn't Clark Fuller.'

Bradman gave Cody's shoulder another squeeze. 'Be sure to give Nathan an extra big white hat,' he said.

Lisa shivered. Lisa sobbed.

They threw a sheet over his body.

They handcuffed her. They searched her. They frogmarched her to a car; and from the car to a helicopter.

Up in the sky she tried to throw herself out. But they held her.

'No one has even said sorry,' she cried.

The FBI men looked at her. Big jaws and sunglasses. 'Just keep calm, miss,' said one.

'He only wanted a drink,' she cried.

'It couldn't be helped,' said another.

'Yes it could!'

She screwed her eyes shut; the tears still sprang, hot, like the drops of blood one of the barmen had wiped off her face as they sat waiting for the other FBI agents to stream into the silent bar.

She saw Alex's dead eyes.

She wanted to hold him one last time.

But they wouldn't let her.

She screamed and dived for the door again.

But they held her.

31

Nathan Jones was buying the biggest round in history.

Nobody was going to get rich, but quite a few were going to get drunk. Across Manhattan apartment blocks emptied, offices spilled out, shops put up shutters. It was New Year's Eve and the moon landing all in one; it was a tickertape parade with a difference. Even the gridlock didn't seem so bad. The President's life somehow seemed more certain, such was the expansiveness of Nathan's wallet, such was the emotion behind his appeal over lost love. The city had been depressed; now there was light. The people had been used to movies with happy endings, the feel-good factor was everything, and now it looked like it was coming to pass. Nathan Jones playing ball.

The wall of money, made up of some $5m, remained undisturbed at the top of the steps. Since his speech to the world Nathan had grown in confidence. He no longer kept an eye on the defensive wall. He knew they wouldn't try another assault. They would find his girl. He had taken a leaf out of Sid's book. He had done it *his* way. He didn't think about the future. He thought about Lisa and he felt nervous; but it was no longer the panic of impending death, he had passed that; it was the uncertainty of a reunion with the girl he loved. He struggled with the words: the first words would be so crucial. He would have to apologize, of course, for dragging her all the way to the top of the Empire State Building when she was probably busy with a new job. She knew he had a temper; she would forgive him. If the truth were known, she had a temper herself. He knew her well enough to be able to say with some certainty that she had probably regretted leaving him almost as soon as she'd done it. Only she was too proud, too headstrong to admit it to herself. In the days and years to come she would realize it; when she visited him in prison, she would tell him; or when she visited his grave. He would hear her, nevertheless, and he would forgive her. Nathan had a bad temper, but he didn't bear a grudge. Not for long, anyway. Not for eternity.

Five million dollars guarding the stairs; the rest of it out the windows.

Despite himself, George was quite enjoying the sensation of throwing it away. They all were, in their own way. If it had been $500 or even $5,000, it would have mortified George, but $5m was such an obscenely large amount that it barely registered on him at all; it was silly money, unreal.

Nathan was having a particularly good time. He had needed the release. 'There you go!' he yelled more than once as the dollars shot up into the atmosphere. 'Home to mama!'

The President was very, well, *presidential* about it. He would have preferred to have been down on the street handing it out to poor people like a Roman senator. He stripped off a single dollar at a time; released it; peeled another. Each note took him six seconds. If he had been left to his own devices, the whole $5m would have taken him three hundred and forty-seven days.

'I don't know what you're laughing at,' the President said. 'Most of them will end up in the sea.'

'But some of them won't. Killjoy.'

Nathan shovelled another handful through the shattered glass. 'Make someone happy!' he cried.

'Each dollar we throw out represents one less school textbook,' said the President, peeling another. 'Each dollar means less welfare.'

'Bollocks,' said Nathan. 'I'm bringing a little happiness into their lives.'

The President snorted. 'That's not happiness. That's greed.'

Nathan nodded to his left. 'Clark, how can a man with millions of dollars in the bank begin to realize what it's like for those of us with nothing? You're the reporter, tell us.'

George shrugged.

'You've no idea what it's like out there,' Nathan continued. 'People will appreciate a couple of dollars in their pocket.'

The President peeled off another dollar and launched it. His voice was steady, angry but calm. 'Not if they have to pick it out of the gutter.' He jabbed a finger at Nathan. 'Don't you presume to tell me about my fellow Americans. They, we, are a proud people – you can't fool them with cheap stunts like this. You know nothing. You are nothing. It's time we called a halt to this charade.' But he peeled off another dollar; he just threw it with a little more contempt.

Nathan raised his gun and pointed it at the President. 'I do believe,' he said slowly, 'that we have discovered a backbone.'

There were two sieges. Nathan, the President and George, at the centre of one. James Morton and Graham Slovenski at the centre of the other. The greater pressure, probably, was on the second. All of the protagonists were dirty and tired. Nathan, the President and George faced the greater immediate danger; but long term, Morton and Slovenski's future was just as murky. Ridicule, hatred, crucifixion; and that was being optimistic. The last thing Morton wanted to see was Cameron appearing in his doorway clutching a fist full of dollars, and whistling that tune.

'You're the fourth person's tried that, Cameron. Knock it off. It wasn't fucking funny the first time.'

Cameron gave a little shrug. 'What's been happening down here?' he asked.

Morton took a pencil from behind his ear and began drumming impatiently on the desk. Cameron wasn't looking one bit frayed. It pissed him off. He jabbed the pencil at him: 'You're the one paid to examine every nuance, every hesitation, every pause. You're the one empowered to negotiate, contain, apply pressure, convince him to surrender peacefully without further loss of life. You fucking tell *me* what's going on!'

Cameron straightened. 'Easy does it, James,' he said quietly.

Morton glared at him. 'Oh fuck it, Cameron. All the textbooks, all the fucking textbooks, none of them legislates for a fucking lovelorn Robin Hood. Next thing we know the bastard'll be getting a humanitarian award.' He rolled his eyes. 'Sorry,' he said.

Doyle got up off his seat and waved Cameron into it. 'I'm going for coffee,' he said. He didn't offer to get him one.

'So?' asked Cameron.

'The usual mixture of bullshit and hard fact. Depends what your interest is. We've had Dreamworks on the phone offering to sign Nathan Jones to a record contract. We have a positive ID on George Burley.'

'Christ.'

'I know. And we've tracked down Lisa.'

'Really?'

'Yup. She's coming in by helicopter from Boston.'

Cameron smiled. 'Something positive, at last. It's about time we had a break.'

Somehow Morton managed to work just his top lip into a snarl. 'There is a downside to it,' he said. 'She was with her new lover when we found her.'

'Won't go down well with Nathan. Of course he doesn't have to know. Yet.'

'He doesn't, no. But it means we're kind of relying on Lisa playing ball.'

'Any reason why she shouldn't?'

Morton gave a little shrug. 'One of our guys got a little enthusiastic.'

'Happens. Cuffed her? Slapped her around?'

'Blew her lover's brains out.'

'God. That's enthusiastic.'

'He did it by the book.'

'What book? *Death Wish*?'

'The guy was ordered to freeze, he reached for . . . well he reached for a glass of vodka, as it turns out, but it could have been anything.'

'And you suspect this will affect Lisa's willingness to cooperate?'

'Put it this way, if you had to pick pieces of your wife's brain out of your hair before going to work, how would you feel about it?'

Cameron nodded. 'A little reluctant.' He took a deep breath, blew it out of puffed cheeks. 'So we have a little work to do.'

'*You* have a little work to do.'

'With your support, James,' Cameron said tartly.

Morton looked to the window behind him. Dollars were still floating past. His eyes felt suddenly heavy; he rubbed a thumb and forefinger into them. 'I don't have any support left to give, James,' he said quietly.

Slovenski heard about Lisa a few moments later. 'God-damn it! God-damn it! God-damn it!' he bellowed, and stormed out of Morton's office.

Doyle reappeared in the doorway with the coffees. 'Tell him the good news?'

Morton nodded.

'What'd Cameron think?' Doyle asked as he set the cups down.

'He thinks Nathan Jones is about ready to give up. Says he's been looking for an excuse from day one. He probably doesn't love her at all, he just wants a way out. The problem really isn't Nathan Jones any more. It's George Burley.'

Doyle nodded. 'As far as we can work out he's not armed.'

Morton shook his head. 'No, as far as we can work out he's not carrying an Uzi, or a rocket launcher or a fucking great spear. We've no way of working out whether he's still armed with the venom of the Nigerian slipper snake.'

'So what do we do?'

'We pray to the great God above for guidance.'

Tara found him fuming in a deserted corridor. As she approached, he pounded his fist into a wall.

'Slo?' she said quietly.

He looked round. He looked about ready to burst into tears. She put her arms round him. 'Slo?'

They hugged. He held her tight.

And then he kissed her and his tongue flitted into her

mouth. And every moment of heaven he waited for her to stand back and slap him and have him arrested. And every moment her mind screamed with the guilt and sickness of this stunt, but her body hurled her into it.

Her hands moved behind him, found the knob of a door, pushed. The office was unlocked. Dark. She bundled him in.

Even in the dark she could see his eyes wide and bright and shocked. He opened his mouth but she put a finger to it.

'Once,' she said. 'Once and then never again. Deal?'

'Deal,' he said.

George looked at his watch. It would be dark soon, and time to act.

32

Midnight, and the thunderstorm that raged about the Empire State Building was the most malevolent anyone could remember. The Met boys probably could have told them it wasn't that special, but it *seemed* special. Like God providing a suitable backdrop to the climax of a drama. Or the Devil.

Below, the denizens of the city huddled together against the pounding rain, still in their summer clothes; there had never been a Blitz spirit in New York, but here it was; positively Churchillian, save for those who took advantage of the huddle to pickpocket or fondle. Those that dared look up saw lightning dance about the upper floors of the Empire and shivered; they knew that this night would be the end of it. In years to come they would be able to say to their kids, *I was there*. And their kids wouldn't give a fuck, but people who buy into posterity rarely consider that.

All was quiet on the management floor. Deceptively quiet. Orders had been given. The idea was to focus attention on one single thing: and that one single thing sat sobbing in Morton's office; bedraggled from the rain, panicked by the drag through the baying throng outside, frightened by the hard-nosed FBI agents, not because they shouted at her, but because they didn't. They were nice. Exceptionally nice. And that made it all the more difficult.

She had sworn not to assist them in any way.

And now she hated herself because already Alex seemed like a lifetime ago; or a fractured dream. He *had* died. There was blood on her blouse. But still it didn't seem real. If they'd tried to deny it or justify it, that would have been the end of it; she would have put up the shutters, just willed herself into a coma. But they'd actually been nice about it. Apologetic.

'The agent involved has been suspended,' said James Cameron, apparently the FBI agent in charge. 'He will lose his badge. He will not work for us again. I know it's not much compensation.'

'No,' said Lisa. 'It's not.'

There were two other men in the room. One introduced himself as James Morton, FBI, the other was Graham Slovenski, the White House Chief of Staff. She recognized him, of course. But if she had not known him she would not have picked him out as the most powerful man in the room; she would have chosen Morton, sitting attentively at the back of the room, half in the shadows. Only occasionally did he lean forward, not to say anything, just to look at her that little bit more closely. It unnerved her in one way, reassured her in another.

'You know what we're going to ask you,' Cameron said. His voice was oddly pitched, a mix of friend and foe, like that of a medical professor who moonlighted as an agony aunt.

Lisa nodded.

'And what's your initial reaction?'

'To tell you to go away and shite.'

Cameron nodded. 'What are your feelings towards Nathan Jones?'

Lisa shook her head slowly. She pulled the back of her hand across her eyes. 'I hate him,' she said.

'Is that really how you feel?'

'Yes.'

'Or do you just hate him for putting you in this situation?'

'It's how I feel.'

'So if none of this had happened, and you saw him walking down the other side of the street, what would you do?'

'I'd ignore him.'

'Why would you do that? Wasn't he your boyfriend for a long time?'

Lisa nodded. 'But I chose to end it.'

'And the only way to end something, even if you still have strong feelings for him, is to end it finally. Not to leave it lingering.'

'Something like that.'

'So you do still have feelings for him, even if they're feelings of hate.'

'Yeah,' she said warily. 'I guess.'

'Okay, that's understandable. You've split up for whatever reason, you still have feelings for him, but you want to get on with your life.'

Lisa nodded. She looked at Morton. There was no reaction from him; his face was blank, neither encouraging or condemning.

'Okay, so look at it another way. You're walking down the street and you see Nathan on the far sidewalk. Someone pulls a gun and puts it to his head. What would be your reaction to that?'

'What does it matter?' She closed her eyes. 'I'm tired of this shit. I'm not going up.'

'I understand that. Okay. I just want to know how you would react in that situation.'

A tear squeezed out. She shook it away. She sniffed up, looked at Morton. 'I'm tired. I'm tired of all this shit. It's got nothing to do with me.'

'Just answer the question,' said Cameron.

'I don't want to answer it! Jesus Christ, your fucking President is stuck up there and you're firing fucking hypothetical situations at me. I mean, Jesus, no wonder he's still there if this is the way you're approaching things.'

'Who said anything hypothetical?'

'You did.'

'When?'

'Stop trying to confuse me. You said. All that shit about Nathan having a gun at his head and what would I do . . .'

'Nathan does have a gun at his head.'

'Aye, the President's took him hostage.'

Cameron shook his head. He looked to Morton, then Slovenski. If it was meant to give what he said gravity, it worked. 'Lisa, the truth is, we stopped being concerned about Nathan some time ago. He's done a bad thing, but he's not the master terrorist we once thought he was.'

'No, he's not.'

'However, as it happens, the so-called second hostage, Clark Fuller, is not Clark Fuller. His real name is George Burley; he's wanted for the murder of two FBI agents. We believe he intends to assassinate the President.'

Lisa looked at him, waited for him to smile, or wink, or something. She looked to the other two. Stony.

'So?' she said.

'So we believe that Nathan is in just as much danger as the President.'

'I can't help that.'

'But you can.'

'This is not my country. He is not my president. He is not my boyfriend. You have done enough to me. I don't want this to continue. I want to go home.'

Cameron shook his head. 'You know that's not possible. You're a smart girl. You've thought about this: no matter what happens, your life will never be the same again. But you have it in your power to decide whether your life changes for the better, or it becomes a living hell. You have the power to be Jackie Onassis, or Mrs Lee Harvey Oswald.'

'Mrs Onassis is dead.'

'You know what I mean. We wouldn't be asking this if you weren't our last hope. We have messed up badly once already, we cannot afford to do it again. We believe that Nathan will release the President once he gets the chance to talk to you.'

'So give me the phone.'

'It's not as simple as that.'

She closed her eyes, swallowed hard. 'Okay. Look. I'll talk to him. There's a concession. I'll even be pleasant, there's another, I just don't want anything more to do with guns. And I don't want to die.'

'You're not going to die . . .'

There came a little cough from Morton. He unfolded his legs, stood, crossed to the desk and sat on the edge. He looked at her for half a minute, nodding his head slowly. When he spoke his voice was calm, measured, scary.

'Lisa, let me tell you our predicament. There's a man up there who's on the verge of killing the President. There's another man who's given us instructions that if anyone other than you tries to go up there, he'll kill the President. By sending you up we kill two birds with one stone.'

Confusion sparked in Lisa's eyes. 'Don't you mean one bird with one stone?'

Morton shook his head. 'We're going to give you a gun. We want you to shoot George Burley.'

If she said no once, she said it a thousand times.

Eventually Graham Slovenski asked to have a word with her alone. Morton looked to Cameron, Cameron shrugged. Okay, said Morton and they left her crying again, her head on her chest, hair tangled over her face.

When the door had closed, shutting out the anxious eyes beyond, Slovenski loosened his tie and sat on the desk where Morton had been. Then he reached across and lifted her chin; he brushed away the hair from her face.

'Y'know, you're going to look very pretty on the front of all those magazines.'

Lisa rolled her eyes. 'Sure.'

'You really will.'

'Aye.'

'Tell me this, do I seem like the kind of man you could trust?'

Lisa shrugged. 'I don't know you. You seem okay.'

'Of course. No reason why you should. But I want to tell you something. Something secret. Something I've never told another living soul.'

'I'd rather you didn't.'

'But I want to. Hear me out, okay?'

'Okay.'

'On a purely personal level, I don't mind if the President dies.'

'Oh.' Lisa glanced behind her. Shadows through the glass.

'Because I have been in love with his wife since the first moment I met her. She is the most incredible woman. The love I have for her is imbedded so deep in my heart that if I ever die and someone gets my heart, that someone's going to love her as well, and he won't have a clue why.'

Lisa nodded. 'I'm not sure I . . .'

'Is there somewhere deep in your heart where you love Nathan?'

'I don't think so.'

Slovenski nodded. 'Maybe not. It doesn't happen to everyone.' He sucked on his lower lip. He looked at the shadows too. 'Lisa, sometimes you have to forget about your personal happiness. Some things are more important. The President is more important. You have to look at the big picture. I know you're not American, you probably don't give a monkey's brass balls about America. There's an awful lot wrong with it. But it's my country, I love it. And if I know anything, I know that he's a damn fine President. If anything happens to him this country is going to fall apart. It will descend into anarchy. Hundreds of thousands of people will die. There will be race wars, civil wars, every type of war you can imagine, because the one thing that binds us together, the American flag, will have been burnt, destroyed. We can't let that happen. You can't.'

Lisa held his gaze. 'I can,' she said. She knew patronizing paternal bullshit when she heard it.

Abruptly Slovenski slapped her. She fell out of the chair. It wasn't the pain, it was the surprise. 'You fucking . . .' she cried.

He jabbed a finger at her. 'Just you listen here, young lady. I've had about as much of you as I can take. Our whole country is hanging in the balance because you're in a bad mood with your ex.'

Lisa pulled herself up to her knees. 'I'm not in a bad—'

He cut her off. He stood, bent, pulled her to her feet. He

held her by the shoulders. Tight. She tensed, waiting for more violence, knowing that this was just the beginning of it. He stuck his face right up close and hissed. 'This is what I'm going to do. I'm going to get you a gun. I'm going to show you how to use it. And then I'm going to put you in the elevator and send you upstairs whether you like it or not. And from then on you're on your own. I don't give a damn who you shoot. Shoot Nathan if you hate him that much. Do me a favour and shoot the god-damn President. Shoot George Burley if you want. Just do *something* instead of moping about here like a spoilt little girl.'

'You killed Alex!'

'I'm sorry! It's done! I can't bring him back! But you can bring us back! You have to!'

They locked eyes. Half a minute. More.

Then he relaxed his grip. She turned slightly, massaged her cheek, wiped some more tears. Then she turned and planted an excellent right cross just beneath his eye.

Slovenski went down.

'That's for Alex,' she said.

33

George's plan was relatively simple. Remove Nathan Jones from his gun. Then shoot him. Force the President of the United States of America to recant his crimes, then throw him through one of the windows so that he splattered on the sidewalk far below. After that he would take his chances with the parachute.

George was more than happy. Everything had worked out so well. He was coming to the climax of one of the greatest acting achievements of the modern era. It seemed a shame that there was no one to record it – a real Clark Fuller, in fact. George grinned at the thought of the reporter, probably still rotting in his car. People in New York just didn't care. He could lie there for a year and a day and still they wouldn't notice. Maybe when he reached ground level he could take a walk past and see if the car was worth salvaging. He could drive back down to Alabama in it; the blood would have dried by now. George tutted. A stupid plan. The blacks would have stolen the wheels and the engine and the radio by now; it would be a skeletal frame, with a skeleton inside it.

The President was standing by one of the smashed windows,

staring out. He was already quite damp from the wind-driven rain. Nathan stood on the other side of the observation floor, his face level with the hole in another window; his face soaked. He turned slightly as George approached him.

'Bout the only thing will keep me awake,' Nathan said.

George nodded.

'Still glad you stayed?' Nathan asked.

George shrugged.

'They'll probably give you a medal.'

'I doubt it,' said George.

'What is it you lot get? The Pulitzer Prize? Didn't Hemingway get that? And that guy from *The Killing Fields*?' Nathan smiled. 'Anyway. It's nearly over. I can sense it. You can go out and make your fortune.' He nodded across at the President. 'What's he up to? Counting votes?'

George shook his head. 'He's looking towards heaven. He thinks that's where he's going. But he's not. He's going to hell.'

'That's a bit profound.'

'It's the truth.'

Nathan nodded. 'Aye. Keep taking the tablets, Clark.'

Nathan took a close look at the reporter. He didn't look well at all. Whatever skin disorder he had, it was beginning to gallop out of control. He was flaking. Perhaps he really should be taking tablets, to control it, but was too embarrassed to say. Nathan chose not to mention it. He had seen how much Clark had been hurt by it before.

The phone rang.

Nathan looked from George to the President. He gave each a slight nod. 'Well,' he said, 'this is it then.'

The President nodded. George didn't react at all. Nathan hurried to the phone. He lifted the receiver, held it against his chest for a moment, took a deep breath.

'Hello?' he said, straining to hear against the howl of the wind.

'Nathan, this is James Cameron. We're sending Lisa up in the elevator. We would like you to send the President down.'

Nathan nodded. 'I will. In good time. Send her.'

He put the phone down. He turned to the elevator. 'They're sending her up,' he said.

George appeared at his shoulder. 'Be ready,' he said, 'it's probably a marksman.'

Nathan shook his head. 'They wouldn't do that.'

Nevertheless, he held the gun out before him, levelled it on the door. Together they watched for the elevator light to begin its climb.

'Oh God,' Nathan whispered, 'let it be her.'

'Get your shot in first,' said George.

'Oh God,' Nathan whispered, 'I'm nervous.'

'Aim for the heart,' said George.

'I had a first line,' Nathan whispered, 'but I've forgotten it.'

The light began to rise. He steadied his gun on the elevator doors. He glanced towards the stairs. There was no movement there.

George shivered. The adrenalin was pumping. He wanted to open his mouth and go *Hahahahaha!*

Only seconds to go.

Only a second.

The elevator came to a halt.

'He's going to kill you,' said George.

Sweat ran into Nathan's eyes. He blinked through it. His hands were shaking.

The door slid open . . . one person within, still masked by the security grille . . . Jesus, dark hair . . . Nathan tried to catch his breath, his finger tightened on the trigger.

The grille began to . . .

'Shoot!' George cried.

Nathan squeezed . . .

'Nathan!' Lisa screeched as she caught sight of him; she cowered back; hid her head in her hands. 'Don't shoot! Don't shoot!'

Nathan jerked the gun away. 'Oh Jesus Christ!' he cried. He blew out hard, his legs wobbled. 'Oh Jesus, Lisa, I nearly . . .'

Lisa peeled herself off the back of the elevator. She stepped gingerly out onto the observation floor, froze again as a bolt of lightning flashed across the sky.

'Oh God,' Nathan said.

'Oh God,' Lisa said.

'Oh God,' George said, and cracked Nathan across the back of the neck.

Nathan gave a little surprised cry and tumbled forward onto one of the money bags. Lisa stopped, her jaw dropped open. She momentarily forgot that she was . . .

George was on Nathan, ramming his head into the concrete floor. Then he stamped on his hand and picked up the gun. George looked up, around at the President standing mesmerized by the window, then at Lisa, frozen by the elevator. George at last went, *ahahahahahaaha!* He felt like Captain Hook.

Nathan tried to scramble away, but George planted a foot in his back and pressed him back into the floor.

He stood that way for a few moments: triumphant. Like Tarzan with his foot on the lion he had just knifed to death.

He looked to the President. 'Well?' he said.

He had half-expected the President to come running to congratulate him, it would have made slamming the gun into his face all the more enjoyable, but he remained where he was by the windows. When he spoke his voice was dry, emotionless; not thankful, not relieved. 'Reporter turned hero,' he said, 'well done.'

'Half right,' said George.

'Reporter?' asked the President.

George smiled. 'You know, don't you?'

The President nodded. 'I guessed. A while back.'

'What gave me away? The nigger skin, wasn't it?'

'The voice. The call to *Oprah*. It took me a long time, but I got there in the end.'

'So there's a sense of satisfaction. That's good. Because now I'm going to kill you.'

'I guessed as much. But not just me. All of us, I presume.'

George nodded. 'But you're the big one. That'll be my sense of satisfaction.' He rammed his foot into Nathan's back again. 'For a while there I thought Nathan might do it for me, but I had him pegged as a wimp the first time I saw him, and I guess I should have stuck with my first impression.'

Lisa stepped forward. 'Please,' she said, 'you're hurting him.'

George mock-widened his eyes. 'Aw. Shucks. I'm sorry.' He rammed his foot in again. Nathan groaned. George grinned, looked her up and down. 'So you're what this is all about. Scrawny little bitch, aren't you?'

Lisa nodded.

'It would almost be touching if it wasn't so pathetic. To risk everything for some piece of cheap pussy. And don't give me that look, or I'll rearrange it.'

Lisa tried to drop the scowl. It barely made any difference. 'Let him go – it's the President you want.'

'Little Missy, it's everything I want, and it's everything I got.' He raised the gun. He pointed it at Lisa's chest. 'Do you want to say a prayer or anything?'

Lisa shook her head.

George removed his foot from Nathan's back, then nodded

down at him. 'Why don't you lie down there beside your loved one? It'll look quite touching, your brains merged in death.'

She stayed where she was.

'Now!'

Her gun was tucked into the waistband at the back of her skirt, covered by her jacket. There had been no opportunity to get it; she had expected some sort of reunion with Nathan and to make her move under cover of that, but it had all happened too quickly. She wasn't a cop. Maybe with training, maybe with experience, but . . . Jesus, to die like this, without even trying. The gun was trained on her, she didn't dare make a sudden move. It didn't seem likely that he would give her permission to scratch her bum once before dying. She stepped forward, then slowly lowered herself until she was on her knees beside Nathan. He turned and looked up at her.

'I'm sorry,' he whispered.

'You will be,' she said.

'Do you want to kiss and make up?' George asked.

Nathan looked at Lisa. Her eyes softened a little. 'Lisa?'

'Hurry now,' said George, 'time's a-runnin' out.'

She gave a little nod. Nathan, grimacing, pulled himself up to his knees. He put his hands on her shoulders. She put her hands around his waist.

He pulled her to him. They kissed. They hugged.

'Awww,' said George.

She turned her face away, buried it in his neck; her mouth moved; she whispered.

'Awww,' said George, 'sweet nothings, sad goodbyes.'

'There's a gun in my waistband,' Lisa whispered.

'What?' said Nathan.

'There's a gun in my bloody waistband.'

Thunder rolled across the sky as they hugged tighter, as Nathan delved in the shadows.

'Okay!' George said sharply. 'That's enough. I've made your little hearts happy again. Now, side by side.'

Nathan made contact. He removed his hand on George's blind side, rubbed his stubbled face against Lisa, and glanced back. Even with the element of surprise it was no good; the gun was trained on them. George had waited too long now; he was itching to kill them.

'Lie down!' George barked and stuck the barrel of the gun against Nathan's ear. 'Lie down!'

Nathan lowered himself. It was now or never.

'What are you, Clark?' the President asked, moving quickly from the window. 'A psychotic or a patriot?'

George kept the gun where it was but turned his head towards the approaching President. 'What?' he said.

'What are you, depraved lunatic or All-American boy?'

'Stay where you fucking are!'

The President kept coming. George shoved Nathan to the ground, then swung round. The gun centred on the President's chest. 'You move another inch, Mr President, and you're a dead man.'

The President smiled, and kept coming. 'Well, there's a possibility I hadn't considered.'

'I swear to God!'

The President stopped. He opened his arms. 'Why don't you, Clark? It's what you're here for, isn't it?'

A light dawned in George's eyes. 'I get it,' he spat, 'you want to die! You want to be a martyr! That way everything you've achieved as President, which is precisely nothing, will be forgotten and you'll be remembered purely for being America's great white hope, cruelly cut down in his prime.'

'You got it,' said the President.

'And you think because I realize that, and I don't want you to be remembered like that, I won't kill you at all!'

The President shrugged.

'Nice try! But never bluff a bluffer, Mr President! You're going to die because I've decided you're going to die! Because it isn't posterity I care about! I know they'll be naming fucking boulevards after you from here to eternity! But I don't give a fuck! All I give a fuck about is America, and you've helped to destroy it!'

'Well,' said the President, 'then I've achieved something.'

'Oh, and wisecracks as well. Laughing in the face of death.' He shook his head sadly. 'You're not funny at all. But you can be. Before you die I want you to sing the National Anthem for me, Mr President. I want you to sing it loud and proud. They probably played it when you were born, now I want you to sing as you die.'

The President held George's gaze for a few seconds. Then he slowly shook his head. 'I think not,' he said.

George smiled. He rammed the barrel into the President's chest.

The President staggered back.

'Sing!' George cried.

The President shook his head.

'Shoot me, Clark. Shoot me dead.'

'That's too easy!' George cried. He almost leapt at the President. He grabbed his lapels and dragged him towards the windows.

Nathan rolled over, still shielding the gun. Lightning cracked above them, blinding them all for a moment. He rubbed at his eyes.

George had the President by the window. Then he had him through the window, holding him by the back of his jacket. 'Sing!' George cried. 'Sing!'

The rain thumped against the President's face. He opened his mouth, gulped at it.

'Sing! Sing! Sing!'

Nathan was up, advancing towards George, gun out before him. 'Oh God,' he murmured. 'Oh God.'

Lisa came behind him, holding onto the back of his jacket. 'Oh please God no!' she said as the wind howled through them.

The President began to sing. Slow, faltering.

'Louder!' George yelled against the wind. 'Faster!'

The President upped the tempo. He started to cough, choking on the wind and rain. 'I can't . . .'

'Sing, you fucker!' George screamed.

Nathan put the gun against the back of George's head. 'Now you sing, you bastard!'

George, shocked, turned slightly. But recovered quickly. 'Ahahahaaha,' he laughed, 'why don't you just say, let him go!' He cackled again and let go of the President who began to scream as he tumbled forward into the storm. Three-quarters of the way out George caught him again; pulled him back. He laughed back at Nathan. 'Fire away!'

Nathan pressed the gun further into him. 'I'm going to shoot you! I'm going to!'

'Shoot me! Shoot me!' George laughed again and jiggled the President. 'I don't hear you singing any more!' he yelled.

Nathan looked desperately towards Lisa. As he did she dived at the window, squeezing between George and the frame. Her hands screwed into the back of the President's soaked jacket as George let go of it, turning in one rapid motion and delivering an elbow into Nathan's stomach. Nathan dropped, rolled, the gun clattered away from him.

'Nathan!' Lisa cried. 'I can't hold him!'

The President was three-quarters, nearly four out of the window.

George laughed again as Nathan scrambled on his belly towards the gun. He turned, laughed some more at Lisa as she hung half out of the window too, clinging to the most powerful man in America.

As Nathan reached the gun, George pulled the trigger.

Nothing happened.

He pulled it again.

Nothing.

He looked at the gun. He shook it. He pointed it at Nathan again. He pulled it six times.

Nothing.

'Nathan!' Lisa screamed.

George looked at her. He looked at Nathan. He opened his hands. 'Well?' he said.

Nathan pulled the trigger.

George staggered back, clutching his chest. He let out a little cry and slumped to the ground.

Nathan raced to the window. He reached over Lisa to grab the President. In saving him, he would save her. His nails dug through the light material, straining to grip. He grimaced, he heaved, he yelled against the pain in his ribs.

And he saved them.

He pulled them back through the frame and they all collapsed soaked on the 102nd floor of the Empire State Building.

34

'Will you marry me?'

'I *hate* you.'

'That's not what I asked.'

'I *hate* you.'

'All of this happened because of you.'

'It was my fault?'

'No. But because I loved you. I was on my way to propose when you ran away.'

'Nathan . . .'

'Will you marry me?'

The elevator slowed, stopped.

It was the end of the drama, but you wouldn't have known it from the cacophony of sound. The storm was reaching its climax. Thunder rolled into thunder, lightning bolts battled it out across the skies. On the streets, far below, dollar bills turned to mush even as people struggled to pick them up.

It was thirty minutes since Lisa had been persuaded into the elevator. Anxiety wasn't the word. Graham Slovenski stood behind the line of marksmen, arms folded, gaze intense.

James Morton was beside him. They had stood helplessly listening to the drama played out above, trying to follow the bizarre mix of scream and thunder, gunshot and lightning, song and sob, relayed to them by the miracle of fibre optic cable. Now they watched the elevator lights.

Along the line of marksmen, someone began to whistle 'Stormy Weather'.

Ordinarily a stop command would have been barked out, but they'd been there too long, too long living on their nerves, too long in the spotlight, trigger fingers stiff. Once in a while Morton had caught one exercising a trigger finger, bend, stretch, bend, stretch and he'd nearly laughed; aerobics for the terminally lazy.

The whistling ceased abruptly. The light had begun to move.

Already erect marksmen became super erect: fifty guns zeroed in.

'Well,' said Slovenski in Morton's ear.

'Well,' said Morton.

The elevator reached the 86th floor. The door slid open. The security grille was pushed back.

'Don't move a fucking muscle!'

They weren't going to. Nathan and Lisa stood with their arms raised.

'Don't move! Don't move a fucking muscle!'

They didn't need to be told twice. The first agents moved cautiously forward.

Nathan kept his eyes fixed on them; he picked out the sweat on their brows, their wide shoulders; two of them were shaking, their guns moving ever so slightly. Nathan tried to breathe through his nose.

'Out! Out!'

They stepped forward. Their legs were pulled from under them and they were pinned to the concrete and searched.

Morton stepped around the line of marksmen and approached. He knelt beside Nathan. 'Where's the President?' he asked.

Nathan turned his head sideways. 'He's still up there.'

'Is he . . .?'

'He's fine. He wanted a couple of minutes to collect his thoughts.'

'And Fuller . . .?'

'I shot him.'

Morton nodded. He stood, he took a deep breath, he turned to the marksmen; he turned to Slovenski, 'It looks like he's okay,' he said, and the emotion cracked on him.

'Oh thank God,' a woman said. When he looked he saw that it was the First Lady and there were tears rolling down her cheeks; she almost collapsed, but Slovenski caught her and hugged her to him. But only for a moment. He saw Slovenski close his eyes for a moment, then extend his arms, pushing her back.

'It's over,' Slovenski said, 'you have him back.'

Tara nodded, wiped at her face. She raised a hand so that it was touching his cheek; she patted. He let go. They nodded at one another, then she turned to Morton. 'Should I go up?' she asked.

Morton shook his head. 'Not until we've secured the area. We've waited this long, we can wait a few minutes more.'

The President ran his hands through his hair, slicking it back. He stood by the window and let the rain wash his face. He rubbed at it, then combed through the three-day stubble for dried skin and dirt. Then he turned to where George Burley lay on his stomach. There was a thin trickle of blood coming from beneath the body. It stopped about a foot away from him, right beside the useless gun. The President bent to retrieve it. He weighed it in his hands for a moment, then detached the empty magazine. From his trouser pocket the President produced the bullets he had removed while Nathan Jones and George Burley slept. He loaded them into the magazine and slotted it back into the gun. Then he placed it on the ground.

The President brushed down his suit, fixed his tie, then clambered over the money bags at the top of the stairs. He was dog tired, but he held himself erect, he pulled his shoulders back. He gripped the handrail for a moment to steady himself, then let go of it and began to descend.

At the first hint of movement from the steps the marksmen snapped back onto the alert. They hit the ground, guns raised as the President emerged around the bend in the stairs. He stopped and looked at them, and they at him.

'Good morning, gentlemen,' said the President. 'I'm sorry to have kept you so long.'

And they roared and cheered and clapped and sang. Tara was in there, under his arm. Slovenski got a hug. Morton stayed at the back, drained. He hurried downstairs to the management floor, fighting against the tide of well-wishers. He tried barking a command or two, but everyone had forgotten about security now in their anxiety to see a living, breathing President, and he was ignored.

Morton entered his office and shut the door. He moved in behind his desk and lifted the phone to call his wife.

It was engaged.

The wind continued to howl through the 102nd floor of the Empire State Building. Even so the sounds of celebration from the 86th could clearly be heard. For a few moments George Burley, easing back into consciousness, didn't recognize what the sound was. He slowly turned from his stomach onto his back. He groaned. He touched his chest and looked at his hand: blood. He tried to wipe it on his coat, but his coat was soaked. *I'm dying*, he thought. He touched the ground beside him. *I am lying in my own blood. I have failed.* Then he looked at his hand, but this time it was not blood, but water. A puddle of rain from the smashed windows. George felt gingerly at his chest; there was a hole in his shirt; there was blood, but it didn't seem . . . he tore at the hole, he stared at the wound. There was a crease mark maybe half an inch wide torn across his chest. It was bloody and messy, but it was not life-threatening. He knew that much. He had studied first aid at night school; only three out of the sixteen lessons, but it had been enough.

George carefully pushed himself up onto his knees. He felt shaky, but he felt *alive*.

God had protected him!

He didn't know why, or how, but God had looked after him. Kept him alive to fight another day.

He knew now what he must do. He tore off his coat. He examined the parachute for a bullet hole; he could find none. Then he hurried across to the steps and listened: he recognized the sound now. They were singing the National Anthem. George spat down the stairs. Let them sing it. He had shown them what he could do, it would be no trouble doing it again. If that was God's will.

George bent and put his hands on one of the bags of money. He dragged it across to the window, the very same window where he had so recently forced the President of the United States to sing his own version of the National Anthem. George grinned at the thought of it. He began to hum it himself.

George wasn't concerned about the weight of the money.

He wasn't concerned about the howl of the wind or the flash of the lightning.

God's warrior had no concerns in the world.

He heaved the bag up onto the ledge, took a firm grip of it, then launched himself out into the storm.

There would be no Jack Ruby.

Nathan was carried out of the Empire State by forty-seven Secret Service agents. He wore a bullet-proof jacket, crash helmet, handcuffs; his mouth was taped, his legs were shackled. But when he hit the open air he could still hear something: people cheering. He wasn't sure what it meant, but it was better than a poke in the eye with a sharp stick.

George Burley gave himself up to the storm.

He plummeted, he pulled the rip cord, he soared.

He cackled. The wind threw him about like a rag doll, but on he cackled.

He sang the National Anthem, was still singing when the lightning struck him. And then he screamed. He was burning, burning, burning.

But he did not die. The rain doused him; the wind cooled him; God guided him.

George landed on the roof of a Korean deli. A deliciously soft landing.

George laughed and laughed and laughed.

He dumped the parachute, then carefully climbed back down onto the street and began walking. He carried the bag of cash over his shoulder. Everywhere people were partying. He joined in. Complete strangers came up to him and offered him drinks. He gratefully accepted.

'He's alive!' yelled a drunk.

'Not for long!' yelled George, but the drunk wasn't a drunk for no reason and didn't understand.

George stopped, untied the bag and removed several

thousand dollars. He closed the bag again; he gave a handful to the drunk. 'Merry Christmas, old Bailey and Loan!' he shouted and heaved the bag up onto his shoulder again. He cackled.

George found a hotel. He paid for his room in cash. They gave him a funny look.

'Sir, your eyebrows are . . .?'

'Burnt, I know. My apartment burnt down. Lightning. That's why I need the room.'

George hurried upstairs. The room was spartan, but he only wanted it for ten minutes. Wash the nigger skin off, then hit the road with his fortune.

George sang as he scrubbed in the shower.

The make-up was harder to get off than he had imagined. The singing stopped. He scrubbed some more. Then some more.

When he started to bleed, George began to realize that the nigger skin wasn't going anywhere.

With an anguished scream he sank to his knees and began to cry.

The lightning had not killed him. It had merely fused his skin and the black make-up into an eternal tattoo. He pounded the floor of the shower with his fists.

God was watching over George okay.

And God was laughing his head off.

New York Newsday 5 April

LOOKING BACK

an occasional column

by CODY RUTTEGER, former Metro News Editor

This morning I took a cab downtown to the Empire State Building. So what, just about every jerk in the city has this week.

It is, of course, exactly five years since the end of *that* siege. You will be pleased to learn that all of the original bullet holes are still in place, lovingly tended by enthusiastic young security guards. All of the original guards are long gone, relaxing on faraway beaches thanks to the profits from their books. In the concession stand, which *has* been restored, I counted forty-six books for sale relating the events surrounding the kidnapping of the President. He, of course, has not yet committed his version of events to print, although it is widely presumed that the recent Oscar-nominated movie by Steven Spielberg, *National Anthem*, received the presidential nod of approval. The First Lady has had little to say on the subject either – on *any* subject, in fact, since little Michael Jnr was born. As well as the official soundtrack to the Spielberg movie you can buy the CD of the Sondheim musical *A Day at the Empire with George*, although don't expect to be able to hum any of the tunes. There are also eight documentary videos, three calendars, Nathan & George dolls and a virtual reality siege kit ($325!). You can pick up a plastic Empire State Building for $3.25.

The best-selling book is, by far, Nathan Jones's *I Did It My Way*, and staff tell me they expect another rush on it both to coincide with this anniversary and then with the publication in *People* magazine next month of the divorce pictures ($3m!). Lisa's book, *He Did It His Way*, has dropped badly away since her TV chat show bombed. Amie Kellerman's *Beaten and Bound: My Night with Nathan Jones*, a surprisingly literate read, is selling well, although *Secure to the End* by former Empire security chief Leonard Maltman hasn't shifted *any* copies at all; one suspects the concession staff keep it there out of politeness. They have also refused to stock Brian Houston's *Suck It and See* for fear of prosecution. FBI director James Morton's *Shield of Honour* is big on facts and figures, but low on emotion and drama – how he managed that, given the material, God only knows, but then you have to remember that he is an accountancy graduate. Much more enjoyable is James Cameron's *Conversations with Nathan*, although since the tapes were accidentally wiped there is some controversy over how the FBI's chief negotiator could have remembered everything in such detail, particularly when you remember the length of time he spent recovering from his breakdown – at one stage he couldn't remember his own name.

Of course the greatest number of books concern themselves with the history of and search for George Burley. As public enemy number one, then and now, his disappearance has not only confounded the law enforcement agencies but intrigued the wider public, as indeed any fugitive with a $1 billion price tag should. The Mitchell Commission line was that George was smuggled abroad by White Armed Resistance, but FBI sources remain doubtful of this. Although privately they believe George either died from his wounds shortly after fleeing the Empire or that he drowned after he and his parachute were blown out to sea, the official line is that he remains at large and should not be approached. The FBI think it's good to have a national boogey man.

And there are those who claim to have seen him. One man, who did work with George at an airport in Alabama, claims to have seen him at the top of the Empire State Building visiting an exhibition dedicated to the siege. A blues singer in New Orleans claims to have enjoyed a six-month affair with him and has passed a polygraph test to prove it, but it is much more probable that George no longer looks like the George who stares out at us from the front of countless books and magazines. The FBI presume he has changed his appearance radically.